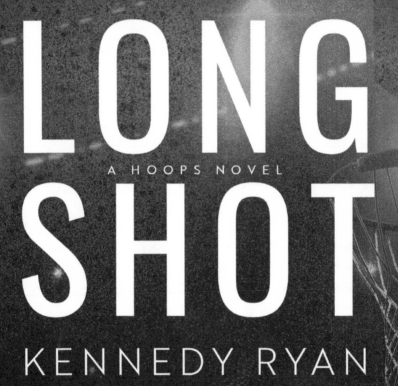

LONG

A HOOPS NOVEL

SHOT

KENNEDY RYAN

LONG SHOT

(A HOOPS Novel)

Copyright © Kennedy Ryan, 2018

Edited by Lauren Clarke Editing
Proofread by Tricia Harden & Emerald Eyes Editing
Cover design by Letitia Hasser & RBA Designs
Book design by Inkstain Design Studio
Cover model: Kevin S
Cover photo © Dominique Spruch & Reach Kennedy

KENNEDYRYANWRITES.COM

AUTHOR'S NOTE

I started writing this book two years ago out of righteous indignation on behalf of a young woman whose journey I didn't understand. I write when I have something to say, and I knew I couldn't say it from a place of judgment and hypotheticals. So I started talking with women who had walked that path. After many interviews, much research and some soul searching, I hope I understand better. I hope I wrote this story from a place of grace and compassion that wouldn't have been possible without the generosity and vulnerability of those with whom I spoke.

With that said, there are aspects of this story that may be sensitive for some readers.

For Natalie, Paula & every woman who ever rose from ashes to tell her story.

FIRST HALF

"The heart speaks in whispers."

CORINNE BAILEY RAE

PROLOGUE

I was there when the levees broke.

Though I was safe in my ward when the monster lost all restraint and unleashed watery havoc on New Orleans, I lived in the city.

I later saw the devastation left in the wake of the beastly storm. We frantically gathered our things, fled our home for higher ground. My family left to survive.

There were those who stayed too long. Remained when they should have fled.

They did not live to regret it.

Now, I'm making the same mistake. I've remained when I should have fled.

I witness the exact moment when this monster loses all restraint. His fury, his rage rush at me like a wall of water. Like a gale-force wind, he blows over me.

I am the devastation left in his wake.

As the world goes black, I see stars. A flash of brilliance. A light I should have acknowledged long ago. As the stars dim and the darkness encroaches, I understand I'm like those who stayed too long, blindly assuming their survival.

I fear that I, like them, will not live to regret it.

ONE

AUGUST

Tomorrow is my father's birthday.

Or it would have been. He died fifteen years ago when I was six, but in the biggest moments, the ones that count the most, it feels like he's with me. And on the eve of the biggest night of my life, I hope he can see me. I hope he's proud.

Tomorrow's the most monumental game of my life. By all rights, my ass should be safely tucked away in my hotel room, not out killing time at some dive. I toss back a handful of bar nuts and sip my ginger ale. At the table next to me, they just ordered another round of beers. God, what I wouldn't give for something strong enough to unwind these pre-game jitters, but I never drink before a game. And tomorrow isn't just any game.

I glance at my watch. Fifteen minutes late? That's not Coach Kirby. He's the promptest man I know. His name flashes across my screen just as I'm considering calling him. I push away the bowl of nuts and the niggling feeling that something must be wrong.

"Hey, Coach."

"West, hey." His voice carries a forced calm that only confirms something's off. "I know I'm late. Sorry."

"No, it's cool. Everything okay?"

"It's Delores." His voice cracks over his wife's name. Basketball is my high school coach's second love. From the day I met him my freshman year at St. Joseph's Prep, I knew Delores was his first.

"She okay?"

"She . . . well, we were at the hotel, and she started having chest pains and trouble breathing." Coach's worried sigh comes from the other end. "We're here at the emergency room. They're running all these damn tests, and—"

"Which hospital?" I'm already on my feet, digging out my wallet to pay the modest bill. "I'm on my way."

"The hell you are." The steel that worked all the laziness out of me for four years stiffens his tone. "You're playing tomorrow night in the National Championship. The last place you need to be is in some hospital waiting room."

"But, Delores—"

"Is my responsibility, and I'm handling it."

"But, I can—"

"Your folks get into town yet?" He steamrolls over my protest to close the subject.

"No, sir." I pause, checking my exasperation. "Matt had to work today. He and my mom are flying in tomorrow."

"And your stepbrother?"

"He's stuck in Germany. Some event for one of his clients." My stepbrother and I may not share blood, but we share a love of sports. Me, on the court. Him, off, as an agent.

"Sorry he won't be there," Coach says. "I know how close you two are."

"It's alright." I play off my disappointment. "I've got my mom and Matt.

4

And you, of course."

"Sorry I can't make it to the bar, though why your ass wanted to go out the night before the big dance in the first place is beyond me."

"I know, Coach. I just needed . . ." What *do* I need? I know the playbook inside and out and have watched so much film my eyes started crossing.

I'm restless tonight. Years of sacrifice, mine and my family's, have gotten me here. And I couldn't have done it without the man on the other end of the line. Coach has invested a lot in me over the last eight years, even after I graduated high school and moved on to college. When scouts and analysts urged me to go pro a year early, he convinced me to stay and finish my degree. To shore up my fundamentals and mature before going to the draft. But the man who passed his DNA on to me—his wingspan, his big hands, his long, lean body, and I guess even his love for the game—is the one I keep thinking about tonight.

My father.

I wasn't sure who this moment should be shared with, but I knew it wasn't my teammates trolling for girls in some rowdy bar. Even though they can only get so rowdy the night before a game, that didn't appeal to me.

"Whatever you need, get it, and get out of there," Coach says, snapping me back into the moment. "Get your ass back to the hotel. Mannard *will* bench you for breaking curfew, even before the National Championship. Don't get too big for your breeches."

"Yes, sir. I know."

Between Coach's take-no-shit leadership and my stepfather's military background, the sirs and ma'ams come naturally. Discipline and respect were non-negotiable in both their regimes.

"I need to go," Coach says. "Doctor's coming."

"Keep me posted."

"I will." He pauses for a moment before continuing. "You know I'll be at the game tomorrow if there's any way it's humanly possible. I just need to make sure Delores is okay. She's the only reason I would miss it. I'm proud of you, West."

"I know. Thanks, Coach." Emotion scorches my throat, and I struggle to hold my shit together. My dad's birthday, the pressure of tomorrow's game, and now Delores in the hospital—I'm staggering under the cumulative weight of this day, of all these things, but I make sure none of it makes it into my voice when I speak again. Coach's got enough to worry about without thinking I'm not ready for tomorrow. "Do whatever you need to. Delores comes first."

"I hope to see you tomorrow," he continues gruffly. "You shoot the damn lights out of that place."

"Yes, sir. I plan to. Call me when you know something."

I don't even bother finding the server or asking for the check. Instead, I leave a twenty on the table, more than enough to cover my tepid ginger ale. I have another few hours to kill before curfew, but if Coach isn't coming to ease my nerves, then I may as well head back to the hotel. I'll try to slip in without running into my teammates.

I'm almost at the door when an outburst from the far end of the bar stops me.

"Bullshit!" a husky, feminine voice booms. "You know good and damn well that's a shit call."

Just shy of the threshold, I turn to see the woman who's cussing like a sailor. Curves punctuate her lean, tight body: the indentation of her waist in a fitted T-shirt, the rounded hips poured into her jeans. She jumps from her stool and leans forward, her body taut with outrage, her fists balled on the bar, and her eyes narrowed at the flat screen. She must be a good seven inches over five feet. A guy my height gets used to towering over everyone else, but I like a woman with a little height. Her hair, dark and dense as midnight, is an adventure, roaming wild and untamed around her face in every direction, drifting past her shoulders. She looks pissed, her wide, full mouth tight, and the sleek line of her jaw bunched.

The beautiful face paired with all that attitude has me intrigued. Even if I'm not getting laid tonight, I can at least get distracted from the pressure that's been crushing me all day. Hell, crushing me for the last few weeks, if I'm honest. I want to shake off the melancholy thoughts my father's death always wrap around me—thoughts of what we missed. What we lost. Seeing her all fired up and cussing at the television, swearing at the refs, lightens some of the load I've been carrying. I find myself walking straight toward the one thing that has penetrated the thick wall of tension surrounding me since we advanced to the NCAA championship a few days ago.

"Asshole," she mutters, settling her denim-clad ass back onto the barstool. "No way that was a flagrant foul."

I take the empty stool beside her, glancing up at the screen replaying the last sequence. "Actually, I'm pretty sure that *was* a flagrant foul." I grab a fistful of nuts from the bowl between us.

"You're either as blind and dumb as the ref," she says, eyes never leaving the screen, "or you're trying to pick me up. Either way, I'm not impressed."

My handful of nuts freezes halfway to my mouth. I have a shot at college player of the year, have been big man on campus for four years, and was on ESPN's *Plays of the Week* by tenth grade. No girl has shot me down since middle school, but I never shy away from a challenge.

"Just making conversation." I shrug and swing my knees around to face her. "Though if you want to be picked up, I might be able to accommodate."

She finally deigns to look at me. Her heart-shaped face is arresting, a contrast of fierce and delicate. She has high cheekbones and dark brows that slash over a button nose and hazel eyes. *Hazel* is too flat a word to describe all the shades of green and brown and gold. I've never seen eyes quite like these. Several colors at once. Several things at once. I wonder if the girl behind them is as multi-dimensional.

"I wouldn't want to wear you out before your big game tomorrow." The corners of her lips pinch like she's trying her best not to laugh at me.

That gives me pause. So she knows who I am. That would usually work in my favor, but I have a feeling she's not your run-of-the-mill ball groupie. "You're a fan?"

Unsurprisingly, one brow crooks, and she rolls her eyes before turning her attention back to the game. The bartender approaches, a bottle of liquor in hand.

"What'll ya have?" He sets the Grey Goose on the bar, toggling a speculative glance between me and the woman ignoring me.

"Could I get a ginger ale, please?"

He smirks, trading out the Goose for a ginger ale he pulls from the fridge under the bar. Filling a glass with the fizzy drink and setting it in front of me, he angles his head to peer under the brim pulled low over my brow.

"August West?" A grin lights his face.

I nod but put my finger to my lips, hoping to quiet him so I can flirt in peace. I don't feel like signing autographs and being pelted with well wishes. I'm not even in the NBA yet, but ever since our team made the Sweet Sixteen, the media has homed in on me for some reason, elevating my profile and making it harder to remain anonymous.

"I get it." The bartender nods knowingly, his voice dropping to a conspiratorial whisper. "Avoiding the crazy, huh?"

"Something like that." I look back to the super fangirl, whose attention remains riveted on the screen. "What's the lady having?"

"A beer she can pay for herself." She slides me a crooked smile and takes a sip of her half-full glass.

"Oooooh." The bartender's beer belly, an occupational hazard, shakes with a deep chuckle. He gives me a commiserating look before ambling down the length of the bar to his other customers.

"So, you come here often?" I can't believe that just came out of my mouth. The face she makes says she can't believe it either.

"Next you'll ask what's a nice girl like me doing in a place like this." The humor in her eyes removes some of the sting.

"You think my game is that weak?"

She side-eyes me, extending both brows as high as they'll go. "We talking on the court or off?"

"Ouch." I wince and tilt my head to consider her. "And here I thought you'd be a sweet distraction until curfew."

"I'm not anyone's distraction," she says. "Especially not some player looking to let off testosterone."

"Assumptions and judgments." I shake my head in mock disappointment. "Didn't they tell you not to judge a book by its cover? You can't possibly know—"

"August West, six foot six, Piermont College starting point guard, deadly from behind the arc, off-the-charts basketball IQ, and Naismith finalist. Six-foot-ten-inch wingspan and forty-inch vertical." Her sharp eyes slice over me from the brim of my cap all the way down to the Nikes on my feet, before returning to the game onscreen.

"Your hops may be Jordan-esque, but your D could use some work." A laugh slips past her lips. "And that's not an assumption. I know that for a fact."

I have to laugh because Coach Mannard has been after me all season—for the last four years, actually—to improve on defense. My three-pointers make the highlight reel, but he's just as concerned with the fundamentals that will make me a better all-around player. Apparently, so is she.

"So they keep telling me." I turn my back to the bar, propping my elbows on its edge, and consider her with new respect. "How do you know so much about basketball?"

"You mean because I'm a girl and should be watching cheering matches?" Her glare is all indignation.

9

"Um . . . you mean tournaments? Even I know they're called cheer *tournaments*, not matches."

"Well look at that." She spreads a thick layer of sarcasm over the words. "You know girl stuff and I know boy stuff. Is it opposite day?"

She turns her attention back to the screen like she couldn't care less that she just impressed the hell out of me. Guys, we talk shit, and never more so than when it's about sports. A woman who can talk sports *and* talk trash? A fucking sparkling unicorn. She gives as good as she gets, this one. Hell, she may give *better* than she gets. There's a spark to her, a confidence I want to see more of.

A lot of girls just reflect. They figure out what you like so they can get in with a baller. This one has her own views, stands her own ground and doesn't give a damn if I like it.

I like it.

"Since you know so much about me," I say, "it's only fair I learn something about you."

She turns her head by slow centimeters, eyes still locked to the screen as if it's killing her to look away from the game. Her expression, those changeable eyes, warm and soften just a little. "What exactly would you like to know?"

"Your name would be a good start."

Her lips twist into a grin. "My family calls me Gumbo."

"Gumbo?" I almost choke on my ginger ale. "Because you have big ears?"

I risk touching her, pushing back a clump of wild curls. The whorl of her ear is downright fragile, and strands of dark hair cling to the curve of her neck.

"Not Dumbo." She laughs and pulls away so her hair slips through my fingers. "*Gumbo,* like the soup."

"I knew that." I really did, but I had to get inventive if I was going to steal a touch without drawing back a stump. "So why Gumbo?"

She hesitates, and for a moment it seems I wasn't breaking through like I thought. She finally gives a "what the hell" shrug and goes on.

"You may not hear the accent now, because it's been years since I lived there, but I'm originally from New Orleans."

Now that she says it, I do detect something reminiscent of that city in her voice. A drawn-out drawl spiced with music and mystery.

"My family moved to Atlanta after Katrina." She gives a puff of air disguised as a laugh. "But I'm NOLA, through and through. I come from good Creole stock. As if Creole wasn't already mixed up enough, my father's German and Irish."

I think the ambiguity of her beauty is part of her appeal. Something elusive and indefinable. I would never have guessed the ethnicities that coalesced to make a face like hers—the wide, full lips, copper skin and striking bone structure. I don't think I've ever seen anyone like her. Hers is not a face you would soon forget. Maybe never.

"I'm a mix of everything the bayou could come up with," she continues, taking a sip of her drink. "So my cousin says I had more ingredients than—"

"Gumbo," I finish with her. We share a smile, and she nods. "So you're a mutt like me."

"I wasn't gonna say anything." Her eyes run over my face and hair, my looks almost as ambiguous as hers. "But now that you mention it . . ."

"Lemme show you something." I pull out my phone, flipping through the photos until I land on a picture of my family from a camping trip a few years ago. "Here."

She takes the phone, her smile fading at the corners. I know what she sees. My mother smiles into the camera, her auburn hair a fiery halo around her pale face in the winter sun. My stepfather and stepbrother stand at her shoulder, both tall blondes.

And then there's me.

My hair cut close to tame the dark curls that can never decide which way to grow. My skin is the color of aged dark honey, and my eyes are gray as slate. I couldn't look less like a part of the family if I tried.

"One of these things is not like the others." I grin over the rim of my glass, sipping my ginger ale. "I guess I'm gumbo, too."

She returns my smile and my phone, but the humor slowly fades from her expression. Curiosity clouds her eyes when she looks back at me, but whatever that question is, she's not voicing it.

"What?" I finally ask.

"What do you mean *what*?"

"Just seemed like you wanted to say something."

For a second, her face shutters, and I think she won't tell me, but she glances up, a smile settling on her lips after a few seconds.

"Did you ever feel like you didn't quite fit anywhere?" Her words come so softly, competing with the revelry in the bar. I lean in to hear until our heads almost touch. "I mean, like you were always kind of in between?"

Her question echoes something I haven't articulated to many people but often felt. I sometimes felt displaced in my mother's new family. I may not look a lot like my African–American father, but I look nothing like anyone in the family I have left. Most kids were one thing or the other and clumped together based on that. It left me sometimes feeling adrift. Basketball—that rim, that rock—became the thing I clung to.

"I think I know what you mean." I clear my throat before going on. "My father died when I was really young, and my mom remarried not too long after. It took me a while to adjust to everything, especially being different when all I wanted was to fit in."

"I get that," she says.

I shrug and turn down the corners of my mouth.

"Thanks to basketball, I started worrying less about fitting in and more about standing out." I roll the glass between my palms. "But even then, yeah,

I sometimes felt . . . I don't know. Displaced."

"Me, too. My skin was lighter than just about everyone's in my neighborhood. My hair was different." She shakes her head, the movement stirring the air around us with the scent of her shampoo, some mix of citrus and sweet. "Most girls there assumed I thought I was better than they were, when I would have given anything to look like everyone else. To fit in. I had my cousin Lo for a few years, but besides her, I kind of just had myself."

What was that like for her? A beautiful anomaly in the Ninth Ward. Maybe I don't have to wonder. Maybe I know firsthand.

"It got kinda lonely, huh?" I ask.

"Yeah, it did." She circles the rim of her glass with an index finger. Her lashes lower like that might hide her memories from me, hide her pain, but it's in her voice. I recognize it.

"Sometimes, even when we had a full house," I say, dropping my voice for just our ears, "I'd end up in the backyard shooting hoops by myself until it got dark."

Like there's some magnetic center, our bodies have turned in toward each other. Our confidences enshroud us, blocking out the ribald conversation, the impromptu karaoke across the room, the wild response to the games on the flat screens. It's just us two misfits. A few minutes with a complete stranger, and I suddenly feel understood in a way that's always been hard to find.

"You get used to being alone," she finally says.

"What about your mom? You guys close?"

"Close?" She squints one eye and tips her head back. "Not really. She's made a lot of sacrifices for me, and it's never been easy. She's strong, a survivor, and I respect that, but I haven't always agreed with her choices. I can't remember my mother ever holding down a job for more than a few weeks."

"How'd you guys get by?"

"She's a beautiful woman." She raises cautious eyes, like she expects me to judge. "She used to say there's always some man willing to take care of a beautiful woman."

I don't know what to say to that. My mom is a beautiful woman, too, but I can't imagine her living that way—relying on just the physical—because she started teaching when my dad died and has worked hard ever since.

"You're a beautiful woman." I nudge her knee lightly with mine. "And I bet you can take care of yourself."

A smile starts in her eyes and eventually spreads to her lips. "Thank you."

I don't have to ask which compliment she's thanking me for.

"My aunt is older than my mom by two years," she continues. "It's what my mom saw her do. It's what they saw their mother do. They used what they had to get what they needed."

She sighs before sipping her drink and going on. "My aunt relocated with us to Atlanta after Katrina, and they might have changed zip codes, but they didn't change tactics. Apparently, men all over will take care of beautiful women."

"Besides your cousin, were you close to anyone else in your family?"

"Just Lotus." A frown shadows her expression. "She went to live with my great-grandmother south of the city and I stayed in New Orleans, but when she moved to Atlanta for college a few years ago, we got close again."

She shakes her head like she's dislodging thoughts, memories. "Enough about my family dysfunction. What about you? Perry West was your dad, right?"

"You know about my dad?" I ask.

"Yeah, sure." Sympathy fills her eyes when they meet mine over our drinks. "Losing him that way—it had to be tough."

"Yeah." I shrug, a casual rise and fall of my shoulders that doesn't hint at how tough it was. "He was a great player."

"He had an incredible long-range shot." She smiles ruefully. "How long was he in the league?"

"The car crash happened in the middle of his second season." I was young, but I still remember his funeral. His teammates were all there, tall as skyscrapers to my six-year-old eyes. "Tomorrow's his birthday."

"No way." Her eyes go wide. "You're playing in the freaking National Championship on your dad's birthday?"

I nod, allowing myself to smile for the first time over this monumental twist of fate. It's a long time since my mom was married to my dad, but she probably remembers that tomorrow's his birthday. We haven't talked about it, though. It feels like I'm the only one who knows it, and now this beautiful gumbo girl knows, too.

"Is tomorrow for him?" Her eyes never leave my face, her intent focus drawing me into her.

"It feels like it. You know? Like what are the odds? I keep wondering if he knows how far I've come. If he can see." I let out a soft laugh, watching her face for signs that she thinks I'm an idiot. "Does that sound stupid?"

"Not at all. I don't know what happens after we're gone, but I hope he can see. He'd be proud of you, no matter how the game goes tomorrow."

"I hope so." I lean in a little closer, giving her the same attention she afforded me. "What about your father? The German and Irish in your gumbo?"

She smiles, but it's a tight curve of her lips.

"He was German and Irish. That's about all I know." Her harsh laugh ripples through the pool of quiet we've made here in our corner of the bar. "Well, I also know he had a wife and kids. My mother was just . . . a side chick, I guess. He paid her rent while they were together, but right after I was born he moved on. So did she. He never came around asking about me. She never offered much explanation for his absence."

"And now? Nothing?"

"We left everything in the Ninth when we moved to Atlanta." Her shoulders lift and fall with a carelessness I don't buy. "He could still be in

New Orleans. He may have died when the levees broke. Who knows? It's never made me much difference."

She flashes me another tight smile, signaling that she's done with the topic.

"How'd we get into all *that* stuff?" She points her finger at me in mock accusation. "*You*, sir, are a good listener. Sneaky way to distract a girl from the fact that her team's losing."

I glance up at the game, grabbing her segue out of deeper waters like a lifeline. "You a Lakers fan?"

"Die hard purple and gold." She folds her arms on the bar and leans forward, her eyes back on the screen. "New Orleans didn't have a team when I was growing up."

"Well they're getting crushed tonight," I offer unnecessarily, hoping to get a rise out of her. Of course, it works, and she goes on a diatribe defending the storied Lakers legacy, though it's taken such a beating lately.

Through halftime and the last two quarters, we squeeze in a lot of conversation between plays. She wants to work in sports marketing and has several internship opportunities that might pan out after graduation. It seems like most of her stories eventually circle back to her cousin Lotus, the ambitious badass fashion student who always has her back. For my part, I avoid rehashing all the things she already knows about me: the numbers on stat sheets and the stories that have been looping on all the sports shows. Instead, I tell her about my mom, about Coach, about the philosophy class that's kicking my ass. We cover everything from minutiae to monumental in the time it takes the Lakers to get blown out.

"What *did* get you so into basketball?" I ask her during a fourth-quarter commercial break.

"I dunno." She studies her beer, probably long gone flat. "One of my mom's guys, Telly, lived with us for a while when I was around ten." She leans one elbow on the bar, giving me a frank look. "He was one of the few good ones who stuck around for a little bit. He loved basketball. Loved the Lakers and we'd watch the games together." She chuckles, making track marks with her fingertips in the condensation coating her glass. "On game nights, we'd order pineapple pepperoni pizza and drink root beer floats."

"What happened?" I sip on my third ginger ale. "To Telly, I mean?"

She answers first with a little shake of her head. "He outstayed his welcome, I guess." Her eyes drift to the screen, maybe an excuse to look away. Or maybe the game really has grabbed her attention. Lakers have the ball. "Someone else came along with more money. Mom traded up."

"You ever see him, talk to him again?"

Her eyes abandon the screen, and for a few quiet moments, she studies the bar top. "No."

The word comes low and husky. After a moment she looks back up, flashing me a half-teasing grin. "But I still like pizza and root beer when I watch the Lakers."

"No pizza on the menu here?" I mumble around a handful of nuts.

"Beggars can't be choosers." The smile she shares with me morphs into a scowl when the final score displays onscreen. "Another one for the 'L' column. Shit calls all night, ref."

"Really? Shit calls?" I glance from the game back to her face with skepticism. "Nothing to do with the fact that the team is aging and plagued by injuries the last few seasons? End of an era, if you ask me."

"Bite your tongue," she snaps, but there's a playful glint in her eyes. "You could end up going to the Lakers. Have you thought of that?"

"Who knows where I'll end up?" I slant my smile at her. "I'm hoping for the Stingers."

"Baltimore?" A frown crinkles her eyebrows before clearing. "Oh! Your hometown, huh?"

"I mean, it happened for LeBron in Cleveland. He played where he grew up, for the Cavs."

"True. Why do you want to stay close to home? You a mama's boy?"

My laugh booms over the TV commentators analyzing the Lakers' loss in the background. "My mom's pretty awesome, but that wouldn't keep me close to home." I stare into my ginger ale instead of at her, a little uncomfortable to express my reasons. "I just want to do something for the place that did so much for me. I was in the Boys and Girls Club. I had amazing teachers, especially in middle school when a lot of my friends started going off the rails. The community center's where I fell in love with basketball."

Self-consciousness burns my face, and I shrug. "My whole childhood was there, and that community made it a good one."

In the beat of silence after I finish, I glance up to find a slight smile on her face and warm eyes that meet mine easily.

"That's cool," she offers simply, and I'm glad she doesn't make it a big deal even though it must be obvious it's important to me. "So, you ready for the draft?"

I appreciate the shift of subject. It's not likely I'll go to Baltimore, and I don't let many people know how much it would mean to me. "I am, but it's all happening so fast." A dry chuckle rattles in my throat. "The NBA was some distant fantasy when I was in the eighth grade. Now it's right here, and unless something goes really wrong, it's actually happening. I just hope . . ."

My words trail off, but my uncertainty remains. It's not even about my ability to play at the next level. I know I'm prepared for that. It's all that comes with it that I'm not sure I'm ready for.

"You'll do great." Her slim fingers close over my hand, gripping the glass. "You'll be an amazing player."

Just that light pressure, just seeing her hand with mine, feels good. Something about the sight levels the unevenness I've felt all day and unlocks words I haven't said to anyone.

"I want to be more than just a player. I want to use my degree. I want a business. I want a family." It feels like a confession. "To be a good husband. A good father. This world I'm entering in a few months, I've seen it devour guys. We work toward this all our lives, and an injury, age, a bad trade, whatever—can end it overnight. If the game has eaten up your priorities, turned you into someone you never wanted to be, what's the point?" I laugh self-consciously. "I probably sound—"

"You sound too good to be true," she interrupts, her hand still resting on mine. "Guys in your position, the night before the big game, right on the edge of the draft—these aren't things most of them are thinking about."

She props her chin in the palm of her free hand, a slow smile working its way to her mouth. "You're special." She bites her lip, lifting her hand away from my fingers, dropping her eyes to the bar top scarred by a million glasses and a million moments before ours. "I'm glad I met you."

That sounds suspiciously like the beginning of goodbye. Like she's ready to close the door on this surreal chapter.

I can't let that happen. A night like this, a connection like this—it's singular. After tomorrow's game, my future will literally be a little ball bouncing around in the NBA Draft Lottery. I may end up playing for a team I don't like, living in a place I won't get to choose.

But tonight, I have control. I have choices, and I choose her. To get to know her. To woo her. To earn her trust. All I need is time.

But time seems to be the one thing we don't have.

"Closing." The bartender drags our empty glasses toward him and wipes down the surface in front of us. "You ain't gotta go home, but you gotta get out of here."

I hadn't noticed the bar emptying around us, but we're nearly the last ones left.

"Good luck tomorrow, West," the bartender says, sliding two checks across the freshly-wiped bar.

"Thanks." I stand and snatch both of them before she can even look at hers.

"Give me that." She lunges toward me, but I hold the check over my head, completely out of her reach.

She stumbles into me, her soft breasts pressing against my chest. I want to wrap my arms around the stretch of sensuous lines and curves that make up her body. With her check still suspended over my head, I slide my other hand down her back, investigating her shape beneath the clingy cotton. I palm the dip at her waist, drawing her a few inches closer until her warmth, her clean scent, surrounds me.

She blinks up at me, bright eyes darkening and widening, the green and gold lost in sable. Desire starbursts her irises. We've barely acknowledged the current humming between our bodies, the electricity running under the surface of our easy conversation, until just now. Until I lured her into me with a little slip of paper.

"Let me buy your drinks." I can't remember ever wanting a woman the way I want her. I don't just want to bury my hands in all that dark hair, or to discover for myself how sweet her lips taste, or to explore her body. I want more of her memories, her secrets—to accept an invitation she hasn't extended to anyone else.

Her lashes lower, shielding her eyes from mine, but she can't hide her body's response—the way all the places she's soft seem to seek out the places I'm hard and unyielding. How her breath stutters over her lips in little pants.

"Um, okay." She steps back until we're no longer touching, clearing some of the huskiness from her voice before going on. "Thanks. I could have . . . well, thanks."

Neither of us speaks on our way to the door. I find myself slowing to match her shorter stride. We watch each other from the corners of our eyes, the silence between us pulsing with possibility. Once outside, we're tucked away under an awning with the still-bustling city just beyond our patch of sidewalk. Inside, surrounded by people and noise and the action of the game, the conversation came so effortlessly. The confessions and admissions I'd never made to anyone else flowed right out of me. And now, it's just us and I'm not sure what to say to keep her here, but I know what I've been feeling, what we've been doing, can't end tonight.

There's this part in *Spanglish*, one of Adam Sandler's chick flicks. He and his kids' nanny share dinner at his restaurant. It's just one meal, a few hours. The narrator, the nanny's daughter, says, "My mother has often referred to that evening at the restaurant as the conversation of her life." I'm pretty sure I rolled my eyes when I heard it and said, 'That was *some* conversation.'

But now, with her, standing at the edge of goodbye, all I can think is . . . that was *some* conversation.

The streetlight and the moon illuminate things the dimness of the bar hid—the amber in her hair I thought was just black, the length of her lashes casting shadows on her cheeks while she studies the ground. We both seem to be searching for words. It's as if we've crammed so much into the last few hours that there are no words left—none left for me, anyway. All I have is feeling. *Need.* I need to touch her, to kiss her—I need something physical to reassure me this encounter really happened. That this isn't the end.

When you're a foot taller than a girl, it's hard to smoothly go in for a kiss, so I don't try for smooth. I'm careful, though. I lift her chin with one finger, persuading her eyes up to meet mine. I cup her cheek and lower my head until I'm hovering over those lips that look so soft I have to hold myself back from devouring them; I have to control my need to taste her right away. My body revs, demands. My heart slams into my rib cage. My dick is hard. Want sizzles through every cell of my body.

"August." She pulls her chin away and presses her hand to my chest, but not to explore. To gently push me back. I hold my breath, waiting to see

21

what this means, this small space she's put between us.

Her head drops forward until the dark cloud of hair eclipses her face, hides her expression. "I'm sorry." She steps back, running a hand through her hair. "I-I can't."

I want to bring her close again. "It's okay. I get it, of course. We just met."

I link our fingers. Even that brief contact stirs my senses. I check the roar of my body, hoping my erection doesn't betray me.

"We can just talk. We can go to your place, if you're not far." I lift her chin so I can see her eyes. So she can see that I mean it. Despite the absolute inferno raging under my skin, it's enough. "We can do whatever you want."

As little, as much—let's just keep doing *something*. Let's just not stop.

"I-I can't. We can't." With a vigorous shake of her head, she takes another step back, dropping my hand, inserting space between us again. "I have a boyfriend, August."

Shit.

I shouldn't be surprised that she's taken. A girl this gorgeous, this funny and smart and authentic—she's all the adjectives I would use to describe the perfect girl for me. She's even the things I didn't know I wanted. But now I know, and I can't have her.

A hole gapes open inside of me wider and deeper than it should be considering how little I know about her, but it's there. And by the second, it fills with disappointment and lost possibilities.

"So . . . is it serious?" I wince internally. If there's anything more douchey than trying to kiss another guy's girl, it would be asking, in so many words, if she's sure she wants to stay faithful to him.

"Yeah." She sinks her teeth into her bottom lip. "We've been dating about a year."

She finally looks up at me, and at least the battle in her expression, the struggle reflected back to me from her eyes, assures me I'm not imagining the pull between us.

"I should have told you, but that would have been weird." She smiles ruefully. "I would have sounded like I was assuming you wanted more than . . ."

We stare at each other in a silence rich with things I shouldn't say.

"I *do* want more than." I manage a smile, though I'm frustrated and not just sexually. I'm downright devastated that some other guy got here before I did.

"I'm sorry." She stuffs her hands in the back pockets of her jeans. "I was enjoying our conversation so much. I didn't want to . . . I hope I didn't mislead you."

"You didn't." I stuff my hands in my pockets, too, to keep from touching her again. "At least I made a new friend."

Friend.

It sounds hollow compared to what I thought we could be, but I can't demand more. I can't *make* her give me more. I'm on the eve of something most men only dream of, and this bright-eyed girl has made me feel helpless.

"Yeah." Her face relaxes a little into a smile. "A friend."

"And you helped take my mind off tomorrow's game."

As soon as I say it, both of our eyes go wide. I check my watch, dreading the time.

Fuck.

Curfew.

Was I so absorbed by this girl that I forgot curfew before the biggest game of my life?

Yeah, I was.

"Oh my God." Her eyes are anxious, worried. "The game. You've missed curfew."

The hunger, the heat, the rightness between us had made me shove every other thought aside, but they all intrude now. *Curfew. The rest of the team, asleep and accounted for at the hotel. Tomorrow's game.*

"Will you get in trouble?" she asks, frowning.

"It won't be the first time I've had to sneak in," I tell her with more confidence than I actually feel. The biggest game of my life, and I lost track of time with a girl in a bar.

But what a girl.

Looking at her, replaying every moment, every joke, every memory we shared over the last few hours, I can't regret it.

"Let me at least walk you home." Curfew or not, there's no way I'm letting her go alone.

"No. I'm really close."

This part of the city is completely commercial as far as I can tell, not residential. "Your apartment is nearby? Or are you staying at a hotel?"

Does she live here? Is she visiting? A student? Is she in town for the game? Will she be there tomorrow? Does she want tickets to come see me play? All the things we *did* talk about are suddenly less important than all the things we never said. I don't even know her damn name. "Gumbo" won't get me very far after tonight. Panic tightens my body into a drawn bow. Even if it's never more than what we had tonight—the honesty, humor, ease, empathy—I want to continue with her. I'll even settle for the dreaded word—friendship.

"I'll walk you home," I insist.

"I'll be fine." She looks down at the ground and then back at me. The end is in her eyes. I see goodbye, and I want to stop it before it reaches her lips, but I don't.

"Goodbye, August. Good luck tomorrow." She turns and starts up the sidewalk.

I want to chase her. To follow and find out where she lives or where she's staying. Even knowing some lucky bastard found her first, I can't imagine having no idea how to find her again.

"Hey, wait," I call after her, forcing my feet not to follow. "You should at least tell me your name. Do you really want me to think of you as Gumbo forever?"

She faces me but keeps walking backward, steadily putting more space between us. Between this night and the rest of our lives. Mischief lights her eyes, and the sly smile playing around her lips makes me think for a terrible moment that she won't tell me.

"It's Iris," she calls back to me. "My name is Iris."

I stay still, absorbing the sound of her name, absorbing the look on her face as she walks out of my life with as little fanfare as she entered it. Her smile dies off, and she's staring at me like she wants to remember my face—like she won't forget tonight either. Like maybe, unreasonably, undeniably, this night meant as much to her as it did to me. If she felt it, too, this connection, she can't be walking away, but she is. I've only known her a few hours. It's unreasonable that desperation bands my chest and panic shortens my breath, like I'm sprinting.

Except I'm standing still. And she's still walking.

Walking and turning the corner, out of my sight.

She takes my hope for more with her when she goes.

TWO

IRIS

Anticipation charges the arena, every breath I draw making my heart race that much faster. I'm sitting in the best seats money didn't even have to buy at the NCAA Championship, yet the basketball game is the last thing on my mind.

"You're as nervous as a live lobster in a boiling pot." Lotus's words are a splash of cold water across my face. Am I that obvious? I feel obvious, like there's a huge neon sign flashing over my head. I keep telling myself that nothing happened with August last night. I have nothing to feel guilty about, but guilt gnaws through my rationale.

"It's a big game for Caleb." I shrug, hoping it looks more casual than I feel. "Of course I'm nervous for him."

"I get that," Lotus says. "But you're downright agitated. Keep bouncing your knee like that and you'll cause a quake in here."

Even after she says it, my knee can't stop hopping, my foot tapping out an erratic rhythm on the stadium floor.

"Bo, what the hell?" Lotus demands, shortening Gumbo as only she does. She presses her hand to my knee, forcing it still. "Seriously, I know this is a huge night for Caleb, but chill."

I stare down at the court, searching for my boyfriend in the clusters of players shooting around and warming up for the biggest game of their lives. I didn't want to distract him before the game by telling him I met August West, but what will I tell him after? A conversation at a bar during a Lakers game is no big deal, but somehow, I know Caleb won't agree.

"Are you even hearing me?" The concern in Lotus's dark eyes jars me out of my head.

"Yeah. Sorry." I finally give her my full attention. "I'll try to relax."

She searches my face, and I force myself not to look away. Braids spill over her shoulders and arms. High, slanting cheekbones and a narrow chin lend her face an almost feline quality. She's slim and emanates strength. I'm not sure if it's the jut of her jaw, her obstinate chin, or her wise eyes. Or maybe it's something beneath her skin, built into her bones.

We come from a long line of Louisiana's famous high priestesses. Our great-grandmother MiMi was the last of them. Her daughter, our grandmother, had no desire to stay in the relative seclusion of a small bayou parish but wanted the excitement of New Orleans. A divide grew between MiMi and the other women of our family, and it seems the mystical power will die with her when she leaves this earth. But sometimes I swear I see traces of it in Lotus.

My skin may be several shades lighter than the smooth cinnamon of hers, but we've never let a little melanin and our one-year age gap come between us. We've needed each other too much. Lotus has been my constant, and I've been hers.

Even the years when she went to live on the bayou with MiMi and I stayed in the city, the miles between us didn't weaken our bond. Though I never keep anything from her, I haven't breathed a word about last night's conversation with August.

The roaring crowd, the scantily dressed cheerleaders, and the swarm of cameras and commentators along the periphery of the court all fade, and I remember last night. August's baseball cap provided a flimsy disguise, and I recognized him as soon as he sat beside me. The lean, powerful body, the chiseled jaw and sculpted lips, the bronzed skin—all dead giveaways.

Caleb has talked about August before, of course, and I know a lot about his game because I stay on top of sports. The media fixated on him during March Madness while his team continued their unlikely road to the Final Four. Caleb and August have been competing against one another since middle school and aren't exactly friends.

None of that prepared me for who August West actually is. I discovered a depth in him that was surprising and refreshing. His vulnerability was so unexpected and at odds with the strength of his public image. Maybe it's the vulnerability that enhances his strength.

A dozen times, I started to tell him I'm Caleb's girlfriend. I have to admit, at least to myself, that I didn't tell him because I thought he might leave. I was enjoying the conversation so much, and that was the last thing I wanted to happen. It won't matter since I'll probably never see him again.

I run a hand through my hair, flat-ironed straight and tamed the way Caleb likes it. I've made more of an effort tonight because this is such a huge milestone for him. I even wore the outfit he asked me to wear, the one he gave me for my birthday, though it shows a little more of my body than I typically would. Left to me, I would have worn his jersey, a pair of jeans, and Chucks.

No, Jordans.

I wiggle my toes in the boots I paired with this tight-ass skirt. The top is cropped just beneath my breasts, leaving my stomach almost completely bare.

Lotus says I look good, but that isn't the point. I'm at a freaking basketball game, not a club.

"Hey, there's your boy," she says, nodding down toward the court. "And he looks as nervous as you do."

Lotus is right. There's a tightness in Caleb's expression and across his shoulders that doesn't bode well for his jump shot. He glances all over the arena, searching for something. It's not until he catches my eyes and smiles that I realize he was looking for me. I set aside my guilt and nervousness long enough to give him the smile, the reassurance, I know he needs tonight.

"Aren't his parents posted up in one of those fancy luxury rooms?" Lotus directs her gaze to the row of VIP boxes elevated above the rest of the arena.

"Yeah, but I like to sit in the stands," I tell her. "And Caleb likes to see me here."

I blow him a kiss, and his smile grows wider, lighting his handsome face. Caleb is the same height as August, six-six, and he's just as powerfully built. His blond hair, tanned skin, and nearly navy blue eyes make him quite literally the golden boy of college basketball. There's nothing to indicate that he won't be just as popular in the NBA.

He turns to practice a few dribbling drills. He'll need all the practice he can get if he's going to outshoot August tonight, though I honestly don't know if he can. I hate doubting him, but we haven't seen a perimeter shooter like August in a long time. Caleb's team is the defending champion. He got his ring last year, but I know beating his longtime rival to win another would be especially sweet for him.

"That man loves you, girl," Lotus says. "And I didn't think any guy could get you out of the library."

"Neither did I."

I had a scholarship to keep and wasn't going to be distracted by any guy. I was working the register when Caleb came into the bookstore needing a book for his psychology class. He showed up every morning for weeks with a cup of coffee for me until I agreed to go out with him. He's practically a celebrity on our campus, so of course I was flattered. I didn't take his interest in me seriously, though. I assumed he was exactly the kind of guy I should avoid, but he wore me down and he proved me wrong. We laughed together. We talked basketball. He treated me well and made me feel special.

"Well you caught yourself a big fish, as our mamas would say." The same bitterness about the men who passed through my life rings in Lotus's voice. "Now just to keep him."

"If anything, he's trying to keep *me*." I grimace at how that sounds. "What I mean is you know I care about Caleb."

"Of course," Lotus says, watching me closely.

"It's just lately, it seems like he's asking for so much more."

I hesitate, not wanting to paint Caleb in a bad light, but Lo lifts her brows and nods her encouragement for me to go on.

"He's been dropping hints about marriage and that he wants me to move with him to the city that drafts him."

"But what if your opportunities aren't in whatever random city drafts him?" Lo's brows pinch together. "He knows you want to pursue your career in sports marketing, right?"

"Of course. Yeah, I've always been up front about that," I say. "But now with the draft approaching, he doesn't want a long-distance relationship, so it keeps coming up."

I've always plotted my path in the opposite direction of my mother's. Independence. Not relying on a man. Making my own way. If there's one thing I know about my course, it's that I have to stay on it.

"Well speaking of." Lotus elbows me. "Your future father-in-law is heading our way." She nods toward Caleb's father and his cousin, approaching through the crowded stands, stopping every so often to smile and chat.

"Would you stop saying that?" Exasperation weights my sigh. "It's bad enough everyone else assumes Caleb and I are already practically engaged."

"To hear Aunt Priscilla tell it, you'll be married and pregnant by Christmas."

"Pregnant?" I scowl. "Mama would love that. The higher Caleb goes in the draft, the more she'll want a grandbaby to hook him for life. That's the last thing I'm thinking about. A baby right now would ruin all my plans."

"What's the rush anyway?" Lotus adjusts an errant lock of hair until it knows its place on my shoulder. "Why's Caleb so eager to get married?"

"I know. What's wrong with a long-distance relationship? I'm not ready for marriage. It's too soon."

"Do you love him?" Lo's eyes pick around the edges of my expression.

"Sure." I shrug, looking down at my knees. "I mean, we say it to each other, but does that mean he's *the one*? I don't know. We've been dating a year. We started as friends, and he's gorgeous and smart and considerate. I'd be crazy not to love him, right? He's perfect."

Lotus puts her hand over mine. "Hey, look at me."

I meet her eyes, braced for whatever she's about to say.

"It doesn't matter if he's perfect, Bo, if he's not perfect for *you*." She squeezes my fingers. "You need a guy who respects your ambitions and your dreams."

"I think Caleb can be that guy."

But even as I say it, I question if it's true. If my ambitions took me to one place and Caleb to another, would he expect me to follow him? Would I lose him if I didn't? I hope I don't have to choose. I know how important basketball is to him, but does he really understand how important my dreams are to me?

"Just be sure," Lotus says, pasting on a plastic smile and aiming it over my shoulder. "In the meantime, here comes papa."

"Good evening, ladies," Caleb's father says, finally making his way to stand in front of us.

Donald Bradley's smile is always as carefully coordinated as his ties and tailor-made suits. The word that comes to mind is calculating, like he's added you up and subtracted you to determine how much of his time and attention you merit. His every movement is smooth, but there is a hardness to him that makes me wonder if there's really a heart beating beneath that silk shirt. He's so much like Caleb physically—the same golden hair and dark blue eyes—but Caleb doesn't have that hard smoothness.

Not yet.

It's a whisper I try to ignore. The thought of Caleb evolving into his father drops a bag of stones in my belly.

"Hi, Mr. Bradley." I glance up at the man beside him, forcing a smile for Caleb's cousin. "Hey, Andrew."

"Hey," Andrew replies politely. Neutral is the word I always associate with him. He's in medical school, so I know he has his own talents, but beside the vitality of his superstar cousin, there is something . . . bland, beige about him. Like he'll match whatever's around him, absorb whatever he needs to in any given situation. Maybe that's not the worst thing, but it makes him hard to read. When you grow up with a series of creepy "uncles" in your house like we did, you learn to read men's intentions. What makes me wary of Andrew is I can never read his.

"You're both welcome to join Barbara and me up in the box," Mr. Bradley says. "We've got quite a spread up there to celebrate after my boy wins tonight."

"I'm fine here for now." I try to warm my lukewarm smile. "I like being close to the action."

"And I'm sure Caleb wants to see you in the stands." He looks at me sternly. "But tonight at the party, work the room some. A beautiful wife is a huge asset for a man like Caleb. We've got as much work to do off the court as we do on it."

My teeth grind together. I have so many things I want to do before I settle down. And right now, none of them involve being a baller's trophy wife.

"I'll support Caleb in every way that I can," I say. "Just as I'm sure he'll support the things I want to pursue."

Mr. Bradley wears a pleased smile and pats my shoulder. "There are all kinds of charities and committees for the players' wives that I'm sure you'll enjoy."

"We'll see how much time I have," I tell him. "I've applied for several internships, including one with St. Louis."

I don't have to wait long for his reaction.

"St. Louis?" His thick brows lower and clump over his eyes. "My team?"

Mr. Bradley, already in the Hall of Fame as a player, is a front office executive for the St. Louis expansion team. He's built many teams from nothing into championship-caliber squads.

"St. Louis is one of the teams I'm interviewing with, yeah." I suppress a satisfied smirk.

"You should probably wait to see where Caleb is drafted before you make any commitments," he says, his tone condescending. "You'll want to know where he lands."

"I'm actually in the final round of consideration for a few internships," I say, keeping my expression placid. "So we'll also have to see where *I* land."

He squints and tilts his head, considering me like I'm a worrisome puzzle. My pieces aren't fitting the way they should. Most girls would jump at the chance to secure a future with an NBA player. So why am I hesitating to marry his golden boy?

"Well, we'd better be getting back to our guests." He nods toward a nearby tunnel. "See you up in the box after the game. Let's go, Andrew."

With one last look, Andrew turns to follow.

"You're marrying into a fucked-up family." Lotus shudders, shaking herself.

"I'm not marrying . . ." There's teasing in her eyes. "Stop pushing my buttons."

"But with my heavy workload at school, it's one of the few joys I have left in life."

"Find new joys."

We share a grin, and she links her arm through mine, leaning her head on my shoulder while we watch the pre-game shenanigans. Mascots for both teams run the length of the court, using trampolines to slam-dunk balls. A kiss cam gets going, and Lotus and I can't stop laughing at an elderly couple kissing like teenagers fogging up a backseat window.

And then I see him. I haven't allowed myself to look for August since the players came on court for the pre-game shoot around. I'm not that close, and you couldn't squeeze a gnat in this building because there are so many people here. Still, I worry that he'll spot me.

I could be worrying for nothing. I mean, he must have girls chasing him all the time. Some inconsequential chick he met in a bar is probably utterly forgettable.

Except it didn't feel inconsequential. Not the things we shared or the look on his face when I walked away. None of it felt inconsequential. And though I know I should forget, I can't stop remembering.

My mom used to say it took a crow bar to pry me open, but with August, I surprised myself. I didn't hold back. When was the last time I talked so openly with anyone besides Lo?

Down on the court, he faces a teammate, dribbling two balls, one with each hand, his posture relaxed. He laughs at something the other player says, his lips spread in a flash of humor and charisma. An indolent swagger hangs on him like his basketball shorts, easy and loose, but a barely veiled energy crackles around him. He's nimble athleticism and latent power on the verge of explosion.

In an instant, he goes from the ease of his teammate's camaraderie to the trademark precision shooting that's inspired awe in basketball pundits throughout this tournament. Eyes fastened on the hoop, he knocks down six three-pointers in quick succession. From wrist to bicep, one arm is sheathed in a shooter sleeve, a compression accessory some ballers use to keep their arm warm and increase circulation. A few colorful tattoos paint the other arm, but the most prominent one is on the ball of his shoulder, the number thirty-three. It's his jersey number, but I remember hearing it was his father's, too.

He's not wearing his jersey yet, and when he tosses the ball back and forth between his big hands, palming and raising it over his head in a stretch, his T-shirt lifts, exposing rungs of muscled abs.

My breath catches. My body flattened to his last night, the check above his head. The rock-hard chest and arms. The gentle hands and eyes. The strength and heat of him, the way he smelled—everything about him made me want to press closer. To be as close as I could get. I wanted to kiss him. The source of all this guilt isn't what I *did* with August. It's what I *wanted*. What I felt.

He looks up into the stands in our direction, and my heart pauses for the space of a beat. I tense, as much from the memory of those eyes fixed on me as from the fear that he'll see me now.

His coach yells, waving the team over to the bench. I should be relieved he didn't see me, but some perverse, masochistic part of me wishes he knew I was here.

My eyes seek Caleb on court, and I wait to feel anything as visceral as what I felt last night with August. I'm glad to see Caleb. I'm proud of him. I'm happy for him, but it doesn't feel like my heart is pinned to a soaring kite. My feet are firmly planted on the ground. My body doesn't go haywire. When was the last time Caleb left me breathless with little more than a look, a touch? For that matter, when was the last time I wanted to tell him so many things there wasn't time for it all?

I have a year invested with Caleb, and we've been happy. After meeting August West once, I'm questioning it?

"So what are you gonna do?" Lo asks softly, breaking into my thoughts. "About this Caleb situation, I mean. If he wants more and you want . . .what you want?"

I turn my head to study my cousin's face.

"Why do I have to know right now?" I answer Lo without actually answering. "I'm about to graduate from college. This should be a time when it's safe to explore, when there's space to figure out what life is on my own. Can't we just be dating? I'm not sure what I know for sure yet, and that should be okay."

The closer we get to the future, the more I feel the weight of Caleb's expectations, spoken and unspoken. I just hope it's not so heavy that it crushes us, crushes what we have completely.

"Don't let him rush you, girl," Lo says. "Better no man than the wrong man. We saw that firsthand."

What would our lives have been like if my mom had married one of the creeps who paid our rent? Except for Telly, I was usually glad to see them go. If she'd married one of those men, I know instead of the security she envisioned, it would have been a trap.

Once the game is underway and halftime approaches, I know Caleb's team is in trouble. It's not in the score, because they're only down by five, still easily within striking distance. And Caleb's performance shouldn't give me pause. He's nearly at a triple-double already. My reservations actually have nothing to do with Caleb and his team, and everything to do with August and his. There's an X factor in sports, probably in life, that doesn't show up in stats sheets or on scoreboards. Jordan had it. Kobe had it. It's that "I will not be stopped" killer instinct. When a player has that, he'll strap the whole team to his back if that's what it takes to win.

That killer instinct blares from every pore of August West.

I've never seen him play live, or I would have known this already. It's in his eyes every time he faces Caleb one-on-one, the crooked grin that says August relishes toying with him. Each time he stops on the dime and spins beyond Caleb's reach to score, he insinuates himself deeper into Caleb's head. And that's where the game will ultimately be lost if something doesn't change in the second half. If I were the coach, I'd assign someone else to guard August because Caleb can't. I suspect Caleb asked to do it, feeling like he had something to prove.

He's not proving it.

If I could have five minutes alone with Caleb, maybe I could help. He's told me before that he thinks about me when the game isn't going his way. Even if I could get to him, I'm not sure I could face him right now. I'd probably just blurt an apology for all the things I *didn't* do last night with August but can't stop thinking about.

Not helpful.

As a fan, I marvel at August's gifts on display tonight—at the show he's putting on for us. As a girlfriend, I wince every time Caleb misses a shot. Caleb can be a little entitled. With all the privileges he's had, how could he not be occasionally? But he's worked hard all season, and August's hot hand is burning all Caleb's work to the ground. Even as I admire August's skill, guilt saws my insides. I should be completely rooting for Caleb, but there's this tiny rebel corner of my heart that wants all of August's hard work to pay off, too. Tonight, on his father's birthday.

The buzzer sounds, and both teams exit the court for halftime.

"They're in good shape, right?" Lo asks.

"Sure." I keep my answer short because if I keep talking, I'll say what I see.

We spend most of halftime at the concession stand. After we squeeze through the bleachers and back into our seats, Lo brings up the last thing, the last person, I want to discuss.

"Caleb's gotta be worried about that August West guy." She sips her soda. "He's something else."

"Yeah, he's an All-American," I answer evenly, keeping my eyes steady on the halftime show while my heart goes berserk. "He'll be a first-round draft pick for sure."

"He's also fine as hell." Lo cocks a skeptical brow. "Don't tell me you were so caught up in stats you didn't notice that dude's ass."

You should see his eyes. You should feel his chest.

You should hear his voice.

I futilely try to forget how being with August made me feel perfectly at ease and wholly exhilarated all at once.

"Is it hot in here?" I fan my face with one hand, trying to cool the heated skin. "And remember, I have a boyfriend. I'm in a relationship."

"In a relationship, not dead." She girl-grunts her appreciation. "Hmmm. And you'd have to be dead not to notice that man."

For a second, all the details from last night collect on the tip of my tongue. It was just a few hours, but it felt then—it still feels—significant. And I've never kept anything significant from Lo. Since nothing happened, I should be able to tell her everything with a clear heart, but I hesitate. Something *did* happen. My stomach lurches with the truth. As much as I don't want to deal with it, something shifted in me last night. I don't completely understand it yet, but it feels seismic.

I don't say any of that to Lo. It was one conversation. She'd think I was crazy to feel that fascinated by August already. *I* think I'm crazy. So instead of saying any of that, I redirect the conversation.

"Game's starting back up."

The score stays close throughout the second half, but ultimately the other team has something we don't. And that something is August. With only two minutes remaining, he does what all the great ones do. He takes over, willing high-risk shots to go in, making the impossible ones look effortless. Frustration radiates from Caleb as he watches the game slipping away. The final blow comes as he's defending August on a possession in the last few seconds. August plants himself in his sweet spot, the far-right corner, just beyond the three-point line. Caleb reaches in to block the shot, and before the whistle blows, I know it's a foul. His last one. He's fouled out of the game. To add insult to injury, August's three-pointer goes in. This could be a four-point play that drills the nail into the coffin.

Shit.

Caleb slams the ball onto the court, sending it rocketing high in the air. He yells at the ref before stomping to the bench. There's a wildness in his eyes, something I haven't seen before. I grew up with volatility, and on occasion, saw violence. Seeing Caleb lose control stirs my instinct to run. But by the time he's on the bench chugging Gatorade, that wildness is gone and he's my golden boy again.

Maybe I imagined it.

August picked his game apart, and Caleb's understandably frustrated. Most guys have those moments when they lose control. If there had been more time left on the clock, and if Caleb was anyone else, he probably would have been ejected from the game. But he's not ejected and has to sit on the bench watching to the very end.

August assumes his place on the free-throw line, his body relaxed like this moment, as big as it is, isn't big enough to swallow his confidence. If he makes this shot, with less than a second left on the clock, there won't be time for us to recover. A four-point game will be out of reach.

With thousands of fans waving and screaming and booing in front of him, creating a human mass of distraction, August seems to block it all out. It's just him and the hoop, and it would take an act of God to stop that ball from going in.

God does not intervene.

A nothing-but-net *swoosh* puts this game in the books. A second later the buzzer goes off, the building erupts, and August's team scatters all over the court in a chest-pounding, body-slamming celebration. August stands in the middle of the floor, absolutely still, the game ball cradled in the definition of his arms against his chest. His head hangs forward, and emotion emanates from him so thickly it reaches me. It touches me.

I tip my head down to hide my face, to hide my smile. I hurt for Caleb, of course, but I know what this means to August—that as he stands in the center, a vein of sobriety running through the jubilation, he's thinking of his father. Wondering if his dad sees him. Wondering if today, on his birthday, he's proud. I have no way of knowing, but somehow, I'm sure he is.

THREE
AUGUST

n one of the earliest photos my mother has of me, my father's autographed basketball rests beside me in my crib. Though shadowy, I know the memories of summer afternoons behind our house, of him lifting me on his shoulders to dunk the ball with my childish hands, are real. I could barely walk when I started dribbling a ball. You could say my entire life has been leading up to this moment.

The fall of confetti, the thunder of the crowd, the lights ricocheting off a thousand camera lenses—it's a prism of sight and sound that doesn't penetrate my private celebration. I've come so far and grabbed the prize, and I want to enjoy this for a moment. Maybe later in life I'll figure out how to turn off the drive that churns like a locomotive inside me, but I haven't yet. And tomorrow it will demand of me what it always does—*more*. I'm allowing myself a moment to savor.

A microphone thrust in my face shatters that nanosecond of contemplation. Questions pellet me like a hail of bullets. Dazedly, I field each question, squinting against the glare of a dozen cameras connected to millions of viewers at home. Coach is probably watching from Delores's hospital room, exactly where he should be. But my mom and my stepfather, Matt, are here somewhere, and I'm consumed by an urgency to share this with the only people who understand all it has required.

As my ecstatic teammates and I finish shaking hands with the other team, my mother reaches me, grabs my arm, and pulls me into a hug that smells and feels like every comfort and encouragement it's taken to get me here. I sink into it, burying my face in her thick, red curls that always smell like strawberries. When my dad died and my world upended, my mother was my constant. When she married Matt and moved us to the suburbs outside of Baltimore, she was my rock. When I got the scholarship to play basketball at St. Joseph's Prep and had to leave my friends and all that was familiar, she anchored me. At every turn, when things have spiraled or changed, she's been the same source of support.

She pulls back far enough to peer up at me, framing my face with her hands. If her watery blue eyes didn't reflect the pride they do, tonight wouldn't mean nearly as much.

"You did it," she says, running her fingers over the sweaty mess of my hair. "Your father would be so proud."

Her words, barely audible over all the raucous celebrating, slip right under the guard I have over my heart and prick me. Before I know it, I'm blinking back fucking tears.

"And on his birthday," she whispers, sadness and joy mingling on her face.

"You remembered?" A laugh trips over the sob in my throat.

"Of course, I remembered." She shakes her head and pats my face. "You're so much like him, you know? But you're even better than he was at your age."

Before I can respond, a hand on my shoulder turns me around. Matt draws me close, pride in his eyes, too. He's not my biological father, but he's the man who taught me so much about discipline and respect. This moment belongs to him, too.

"Hey, West." Coach Mannard approaches, grinning more broadly than I've seen him do in four years playing for him. "You saved us tonight more than once. It's been an honor to coach you."

"Thank you, sir."

I shake the hand he extends to me, and we both laugh and end with a hug. Coach Mannard and I have butted heads several times. Fortunately, last night's curfew violation wasn't one of them—I slipped in unnoticed. Even when we haven't seen eye to eye, we've had one thing in common: we both want to win. And tonight, as our road together ends, we have.

"The boosters have a celebration reception for us in one of those fancy boxes upstairs." Coach Mannard addresses me but raises his voice and then looks around to my teammates who have gathered around. "I'm sure all of you have your own plans to celebrate."

That comment is met with wolf whistles and laughter. Fifteen college guys who just became national champions can get into a shitload of trouble, and a lot of us plan to find out how much firsthand tonight.

"But," Coach Mannard says, pausing until he has our attention, "these are our boosters and they want to see you. Shake your hands. This is the school's first basketball title. You made history tonight. It's a big deal. *You're* a big deal, and the people who pay the way want to see you."

He looks at his watch and then back at us.

"I know some of you have interviews to do." His eyes drift to me and then away. "And we'll have the trophy ceremony here in a little bit. After that, shower and get your asses up to the box. Just gimme an hour or two. Sing for your supper, and then I don't care what you do as long as I'm not reading about it tomorrow."

The next hour or so goes quickly, a stream of people demanding my attention. I lose count of the reporters with their recorders and microphones, all asking the same questions.

The trophy ceremony is a blur of emotions, but I see it all in stunning Technicolor detail. My mind takes a snapshot. I'll never forget hefting that trophy over my head in front of thousands of screaming fans.

It's only after I'm showered and in my dress shirt and slacks that it all starts to sink in. I'm a national champion. I may win the Naismith award, Player of the Year. I may have just sealed a top-five spot in the NBA draft. Implications inundate my mind—the money, the fame, the opportunities.

I'll be back in class in a few days. Finals are coming soon. Besides an upcoming visit to the White House, life will return to normal. But there's a new normal waiting for me after graduation, and I'm not sure I'm ready.

I hang back a little and let the rest of the team go ahead to the booster party. When I board the elevator to the luxury boxes, I'm alone, considering the things I told Iris last night about not wanting to lose myself in all of that madness. I want to hold onto that.

I step off the elevator, and my heart stops. Thuds. Drops

Iris.

Like my thoughts delivered her to me, Iris is standing right there, tucked into a group of people clustered at the entrance of the box not too far from ours. Is it my imagination? No, a figment of my imagination wouldn't charge the air and heighten every detail. Everything is clearer, sharper, crisper. For my senses, she's a magnifying glass. She's a megaphone.

And she's standing right there.

Her hair is different. Tamed. It's long, straight, and hanging to the middle of her back. Color splashes her lips, eyes, and cheeks, layered over the beautiful nakedness of last night's face. Instead of the casual clothes from the bar, she wears a short top that stops right under the roundness of her breasts.

The skirt sits low on her hips, molding to the length of her legs and the curve of her ass, leaving a stretch of toned stomach bare. I could tell last night she had a great body, but the reality of her shape, her soft, coppery skin—it shames my imagination. She looks different, but it's still her. My gumbo girl. Every cell in my body confirms it, and my feet are taking me toward her before I realize where I'm going.

"Iris?"

When I call her name, she searches the space around her, sifting through the knot of people until her eyes meet mine, widening with surprise. She quickly picks her way through the small crowd gathered at the entrance to the box, crossing the space until she reaches me. She smells the same, and the effect she has on me, it's exactly the same. A lightning strike. A power surge. Our eyes tangle in the tight space, in the brief silence. Those eyes are the color of whiskey tonight, and they're just as intoxicating. She goes right to my head.

"Hey." My voice comes out raspy and labored, like I took the stairs at top speed instead of the elevator to get here.

"August, hey."

She sounds breathless, too. It must be the live wire running from me to her because she hasn't exerted herself. As a matter of fact, she couldn't look more perfect. "You look . . ."

I stop to steady myself. Adrenaline courses through me like I'm in the heat of a close game, a nail-biter. Like the ball is in my hands for the last-second shot.

"You look beautiful, Iris."

"Oh . . . um, thanks." She tugs at the top like maybe she's self-conscious. Then her eyes go wide again when she looks up at me. "Oh, God, August. Congratulations! Incredible game. I'm sure your father's proud of you today."

Her softly spoken words move me. All the pieces of myself that never seemed to quite fit lock with this girl. I recognized it last night, and I know it now. Maybe it's because we grew up with some of the same challenges, of never feeling like we belonged. Maybe it's the nitroglycerine chemistry boiling between us, just waiting for the strike of a match.

"Thanks." I clear my throat, not sure what to say next except the obvious. "What are you doing here? I mean, I'm glad. Really glad, I just—"

"Iris."

The sharp voice just beyond her shoulder captures my attention. She stiffens, her lashes drifting down for a second before she glances back up.

"August, I—"

"Hey, baby. I was looking for you." The tanned arm that wraps possessively around her waist belongs to the guy I just defeated.

"Caleb, hey." Iris flicks a glance between the two of us.

What. The. Fuck.

Caleb Bradley is Iris's boyfriend? It couldn't be worse. I hated the *idea* of the guy lucky enough to have Iris before. Now I hate the actual guy. The one everyone calls "the golden boy" is, from my experience, an asshole. He certainly doesn't deserve the girl I met last night. I've never envied his family's money or all the attention the media showered on him. I've never envied the advantages he's had, but now he has her. I envy him that. It boils under my skin and churns in my gut.

"Good game." I fix my eyes on his face so I don't have to look at Iris.

"You, too." Stony blue eyes collide with mine. Bitterness twists his lips. "Congratulations."

It's the most grudging congrats I've ever heard, but I can't blame him. No one wants to see the winner so soon after losing.

"You know my girlfriend?" His eyes connect dots between Iris and me, suspicion laced tightly into the words.

When I finally look at her, the guard over her eyes that dropped so quickly last night is back. I'd almost forgotten it ever existed. Is it back because of me? Or because of him? I have no idea how she wants to play this. Nothing happened last night. Not because I didn't want it to, but because she stopped it.

For him.

For a moment, I want to ruin it. To wreck their relationship by planting doubts in his mind. It's a passing thought I won't follow through on. That's not how you win a girl like Iris.

"We met last night at a bar." Her voice is even. Her eyes, when they meet his, are clear.

"At a *bar*?" A frown jerks his eyebrows together. "What the hell?"

"I wanted to see the Lakers game," she says with measured patience, "and the hotel wasn't carrying it. So, I went to the bar around the corner to watch."

"We ran into each other there," I finish for her. "Just talked for a little while. No big deal."

"Right. No big deal." Her eyes meet mine for a charged second before swinging back to Caleb. "I hadn't had a chance to tell you."

"Well, you won the game, West." There's a phony lightness to Caleb's voice while his eyes remain flinty. "Next thing you know, you'll be trying to win my girl, too."

"Oh, you're not that insecure, are you, Bradley?" I deliberately relax my posture, sliding my hands into my pockets and rocking back on my heels, laying a wide winner's smile on him. "If she doesn't want to be won, she won't be."

"She doesn't want to be." He strips all the lightness from his voice, and if his eyes were stony before, now his whole face is granite. The arm around her waist stiffens to steel.

"Both of you, please stop." Iris exhales sharply, her words, soft but firm, refereeing the tension snarling between Caleb and me. "Caleb, we just talked."

His face broadcasts his displeasure. Seeing his hand spread over Iris's waist, mine might, too. *Asshole.*

I've known him since the eighth grade. Most guys don't just stumble into an NBA career. They pursue it relentlessly for years. We started attending the same preparatory camps and tournaments years ago, and though everyone's fawned all over him, he and I have never clicked. Dirty plays when he thought no one was looking, jockeying for positions, whining when he lost and boasting when he won—those are things that have kept us from being friends. Even though the press constantly compares us and pits us against each other, the hostility has never been open . . . until now.

Until her.

"I guess I won't see you again until the draft, huh, West?" Caleb's tone stays smooth, but he can't hide the lumps from me—the frustration in his eyes, the anger bunching his jaw, the tight fists at his sides.

"Probably not." My eyes stray to Iris. As tall as she is, the two of us dwarf her. I give in to temptation and rake my eyes deliberately over her body again. "I'd wish you luck, but you're obviously a very lucky man."

She draws a deep breath that lifts her breasts under the cropped top. Caleb's narrowed eyes shift between the two of us, like he suspects there's a silent, secret message we're passing between each other under his nose. I wish there was a way for me to telegraph to her what I'm thinking: to ask why she'd fall for the act he dupes everyone else with. And why, knowing the well-documented rivalry between us, did she not tell me who she was last night? For the first time since I saw her at that bar, I wish I hadn't. It would have been better to never know there was a girl out there who could make me feel this way after only one night than to know she chose a guy like him.

"Congratulations, again, August." Iris's smile is starched and stiff, but I know she's sincere. "Caleb, we should get back to the party. Your father's probably looking for you."

Iris tugs his arm, but he doesn't budge for a second, watching me.

Silently warning me. I grin at him, so he knows I don't give a fuck and that he doesn't intimidate me.

After another second, he nods at Iris and they head toward their box. They're absorbed into the press of people, and I'm left standing alone. The sense of loss I felt when she walked away the night before is nothing compared to what I feel now. Now it's not just that I can't have Iris. It's that I can't have her because *he* does. And the girl I met last night, she deserves better than Caleb.

My teammates, Coach Mannard, the boosters—everybody's celebrating, and I'm determined to join the party. This is everything I've worked for, and I refuse to allow Caleb and his girlfriend to spoil it for me. A few of the cheerleaders have thrown clear signals they'd love to find themselves under a national champ tonight. Or on top. Or on their knees. I'm not picky, and I could use the distraction.

After half a bottle of champagne, I'm game for whatever. Who needs Caleb's leftovers when I can have something hot and fresh right here? I'm at the bar in our box still convincing myself when Iris joins me.

"What's a nice guy like you doing in a place like this?" She stares straight ahead at the bottles lining the wall behind the bar for a moment before she turns to me.

"Where's your boyfriend?" I tip the half-empty champagne bottle up to my lips. "I'm surprised he let his consolation prize out of his sight."

"Wow." She shakes her head, a humorless smile resting on her lips. "I probably deserve that, but . . . wow. To answer your question, Caleb and his dad are talking with a potential agent."

"And you decided to sneak over here to check on me?" I slide her a glance as cold and hard as glass. "To make sure I've recovered from the shock of seeing you with the golden boy?"

Iris rests her elbow on the bar, watching my profile for a moment before speaking. "No. I came back to say I'm sorry, August." Her voice holds genuine remorse. "I should have told you about Caleb."

"Yeah." I turn toward her, hoping she feels at least an aftershock from the irritation rumbling inside me. "You should have."

I'm being an asshole. I know it, but I can't seem to stop even when I see the hurt accumulating in her eyes. I'm too drunk. Drunk on disappointment. On frustration. On anger. The half-empty bottle is merely my excuse to show it.

"When you first sat down at the bar last night, I thought maybe you were just a jerk." Her eyes tease me from under her lashes.

I bark a laugh and take another swig from my bottle. "Thanks for that."

"You know what I mean," she says, loosening into a small smile. "Then once we started talking, there didn't seem to be a good place to say, 'Hey, I'm Caleb Bradley's girlfriend.'" She traces a pattern on the bar, dipping her head until a fall of hair conceals much of her face. "After a while, it didn't seem to matter anymore."

If I had known she was Caleb's girl, I wouldn't have sat down. I would have kept walking out that door and made curfew in plenty of time. But she's right. Even just a few minutes into our conversation, knowing about Caleb wouldn't have made me leave. Not once we started. Not once I knew her.

"So . . . it's serious?" I carefully set down my bottle of champagne. "I mean with him. You said it was serious. Like are you guys talking marriage or what?"

Knowing that she was serious about "some guy" was one thing. Knowing she's serious about *him* is quite another. Caleb and I will move in the same circles, play in the same league, attend the same events. I may see her from time to time, wearing his ring and raising his kids. Maybe I've just had too much to drink, but my stomach turns.

She shrugs, dropping her eyes to the floor and shifting her weight from one foot to the other. "He wants to marry me, yeah. Someday."

"And what do you want?" I ask, watching her closely.

"The same things I told you I wanted last night." A frown crinkles her expression. "I want my career. I want the chance to prove myself."

"Good." I pick up my champagne. I need it. "Remember how I said guys lose themselves in that world? The one Caleb and I enter in a few months?"

I wait for her to nod, to acknowledge that she remembers. "So do girls," I say softly. "I would hate to see that happen to you, Iris."

"Thank you." She pushes her hair behind her ear, her lashes lowered. "I'll keep that in mind."

I hope she does. A girl with that much spirit shouldn't be crushed. A girl with that much character shouldn't be swayed. I'm afraid a man like Caleb could do both.

Regret tinges her smile when she looks at me. I don't know if it's regret for not telling me about Caleb last night or if it's regret for what we've lost before it has even begun. Whatever it is, she tucks it away behind her eyes and steps close to me.

"You're a great player, August." She tips up on her toes until her lips are at my ear. "But I think you'll be an even greater man."

Her words zip like an arrow to the very heart of everything I've wrestled with tonight, soothing my uncertainty about how I'll handle the future. My hand slips to the small of her back, to the silky skin above her skirt. I want to pull her closer so badly, but she steps back until my hand falls away. Clearing her throat, she flashes me one last heart-stopping smile. "Bye, August."

And with that, she turns and leaves the bar, retracing her steps from my box back to Caleb's. My fingers seize around the gold-foiled bottle of champagne in unreasonable frustration. I met this girl last night. I shouldn't feel this intensely so quickly. I shouldn't feel like Caleb stole something that was never mine. I out-shot him tonight. I out-rebounded him. I flat out outplayed him. I'm the one who raised the trophy over my head. I won.

So why in God's name do I feel like the loser?

FOUR

IRIS

When I FaceTimed with Lotus last night, showing her my outfit options for this interview, we agreed this pencil skirt was perfect. Now it feels too tight, like it's highlighting all the assets on my body and overshadowing the ones on my resumé. And did this blouse cling to my breasts like this before? Did they grow overnight? I check the pins securing my hair into a knot at my neck. A light dusting of powder and a few touches of color are my only concessions to makeup. Anxiety knots the muscles of my stomach.

"You've got this," I mutter under my breath. My GPA is high. Armed with several semesters' worth of training and experience, plus letters of recommendation from all my professors, I should feel confident. This is the one, though. The opportunity on my list that I want more than all the rest.

I did my homework. Richter Sports is up and coming, and Jared Foster is one of their hungriest agents. Seeing his name on the interview list only ratcheted my nervousness.

I match the number on my interview guide to the one on the door. Today is a sports market job fair of sorts, and everyone who is anyone in the business is here looking for fresh, cheap talent. That's me. I'll work for nearly nothing. Just give me a chance, and I'll make the most of it.

I knock, tensing while I wait for a response.

"Come in," a deep voice calls beyond the door.

Inside, a broad-shouldered man, maybe in his early thirties, sits behind the too-clean desk taking up so much of the borrowed space. Something about his shock of blond hair and his ruggedly handsome face tug at my memory, but I can't place him. I can't think where we would have met.

"Hey." His eyes slowly slide over me from top to toes, masculine appreciation quickly replaced with professional indifference. "On-air talent is up the hall, I believe." He returns his attention to the papers in front of him, offering me a dismissive nod. "Close the door on your way out if you don't mind."

Gritting my teeth, I tighten my fingers around the folder holding my resumé. "I'm . . ." I clear my throat and start again. "I'm not here to audition for television. I'm here about the sports marketing internship."

He lifts his head, assessing me with new eyes, and I hope seeing past the things on which men always seem to place a premium.

"Is that right?" The seat creaks when he tips it back. "My apologies. I'm Jared Foster, resident chauvinist douchebag."

An involuntary smile quirks my lips at his roundabout apology for the presumption.

"And you are?" he asks, his firm lips yielding to a smile of his own.

"Iris DuPree."

"Well, Iris DuPree." He nods to the straight-backed chair across from him. "Let's get started and see what you got."

With every minute that passes and each question he poses, my nerves dissolve into the calm that comes with competence—with knowing you are fully capable of meeting the challenge ahead. I haven't wasted the last four years. When I wasn't working at the bookstore, I was studying the industry, working for free when need be, to learn the ropes and practice what the sports market experts preached. His demeanor goes from indulgent but skeptical, to shrewd and speculative. And finally, to impressed.

"So, Iris," he says, meeting my eyes with more respect than when he assumed I was only good for a close-up, "I always end my interviews with this question. What's a moment in sports that inspired you?"

I don't even have to think about it. I've had to familiarize myself with most sports, but basketball is my first love.

"Ninety-seven NBA Finals," I answer, relaxing my shoulders and unknotting my fingers. "Utah Jazz and Chicago Bulls."

"Game five," we say together, sharing a smile because he knows exactly where I'm going.

"Jordan was sick as a dog," I say, "but somehow, he dug deep into reserves that most people don't even have and willed that game into the win column. It was Herculean."

"Good one." Jared nods approvingly. "And what did that say to you?"

"Let nothing hold you back or keep you down." Conviction rings in my voice because those are lessons I had to learn growing up, a child of the Ninth Ward. A Katrina refugee from a city that had to reincarnate itself more than once. "Even when you think you're defeated, dig deeper. Go harder. Press, because there is something worth it on the other side."

"Good lesson." Jared glances down at my resumé, lifting his eyebrows and nodding. "You've been busy. This all looks good."

"Thank you." I fight back a premature smile.

"If offered the opportunity," Jared continues, "you realize it pays next to nothing, will take over your entire life, and requires you to relocate to Chicago."

The money, or lack of, doesn't matter. I've learned to live with less than most. Hard work has never scared me.

Caleb's face flashes through my mind, creased with disappointment if I make a decision before we know where he'll be drafted. And for some reason, August's face follows soon after. And his words, cautioning me not to lose myself in the world he and Caleb will enter soon. It's been two weeks since the championship, but I've thought of him more than once, and his advice in my head is exactly what I need to hear.

"I'm willing to do what it takes for this chance." I infuse the words with confidence and meet his eyes without hesitation.

"Good." He stands and walks around the desk, prompting me to stand, too. "We have a few more of these job fairs to do, and we won't make selections for the next couple of months, but you definitely impressed me, Iris. I'll be in touch."

"Thank you." I force myself to breathe evenly, but my heart is sprinting. A job like this is exactly the kind of opportunity I need to launch my career in the business of sports.

Jared grabs my hand for a firm shake. "And, hey. I'm sorry again for starting on the wrong foot. Assuming you were on-air talent—"

"Nothing wrong with on-air talent," I interject with a forgiving smile. "Some of the smartest people I know sit in front of the camera. I just don't happen to be one of them."

He releases my hand and walks over to the door. I'm following him when my stomach roils like an angry ocean. Nausea washes over me, so strong it takes my breath, makes my mouth water and dots perspiration across my skin. My eyes stretch when I feel my breakfast reversing, making its way up my throat. I part my lips, prepared to give a quick goodbye and make a hasty departure, but it's too late. It's sudden and inevitable. Everything in my stomach ejects from my mouth in a putrid stream.

And splatters all over Jared Foster.

FIVE

IRIS

"I can't be."

The words tumble past my numb lips. I stare at the urine-stained stick, predicting that in a few months I'll be the last thing I want to be at this stage of my life—a mother.

"Yeah, well four positive pregnancy tests say you are," Lotus replies from the screen turned to face me, her concern evident even over FaceTime. We live in the same city, but we're on different campuses. With our hectic schedules, we FaceTime like we live in different countries.

"How'd this happen, Bo?"

"What do you mean?" With wobbly knees, I sit on the bed, careful not to disturb the laptop displaying Lo's face, the only reassuring thing in this unexpected shit storm. "It happened the usual way."

"I know, but the usual way for people with a shred of common sense involves condoms or shots or pills that keep this from happening."

"The pills made me sick. The shots made my hair fall out, so Caleb used condoms."

"Apparently not every time," Lo mutters, eyebrows sky high.

"Yes, every time, Lo." I swallow another wave of nausea, this one less to do with my pregnancy and more to do with the tough choices ahead of me. "We were always careful. We didn't want to jeopardize our future plans."

"You didn't want to jeopardize *your* future plans," Lotus says, doubt leaking into her voice. "This pregnancy means you might have to depend on Caleb more. It makes it harder for you to be independent and live apart from him. Maybe he was less careful than you thought."

"No." I shake my head in adamant denial. "And don't you think I would have noticed if he skipped the condom? Caleb wouldn't do that. He didn't want me living somewhere else and working in another state, but he would never do this on purpose."

"He wrapped it up?" Lo lifts a skeptical brow. "Every time?"

"Every time," I say with confidence, because to even entertain what she's suggesting would make Caleb a stranger to me—a manipulative person willing to sacrifice my future, my dreams for his wishes. And I can't believe I'd be intimate with someone like that and never know. I can't have been that wrong about him. It's just not possible.

"What're you gonna do about it?" Lo rests her chin in the heel of her hand and watches me steadily.

"I'll talk to him, of course," I tell Lo, glancing at my phone on the bed to check the time. "He's coming over. We'll talk and decide what to do together. I'll figure it all out. This pregnancy won't slow me down."

The words ring hollow. It *will* change things. It has to impact my plans, of course, but I know I can make it work. I have to.

I sign off, promising to call Lotus once Caleb and I finish talking. We've both always been afraid of ending up like our mothers—depending on a man for everything, taking his scraps. This isn't that. I know it, and I hope

Lotus knows, but she still wants to make sure. And when I face Caleb on my doorstep, so do I.

When I tell him, his laugh booms in my small room. A wide smile crinkles his eyes and creases his lean cheeks.

"This is awesome." He grabs me by the shoulders and dusts kisses all over my face. "Baby, this is the beginning of our future together."

Or the end of the one I envisioned for myself, if I'm not careful.

I press my hands to his chest, carving out a small space of breathing room.

"It's not awesome, Caleb," I say softly, firmly. "It's a problem. I'm about to start my career. I've been interviewing for positions and feel really good about my prospects. This is a major wrench."

"Baby, you don't have to work anymore." Arrogance stamps his face. "You never really needed to. Even without an NBA contract, I can take care of you. You don't need to worry about anything. Just move with me, and you and the baby will be taken care of."

Taken care of.

That's one thing I promised myself I'd never be. I remember my mother emerging from the bedroom at the back of our small apartment, a robe hastily tied over her nakedness. A near-stranger walked out after her, zipping his pants, tucking in his shirt, counting off bills for her waiting hand.

"But none of the positions I'm in the running for are in the places you'll probably go," I say firmly. "There's one in New York, and I had a great interview today with Richter Sports. I think they may offer me a job with their Chicago office."

A cloud darkens his expression.

"Chicago!" He levels a glare at me, the blue of his eyes going almost black. "The odds of me being drafted by Chicago are next to zero, Iris. How could you even consider it?"

"I considered it because it's a great opportunity." I step away from him altogether, escaping the anger vibrating off his body. "One I should take before I have a family and obligations. This is the time for us to risk and explore, and figure things out."

"What's there to figure out?" he demands. "I love you. You love me."

I just blink at him. We've said those words, yes, but this relationship isn't the filter for all my decisions, just like it can't be the filter for all of his. Why can't he see that both things are true? That I can love him, but not be ready for this? Not be ready to hitch my entire future to him? That I'm not sure, and that I shouldn't have to be yet.

"We're having a baby. We should be together," he continues, apparently not concerned by my silence. "And you and my child will go with me to the city that drafts me. It's the only thing that makes any sense."

"What about my dreams?" I watch his face for any sign that he would mourn my ambitions at all. That my hopes mean more to him than getting his way. "I don't want the last four years of college, all my hard work, to go to waste." I lick my lips nervously. "Let's just weigh our options, Caleb. We *have* options.

"You don't mean abortion?" Caleb goes still, and his eyes ice over. "Don't even think about it."

Would I? The space between theoretical and actual makes you consider things you never thought you would.

"No." I shrug. "Not really. I don't know, Caleb. This is just a lot."

"I know." He walks me to the bed, sitting down and pulling me onto his lap. "But this only accelerates the plan. You know I want to be with you, want to marry you. I want you with me when I'm drafted, and I want us to have a family. I've known this for a long time."

How? How do you know?

The question rattles in my brain, my uncertainty butting up against his confidence. I care about Caleb. He wouldn't have been my first, wouldn't have gotten past the walls I used to protect myself if I didn't care. But forever? Marriage? Children? Somehow, even as I stare into his dark blue eyes and lean into the gentle stroke of his hand in my hair, I have trouble seeing the rest of my life with him. And I shouldn't *have* to see it right now.

"Caleb, I can have this baby even if we aren't married. Even if we live in different states for a while. People do long-distance relationships all the time."

"Are you not happy in our relationship?" Hurt creases his expression into a frown. "Am I missing something?"

I leave his lap to pace in front of the bed, fixing my eyes on the thin, cheap carpet. "It's not that. I . . . we're young. We have a lot of life ahead. We don't have to chain ourselves—"

"Chain?" He expels the word on an outraged breath. "A lot of girls wouldn't see marrying me as a punishment or a prison."

"A lot of girls would see this baby as an opportunity, Caleb." I look up to meet his eyes frankly. "I don't. When and if I marry someone, I don't want to feel trapped into it."

"Trapped?" His disbelieving laugh fills the room. "Not to be arrogant, but I'm the one who has to worry about being trapped by a woman with a baby."

"Not *this* woman, you don't," I fire back. "I'm not asking you to marry me. If you would listen, I'm telling you I'm not ready for that."

"And our baby?" His tight lips barely let the words out. "I suppose you're not ready for that either?"

At his question, Lotus's concerns echo in my ears.

"How, um . . ." I swallow my reluctance and force myself to go on. "How did this happen? We were always so careful."

I risk a glance at Caleb's handsome face. "Weren't we?" I ask softly.

Something flickers through his eyes so quickly there's no time for me to read it. Guilt? Anger?

"I'm pretty sure you were there, too, Iris. Wouldn't you know just as well as me if we were always careful?"

I don't wear the condoms.

It screams through my head, but I can't make myself say it. Anything close to an accusation would only worsen this already tense situation. Honestly, I can't ever remember a time when we didn't use protection. Does it really matter whose "fault" it is? Condoms aren't fail-proof. Even though Caleb has been pressuring me to discard my plans and get in line with his, I can't imagine him going to these lengths.

Besides, it's like he said: men in his position are the ones worried about being trapped by a grasping female securing a bright future via uterus. Even though I'm being dragged into this situation kicking and screaming, people will assume that's what I've done. That I've "trapped" Caleb. They'll have no idea that I can barely breathe with this baby growing inside of me. That my palms practically drip sweat when I think of Caleb's ring on my finger. That it's not satisfaction I feel knowing I'm pregnant by an NBA draft shoo-in.

It's claustrophobic.

SIX

AUGUST

've been under bright lights a lot the last few years. I should be used to them by now, but squinting into blinding bulbs on the set of *Twofer*, the sports show hosting the Draft Class Special, I'm not so sure.

"Nervous?" Avery Hughes, one of the hosts of *Twofer*, asks.

Uh . . ." I glance around the set, taking in the huge cameras, the sleek furniture, and the crew scurrying around and preparing for the show. "Nah. What's there to be nervous about?"

"Nothing at all." Avery's dark eyes and the smirk tilting her mouth convey amusement. "Thanks for coming on."

"No problem." I fill a Styrofoam cup with the dark roast coffee on the table. "Thanks for inviting me."

Lloyd, the agent I just signed with, would have had a conniption if I'd refused to appear on *Twofer*, one of the most popular sports shows around. He thinks the higher my profile is as we approach draft night, the better. I'm just ready to get it over with.

"You were first on my list of guests," Avery says, drawing my attention back to our conversation. She's a beautiful woman, but she's best known as a tough journalist. A smart one, too. "You and Caleb Bradley."

"Wait." My hand pauses with the coffee halfway to my mouth. "Is Caleb on today's show, too?"

Just the sound of that dude's name scrapes my nerves. I've thought of Iris more times than I want to admit in the last three months. Unfortunately, that also means thinking about her punk-ass boyfriend. The media can't seem to say my name without saying his, and vice versa, but thank God Caleb and I haven't actually been in the same place at the same time.

"Yeah, Caleb's on the show, too." A frown crinkles Avery's smooth skin. "Your agent didn't tell you?"

My eyes lock with Lloyd's as he walks on set with MacKenzie Decker, president of basketball operations for the San Diego Waves, the latest expansion team approaching their first season. My agent glances away almost immediately. He knows there's no love lost between Caleb and me and probably assumed I would have declined this appearance had I known Caleb was booked, too.

My stepbrother, an agent himself, didn't want to mix blood with business, or he would have repped me. Technically, he's not blood, but most in the league don't even know we're connected. He recommended Lloyd with only a few reservations. Right now, facing an hour on camera pretending not to hate Caleb, I have even more reservations about my agent.

"Lloyd has a lot going on," I reply, smoothing my expression into a blank slate as he and MacKenzie Decker approach. "He must have forgotten to mention it."

Deck, as everyone calls him, ignores me and reaches for Avery immediately, pulling her close to kiss her cheek. She glances at me self-consciously, but a smile spreads over her face and affection warms her eyes when she looks way up at the basketball executive and former baller. I've heard rumors about them dating. It's obviously true, because Deck looks like he might scandalize us all and bend her over the nearest couch any minute now.

"Ahem." Avery puts a little space between her and Deck but doesn't step completely from the crook of his arm. "August, have you met MacKenzie Decker?"

"I'm a huge fan, sir." I extend my hand to one of the greatest point guards to ever lace up. "It's truly an honor."

"You can drop the 'sir' and call me Deck," he says, accepting my handshake. "You have a bright future, August. I've been watching you for a while now."

I glance between Lloyd and Decker. I don't want to play for an expansion team. Even Deck, one of the most brilliant basketball minds of our generation, can't skip the slow start any expansion team inevitably experiences. It'll be awhile before the Waves start winning. Spending my most productive years in a brand-spanking-new, dead-end situation is not how I envision my run as a professional basketball player.

If I thought Lloyd was avoiding my eyes before, he's damn near hiding now. There are several things we haven't seen eye to eye on already, and if he was expecting some wet-behind-the-ears pup who would blindly do whatever he said, he's got another thing coming.

"Congrats on the championship." Deck sips his coffee, one arm still resting lightly around Avery's waist. "And on the Naismith. That's quite a senior year you had there."

"Thank you, sir." The lift of his eyebrows reminds me he doesn't want the formality. "I mean, Deck."

"You took a risk staying all four years," he says, watching me closely.

Most players with my prospects leave college after their sophomore or junior year. They want to start earning as soon as possible, and the risk of injury before we reach the NBA always hovers over every year we remain in college.

"I wanted my degree. Wanted a thorough education." I toss the half-full cup of coffee into a nearby trash can. "On and off the court. Coach Mannard's program was great to shore up my fundamentals."

"True. And frankly, I wish more players stayed in college longer. The one-and-done era has weakened fundamentals overall." Decker nods, his mouth quirking in a one-sided grin. "There's no education like playing against elite players, though. There's no preparation for that. You just gotta dive in, sink or swim."

"I plan to swim." The assured words leap out before I catch them. I don't want to seem arrogant, but if there's one thing I have, it's confidence.

If there's one thing I *don't* have, it's tolerance for the douchebag who just walked on set with his new agent. I catch myself glaring at Caleb and make a conscious effort to relax my facial muscles.

Caleb may have missed the animosity on my face, but Deck didn't. He glances over his shoulder in the direction of my glare before turning back to smirk at me. He probably thinks it's simply juvenile rivalry between us, but it's become more than that. In only two encounters, Iris made it more.

I deliberately offer Caleb a jaunty salute, my teeth gritting when he gives me that slick crocodile grin, the kind that spreads open all friendly, only to chomp you between its teeth when you least expect it.

"If you'll excuse me," Avery says, nodding to a production assistant who's just handed her a stack of papers. "I need to review a few things with my co-host before the show starts."

She walks off, stopping beside Caleb and his agent to give them both a smile and a few words before moving on.

I want to put some distance between Caleb and me.

"Where are the restrooms?" I ask, looking from Deck to Lloyd.

Deck gestures to a dimly lit hall a few feet away.

"Over there." He pats my shoulder in an almost avuncular manner. "I hope we'll get to chat some more before you leave New York."

I assure Deck I'd love to have dinner and talk, and that he can set it up through Lloyd. I'm so ready to get away from Caleb's cocky grin. The bathroom door swings closed behind me, and I draw a deep breath. I've known Caleb since middle school, but not once been jealous of him. But knowing he has Iris, I'm jealous. It's ridiculous, considering I've only met the girl twice. I certainly don't know her well enough to feel this intensely about Caleb kissing her. About him fucking her. About him probably marrying her someday. My hands sting under the hot water while I wash them unnecessarily. I switch the faucet to cold and splash water on my face, a lame attempt to cool down the temper that flares the more I think of a cretin like Caleb with a girl like Iris.

"Fancy meeting you here," Caleb says from the door.

I meet his eyes in the mirror for a moment before looking away, devoting my attention to turning off the water and drying my hands.

"I didn't realize you'd be here today," he continues, though I haven't said a word in reply. "Maybe they thought I wouldn't show if I knew you were coming, but they were wrong. I'm really glad we have a few minutes to talk."

I still don't dignify anything he says with a response but hold his eyes in the mirror for another few beats.

"My new agent has his ear to the ground." Caleb pushes away from the door, walking deeper into the bathroom until he stands right in front of me. "Seems your hometown Baltimore Stingers want me."

Disappointment settles in my chest. It might be a lie, but Lloyd and Decker looked a little too cozy when they came in. I bet they were talking about a possible deal with the Waves. I have so little control over this next

66

phase of my life, and it frustrates the hell out of me, but it's the nature of the NBA. Rookies don't get to choose.

"Oh!" Caleb snaps his fingers. "Before I forget, I wanted to show you something."

He pulls his phone out and scrolls over a few pictures until he finds the one he wants. There's no chance this is benevolent. I've seen his "up to no good" innocent face since we were twelve in our first basketball camp together.

He turns the phone to show me the screen. At first, I don't know what I'm seeing, but then, as my brain and my eyes connect, I get it.

And what I wouldn't give to slam his face into the urinal.

An ultrasound.

This isn't happening. Not to me, and I wish it wasn't happening to Iris.

"Aren't you gonna congratulate me?" Caleb stares down at the little cloudy image before sliding his phone back into his pocket. "I'm gonna be a dad. Iris and I are ecstatic."

I can't do it. The image of Iris pregnant with this man's . . . *spawn* . . . strangles the words in my throat. I just stare at him, nauseous, before nodding and walking to the door with still-not-quite-dry hands.

"I feel like I should apologize," Caleb says at my back, rushing the words because he probably realizes I'm not pausing to hear him out. "I mean, first the Stingers. Now Iris. I just keep taking the things you want, don't I?"

I do turn then, meeting his mockery head-on.

"What makes you think I want her?" I ask, cocking one brow for good measure.

"Oh, come on, West." Caleb laughs, sliding the phone back into his pocket. "How long have we known each other? I've never seen you look at a girl the way you looked at *my* girl."

"You're such an asshole."

"An asshole who has the girl *and* the team you want." A bright smile breaks across Caleb's face before he turns toward the urinal and I hear his zip slide down. To the sound of him whistling and pissing, I stalk out of the bathroom, ready to blast Lloyd for putting me anywhere near Caleb and his damn ultrasound. My teeth ache biting back curses. What I wouldn't give to punch this dude's pretty face.

What I wouldn't give for a few moments with Iris to remind her of our last conversation.

Don't lose yourself in him.

Don't forget your dreams.

Don't follow him.

Most of all . . .

Don't choose him.

I didn't have a right to say those things before, and I certainly don't now that they're having a baby together. He'll convince her to marry him. I know it in my bones the way you know two trains racing toward one another will collide. With this baby in the picture, it's a whole new ball game.

For the first time in my life, I'm riding the bench.

SEVEN

IRIS

The bleeding hasn't stopped. It's been heavy, constant since last night. I didn't want to, but I called Caleb, who predictably freaked out. I'm freaking out, too. Is it anxiety twisting my stomach into knots, or am I miscarrying? Are my breaths short and quick because of fear, or is it something else? What's happening to me? To the baby?

My OBGYN told us to meet her at the hospital. I'm nearing the end of my first trimester, when miscarriages are most likely. God forgive me, but there is a small part of me that would be relieved if I miscarried. Like I'd dodged a bullet and could go on with my plans undisturbed.

I know there are women, probably on this very floor, so joyful and grateful to be pregnant. Some of them made sacrifices, lost babies along the way, underwent fertility treatments to have what I don't want and never asked for, but I can't argue with that renegade part of me that sees this as a possible escape.

The door to my room swings open slowly, and Lotus pokes her head in.

"Hey, Gumbo." Her smile belies the concern on her face.

I wave her in, tears leaking from the corners of my eyes. She hurries over and plops onto the bed beside me, her arms encircling me. I bury my face in her shoulder and try to hold all the emotions in—the anxiety, the guilt, the hope, the frustration. They all swirl inside of me, as mixed up as the soup I'm nicknamed for.

"How you holding up?" Lotus asks, pulling away to study me closely.

"I'm okay." When she levels a skeptical look on me, I give up the pretense. "Alright. I'm losing my mind."

"What do they say?

"They're running tests." I sniff and swipe at my wet cheeks. "They should be back in soon."

"Where's Caleb?" She looks around the room like he might be hiding in the closet or under the bed. "I'm sure he's not far since this is his heir apparent."

I laugh, but Caleb *is* slightly obsessed with this pregnancy. I may still feel ambiguous about this baby, but he certainly doesn't. The only thing I've ever seen him want more is basketball.

"His agent called and needed to go over a few things, so he stepped out for a sec."

"I guess he's excited about going to Baltimore, huh?" Lotus asks.

The Baltimore Stingers took Caleb in the draft. August wanted to play for his hometown team, but the San Diego Waves drafted him instead. Somehow, even though he smiled for the cameras and pulled the team's cap over his dark, caramel-streaked curls, I knew he was disappointed. He and Caleb keep trading victories and losses.

Score another for Caleb.

"Yeah," I finally answer Lotus's question. "He's looking for a place in Baltimore now. He'll be moving in the next few weeks."

"And you?" Lotus studies my face. "Where will you be moving?"

"I have to be out of my place in the next couple of weeks." I try to ignore my anxiety. "Since it's an on-campus apartment, and I'm graduating . . .well, I gotta go."

"If my scholarship didn't require me to live on campus—"

"I know," I cut in. "Don't think twice about it. That still wouldn't solve everything. Having a baby with no job? I was hoping to have heard from Richter about the internship by now."

Unless vomiting on Jared ruined my chances. Couldn't blame him for thinking twice about hiring me.

"Maybe I can work at the bookstore for a little longer," I say.

It sounds ridiculous even to my ears. Work at the campus bookstore instead of living in luxury with Caleb when there's nothing holding me in Atlanta? I'm in some kind of limbo until I hear back from Richter, but a hasty move could be the wrong one. It could change the course of my life, and as much as Caleb keeps pressuring me, I won't be rushed. I know if I want to move when he does he'll pay all my expenses, but that would feel like one more step in the direction I promised myself I'd never take.

Needing something to do, I press my phone home button. Two missed calls.

"Hmmm. I missed a call from Mama," I murmur. "And some number I don't know."

"How is Aunt Priscilla?" Lo's voice is a polite query, but I know she doesn't enjoy discussing my mother, and her mother even less.

"She's fine." I sigh, my heart as weary as my body. "Of course, she wants me to 'make the most' of this pregnancy. Wants me to marry Caleb and do anything I can to secure my future. At least, the only future she imagines for me."

"Hey, our futures won't look like our mamas' pasts," she assures me. "Don't you worry about that." Lotus grips my hand, the green stone of the ring she wears glinting under the hospital's fluorescent lights. I link our fingers so my ring, identical to hers, winks back at us, too.

"Remember when MiMi gave us these?" I ask, a tiny smile tugging at my lips as I remember one of the few times our great-grandmother visited us in New Orleans.

"Of course I do." She scrunches her face and clears her throat, signaling she is about to do her famous MiMi imitation. "*Mes filles*, wear these always and have my protection."

I giggle at Lo's heavily accented, but spot-on, imitation. I haven't been around MiMi much, but when I am I only ever understand half of what she says since she switches seamlessly from French to English. She blends her languages the way she blends her faiths, saying Hail Marys one minute and praying to the Great Spirits the next. She wears rosaries around her neck and scatters her potions and *gris-gris* throughout the house.

"These rings haven't failed to protect us since we put them on," Lo says, the laughter leaving her face. She lays her hand against my stomach. "It'll protect you now."

I barely stop my eyes from rolling. To be a college-educated, sophisticated millennial, Lo puts more stock in MiMi's voodoo mumbo jumbo than she should. She *did* live with the woman for years, so some of the superstitions were bound to rub off on her, but I think it's a load of crap that pulls the wool over people's eyes and preys on their fears and ignorance for monetary gain. I don't say any of that because Lo gets defensive, and I get irritated, and right now I need the harmony between us more than anything.

"You're right." I rub my thumb across the gold band on my ring finger before continuing quietly. "It's just . . . there's a part of me that wants this pregnancy to be over, Lo."

Her eyes snap to my face. My confession might draw judgement from someone else, but Lotus's face softens with sympathy. She understands how hard I've worked.

This baby is a life. I know that. I respect it, but my dreams are alive, too, and I wonder if one must die for the other to thrive.

"I get it." She pulls one knee up under her on the bed. "We'll know what's going on soon and go from there."

I nod, my stomach muscles clenching while we wait. What if the baby isn't okay? What if the baby *is* okay? The two possibilities send my life spiraling in radically different directions, and my fear spirals with them. To distract myself, I tap the unknown number alert and see a voicemail. I open the voicemail and put it on speaker.

"Iris, hi," a vaguely familiar, deep male voice says from my phone. "It's Jared Foster."

My eyes go wide.

"The internship," I whisper-hiss at Lotus, who stretches her eyes wide back at me.

"I hope you're feeling better since the last time we saw each other." Jared's voice holds a touch of humor. "I know you felt bad about what happened. Don't. My dry cleaning was tax-deductible."

Even though I'm not in the same room with Jared, embarrassment burns my cheeks. Vomit. Seriously?

"I'll just get right to it," Jared continues. "Richter is offering you one of the internship spots. We'd expect you in Chicago in the next month, and we'd need you ready to travel pretty much right away. There's several deals we're about to close, and you'd have to jump right in."

His low chuckle interrupts the list of expectations. "You said you were ready to work, to do whatever it took," he says. "I hope you meant it. Give me a call so we can talk details. Congratulations."

My fingers tremble over the phone, and I immediately want to replay the message. I've been anxious, biting my lips all day, but now they stretch into a wide grin. In the midst of so many things going wrong, something is going so right.

"Oh, my gosh." Lotus squeals, her eyes lit with as much joy as she'd have for her own good fortune. "This is amazing, Bo."

"I know," I squeal back. "He told me it would take a couple months to decide, but I had almost given up—"

The door swings open in the middle of my sentence. The doctor walks in, followed by Caleb, who lowers the phone from his ear and slides it into his pocket, obviously just finishing a call.

It all comes crashing back. I'm in the hospital, three months pregnant, and bleeding heavily. What felt like the greatest moment of my life now feels like a cruel joke—a carrot dangled in front of me and snatched away. Lotus grips my hand again, lining our rings up and giving my fingers a reassuring squeeze.

"We've looked at everything, Iris." Dr. Rimmel's eyes are kind, and her expression is serious. "You have a rather large subchorionic hematoma."

"English, Doc," Lotus says with a wry look. "No speak medical-ese."

Dr. Rimmel's lips twitch, and I'm so glad Lotus is here, or I'd be going crazy. Caleb comes to sit on the bed beside me, his concern and frustration all over his face.

"Yeah, what's that actually mean?" he demands. "We've been waiting forever."

Where Lotus's comment lightened the atmosphere, Caleb's injects so much weight, Dr. Rimmel's slight smile disappears, and her shoulders square.

"To put it simply," Dr. Rimmel says, giving Caleb a pointed look, "the placenta detaches from the uterus, which causes clots and the bleeding we're seeing."

"The baby?" I force myself to ask, not sure what I want to hear her say. "Is the baby okay?'

"Yes, the baby's fine, but we need to put you on bed rest to make sure everything *stays* fine."

"Bed rest?" I croak. "I . . . like full-on stuck in the bed? For how long?"

"As long as it takes, Iris," Caleb interjects sternly. "We'll follow instructions to the letter."

We don't have to lie in bed for God knows how long. *I* do. Of course, I'll do whatever the doctor recommends, but Caleb has no right to be cavalier about *my* life, *my* time, *my* body.

I bite my tongue because this isn't the time to assert myself. I need to understand what is required and set Caleb straight later.

"For how long?" I ask again.

"We'll start with full home bed rest," Dr. Rimmel says. "And assess in a few weeks."

The word *home* hits me hard. I have to be out of my on-campus apartment. The university has extended as much grace as possible, and I've got a few prospects, but noth*ing in stone.*

Full home bed rest?

I don't have a home, much less a bed to rest in.

"I'll take care of her and the baby." Caleb glances at me. "We'll get your things moved into my place right away."

A sense of helplessness washes over me. I clench the hospital gown in my fists. I hate feeling out of control in my own life, like an actor on someone else's stage, my every move directed.

"It's not just bed rest, but pelvic rest, too." She gives Caleb a stern look. "That means low activity and no sex."

Caleb's face falls, but for me it's a little bit of a silver lining. I haven't wanted to have sex for weeks. I chalked it up to hormones, but maybe it's Caleb's high-handedness that's been turning me off. At least this baby and this damn bed rest give me a good excuse to abstain.

I hate to think this way, but when I glance at my phone and remember Jared's voicemail about Chicago, no sex feels like the only good thing coming out of this. MiMi's talisman ring winks at me from my lap. I don't know if it's working or not. For now, the baby is protected, but my plans for the future are in definite jeopardy.

EIGHT

AUGUST

Make the best of a bad situation.

That's not completely fair or accurate. I'm living in San Diego, a city with near-perfect weather year-round. I signed a thirty-million-dollar NBA contract. You'll find countless dead hoop dreams in every high school gym and on any neighborhood playground. I'm one lucky son of a bitch.

I get it.

But beginning on a team that probably won't have a winning season for years sucks. I'm already thinking ahead to the end of my rookie contract and how I'll get out of San Diego. Coach Kirby's voice in my head calls me spoiled, ungrateful, *and* a pussy. He would never tolerate this kind of defeatist attitude. And there are some plusses here.

For one thing, I'm playing with a veteran who knows how to win at this level. Kenan Ross is a beast. I've admired his game for years. I watch him during our first team meeting and have to admit it's a great opportunity to play with him, even if I'm not sure he wants to be here either. He left a contending team, who won a championship just a few years ago, to come here and start from scratch.

"In my nose or in my teeth?" he asks under his breath while our head coach reiterates the privilege we have of building a team from the bottom.

"Huh?" I shoot him a perplexed look. "What're you talking about?"

"You checking me out like a chick," he says with a crooked grin, his teeth startlingly white against his dark skin. "So either you wanna ask me out . . ." He gives me a quick side-eye. "And the answer is *hell* no, by the way."

I snort-snicker, glancing up to make sure Coach hasn't noticed us *not* paying attention.

"Or there's a booger in my nose, something in my teeth."

"Uh . . . neither," I assure him. "Nose and teeth all clear, and rest assured, you're a little hairier than my usual."

"Bigger, too, I assume," he says with an easy grin.

Dude is huge. At six foot seven inches, he's one of the best power forwards in the game. And swole with it. He's as hard as marble, and at thirty years old, in the best shape of his life. He picked up the nickname "Glad" in college, short for gladiator. He throws bows down low, and he's known for his aggressiveness in the paint. He battles for every possession, goes after every rebound. He's an excellent two-way player, defense and offense, and as someone who has been accused of needing work in the defense department, I have much to learn from him.

Iris busted my balls about defense.

Fuck. I promised myself I wouldn't think about her. She's pregnant with another man's baby. A jerk's baby.

"Now you all pouty," Kenan says from the side of his mouth. "Okay. I'll go out with you. Damn."

I chuckle and shake my head.

"Keep your pity date, man." My smile disappears. "Though I was thinking

78

about this chick I promised myself I *wouldn't* think about anymore."

"Yeah." Kenan's smile fades as fast as mine did. "I can relate."

I'm an idiot. Kenan requested a trade when his wife cheated with one of his teammates on his last team. "Shit, Glad," I say, inwardly kicking myself. "I didn't mean to—"

"It's aight." His smile is manufactured, nothing like the natural one of a few minutes ago. "She's not worth discussing. Neither is he."

"But she was worth leaving a championship team to come here?" I ask.

"What's wrong with here?" Kenan asks, his brows lifted. "I'm making the same money."

"Yeah, well some of us don't have rings yet," I say, hoping I keep the bitterness out of my voice. "So money's not everything."

"What you thinking about rings for already?" He blows out a puff of disgusted air. "It's only October. Season one. You just got here, Rook. You got a lot to learn *and* earn. You think because you were the man on your campus, you'll come in here taking names and leaving your mark and shit?"

"No, it's not that."

"It *is* that." Kenan's eyes go hard. "I've played with entitled pricks before. Don't be one."

I bite back my defensive response and leave space for him to say more if he wants. He's right. I *have* been acting like an entitled prick.

"How many guys from your high school are playing pro ball?" he demands.

"Just me," I reply quietly.

"And from your college team? Any of them in the NBA?"

"Nah," I admit with a shake of my head, remembering all the great players who just weren't great enough to be here. "None."

"Right, so quit thinking about what you don't have and be grateful for what you do. You gotta pay some dues." He stands when the coach dismisses us and tells us to report to the gym. "Starting now." He points to the gym bag at his feet.

"That's you," he says.

"Uh . . . excuse me?" I point to my bag a few feet way. "No, that's my bag over there."

"I know that, Rook." His grin is back, and this one is not only natural, but at my expense. "Since you've been here all of a day, but already think you should be winning rings, let's see you carry bags for someone who actually *has* a ring."

"Oh. You want me to . . ." My voice trails off as he walks away, leaving his bag for me to haul.

Another veteran player heads over and hands me his bag.

"Glad said you got this, Rook." He smirks and drops the bag at my feet.

"Yeah, but—"

"This you?" another vet asks, dropping his bag and walking toward the gym.

"Um . . . no, I was just trying to tell Glad that—"

"Thanks, Rook," he says and walks away.

By the time I make it into the gym, I'm struggling with seven bags, none of them mine. I drop them unceremoniously by the benches and jerk the sweatshirt over my head to join my teammates for practice.

"I wondered what was taking you so long," Kenan says, bouncing the ball in a dribbling drill.

"So are you, like, hazing me or something?" I try to keep my voice light, but maybe I do resent that stunt a little.

Kenan stops dribbling to look me in the eye. "Everybody knows what you can do, Rook. We may be vets, but Deck is building this team around you. You're young, but you're the franchise player. We get that," he says quietly. "But when you're in the trenches with somebody, you don't just need to know what they can *do*. You need to know who they *are*. I wanna know more about your character than I do about your game right now."

80

His penetrating stare assesses me. "So yeah, you'll carry bags for vets from time to time. Nothing wrong with staying humble before all the rings start rolling in."

"It's the least I can do," I grudgingly concede, offering the smallest grin.

"Count yourself lucky." He takes a shot that's nothing but net. "They made me clean jock straps."

"Shit." I twist my face in disgust. "Ball sweat?"

"Ball sweat."

Give me bags any day.

NINE
AUGUST

Life doesn't always deliver on its promises, and some dreams taste sweetest before they come true.

Such is my NBA career so far. It's February, halfway through my rookie season, and we have the sub-five hundred year you'd expect from an expansion team. No way we'll win half our games at the rate we're going. Kenan keeps reminding me we're just starting out and to be patient.

Another thing that's overrated? The all-you-can-fuck pussy buffet. I admit I've taken advantage of it. Had a threesome or six. Hell, I was with four girls at once a few weeks ago. I think one chick just sucked my thumb because the other three had all the vital bases covered. It's a rite of passage for most professional athletes, the overindulged dick. Wilt Chamberlain claimed he slept with twenty thousand women. I just have to wonder did it get old this quickly? Did he lie in bed some nights, a woman on each side, and feel utterly alone? Did he think about one particular girl while he was fucking all the others?

'Cause that's my present dilemma.

Caleb and I have only met on court once this season. It was my best individual performance so far because our mutual dislike brings out my best play. It's a team sport, though, and his team, my hometown Stingers, had a better night and are the better team. We lost in overtime by two points.

Caleb and I barely spoke that night. I forced myself to shake his hand before leaving the court because Coach Kirby would ream my ass for bad sportsmanship if I didn't, but I couldn't look him in the eye. I would have lost my shit if I'd seen his smug satisfaction. He's on the team I wanted to play for in my hometown. He's got the girl I can't get out of my head. News travels fast on the NBA circuit, and a few months ago, the golden boy having a baby was all anyone wanted to talk about.

Every time I think of them having a kid, building a life together, I want to punch a hole through the wall.

Or through Caleb's face. Whatever's closer.

It's All-Star Weekend, and by some miracle, I was voted into Sunday's All-Star game, albeit third string, but I hadn't expected even that as a rookie. Of course, Caleb was voted in, too. I just can't escape that guy. The media is carrying the "rivalry" on from high school and college, perpetuating it every chance they get. They've created this narrative of us being in a two-man race for Rookie of the Year. I don't even want my name in the same sentence as his, and people can't seem to talk about me without talking about him. At least he's not in tonight's three-point contest.

I have a couple hours before I need to show up for my next All-Star commitment, an appearance at a local homeless shelter. The league is big on players giving back. I love the city of San Diego and will definitely do some charitable work there, but I've already spoken with the league's charity coordinators about doing a few things in the community where I grew up. Baltimore may be Caleb's team, but it's my town. My childhood was there.

My family is there, my history, and my friends. That core group of people nurtured me to help me get where I am, and I want to contribute there *and* to the city that drafted me.

Right now, in the madness of All-Star Weekend, I just need a minute to myself. There will be cameras at the homeless shelter this afternoon. I've been signing autographs and taking pictures with fans all day. There will be interviews on court and off tonight at the three-point contest. Everywhere I go, I have to be *on*, and for just a minute, I don't want to be. I rush down a back hall of the arena where the festivities are being held.

Glancing over my shoulder to make sure no one sees me, I try a few doors, all of which are locked. The knob on the last door turns easily, and the door swings open into a dim room, a lamp in the corner providing soft light.

Perfect. Maybe I can even grab a few winks. I sink gratefully into an overstuffed recliner, pushing the button to elevate my feet.

A soft sigh from a chair in the corner startles me. I squint, visually picking through the shadows and find the last person I expected to see.

"Iris?" I ask disbelievingly.

"Shhhh!" She raises an index finger to her lips.

God, her lips.

I'd forgotten how full they are, how wide and luscious. I'd forgotten that her eyes hold a dozen colors hostage and that her hair is a pitch-dark fall of silk. Maybe I didn't forget as much as didn't allow myself to remember—I blocked the memory of how this woman is exactly what I would wish for. My imagination, my memory, did her no justice.

She gestures to a blanket-covered lump at her chest.

"Sorry," she whispers. "Didn't mean to shush you. She just fell asleep, and I didn't want to wake her."

Her.

For the last few months, I've thought of the baby as Caleb's *spawn*. Now that I'm in the same room with Iris feeding her baby, I can only think of the baby as . . . hers.

Feeding.

"Oh, shit," I mutter, lowering the footrest. "I'm sorry. You're . . ." I gesture to the baby on her chest. "And I'm just sitting here like—"

"It's okay," she interrupts, smiling. "I'm decent. She's finally sleeping, and I could use a few minutes of adult company." She licks her lips and then bites the corner of her mouth. "Stay."

Even though she asks, I know I should leave. Not to preserve her modesty. She's right. The blanket completely covers her chest and the sleeping baby. I should leave because I want to stay too badly. Because after more than a year of not seeing her, I have a million things to ask her and a million things I want to share. We're different people than we were when we first met. I've signed a huge contract. I'm on a box of cereal out there somewhere and have been animated in a video game. My life is completely new. And Iris has a baby now, for God's sake. There's a part of me, though, that will always think of her as the gorgeous girl swearing at the television in a sports dive, sipping flat beer and pulling for her Lakers. We're different, but I wonder if the quick, deep intimacy we shared that night is still there. If it's still the same.

"So how've you been?" she asks.

I sit back, raising the recliner again, and grin. "How much time ya got?"

She glances down at the blanketed bundle. "She'll be in a milk coma for a little while, so probably plenty of time to hear about all your rookie adventures."

"It's been a wild ride," I say, hastily trying to fix the bad impression I probably gave. "I mean . . . I don't mean wild like chicks or whatever. Not like that."

One knowing eyebrow elevates.

"Okay." I chuckle self-consciously. "Maybe a little like that."

She rolls her eyes and twists her lips.

"Alright. You got me." I allow myself a wolfish grin. "A lot like that."

"It's to be expected." She shifts a little, tipping her head back against the cushion of the leather couch. "You're rich, talented, handsome. Single. I wouldn't believe you if you told me any different."

"So you think I'm handsome?" I tease her.

She looks away and to the side, shaking her head and laughing softly under her breath. "Like you don't know." She pats the little bottom under the blanket. "I'm sure you had no trouble finding . . . *companionship* . . . before your fat contract. And I'm sure you have to fight 'em off now."

My smile freezes on my lips. We can laugh a little here in this barely lit room. I have a few minutes with her in a year, but she's going home with Caleb. She'll be in his bed tonight. Even now, she's feeding his child.

My good humor circles a drain until it's gone, and all that's left is my futile resentment.

"I'm certainly not fighting 'em off," I say pointedly, linking my fingers over my stomach.

She stiffens for an almost-imperceptible second, before resuming her smile and meeting my eyes directly. "I'd be surprised if you weren't taking advantage of every perk the NBA has to offer."

"Yeah, well, when you can't have what you really want," I say, locking our eyes together, willing her not to look away, "you settle for whatever's available."

She laughs, but it rings false before she glances away and adjusts the blanket around the baby. "A man like you should never have to settle, August."

"Same goes for a woman like you, Iris." I plow through my hesitation to ask her the question I hope she would ask me if she saw me compromising my ambitions. "*Are* you settling?"

She swallows, the muscles moving in her slender throat, and takes a deep breath before looking back to me. "I'm not settling. I'm doing the best I can with the hand I've been dealt."

I don't know everything that has transpired in the year since I last saw her, but it doesn't matter. She got pregnant. I know she has to be responsible, but putting all of her eggs in Caleb's basket is a mistake. It's one I can't allow her to make, at least without warning her again. We've only met twice, but she feels like my friend. A friend I'd probably enjoy kissing and fucking, but a friend nonetheless.

I get up and walk swiftly over to the couch, squatting and looking up at her. If you didn't look closely, you'd assume she was as serene as any mother nursing and nurturing. But she's not any mother. And when I look into the turbulence of her eyes, she's certainly not serene.

"Iris, don't lose sight of what you want." I risk touching her, gripping the hand in her lap. "You got pregnant, but that's not the end of your dreams. You're too young and talented and amazing to abandon your ambitions running after Caleb while he pursues his."

"I'm not running after him," she says stiffly, snatching her hand away. "You don't know the choices I had, the hard calls I had to make."

"I'm sure you did what you had to do because that's the kind of woman you are." I recapture her eyes but don't try to recapture her hand. "But you're only proving my point. You did exactly what you had to for this baby. Now do what you have to do for *yourself*."

She looks at me, her emotions naked and spread across her face, watering her eyes. Her lips part, but whatever she plans to say gets cut off when the little bundle on her chest squirms, shifting, and the blanket falls away.

And holy Shit. I'm looking at Iris's breast.

The nipple is piqued and the color of fresh plums against the dark gold of her skin. A milky drop clings to the tip. I can't swallow or breathe, but my mouth automatically opens, my body demanding I suck. I should look away. I'm probably creeping hard, but I can't help it. My fingers fold into my palms, aching to trace the blue–green network of veins just under her skin.

When I finally look up, Iris is as paralyzed as I am, watching me watching her. Her mouth falls open, her breath coming hard, heaving her breasts, one covered and one exposed to my greedy eyes. The air thickens with all the urges I've been suppressing and drowning in meaningless sex with other women. This is the woman I want. Crazy as it may be, this is the one I want. I couldn't move from this spot if the place were on fire.

"You are so fucking beautiful." My voice is hoarse and urgent. "We barely know each other. I get it, but I can't stop thinking about you, Iris."

My words snap the thread tying us together, and she hastily, belatedly jerks up the bra, fastening a flap and pulling her blouse together.

"August, don't." She runs a hand over the back of her neck under the hair spilling past her shoulders.

I saw her nakedness, but I'm the one exposed. I can't hide how much I want her. I've felt more connected to her in the little time we've spent together than I have to any of the women I fucked this last year.

"Do you think about me, too?" The question I promised myself I wouldn't ask forces its way out.

"I can't think about you." She squeezes her eyes shut, clamping her teeth tightly on her bottom lip. "I'm with Caleb. We have a daughter, a future."

"A future?" I snap. "With him? Gimme a break. He's probably cheating on you already."

A muscle clenches along the smooth line of her jaw. I'm on the road enough to know the married players get as much ass as the single ones. I've known Caleb a long time. That man always wants his cake and to eat it, too. No way he isn't tapping anything he can pull when he's away. If Iris were mine, I'd be faithful to her. There's not a woman alive who could tempt me if I were hers. I want to confess it all to her, but she wouldn't believe me.

"I have to try to make this work, August." She rubs the downy hair of her daughter's head. "There's a lot at stake."

"Your future is at stake."

"August, we've met all of twice and—"

"Correction. Today makes three," I say, adding a smile to show I know how ridiculous it sounds.

The tight lines around her mouth loosen some, too. Humor softens her eyes.

"I stand corrected. Today makes three," she says, slowly sobering. "But you can't expect me to walk away from the man I've been with for two years. For what? A feeling? An attraction?"

"So you *are* attracted to me?"

She aims an exasperated look at me, shaking her head. "It doesn't matter. I can be . . . attracted to someone without acting on it. That doesn't mean I'm walking away from my relationship, the father of my daughter who's taking care of me and my baby."

"I'd take care of you, if that's what you wanted." I force myself to stand, though I'd be content to sit at her feet all night. "But the girl I met in that bar didn't want to be taken care of. I'd do everything in my power to help you follow your dreams so you could take care of *yourself*. And then we'd both know you were with me because you wanted to be, not because you had no other choice."

I pause, letting my words linger in the air, letting her hear the truth behind what I've said. "Ask yourself if Caleb would do the same."

I'm about to press my point a little more, take advantage of these few, rare moments as much as I can, but the baby chooses that moment to open her eyes.

I'm lost all over again.

Her complexion hovers between the lighter tan of her father and the deeper gold of Iris's skin. Dark curls frame a tiny face with a button of a nose and a rosy bow of a mouth. The daughter captivates me at a glance, just like her mother did, and my heart falls right out of my chest and lands at this baby's feet.

"She looks just like you," I whisper, unable to look away from the little dusky-haired angel in Iris's arms.

Caleb's eyes stare back at me, though, a blue so dark they're almost violet. "But she has her father's eyes," I say, my teeth gritted and my jaw clenched.

"Yeah, she does." Iris stares down at the baby. Her expression doesn't soften or hold that maternal adoration I'd expect.

For the first time, I see past how beautiful Iris looks, and I see something else. Or maybe I notice the absence of what I've seen before. A spark. Life. Vitality.

"Are you doing okay?" I ask softly. "I mean, really okay? What's going on with you?"

Surprise flits across Iris's face at my question before she blanks her expression. "I'm fine."

"Not overjoyed? Deliriously happy?" I tweak one of the baby's curls, grinning when she gurgles with something close to laughter. Caleb may be an asshole, but his daughter is gorgeous. Perfect

"I just . . ." She sighs and twists her lips into a grimace. "I don't know, August."

"Hey. You can talk to me." I smirk and shrug. "After all, this *is* our third conversation. Surely we're past keeping secrets by now."

A husky laugh is her only answer. For a few seconds, I wait in the silence, unsure if she's going to tell me anything. She presses her lips together, and blinks rapidly, but not before a few tears escape over her cheek.

"I don't *feel* like a mother. I feel . . ." She pauses, maybe searching for the right words. Maybe she already has the right words and doesn't want to say them.

"You talk about that girl you met in the bar," she continues, brushing impatiently at her tears. "She's gone. I was offered the job of my dreams, the opportunity I've been working toward for years, and I had to turn it down because of this pregnancy."

"I'm sorry," I say softly. "I know how badly you wanted to get into sports."

"I still do." She sniffs and lifts eyes liquid with disappointment. "But what if I never—"

"You will, Iris," I cut in.

"I feel like I'm becoming everything I never wanted to be, and I'm not sure how to stop it. I didn't want this pregnancy." Her voice pitches low as if, even though her daughter couldn't possibly understand yet, Iris doesn't want her to hear. "I didn't want . . ." She doesn't say it, but she glances down at the baby snuggled into her chest, and the unspoken words come across loud and clear.

She didn't want *her*. The baby. She didn't want her.

"I'm an awful person," she says, her words tortured and choked in sobs. "But I'm determined to take care of her. I want it to be enough, for her to be enough, but I resent everything all the time. It's all I feel. Everything else seems . . . faded. One minute I'm completely numb, and the next I feel too much, and I'm a blubbering mess."

An ironic smile quirks her lips, even as tears streak down her face. "See what I mean? I'm all over the place."

"Maybe you should talk to someone."

"You're probably right, but Lo's so busy with her own life, and my mother . . . God, she's too happy I've 'snagged' myself a baller. She thinks I'm whining and complaining about nothing. Why would I need a job? Why would I want to work when this is the meal ticket most women would kill for? I can't talk to her."

"I was thinking more like talking to your doctor," I say quietly. "I'm no expert, obviously, but maybe it's depression or something. You're not a bad person, and I don't think you're a bad mother. Maybe you're someone who hates she had to put her dreams on hold and whose hormones are out of whack."

Her eyes widen, and she glances down at her daughter, biting her lip.

"Maybe," she finally mutters. "No one's suggested that before. Not that I've talked to anyone about it."

"Might help. What's her name, by the way?" My voice is practically polite, not giving away a hint of how seeing this beautiful baby affects me, of how her mother affects me.

"Sarai," Iris replies, a small frown crinkling between her eyebrows. "It means princess."

"She looks like one." I quirk my lips when Sarai seems to smile at me. I don't know if babies actually smile at this stage, but warmth washes over me just the same.

"August." Iris's pause is loaded with hesitation and resolve. "I meant what I said. Caleb is taking care of us. He has to until I'm in a position to get back on my feet. I need to try to make it work. You understand that, right? I can't . . . we can't . . ."

Her lashes drop, and she shakes her head. She doesn't need to say anymore. Her gorgeous face is so earnest.

She's too good for him. I knew that right away. She wouldn't be the girl I can't stop thinking about if she were disloyal. If she were a cheat. Still it's only a matter of time before Caleb shows his true colors.

After I walk out this door, Iris and I will keep living our lives, going about our business as if these few moments didn't shake my foundations, but one day she'll walk away from him. She's too smart and too good not to.

And when that happens, I'll be there.

TEN

IRIS

There have been days I've wanted to hurt myself. Maybe even hurt my baby. I'm an awful person, but an honest one. All I can do is hope these feelings aren't who I really am. I hope this isn't the mother I will be forever, but this is who I am today.

I read the lines I wrote weeks ago. My counselor recommended I write my unfiltered thoughts down in a journal. That advice came with a prescription that had me feeling better about life in general relatively quickly.

All-Star Weekend was a turning point in so many ways. I was feeling low that day in the room designated for nursing mothers. My conversation with August, his suggestion about post-partum depression, opened me to the possibility that maybe there was more to what I was feeling than just my own selfishness. Than just resenting my circumstances. It prompted the conversation with my doctor that has led me out of that dark, desolate place.

I close the journal and lock it in the nightstand on my side of the bed. I'm not that woman anymore. It has only been a few weeks, but Sarai, my princess, has shifted to her rightful place—the center of my world.

"You're mommy's princess, aren't you?" I coo down to her, going through the motions of changing her diaper. I nuzzle the soft pads of her tiny feet, eliciting a little snicker from the gorgeous baby on my bed. Maybe I'm a biased mama, but I think she's the most beautiful baby I've ever seen.

But August thought so, too.

When August walked in, I was shocked but also so pleased to see him. So pleased I haven't been able to get him out of my mind. Those charged moments when the blanket fell from my breast and I gaped at him like a hussy instead of immediately covering myself. I was frozen with shock, and if I'm honest . . . God, I hate admitting this even to myself. The way he looked at me, so hungry and reverent, I just wanted more of it.

When I saw August, I was still carrying fifteen pounds of baby weight. My hair hadn't had a good condition and trim in weeks. The bare minimum makeup I'd forced myself to apply was long gone, but he'd looked at me like I was a goddess. Like he'd eat me whole if he got close enough.

And I'd wanted him close enough. So much closer. My nipples stiffen under my T-shirt, recalling the heat simmering between us for those electric seconds.

This is not good.

I have to get these thoughts under control.

I've deliberately avoided the sports sites I usually stalk and have tuned out the basketball world as much as I can. I don't want to know about August—don't want to hear about who he's dating or how well he's playing or how his life is just perfect.

Because mine isn't.

Besides my daughter, whom I don't think I could love any more than I do now, my life is in shambles. I'm living in a city with no friends or family, completely dependent on my baby's daddy, whom I'm not sure I love.

There. I said it. At least in my head I've said it.

I don't think I love Caleb.

How could I feel what I did with August in that room—how could I think about him so often—and love Caleb? I mean really *be in love* with Caleb? I refused to believe my heart is that fickle.

I'm not sure Caleb loves me either. I'm pretty sure he's cheating on me, but I can't make myself care, much less ask. Even though my new OBGYN found a birth control that works with my body, I didn't tell Caleb. If he's out there cheating on me, he'll wear condoms. Further evidence that I cannot be in love with him.

A snippet of gossip penetrated my social media boycott the other day. Apparently, August has been seen with tennis star Pippa Kim on more than one occasion, and everyone's speculating that they're dating. It's unreasonable, but I resent that. It makes me . . . *angry* is the wrong word. I don't have a right to anger, but I don't like it. Whatever this feeling is, it burns in the bottom of my belly all day like a smoldering coal.

I should be jealous of the numbers I find scrawled on slips of paper in the pockets of Caleb's pants, but I'm not.

My phone rings, interrupting the plans that have cycled through my head constantly lately.

I glance at the screen. Lo is the only person I really talk to anymore, besides my mother from time to time.

"Hey, Lo," I say, propping Sarai on my hip and crossing the heated floors barefoot. I certainly won't have heated floors and a mansion with a parking garage full of cars if I leave Caleb, but I'd have my life back and some semblance of control over my existence.

"Hey, Bo. What the hell is *up*?" Lo's voice is half-amused, half-irritated. "You forget your girl or what?"

"Course not." I place Sarai in her high chair and pull ingredients out to prepare her lunch in the food processor. "Just busy being a mom, I guess."

"I get that, and you know how much I love my princess, but I'm feeling a little neglected."

"I'm pretty sure of the two of us, you have the more demanding life. Every time I call, you're in some fashion show or at a shoot."

"True that," Lo says with an unabashedly satisfied chuckle. "This life *is* fly."

I roll my eyes, a smile tweaking my lips.

"You need to figure your shit out, too," Lo says sharply. "You can't stay in this rut forever."

I was excited about bouncing my plans off her like we always have, but her comment stifles my enthusiasm.

"Rut?" I ask. "You call having a baby and devoting myself to her a rut?"

"Don't go getting all sensitive," she says teasingly, though I'm not in the mood to be teased. "You never leave that big ol' house. You haven't made any friends there. You aren't getting your career back on track."

"I will," I say with more confidence than I feel.

"Don't let Caleb run all over you," Lo plows on. "There is only one thing I take lying down, and that's the good dick. Even then I'll probably end up on top."

Her audacious chuckle from the other end has me chuckling, too. God, I miss her. I miss this.

"I've met Caleb," Lo says. "I doubt very seriously you're getting the good dick."

"Oh my God. You did not just say that."

"Oh, yes I did, honey. I gets *the good dick* no matter what is going on. That's a priority. And I'm not talking about that rich-man dick."

"Ex . . . *cuse* me?" Laughter defies my good intentions and barges out of my mouth.

"I'm just saying I haven't met a rich man who can really fuck, ya know?"

"Um, no, I don't know."

"Well, Caleb is the only man you've ever slept with, so you've only had rich dick. You don't have anything to compare it to. Gimme some of that broke dick. That unemployed, still-living-with-his-mama, sleeping-on-her-couch dick."

I'm laughing uncontrollably now, and it only spurs her on more.

"That phone-just-got-turned-off dick," Lo continues, warming to her subject. "Gimme a man who grew up on food stamps and never knew where the next meal was coming from. The rich ones fuck like they're entitled to your pussy. Fuck me like I'm survival. Like your life depends on my shit. That's some grateful dick, right there."

"And yet I've never known you to date anyone like what you're describing," I remind her.

"Date?" Lo asks, her voice indignant. "Who said anything about dating? I'm talking about *fucking*. I only deal with those dudes between the sheets and for as long as it takes to give him a ride to the check-cashing store the next morning. You don't *fall* for broke dick. Honey, you just get it while you can and ride it while it's good."

"God, you never change, do you?" I ask, feeling more lighthearted than I have since the last time we spoke.

"I do change." Some of the humor leaves Lo's voice. "Actually, a lot is changing. That's why I'm calling."

"Oh, yeah?" I ask absently, dumping steamed sweet potatoes and green beans into the food processor. "What's up?"

"I have the opportunity of a lifetime!" The excitement Lo has been holding back bursts across the line, giving me pause.

"What kind of opportunity?"

"You know I hustle, right?" Lo cackles. "Like, take side jobs to make ends meet? Well, I was on this shoot for a friend who was paying me in pizza, and Jean Pierre Louis, that new designer everyone is raving about? You know him?"

I glance around my gilded cage, the walls of Caleb's house that basically define my existence. My T-shirt is stained from the peaches and peas Sarai had for breakfast. My hair hasn't been washed in days, and I smell strongly of spoiled milk.

"I haven't exactly been keeping up with the latest in fashion," I reply dryly.

"Oh." Lo sounds deflated for approximately a quarter of a second before bouncing back to full-force enthusiasm. "Well he's the bomb, and I didn't realize it was his shoot. I threw some of MiMi's French on him, followed instructions like a good little minion, and kept him cracking up the whole time. At the end, he offered me a job in his New York atelier. Can you believe that?"

The information zooms through my mind at warp speed, bits of it clinging to the sides of my brain while some of it doesn't stick at all.

"But . . ." I flounder a little. "But you have one more semester left at Spelman. Is this a summer job?"

"No, it starts right away. I can finish school anytime." Lo's energy crackles even over the phone. "This is a once-in-a-lifetime opportunity."

"It's a bit of a risk, isn't it?" I ask tentatively, not wanting to upset her but feeling like I need to offer a level-headed perspective. "I mean, you spend one afternoon with this guy and you uproot your whole life, all your plans, for him?"

"You mean the way you uprooted your whole life and all your plans to follow Caleb?" Her voice comes sharp and pricks me. It's quiet for a few moments as I find my way in this foreign land where Lo and I may be at odds.

"It's not the same," I say quietly. "Our situations are not the same, and you know it."

"No, they're not," Lo fires back. "Because unlike you, I won't hand my life over to some man. I'm taking this opportunity by the horns and following my dreams. I would never allow myself to end up trapped in somebody else's plans for me."

"Trapped?" I cannon back. "What are you saying? I should have had an abortion?"

"You know I love Sarai." She pauses. "But I would've been more careful about what was going in my lady business and made sure he was wrapped up tight."

"I'm not the first woman this has happened to, Lo. You know condoms aren't a hundred percent."

"I know, but . . ." The quiet on the other end swells with her hesitation.

"But what?"

"I don't trust Caleb."

I abandon the vegetables altogether, my hands dropping and falling limply at my side. "Did someone say something to you? You heard something about him?" I ask, dread gathering in my stomach.

"No, nothing like that," she says quickly. "I saw a shadow."

My head tilts as I try to discern what the hell this means. "A shadow? I don't understand."

"On his . . . soul," she says, her voice lowered to a whisper. "I think I saw a shadow on his soul."

"What do you-you . . ." I can't even stutter right. This is so ridiculous. "What the hell does that even mean? A shadow on his *soul*? He's the father of my child, Lo. This is serious. It's not time for some voodoo shit you caught from MiMi."

"Maybe if you'd taken the time to learn some of that voodoo *shit*," Lotus says, her voice crackling with disapproval, "you wouldn't be with him right now."

"Look, you keep that superstitious crap to yourself. I love MiMi just like you do, but—"

"Oh, I doubt that," Lo scoffs. "You barely know her. Your comments prove that."

My hurt swells and builds until it makes my eyes wet and my jaw clench. "Just because I didn't live with her like you did doesn't mean I don't love her."

"Whatever." A door slams shut between us. We rarely talk about the circumstances which led to Lo leaving New Orleans and living with MiMi. I know it's a sensitive issue. How could it not be? But all of a sudden, it feels like we should have talked about this more. It feels like something our family swept under the rug for years is about to break us.

"Lo, wait. This whole conversation has gotten out of control. Let's . . ." *I don't know what.*

"Let's what, Bo? Start over?" Bitterness cracks Lotus's voice. "Some things don't get do-overs. Not some forty-year-old man taking your virginity before you even have your first period. Not your own mother choosing him over you and shipping you off to the bayou to live with your great-grandmother."

That incident will probably haunt us both for the rest of our lives. It was the thing that took Lo away from New Orleans. She'd fight to her last breath for me, and I'd do the same for her, but I can't form words to soothe her deep wounds. I don't know what I can say to get us where we were before this awful conversation happened.

"But the joke's on Mama," Lo continues with a harsh laugh, "because getting away from her was the best thing that ever happened to me. I learned a lot that I never would have if I'd stayed in the Lower Ninth. Now, I can see when a man has a shadow on his soul, and I'm telling you that I saw a shadow. Do with that whatever you please."

"It just doesn't make sense to me, Lo," I say, pleading for her to understand.

"Something's off. I don't know what it is, but it is, and I, for one, am not gonna sit by and watch you barter yourself the way our mamas did."

I swallow the hot knot of hurt that almost chokes me. "Wow. Is that what you think I'm doing?" I ask, my voice pitched so low I barely hear myself. "What our mothers did? You think I'm like them now?"

"I didn't mean it that way." Lo sighs heavily. "I do think you could have done things a little differently, but I get it. It's hard to think of doing things on your own."

"That's not why I'm here, Lo." My voice assumes a hard edge. "Caleb is Sarai's father."

"Yeah, but not yours," Lo snaps. "So why have you allowed him to dictate everything? To manipulate you into this situation?"

"Manipulate?" An outraged breath puffs from my chest. "I haven't let him manipulate me. You were *there*. You know I was on bed rest. I couldn't work. I couldn't even leave the house. I had nowhere to go."

"You don't see it." Her words ring bitter. "Just like your mother never saw it. Just like mine never did either."

"How dare you compare me to them?" Every word lands somewhere it shouldn't. On my heart. Through my soul.

"How are you different? Living off a man's wealth to keep a roof over your head and clothes on your back. Fucking some rich man so he'll provide for you."

"Everything I've done . . . or not done . . . has been for Sarai, and you know it. I had so few choices. I'm doing the best I can."

"I know, Bo. I wish . . ." Her voice peters out, and I can feel some of the enmity we've flung at each other over the last few minutes draining away. "I wish you had gotten away from them, too. I hope they didn't influence you more than you realized."

"That's an awful thing to say." Hurt cracks my voice.

"I know you would never choose him over Sarai," Lo rushes to say. "I don't mean it that way. I meant—"

"I think we should end this," I interrupt. "This conversation is only getting worse, and we may not be on speaking terms by the end of it. Drop out of school. Move to New York for the atelier or whatever you call it."

The silence between us is unlike any we've shared. It's a wall of invisible bricks, layered with the mortar of our hurtful words.

"Okay," Lo finally replies. "Just remember if you need me, if you need anything, hopscotch."

Tears prick my eyes when she says that word. She could never get hopscotch right for some reason when we were little girls, so I helped her. I'd hop first, and she'd hop behind me, mimicking my steps until she got it herself. Silly as it seemed, it worked, and long after she could fly across the chalked squares by herself, "hopscotch" was our code for when we needed each other.

I'll never forget the bloodcurdling scream bellowing through the air at our family reunion. It wasn't my name she called when that man was on top of her. In her panic, she yelled hopscotch, and I ran. Before I saw them, I heard his grunts. And I heard Lo saying one word over and over.

Hopscotch. Hopscotch. Hopscotch.

I swore then, no one would ever hurt Lo again, not if I could help it. MiMi protected her for years living on the bayou, but when she moved to Atlanta for college, I took up the protective mantle personally. We haven't actually said the word "hopscotch" in a long time, so hearing it from Lo now, when I'm the one hurting her and she's the one hurting me, I have no idea what to do.

I mumble goodbye and rush off the phone. Knowing that's what she thinks about me, after all these years, after everything I've seen her go through—right now, I can't say hopscotch. Lo would be the last one I'd call for help.

ELEVEN

IRIS

I faked an orgasm.

Between bed rest, pelvic rest, the mandatory post-baby abstinence, and Caleb's hectic practice and travel schedule, I haven't had sex with Caleb in months. And the first time we do, I fake an orgasm.

When I told August I had to try to make my relationship work, I meant it. I had every intention of making this work, but I can't ignore the signs anymore. I don't love Caleb. I know it now, and I have to tell him.

It would be so convenient if I did love him. Leaving him will upset the apple cart. Hell, it will toss the apples into the street. Things are simple if I stay with Caleb, if I pretend this is what I want. Sarai and I will keep a multi-million-dollar roof over our heads, I'll have more money than I know what to do with, and custody remains simple. I'll have a partner to help raise my child. Though, despite Caleb's initial obsession with my pregnancy, he has been surprisingly laissez faire about actually parenting. Maybe it's just all the travel and the demands of his first NBA season. Maybe this summer, when he's off, he'll come into his own as a father.

I struggled at first, too. It took therapy and a prescription for me to be all in, but I am now. And the worst thing I could do for my daughter is turn a bad relationship into an awful marriage. I've always been determined I wouldn't settle for all the crap my mother took, and Sarai won't ever see that in me. I just have to figure out when to tell Caleb and how.

"Damn, that was good, Iris," Caleb mutters into my neck, still inside of me. "I needed that so bad, baby."

I just nod, willing him to get up so I don't have to ask him to. Caleb has never been a gentle lover, and I know it's been a long time, but he was rough, and I'm sore.

"The stress of this first season has been more than I realized." He lifts his head and peers down into my face in the dim light from the lamp by our bed. "I may be Rookie of the Year. Do you have any idea how my dad would feel? How proud he'd be if that happened? But with us losing the last few games, I'm so on edge. Fucking commentators speculating and criticizing."

He pushes the hair out of my eyes, his touch gentle.

"You take the edge off like nothing else, Iris."

He frowns, and I follow the direction of his stare. There's already faint bruising on my breast. Probably on my thighs and hips where he gripped them too hard. "Did I hurt you?"

He did. I wasn't ready for him, but he shoved into me. He never makes sure I'm satisfied. Never makes sure I'm pleased first, just . . . takes. He always takes and never looks for ways to give me what I need. I'm always the one yielding, compromising, left wanting. When did I start noticing it? Why didn't I notice it before?

"It's okay." I squirm beneath his weight. "You're a little heavy, though."

He shifts off my sore body. I've heard women say they like it rough, that they like hard fucks, but I don't see the appeal. I don't get how these bruises and aches are sexy. But as Lotus was quick to remind me, I've only ever been with Caleb. I have no one else to compare him to.

Only I find myself comparing him to August all the time, which is unfair. I haven't lived with August. If I spent more than a day with him, maybe he wouldn't be solicitous, and kind, and gentle, and considerate, and easy to talk to.

And sexy as hell.

I can't keep thinking of another man, of Caleb's rival this way, and continue living here, continue in this relationship. Maybe I should wait until his rookie season is over. He just admitted how stressful it's been. That's the most Caleb's revealed to me in a long time. We've been like satellites, just kind of in each other's orbit but not close enough to touch. The distance between us—doesn't he *feel* it? Does he even care?

"Hey, there's something I want to ask you," Caleb says from his side of the bed. He's lying on his side, his chin propped in his hand.

"Okay." I lick my lips nervously and pull the sheet more tightly around my nakedness. "Shoot."

Mischief lights his eyes and widens his smile, and for a moment, he's that guy who showed up at the bookstore every day, with coffee, wooing me to go on a date with him. He turns over and reaches into his nightstand. When he comes back, his eyes dart between my face and the ginormous diamond he's holding. "Iris, will you marry me?"

I always dreamt that when those words were spoken to me, I'd be elated. There would be no hesitation. I would fling myself into that man's arms and weep for joy. Only the weeping part is turning out to be true. I blink back tears of frustration and regret. We are obviously nowhere near being on the same page since I was just contemplating how to leave him. This will be more difficult than I thought.

"Caleb, I don't know what to say," I mumble, biting my lip until it matches my other aches. "I'm . . . well, are you sure about this?"

"What the hell do you mean am I sure?" The ring trembles between his fingers with the anger I see clearly on his face. "We live together. We have a baby together. Of course, I'm sure. What kind of question is that?"

I wish he was being rhetorical, and I didn't have to respond, but he's clearly waiting, not too patiently, for my reply. "I mean, things haven't been the same, have they?" I ask, searching his face for some answering understanding. "There's been this distance, and I—"

"We couldn't have sex for months, Iris, while you were on pelvic rest or whatever. And then we had to wait another six weeks." He rolls away, tossing the priceless diamond onto the nightstand as if it's one of those candy ring pops. "I've been on the road. Hell, you were moping around here for weeks like you'd lost your best friend. You didn't even want our baby. Of course, there's been distance."

"What did you say about Sarai?" I pick the most disturbing thing from his list of grievances. "Of course it was hard at first, and I was sorting through a lot, but—"

"Forget I mentioned it." He stands and walks into the bathroom, turning on the light and illuminating his well-conditioned body. He's an elite athlete. At six foot six, he's as tall as August. With his classic blond hair and navy blue eyes, he's just as handsome in a completely different way. But there's no thrill when I look at him naked. I suddenly scan my mind, my heart, for the last time there was.

I slip on my robe and follow him into the bathroom, determined to hash this out so we can end this chapter of our relationship and move on to the next. Figure out custody and co-parenting and all the details that come with a separation I hope won't be messy.

"Caleb, can we talk?" I ask softly.

He's silent, his broad, tanned back turned away from me, his posture stiff.

I touch his shoulder. He flings my hand off. I stumble back from the force of it, and my hip bumps painfully into the sharp edge of the counter.

"Ow." I wince, squeezing my eyes shut against the brief, blinding pain. "Caleb, God. That hurt."

I wait for an apology that doesn't come. His eyes run dispassionately over me, his inspection starting at my bare feet and climbing over every inch until he meets my eyes. There's a frigid possessiveness there, as if I'm a misbehaving pet he owns but isn't too fond of. One he needs to make sure gets back in line.

I shiver under that icy stare. I still feel it when he looks away. The cold has set in.

"Hey, we've got time." He tugs me into him, even though he must feel how stiff I am in his arms. "Let's not talk about marriage again until the season is over. Can you just give me that? I have a string of tough games coming up, and I need to focus."

Everything in me screams to get this settled, because it's lingered long enough, but I nod. I can give him that, but he's never fucking me again. I felt like an object tonight—like he was collecting rent money. It was a transaction between our bodies, one where I got nothing, and he took everything. As I look back over our relationship, I have to wonder.

Has it been that way all along?

TWELVE

IRIS

"We need to schedule some charitable work for you, Caleb."

Sylvia, the Stingers' community outreach coordinator, bites into the beignet I offered her with a cup of coffee.

"These are incredible." She groans and closes her eyes in what looks like rapture. "Did you make these yourself, Iris?"

"Yeah." I laugh and wave a finger in front of my mouth. "You have some powder."

"Oh." She brushes away the white powder. "Thank you. I didn't know people actually made these at home."

"Well, I'm from Louisiana." I smile, thinking about the time MiMi showed Lo and me how to make them. "It's one of the few recipes I follow pretty well."

"I need to leave for tonight's game in a little bit," Caleb interjects, a small frown marring his expression. "What are the charitable opportunities?"

Sylvia's smile dims a little, and so does mine. Caleb has been uncooperative and surly all day. I hoped he would shake the funk for this meeting with Sylvia, but he's been distracted and abrupt the whole time she's been here.

"Um, we have a great one at a community center downtown," Sylvia says. "The heroin epidemic in Baltimore and the surrounding counties is unbelievable. We had twice as many overdoses as murders last year."

"Oh, my God." I lean forward and press my elbows to my knees. "That's awful."

"And what exactly does this have to do with the Stingers?" Caleb asks, sipping the coffee I poured for him. "Iris, what the hell is this? Since when do I take sugar in my coffee?" He shoves the cup at me. Some of it sloshes over the side, scalding my hand.

I gasp, wiping the wetness away on my jeans and rubbing at the tender spot.

"I'm sorry, babe." He looks concerned for half a second. "If you could bring me a coffee the way I take it, I'd really appreciate it."

I glance at Sylvia before walking into the kitchen to get him a fresh cup. Our eyes meet briefly, hers wide with surprise, but she glances down at her purse right away. She's as shocked as I am by Caleb's inconsiderate behavior. This has been his MO since our argument about marriage a few weeks ago. Rude. Inconsiderate. Asshole. It seems to worsen by the day. His patience is thinner, and mine is nearly gone. The season is almost over, but I'm not sure we'll last until then.

"Downtown?" Caleb is asking when I re-enter the living room. "Downtown Baltimore? Wow. I'm pretty sure I'm traveling around then."

"We haven't set any dates yet Caleb," Sylvia says, pinching her lips together and glancing down at the pad in her lap. "The community center is a great chance to interact with some of the local youth. Maybe doing some basic drills with them, maybe working on a beautification project at the center. Things like that."

"Could I help?" I ask before I think better of it. Sylvia and Caleb both turn surprised looks my way. "I mean, if I can help, I'm willing."

Caleb frowns, his lips already parted and denial in his eyes. Sylvia steps in before he can voice his displeasure.

"I think that's a great idea." Her warm smile eases some of the regret I feel for speaking. "We've been trying to get more visibility for players' wives."

"Oh, Iris isn't my wife," Caleb cuts in, his eyes dropping to the ring MiMi gave me. "We're not even engaged."

He and I lock stares, both defiant. He's determined to get his way, and I'm determined that he won't.

Sylvia clears her throat.

"But you're a family," she says, glancing at me reassuringly. "You have a daughter together. Lots of players' girlfriends are involved. I think it would be great. If you aren't too intimidated by downtown Baltimore, Iris."

"I grew up in the Lower Ninth Ward." I set Caleb's coffee down in front of him with a clang, looking at him when I say my next words. "I'm not easily intimidated."

With his eyes narrowed and his mouth set in a hard line, he sips and nods his grudging approval. "Community center, huh?" He bites into a beignet, stops mid-chew and squints. I've seen just that look when he and his agent are assessing if something will be good for his career. That's what he's doing now: weighing how me doing this will reflect on him.

I don't know where that comes from. I'm being petty.

"You're right. It'll be good for my image in the community," he finally says to Sylvia, confirming my suspicion. "For people to see us active and involved. Goodwill for the team. Iris can represent us."

Permission granted.

Irritation snaps my teeth together. He makes me feel invisible all the time or like he's running my life by proxy, making decisions on my behalf. Does he even realize this is the kind of thing I might have been organizing if my career were on track? That I could do Sylvia's job with my eyes closed? In my sleep?

"Then it's settled." Sylvia stands and gathers her purse and jacket. "I'll call you with details, Iris. Thank you both."

"Sure." Caleb turns toward the stairs and throws a comment over his shoulder. "I need to leave soon for tonight's game. See you later, Sylvia."

"I'm really excited about this opportunity," I tell her at the door. "I've been wanting to do something meaningful for a while now."

"Then this could be a great fit. Oh, and there is a daycare onsite if you think your daughter would be fine there for an hour or so," Sylvia says, making her way down the short set of steps to her car parked in the circular drive. "I'll be in touch."

Once she's gone and I'm back in the kitchen, I allow myself the simple pleasure of anticipation. I'm going to do something outside of this house, at least for an hour or so. Something that doesn't involve mammary glands or diapers or mashed vegetables.

But not today.

The dishes in the sink, mostly bottles and baby spoons and bowls, remind me that at least for today, this house is the scope of my existence.

I start setting the kitchen to some kind of order, cleaning the food processor and mopping up the clumps of Sarai's breakfast that didn't make it to her mouth.

Caleb will be heading to the arena soon. I can't decide if I like things better when he's on the road or when he's home. It's just as lonely in this huge house when he's here as it is when he's gone. Surely this isn't what he wants in a marriage? We're just co-existing. There's no real connection, no friendship. We at least used to have that. We started as friends, but even that's hard to remember now.

"What's this?"

I look up from washing Sarai's bottles to see Caleb in the arched kitchen entrance holding a few sheets of paper.

"Where'd you get those?" I know exactly where he got them. I'm just delaying the questions those papers lead to.

"In my office," he says abruptly. "On the printer. What's this about, Iris?"

His office. Everything in this house belongs to him. His eyes roam over my breasts and hips and legs, reminding me that I belong to him, too. At least, he likes to think so. We sleep in the same bed, but I've managed to avoid having sex again. He hasn't mentioned getting engaged again either. We're both tiptoeing around issues that will lead us to crossroads. I'm not ready to go out on my own, not without a job, a home, resources. Something to ensure Sarai and I will be straight.

I know if I leave now, Caleb will provide for Sarai. Legally he has to, but I don't want to get into all of that right now, not when Caleb is under so much pressure. So we're in limbo, but I'm researching the next steps to secure our future, mine and my daughter's. And that's what he's holding in his hand.

"It's just some information about an online certification program for sports industry essentials." I push a chunk of hair behind my ear before meeting Caleb's icy blue eyes. "I'm thinking about enrolling."

"No." His harshly spoken word freezes me against the sink. "Not happening."

"Sarai is getting older," I say carefully, not wanting to fight before Caleb's game. "I have to think about what I'll do with the rest of my life."

"What the hell does that mean?" In a few strides he's beside me, towering over me. Glowering at me. "The rest of your life? You'll marry me and raise my children, Iris. Nothing to think about."

"Children?" Shock hushes my voice. "I'm not having more kids."

The quiet following my words swells with the fury in his eyes.

"What did you say?" he asks, his voice deathly quiet.

"I mean, not until I get my future on track. Caleb, you know I never planned to get pregnant at this stage of my life. I love Sarai, but I still have the same hopes and dreams I had before she came. I want to resume my *life*."

His eyes soften, but it's a false soft. A curtain he draws over his true feelings, but I see them clearly. I'm not sure why I haven't recognized this trick before, but I do now.

"Baby, I think once we're married," he says, resting his hands on my hips, "we can revisit this, but for now, it's not something we should do."

"You're right." I keep my voice soft and even, but I slip through his fingers, stepping away. "You have a game tonight. Let's discuss it later."

His expression goes flat and hard like the face of a cliff. He grabs my hand and twists it, shoving my ring finger in my face.

"I don't understand what you want," he spits out. "I offer you a ten-carat diamond, and you're still walking around wearing this cheap junk jewelry where my ring should be."

"It's not junk." I jerk my hand away, rubbing at the pain in my wrist. "It's from my great-grandmother." I narrow my eyes at him and lay my words out with care. "For protection from anyone who wants to hurt me."

"Hurt you?" Frustration darkens his handsome face, and he grabs both my arms tightly. I've never felt the disparity between our heights and weight more than now. I'm not a tiny girl, but when held by a basketball player with more than a foot on me, whose body is honed to compete at the highest level, I'm practically defenseless.

"I *love* you, Iris, but if you don't know the difference between love and pain," he grits out. "maybe I should teach you."

He shakes me, and my head snaps back on my neck with every jerk. My arms throb under the vise of his fingers.

"Let me go," I gasp, pressing my hands to his chest. "Right now, Caleb."

For a moment, refusal flares in his eyes. He tightens his painful hold a few seconds more, letting me know without words that he could keep doing it if he chose. Slowly, his fingers ease, but the intensity of his eyes doesn't let go.

As soon as he releases me, I walk swiftly across the room, putting as much distance between us as this kitchen will allow. I almost limp with relief being away from him, and lean against the sink, forcing myself to look at him.

"Put your hands on me like that again," I say, my voice leaden and sure, "and I will walk out that door with my daughter, and good luck finding us."

The storm in his eyes settles into something that resembles fear and masquerades as remorse. Whatever it is in truth, I'll never know because he quickly shutters that look.

"I'm sorry," he says quietly. "It won't happen again. I'm just under so much pressure right now. We're close to making the playoffs. Tonight's game is huge for us. I'm feeling it, but that doesn't excuse me taking it out on you."

I want to believe him. He's never hurt me like this on purpose before.

"I understand the pressure, but . . ." I drop my eyes to the floor. "I saw my mom and aunt take a lot of crap from men when we were growing up. I have no tolerance for it."

"It won't happen again." He takes a deep breath, as if clearing the air. "Now that we got that out of the way, would you come to tonight's game? It would mean a lot to have you and Sarai in the stands for me."

"Sure." I slide my hands into the back pockets of my jeans. "Who are you guys playing?"

"The San Diego Waves," he says, watching my face closely as if for a reaction, one I refuse to give him, but inside my heart stutters and thumps.

So much for avoiding August.

THIRTEEN

AUGUST

"Hey, West. You got a second?"

I turn to face Deck. In addition to being the San Diego Waves' president of basketball operations, he'll also be first-round Hall of Fame. When he calls, you answer.

I hang my coat up in the locker and meet his eyes over my shoulder. A few guys mill around the Baltimore Stingers' guest team locker room, but for the most part, we have this corner to ourselves.

"Yeah?" I stopped trying to call him 'sir' long ago. "What's up?"

"I know this is a big game."

No game is a big game because it's almost the end of the season, and we've got an icicle's hope in hell of making the playoffs. It feels like the last few games don't matter since there won't be a post-season for us. We're an expansion team, so that's to be expected in our first year, but it still bites with teeth.

I've never been on a losing team in my life. The fierce competitor in me has never allowed that to happen. I've always been able to pull any team I was on across every finish line—*first*. But this is the NBA. Every man out there is the best in his neighborhood, the best in his high school and college. One man can do a lot, but in this league, one man can never do it all.

"What's so special about this game, Deck?" I close the locker and turn to face him.

"For one, you're playing in your hometown," Deck says. "I assume your family will be here to see you."

I allow a genuine smile, thinking of my mom and stepfather in the stands tonight. "Yeah, they'll be here. My mom's invited the team over for dinner after the game since we don't fly out 'til morning. You're welcome to come."

"Nah." An almost sheepish smile looks out of place on the strong planes of his face. "I'm flying to New York to see my girl, but thank your mother for me."

Deck and Avery make long-distance love look easy, though I'm sure it has its challenges. "Give Avery my best." I shoot him a knowing grin.

"I haven't seen her in three weeks, so I'll be busy giving her *my* best and not thinking about your punk ass." His roguish laugh makes me laugh in response.

"Lucky man." I lean back on the locker and wait for him to get to the reason he came, which has nothing to do with my hometown, my mama, or his girlfriend, for that matter.

"So the media has been hyping this game because it's you and Bradley," Decker says, the humor fading from his expression. "Everyone's saying it's a two-man race for Rookie of the Year." Decker lifts both brows. "Or are you so caught up in your tennis star girlfriend you hadn't noticed?"

A chuckle rumbles from my chest, and I offer him a slow head shake. "Don't believe everything you read, Deck. You should know that better than anyone."

"Oh, so you're not fucking Pippa Kim?"

I zip a finger across my lips. "A gentleman never fucks and tells."

Truth is, I did fuck Pippa months ago. It was good, but not something I wanted to repeat. We're both new to the sports spotlight, me with basketball and her with tennis, so we understand unique challenges most people can't even imagine. We clicked as friends and have attended various functions together. I never comment when people ask me about Pippa, and she never comments when people ask her about me. Apparently "no comment" is a comment in itself because now everyone assumes we're together.

Pippa was during my "how many holes can I squeeze my dick into" phase. I probably would have screwed a hole in the wall if I had thought it might help take my mind off Iris.

Which brings us to the *actual* reason Deck should worry about tonight's game.

"Me and Caleb are cool." The lie comes smoothly. "But if the media makes shit up, why should you care? More butts in seats if they think there's drama, right?"

Deck's too sharp for my own good. He narrows his eyes and crosses thickly muscled arms across his broad chest. I always think of him like a lion with his tawny hair and eyes. Dude is still cut up even though he's a few years out of the league. My eating and workout regimen were the first things he adjusted when I joined the team. He may be a front office executive now, but he was a baller first. He's hands-on with the players, and right now he's trying to wrap his hands and head around this Caleb situation.

"If you say so, I believe you," he finally replies after a few seconds. "But I'm trusting you to be the bigger man if he starts shit on the court tonight."

I will my face into not giving a damn and shrug carelessly, faking nonchalance like a motherfucker. "At least you picked up on the fact that he's an asshole," I say. "Most are fooled by the golden boy act."

"Why do you think I didn't draft him?" Deck dips his head, a cynical brow raising an inch. "I know a carefully crafted image when I see one, and Caleb's daddy's been carefully crafting that boy since he was in diapers. Now he's used to getting everything he wants. I'd hate to see him when he doesn't." He points a warning finger at me. "Thus, this little talk. The two of you always go at each other hard, and you seem to always come out on top."

"Not always.,"

He got the girl.

And I deeply resent him for that.

I'm gonna hold my shit together with iron will and rubber bands tonight, though, no matter how he provokes me. It'll require complete focus. I haven't allowed myself to wonder if Iris will be at tonight's game. It'll be packed, and I probably won't even know if she comes. I assume she attends his home games.

That damn lucky bastard.

To look up in the stands and know that woman is pulling for you must be the best feeling in the world. Maybe one day I'll find out for myself, even though I know it's not likely. They're two shakes from getting married. They're living together and have a kid. I understand all the odds are stacked against me, but something inside doesn't give a damn and keeps holding out hope.

"I know you, August," Deck continues softly. "Whatever it is that has you and Caleb snarling at each other every time you meet, keep it locked down tonight. I don't want flagrant fouls, ejections, fights—none of that shit. *Capisce?*"

I swallow the defiant response swelling in my throat, a rebel yell that wants to declare I'm gonna wipe the fucking floor with Caleb. Not in a fight. Not playing dirty. No, I want to humiliate him fair and square. I want to outplay him.

Like I always do.

"*Capisce*," I assure Decker before suiting up.

FOURTEEN

IRIS

"I'll be fine on my own," I tell Ramone, the bodyguard Caleb assigned to Sarai and me for tonight's game.

It's not unusual for professional athletes as popular as Caleb to have security for them and their families, but we've never used it before tonight. We don't need it, but Caleb insisted.

"Really, you don't have to sit with me," I say, holding onto my patience.

Ramone's face goes from impassive to obstinate. "Protecting you is my job, Ms. DuPree," he says, his voice as stiff as the collar of his heavily starched shirt.

"Your job?" I shift Sarai on my hip and juggle the nachos I bought as we make our way to the seats Caleb secured. "You mean just for tonight, right?"

He blinks at me as if I've asked him a hard question. He's saved by the bell when someone calls my name from behind.

"Iris?" the deep voice asks again, prompting me to search the cluster of people around us. "Is that you?"

A huge smile overtakes my face when I spot Jared Foster.

"Oh my God, hi." I take a few steps in his direction, side-eyeing Ramone, who is with me every step of the way. "So good to see you."

"I thought that was you but wasn't sure." He smiles warmly, looking from me to Sarai. "And who's this beautiful girl?"

"My daughter, Sarai." I brush dark curls back from her forehead and drop a kiss there.

"So *you're* the reason Mommy wouldn't come work for me," Jared says, bending to peer into Sarai's dark blue eyes.

"Pretty much." Regret spears through me right alongside the pride I feel when I look at my little girl. "I can't exactly hustle and grind and travel and do all the things the internship would have required right now."

"True." Jared reaches into his pocket and takes out his wallet. "But maybe circumstances will change, or the job will."

He proffers a business card to me, which I stare at like it's Willy Wonka's Golden Ticket. I don't have a free hand to take the card, and I'm too shocked to, anyway.

"I'm not with Richter anymore." He realizes my small dilemma and slides the card into the open front pocket of the baby bag hanging from my shoulder. "My cell's on the card. When things settle some, call me."

I glance from the card poking out from the bag to Jared's handsome face. "I'm with Sarai's father, Caleb Bradley, and we live here in Baltimore, so I'm not sure when I'll be able to . . . that is to say . . ." A brittle little laugh breaks over my lips. "There are just a lot of obstacles."

"Let nothing hold you back or keep you down," he says, kindling my memory. "Isn't that what you told me in our interview?"

"Yeah." I return his smile. "I guess it is."

He smiles, his eyes curious. "Bradley, huh? Would never have guessed."

"You know Caleb?" Of course. Everyone knows him. *"I mean, personally?"*

"No, only by reputation." Jared grimaces as if that reputation isn't great, which makes no sense. Everyone loves Caleb. Living with him, I've seen the holes in the polished façade he projects to the world, but few do.

"We should get to your seats, Ms. DuPree," Ramone says firmly, aiming a sharp look at Jared.

"Don't let me keep you," Jared says easily, addressing me and ignoring Ramone. "You have a beautiful daughter, Iris. Call me when she's a little older if you decide to venture back into the workforce."

"I will." I hesitate a beat before asking the question that keeps turning in my head "Why? Why would you want me to come work for you? We had one interview, and I—"

"Impressed me," he cuts in. "It wasn't just what was on paper. It was you. Your passion for sports. Your love for basketball and your grit. Your intelligence. It all showed in that interview. A lot of people would love having you on their team, and I'm one of them."

He looks at Ramone, who shifts impatiently from one foot to the other.

"I'd better let you go," Jared says, amusement in his eyes. "Remember. Call me when you're ready."

I try not to glare at Ramone as we take our seats just a few rows behind the Stingers' bench. He's just doing his job. I get it, but Caleb and I definitely have to talk about this.

Even Ramone's overbearing presence can't dampen my spirits. Jared Foster wants me on his team. I may be closer to independence than I thought.

FIFTEEN
AUGUST

From tip-off, I know something is wrong with Caleb. I've been facing him since we were bare-faced adolescents whose voices hadn't changed yet. I've studied him and know his every tell and all his triggers. Something's different. Something's changed. He's even more aggressive than usual, but he's not hiding it in sly side-plays the refs and the cameras miss. He's more blatant and less controlled than I've ever seen him. Almost unhinged. Sloppy. Picking apart his game isn't even a challenge this time, and his frustration boils to the surface and over the sides quicker than usual.

Me—I'm having the game of my damn life.

Tres. Trois. Triple.

Any way you wanna say it, I'm raining threes. There's a zone a shooter enters where the hoop feels closer and wider, like a woman spreading herself open and making it easy for you to slip in. You hear *swoosh* before the ball leaves your hands. It feels like you could close your eyes and make every shot—you're that in tune with the net. That's the zone I'm in tonight, and for some reason, the Stingers coach leaves Caleb on me when *we all know* he couldn't guard me with a sword and shield. He's never been able to, but he always insists on trying. His ego is not only his downfall, but his team's, because remarkably, we're up at the half. This game *does* matter for them. They'll probably make the playoffs, but they're in the wild card position. They need to win, or other teams need to lose for them to make it. And if I have anything to say about it, they ain't winning *shit* tonight.

"You guys are killing 'em," Coach Kemp says when we huddle after halftime before the third quarter starts, his eyes fixed on me. "Keep it up."

He's a good leader, but everyone knows his assistant coach, Ean Jagger, is the brains behind this operation. A college injury ended Jagger's pro hopes, but he's a basketball savant. With his dark, closely cropped hair and black-rimmed glasses, he's got a little bit of a Clark Kent vibe going on. Around Deck's age, he's one of the most respected minds in the league. Every team wooed him, and I have no idea how Decker cajoled or bribed him to slum it with an expansion squad, but thank God he did.

When we break, Jagger waves me over. I join him by the bench, tucking my jersey into my shorts.

"'Sup, Jag?" I don't have to bend because at six foot seven, he's got an inch on me.

"I know you're in the zone right now." His deep timbre rumbles low under the collective hum of the waiting crowd. "And every shot is falling, but if you go cold, we're fucked."

"'Scuse me?" I glance at him with a frown.

"Yeah, since you're taking every shot, you're the only one in rhythm," Jagger says, the calm demeanor he's famous for unruffled. "You start missing, no one else is ready. We all know you're a gifted athlete, August. Don't just show off. Show us you can *lead*."

He taps his clipboard for emphasis, nailing me with a look from behind his glasses.

"You're the point guard. The floor general. Involve your teammates more," he says. "Slow the game down so they can catch up. Open the floor. What happened to the passing we've been working on all season? You've reverted to hoarding the ball. Where's your head, man?"

Only Jag would hone in on these issues when, from the outside, it looks like things couldn't be better and I'm having a stellar game.

Everything he's said is spot on. I'm playing well, but I'm the only one playing well. That's not the kind of team we want to be, and that's not the kind of player I want to be. I promised myself I wouldn't let Caleb take me out of my game, and even though I look good, it's selfish play that's doing it. And that's his game, not mine.

"Good looking out." I fist-pound him and nod. "Thanks, Jag."

"No problem." He pushes the glasses up his nose, looks back to his clipboard and starts marking up our next play.

I'm headed toward the floor to start the second half, when I happen to look up at the jumbotron. Some cameraman has a great eye because out of all the people in this arena, he found the two most beautiful.

Iris doesn't seem to realize the camera is on her. "Shot Caller" is emblazoned on the front of her red T-shirt, and she bounces Sarai on her knees, making animated faces to coax her into laughing. Sarai's little hands flap, and her fingers close around her mother's nose. I can't hear Iris's laugh, but even the memory of it is like warm honey pouring over me. Her laugh is husky and full-bodied and genuine—something her soul cooks up and her heart serves.

When she finally realizes the camera is on her, and she and her daughter are on the big screen, she looks embarrassed for a second but recovers. Like the perfect baller's chick, she looks into the camera and waves Sarai's hand. The most angelic smile lights up the little girl's face, sparks in those violet-blue eyes.

Even with my team up, and my highest-scoring game already on the books by halftime, disappointment singes my insides. I'm about to turn away and walk on court when Iris looks right at me. Only a few rows behind the bench, she's close enough for me to see her eyes widen, and that gorgeous, fuckable mouth falls open the littlest bit.

If I'm off my game, so is Iris. She should have looked away by now to hide this. The camera is still on her, and in seconds, someone will connect the dots between me staring up at her and her staring back at me, but neither one of us looks away. On lonely nights, drowning in pussy instead of booze, I've lain awake and tried to convince myself I imagined this pull between us. But this thing that connects us may as well be a neon thread, lit up for everyone to see. It's so tangible you could pluck it. I'm tangled up in it and can't seem to work myself free.

"West!" Kenan calls, finally jerking my attention away. "You playing or what?"

Shit.

Our starting line-up is already on the floor, and so is the Stingers'. I'm the only one not out there. I take one last look at Iris, who is now looking at her daughter and not me, before going on the court.

When I take my spot, Caleb's eyes are slitted. He looks from me to the stands, and there is no question he noticed the long look I shared with his baby's mama.

What-the-hell-ever.

I put the incident behind me and grab hold of Jag's advice. Getting my team involved, spreading the floor, and slowing down the game helps me to shake off the moment with Iris that rattled my insides.

One of our players is at the free-throw line, and Caleb and I are standing beside each other, waiting for him to take his two shots.

"You see something you like up in the stands, West?" he asks, watching the ball circle the rim before falling through the net.

I don't respond. I think that's best. He knows what he saw, and I don't feel like lying to him.

"I fucked her in the ass before the game," he says, so low only I'll hear. "No one's ever had her like that before. I get all her firsts. Did you know I was her first, West? I'll be her only and her last."

Outrage and disgust rise like bile in my throat. I glance at him, my eyes burning with hate. I squelch my fury and reach for the coldhearted, ruthless competitor who always finds a way to ruin this man's night.

"You talk that way about the mother of your child?" I tsk and shake my head like it's a shame. "I was gonna ease up on you, show some mercy, but now I'm gonna wipe the floor with your bitch ass."

And I do.

For the next twenty minutes, I take Maverick's advice to a degree, but I shake Caleb, deny him the ball, do everything in my power to pick him apart.

With only a few minutes left, this home crowd is stunned that we're up by ten points. Caleb attempts a dunk. Not on my watch. I leap to trap the ball against the backboard, and the ref calls it a clean block shot. None of Caleb's shouting and whining gets the call overturned. The building is as quiet as it's been all night, and some fans are even starting to leave.

Next time down the floor, Caleb tries to return the favor, but my shot goes in, even though I fall on my back in the act of shooting. I'm about to get up, when he comes to stand over me, legs spread and groin above my face, a not-so-subtle "suck my dick" message—a blatant disrespect among ballers.

I'm on my feet and in his face before my brain can catch up to the rest of my body. We're head to sweaty head, chest to chest, nose to nose, growl for growl. Teeth bared and tension unleashed in the tight space between us. A leanly muscled arm shoves me back.

"What the hell?" Kenan demands, his nose now at mine. "You trying to get suspended for the next game? Keep your shit together, Rook."

Caleb looks over the shoulder of a teammate, his eyes baleful and malevolent. Indignation drains out of me every second I hold his stare. I glance from him to the scoreboard and back, my smirk telling him without words that he may go home with Iris, but it's as a loser who got his ass handed to him on the court. I made him my highlight reel bitch, and she witnessed every second of it.

Fuck that in the ass, you pussy son of a bitch.

I turn away, as disgusted with myself as I am with him. I give Kenan a curt nod, letting him know I have my emotions on lock again. With only a minute left in the game, we're almost home free. In the last time-out huddle, Decker stands behind the bench.

"Game's over, Coach," he says, his eyes trained on me. "Do we need August out there? It's sewn up, right?"

Coach Kemp looks at me speculatively. "It's true, West. Why don't you sit out this last—"

"No," I cut in, looking from him to Decker and back again. "Let me finish."

I want to be out there when the buzzer goes off. I want that asshole to shake my hand like a good little golden boy when this is over or risk everyone seeing him for the whiny little bitch he is.

"Up to you," Decker says, disappointment flickering over his expression before he clears it. "But I'd prefer you sit out."

I don't wait for them to reconsider. I leave the huddle and walk onto the floor.

It's our final possession, and I've got the ball. Me and Caleb, one on one. I fake left. He dives. I turn right. I'm gone. Dodging defenders, in the paint, penetrating to the goal. I leap and scoop the ball in. I'm high. Caleb's below, and our eyes connect.

Nail in your coffin, motherfucker.

When I come down, Caleb's still standing there. Our bodies collide. I plummet to the floor, my leg twisting awkwardly when I land.

White-hot pain lances through my leg, and my vision goes black around the edges.

The team trainer is immediately at my side and tells me not to move. I try to sit up, but my head swims from the pain.

"Shit," I mutter, collapsing back onto the court.

"He said don't move," Decker orders from my right, his furrowed brows and tightly held lips a map of concern. "And don't look."

Don't *look*? What is there to see?

I glance around the tight circle of grim-faced players surrounding me. The emotions warring on their faces range from horror to pain to pity.

My heart batters my chest, not because of the pain, though it's excruciating, but because of the pity in their eyes. So few people can play at this level, and we're an elite fraternity of sorts. We've all worked unimaginably hard for most of our lives to get here, and it can all disappear in an instant. One bad fall can ruin a career.

I need to see my leg.

They bring a stretcher, and I shake my head. No way I'm going out like that. Even if I have to hobble off the court, I want to go under my own steam.

I sit up to tell them so and another wave of dizziness overtakes me, but not because of the pain. Because of what I see.

The large bone in my right leg protrudes through the skin. Nausea roils in my stomach at the gruesome sight. This isn't a strain or a tear or something you bounce back from easily. It's a break, and recovery will take incredible effort and time, if it can be accomplished at all.

Through a haze of mind-numbing pain, my first memory of handling a ball rises up as they lift and strap me to the stretcher. I'm in the backyard and barely able to hold onto the ball because my hands are so small. Perched on my father's shoulders, and with his great height, I can just reach the goal and drop the ball through the net. He and my mother cheer, and even at that age, the approval is a warm rush I hold close and immediately want more of.

Will a crowd ever roar for me again?

It's not our home crowd, but everyone cheers as I'm hoisted on the stretcher and taken toward the locker room. Every face I pass shows sympathy, even the Stingers' players. When I pass Caleb, though, a black satisfaction darkens his blue eyes. There's retribution in the curl of his lip.

The defending player is supposed to give the player with the ball room to land. Caleb didn't do that. It was a dirty play. No reasonably informed person watching what just happened would say otherwise.

His scorn and cruelty cover me under the blinding lights and flashing cameras, and I wonder if Iris is still here. If she saw the play. Caleb did this to warn me, but I hope Iris takes it as a warning, too.

SIXTEEN

IRIS

Oh. My. God.

Dirty play.

The two words start as a whisper of speculation and disbelief, but grow louder and more certain around me until it seems everyone is saying what Caleb just did was a dirty play. Shaken, I watch them carry August off the floor on a stretcher. Once he's been swallowed up by the darkness of the guest team tunnel, I shift my eyes back to the court. Caleb is staring at me, and the anger, the malevolence he's hidden is on full display in his eyes. It takes my breath hostage. I don't even recognize him for a moment, and I know what he just did was about me. About me and August.

August put on an amazing performance, recording a personal best in points, but at what cost? His injury is obviously serious, but how serious? Will he miss the rest of the season? Could it end his career?

Is it my fault?

"I'm ready to go," I tell Ramone.

His frown is quick and stern and not scaring me even a little bit. "But Mr. Bradley wanted us to meet him at the—"

"I'll see Mr. Bradley when he gets home." I stand with Sarai asleep on my shoulder. "You can walk me to the car, or I can go on my own. Those are the only options."

He hesitates, glancing down at the court. I follow his eyes to Caleb still watching me. I start down the row, not looking back to make sure Ramone is following. The quick thud of his steps behind me confirms he's coming.

"Ms. DuPree." He grabs my elbow, looking down at me. "I'm escorting you to your car and will drive you home."

"Look, I don't need—"

"I insist." His fingers tighten around my bones to a point just short of pain.

"Let me go." I snap a look from my elbow to his implacable expression. "Or I'll scream for the cops."

His fingers drop immediately, but his bulk still crowds me, and I clutch Sarai closer. What was supposed to be protection now feels like capture. He points toward the exit, to the private garage where my car is parked.

Without him asking, I let him take the wheel of the G-Class Mercedes SUV Caleb gave me, and I climb in the back, buckling Sarai into her car seat. I don't say a word to Ramone, and he doesn't say a word to me, but something has shifted, not just between Ramone and me, but between Caleb and me. That dirty play was an act of war, a shot he fired at August, but it struck me, too. It passed right through my heart, and I'm aching for all that August may have lost tonight.

I pull out my phone and Google him to check for an update on his injury. Nothing much more than I already know, except that they've taken him to the hospital for tests. There are only a few games left in his rookie season, and this has happened.

Because of me?

I choke on guilt, and the bright lights of the skyline blur through my tears while we travel the city's streets. As soon as we pull into the garage, I unsnap Sarai and scoot to the door. Ramone is already there, holding it open for me. I don't even look at him, but rush inside and up to the nursery, laying her down in her crib and making sure her monitor is on.

I turn on the huge television in our bedroom built into the wall over the fireplace. Avery Hughes, one of SportsCo's most popular anchors, shares a split screen with a reporter in the field.

"What can you tell us, John?" Avery asks. "Any news on August West?"

"He's inside." John points a thumb over his shoulder to the hospital behind him. "All we've heard is that they're doing tests to gauge the extent of the injury. It looked pretty bad, but we won't know until the results are in."

A small commotion off-camera distracts John for a second, and then he jerks his attention back to Avery.

"We may have something." He gestures for the cameraman to follow him. "It's MacKenzie Decker, San Diego Waves president of basketball operations."

The reporters gathered at the hospital entrance slow Decker's progress, clustering around him with boom mics and recorders and curiosity.

"What can you tell us, Deck?" one reporter yells. "Is August out for the rest of the season?"

"How bad is the injury?" another asks before he has time to answer.

"Is the leg broken?" The question is hurled at Decker, prompting a quick frown on the handsome face.

"I played basketball, not baseball, guys," Deck says, stopping to answer their questions, a strained smile canting one side of his mouth. "You keep zinging these fast balls at me. Gimme a chance to answer one."

A few of the reporters chuckle, but no one moves, waiting for answers to their questions.

"It's too early to say how serious the injury is," Deck continues, his eyes graver than the smile firmly planted on his face. "As a precaution, it's safe to say August probably won't return for the last few games of the season, which is tough. Everyone knows he's a once-in-a-lifetime player. I have no doubt he'll be just fine." He glances past them to the hospital entrance. "Now I better get in there and check on our boy." He waves, ignoring the follow-up questions, and makes his way inside.

When the camera cuts back to Avery, it catches her in an unguarded moment, and genuine concern shadows her pretty face. It's been rumored for months that she and MacKenzie Decker are dating. I wonder if she knows August personally. Her expression definitely goes beyond the bounds of professionalism.

She looks into the camera, composing herself and slipping her reporter's mask back on. "Keep us posted, John. Now, I think we have a comment from the other side of the court. Speculation around the league about a dirty play by Caleb Bradley started almost before West hit the floor. I think we have some sound on that from the Stingers' locker room."

Caleb's face comes onscreen, his expression concerned and contrite as he stands by his locker, grabbing his leather jacket. His hair is still damp from the shower.

"I can't say how sorry I am this happened." He gulps as if it's hard to swallow, his eyes blue, free and clear of malice. "August and I have been playing together since we were kids, and of course there's a friendly rivalry between us. We bring out the best in each other on court. I respect his game, and he's a great guy. I unequivocally deny that it was a dirty play. I would never do something like this, and I think my reputation speaks for itself." He looks down at the floor, shaking his head and running a hand over the fair hair curling at his collar.

"He's in my prayers, and I hope he's gonna be okay." He slides his jacket onto his powerful shoulders and looks solemnly at the reporters circling him.

"If you'll excuse me, I need to get home to my fiancée and baby girl."

Fiancée?

We're not engaged, and he's never said that publicly.

Yeah, something has definitely shifted. I sit on the edge of our bed and wait for him to come home so I can find out what it all means.

SEVENTEEN
AUGUST

"**Y**ou stupid motherfucker."

Decker's anger hurts almost as much as my leg. They gave me painkillers before we even left the arena, so the blinding pain has dulled to a persistent throb. I struggle to focus on Decker's words as the drugs sap my lucidity.

"I told you, West," Decker says, drawing a deep breath through flaring nostrils. "I warned you about this shit with Bradley."

I don't speak. I fucked up, and I have to take this.

"And when we had the game won and I advised you to sit out the last minute, you what?" Decker demands rhetorically. "Needed to piss a circle around Caleb to prove you got the bigger dick?"

My mom clears her throat from the corner.

Decker grimaces. "Sorry, ma'am."

"No problem," Mom says. "But maybe you can save the recriminations for when my son is not in unbearable pain and waiting for the surgeon to arrive."

"Yes, ma'am." Decker dips his head in deference to her. "You're right. I'm just a little frustrated."

"I understand. We all are, but August getting better is the priority, and the only thing I care about," my mother says quietly. "Now, I'll leave you two alone. My husband is on his way. I'll go meet him."

The door closes behind her, and Decker looks back to me.

"She's right, and I'm sorry." Disappointment and fury wrestle in the look he lays on me. "I feel bad for you, but I'm also so damn angry with you."

"Not as angry as I am with myself." I bang the bed with my fist, shaking my head at my own recklessness.

The door opens, and the orthopedic surgeon walks in, Dr. Clive.

"How you feeling, August?" he asks, glancing at the folder in his hands.

"High as a kite. They gave me some painkillers." I release a heavy sigh and wince at the needles of pain in my leg. "But it still kinda hurts like hell."

"What are we looking at, Doc?" Decker leans against the wall and shoves his hands in his pockets.

Dr. Clive's brows lift over the silver rims of his glasses. If the bone jutting from my leg didn't tell me this can't be good, the twist of his lips and the reluctance in his eyes do.

"You've got a compound fracture, August." He steps over to the wall, places a film on the mounted X-ray monitor, and points to the image. "You see the break here and here in the tibia and fibula? Good news is that the break is clear. No damage to the nerves, tendons, or ligaments."

"Why do I feel like there's bad news, too?" I need to pay attention, but between the drugs and the pain that persists despite them, it's hard to focus.

"We need to start prepping for surgery right away," Dr. Clive says. "The bone broke through the skin and has been exposed to air. There's risk of infection. We need to do immediate intramedullary rodding of the tibia. We'll place a titanium rod down the center of the tibia and then further stabilize it with small screws in between the rod and the bone above and below the fracture site."

"A rod?" I tip my head back into the pillow. "Will I have that forever?"

"Yeah, afraid so." The grim line of Dr. Clive's mouth eases the smallest bit. "Think of it as another bone, but one that'll never break."

"What's the recovery like on this, Doc?" Decker asks. His frown has grown heavier with every word Dr. Clive speaks.

"Being optimistic, it could take anywhere from six to twelve months to return to fully competitive basketball after something like this." He pulls the images down and shoves them back in the file. "You'll be in an Aircast for about two months, August. And, of course, aggressive rehab from there. Most athletes can return to pre-injury levels. It just takes a lot of time and hard work."

"I'll be ready for rehab, no matter what it takes," I assure the doctor, but mostly Decker. I know he's concerned for me, but basketball is a business, and I'm a commodity—one in which the team has invested a lot of money.

"Let's get the surgery behind us, and then we can talk about rehab," Dr. Clive says, walking to the door. "I'm going to prep. We'll be back for you in twenty minutes or so."

The prognosis is better than I thought it would be, but I still feel like an idiot. If I could take that last minute back, if I could reconsider rubbing the win in Caleb's face, I would.

"Look, Deck, I'm sorry." I force down my shame and regret. "I know it was stupid. I just . . ."

What can I say? Caleb has the girl I want? I jeopardized a thirty-million-dollar contract for a woman who lives with another man, has had his baby, and already turned me down? A woman I've only seen four times? If I ever see Iris again, I'll walk the other way.

Who am I kidding? In that charged moment Iris and I shared tonight, I couldn't even look away. What makes me think I could *walk* away from her?

And that makes me a fool so many times over I lose count.

"Just worry about getting through the surgery." Decker forces a half-hearted grin through his obvious concern. "I'll rip you a new one when you can take it a little better."

The door opens, and my mom and Matt come in, accompanied by my stepbrother. He's tall and blond, practically Matt's spitting image.

"Hey, you can't be here, Foster," Deck tells him sternly. "We don't need agents sniffing around. Not even sure how you got in. Team and family only."

We've been so careful to keep our connection discrete, I forget even Decker doesn't know.

"It's okay, Deck," I tell him. "He *is* family. Jared's my stepbrother."

EIGHTEEN

IRIS

I stand as soon as Caleb enters our bedroom. We watch one another in wary silence for a few moments before he walks over and drops a kiss on my cheek. I jerk back, glaring up at him. "Don't, Caleb."

His eyebrows arch over the hard humor in his eyes before he shrugs and walks toward the closet, taking off his jacket. I follow him closely, determined to have this out.

"What was that tonight?" I ask, my voice brittle.

"What was what?" he asks, a little too casually, too easily, but his shoulders tense beneath the thin cotton of his shirt.

"August."

At his name, Caleb meets my eyes in the closet mirror. He sneers and huffs a breath. "Oh, you mean his little fall?"

"Little fall?" I walk to stand in front of him, staring up and searching his face. "His career could be over, Caleb. Why would you do that?"

His eyes are blistering cold blue. "And what exactly are you accusing me of, Iris?"

"It was a dirty play."

The back of his hand slams into my mouth, shoving any other words down my throat. I stumble. My back hits the mirror, sending spikes of pain through my shoulder.

I've never been hit in the face. My mother didn't bother disciplining me. Though I saw men hit her and my aunt from time to time, no man has ever hit me, so I didn't know. I couldn't have known that the first hit, that baptism into violence, doesn't just sting the flesh. It startles the soul.

For the space of a broken heartbeat, I stare at him. Every sensation and emotion—pain, anger, fear, panic—converge into the ache of my teeth and the throb of my lips. I touch my mouth, feeling the smear of blood, but not taking my eyes off him in case he strikes again.

As the shock wears off, my fingers twitch, every muscle longing to strike back, but I have the presence of mind to know I can't. Lotus said she saw a shadow on Caleb's soul. Well, I see a snake—a boa constrictor of lean muscle who could crush me with barely exerted effort.

"I'm sorry, baby." He looks contrite. "I was just so upset that you would accuse me of a dirty play. It was instinct. It won't happen again."

He steps toward me, his hand reaching for my face.

My hand raises to ward off another blow. He frowns and takes another step, trapping me between the mirror and his huge body. I swallow my fear and shock so I can speak. "I told you what would happen if you ever did that, Caleb." My voice sounds strong, but every cell in my body is trembling. It's an act I have to hold up because I know he will exploit any weakness.

As soon as my words hit the air, I realize I've made a tactical error. The phony remorse melts like a plastic mask in a furnace. And from the fire, his true face appears, all bolts and steel.

"Oh, now I remember." He folds his arms across the width of his chest.

"Something about you leaving with my daughter if I ever hit you, and good luck trying to find you. Do I have it right, Iris?"

"I *am* leaving." I slide away from the mirror, my back straight and my stride confident, even though the very blood in my veins is shaking. He's twice my size. The force of his hand against my lips—that strike still hurts.

I ignore the pain and focus on getting Sarai and me out of this house unscathed. I grab an overnight bag and toss a few items of clothing in, not looking at him as I shove a pair of Chucks in, too.

"What do you think you're doing?" Laughter threads through his words.

I don't bother answering, but walk swiftly into the bedroom, scooping my purse as I go. I make my way silently into the nursery down the hall, and in the faint light of the half-lit sconces on her wall, grab the essentials and a few outfits for Sarai. I pick her up carefully, praying she doesn't wake.

When I step into the hall, Caleb is there, leaning against the stair banister.

"You actually think I'll let you leave me." He chuckles, shaking his head.

"We can discuss custody," I reply emotionlessly. "But this is over. We're over, Caleb."

The cruel amusement fades until all that's left is cruel.

"Try to leave me." His words are wrapped in nails and heavy with warning. The darker centers of his eyes, the irises, are shards of glass. "I want to see you try."

I don't pause to contemplate what that means, but rush down the steps. I freeze in the foyer, surprised to see Ramone still here and hovering as if waiting for direction. He looks up the stairwell at Caleb watching from the landing. I glance up to see Caleb shake his head once. Ramone steps back. I race to the garage, my heart pounding as if I'm in a fox hunt with hounds nipping at my heels, but no one follows me.

I snap Sarai into her car seat, amazed that she hasn't even stirred, and stow our bags in the back of my car, shooting furtive glances at the garage door the whole time. No movement.

I start the car and pull out, rounding the circular driveway and gunning it as soon as I hit the road. I check my rearview mirror every few seconds, certain Caleb must be following, but there are no lights trailing me. The frigid certainty in his voice haunts me. Like he was so sure I wouldn't get away. My sore lips pull painfully into a crooked, relieved smile. I shake a metric ton from my shoulders and tip my head back into the buttery leather of the headrest. Things haven't been right between us for a long time, but I had no idea how wrong they would go.

He hit me.

I'm still reeling inside and aching where he hit my mouth with the full force of his body behind his hand. I didn't think this through beyond getting out of the house, but it's so late. I'll find a room for the night and get a fresh start tomorrow.

I pull into the parking lot of a Holiday Inn off the interstate. It's not the expensive hotels Caleb always reserves for us, but I never cared before and I certainly don't care tonight. My freedom is the only luxury on my mind.

I park, wrangling my bag and Sarai's while bundling her in the blanket against my chest. I juggle everything in my arms, struggling to get the door open without waking her.

"I need a room for the night, please," I whisper to the front desk attendant. I would love for Sarai to sleep through this entire ordeal.

"Of course." The young man's eyes narrow, and a smile breaks through his professional demeanor. "I know you."

"Excuse me?" I ask cautiously, patting Sarai's little bottom.

"Well, not *know* you." He offers an almost shy smile when he takes my credit card. "I saw you and your baby on TV tonight."

The jumbotron.

I can't think about being on the big screen without remembering the moments after when, in an arena of twenty thousand people, it felt like August and I were alone in an electric bubble. Each moment I've ever spent in his company had played through my mind, and I'd cherished every one. The kind, funny, thoughtful man should have seemed at odds with the feral competitor on the floor, but he wasn't. All the disparate parts fit snugly and rightly to form this man I desperately want to know better.

And maybe now I will.

It's an ill-timed thought, but I'd be lying if I didn't at least admit to myself that with things over between Caleb and me, there will be *something* with August. Even if I don't pursue it, he will. The knowledge sends a tiny thrill through me.

"Um, ma'am, your card has been declined." The awkward phrase snatches me from my thoughts.

"Oh. I'm sorry." I glance from the black card extended between his two fingers to the frown on his face. "Are you sure? There's no limit on it."

"Right. It's a Black card, but . . ." He hesitates, his eyes speculative. "This card has been reported stolen."

"Stolen?" The word emerges loud and harsh in the quiet lobby, garnering the attention of two people at the other end of the desk also checking in.

"That's impossible," I say in a softer voice.

"We can't use this card." His voice stiffens. "Did you have another we can try?"

"Uh, yes." I reach into my wallet and hand him my debit card. "Here you go. I know that one is fine. I'll have to call about the other one to figure it out."

My words trail off when his brows bunch into a frown, and he glances at me suspiciously. "This one doesn't work either."

"That can't be right because I . . ."

Both of those cards, though in my possession and I've used them a hundred times, are technically in Caleb's name. Caleb's accounts. He may not be on my tail with high-beam lights, but he's chasing me nonetheless.

I extend my hand, requesting the card back. He reluctantly gives it to me like I might be running some elaborate fraud operation.

"It's a misunderstanding," I assure him. "You take cash?"

He nods, but still looks doubtful. I flip through the compartments of my wallet, searching for cash.

Dammit. Nachos and parking at the game took most of my cash. I only spy a solitary ten-dollar bill.

I don't have enough money for a room, and I don't have enough gas to make it all the way to Mama's house in Atlanta or to Lotus's place in New York. If we were speaking, which we aren't. I don't even know her new address there.

I can't just stand here while the attendant decides if he should call the cops or kick me out. I avoid his eyes, shift Sarai in my arms and walk back out to the car. My purse, overnight bag, and Sarai's diaper bag weigh me down, but not nearly as much as the reality of my situation. Caleb shut down my cards. Knowing I'm out with his daughter in the middle of the night, he shut down my cards. Maybe I should have waited until the morning, but getting away from him was urgent. Something in his eyes told me to escape while I could.

I'm driving somewhat aimlessly, unsure where to go and what I can afford to do, when flashing blue lights and the "blip" of a police siren grab my attention. For a moment, I wonder who they're pursuing, but I'm the only one on the road.

Dammit. Those blue lights are for me. Fuck my life. Could this night get worse?

With my heart hammering, I pull off to the shoulder. I *was* distracted, so maybe I *was* speeding. I roll down my window, already wearing the practiced self-deprecating smile reserved for traffic stops.

"Officer, I'm sorry if I—"

"Out of the car, ma'am." His clipped words take me aback.

"What . . . was I speeding? A busted taillight? What's going on?"

I'm still trying to process everything when two more police cars pull in, lights flashing and cops climbing out cautiously as if this is *America's Most Wanted*.

"This vehicle and license plate match the description of a car reported stolen." The officer glances in the back seat. "And reported in a child abduction."

"Abduction?" The word blasts from my mouth like a rocket. Anger clenches my hands into tight balls. "What the hell is going on? My daughter is safe, sleeping in the back seat."

"Ma'am, please step out of the vehicle with your hands raised."

I gape at him for a few more seconds, not even sure if this is legal. Not even sure if I should get out of my car on a dark, deserted road at night. Shaking myself from the stupor, I reach over to the glove compartment.

"Ma'am," he snaps, eyes sliding to my arm reached across the passenger seat.

"I'm just getting license and registration," I assure him. I hand over the paperwork, watching as he shines his flashlight on the documents.

"Registration says Caleb Bradley." He taps the door. "Step out of the vehicle, please."

This is a nightmare. The other two officers approach, one of them speaking into the intercom on his shoulder. On rubbery legs, I climb out of the SUV, stepping to the ground with my hands raised.

"There has been a terrible misunderstanding." I will my voice to stop shaking. Fear coats my throat. I'm on a dark road with three men. Cops, yes, but men nonetheless. "Like I said, it's my daughter in the back seat, and this is my car."

"But the registration—"

"Caleb Bradly is my boyfriend," I say hurriedly. "He gave me this car months ago. The baby is our daughter. There are a dozen ways to verify what I'm saying."

"Ma'am, in cases of suspected child abduction," one of the other officers says, "we have to protect the child. I'm afraid we'll need to take you into custody."

"The hell you will!" I step back, my calves bumping up against the car's running board. "My daughter—"

"We've already contacted her father," the officer says. "He's on his way."

"On his way?" I snarl. "He can be on his way, but he's not taking my daughter anywhere."

The cop turns me, and my body flattens to the car as he slips cuffs on my wrists. The click of the cuffs sets off panic in me.

Where will they take Sarai? What's about to happen to her?

I strain against the iron circlets, twisting my shoulders and kicking my feet back.

"Ouch." The officer curses under his breath. "Look, lady, you're this close to adding resisting arrest and assaulting an officer to the grand theft and abduction."

"I haven't done anything." My voice quakes, and tears leak over my cheeks. "Oh my God. You have to listen to me. She's my baby. I haven't taken her! She's mine. Please don't take her. Please just listen to me."

Sobs shake my shoulders. Frustration, anger, and fear light a match to my blood and speed my heart. I rest my forehead against the cold metal of the expensive car that I never even thought about leaving behind. The credit cards, the car, the money—each thing he's given me is simply a bar in my cell, imprisoning me.

Another car door slams, and I jerk my head around. In the darkness, Caleb's broad shoulders cut through the small circle of men surrounding me.

"Where's Sarai?" he demands, his voice, his face panicked. "Did she hurt her?"

A growl rumbles in my belly and springs from my throat. I hurl myself at him, even with my arms cuffed behind me.

"You bastard!" Hands trapped behind my back, I head-butt his chest and kick his shins. "What did you do?"

My raised voice bounces off the night sky, echoing around us like a screech in the jungle.

"You see what I mean?" he asks the officer closest to him. "She's been like this for weeks, ever since she stopped taking the medication the doctor prescribed."

"Motherfucker!" The word scratches its way out of my chest and scrambles over my lips.

"You don't believe me?" he asks the officer. "This is my car she's driving. I'm just going to reach inside for something that will prove what I say is true."

He steps away for a moment but returns with my purse. My heart stills in my chest when he holds up a bottle of tiny pills.

"See?" He holds them out to one of the officers. "Her name's right there. Ever since she stopped taking these pills, she—"

"I'm gonna kill you!" The words blast from me with propulsive force. "You lying son of a bitch." I lunge forward again, but the cop catches me before I can ram Caleb.

"I promise you, officers," Caleb drawls, "she's not always like this. When she takes her meds, she's a different woman, but you can see why I was concerned when she left with my daughter. She's in an unstable state, and I feared for our baby's safety."

"Her safety?" A sob-laugh hefts from my chest. "*He* hit *me*!" I look up over my shoulder, pleading with the officer closest to me. "You have to believe me," I rasp. "I left because he hit me."

"Oh, I hit you?" Caleb cuts in. "Where? I don't see a scratch on you."

My lips, still aching from his blow, tremble. "He hit me in the mouth," I tell the officer, my voice desperate. "Please don't let him take my baby. Oh, God. Please listen. I'm begging you."

A wail cuts through the air.

"Sarai." My glance darts between the officers. "She's hungry. I need to feed her."

Four sets of eyes drop to my breasts, straining against my T-shirt. I hate every creature walking this earth with a dick.

Caleb opens the back door and reaches in to coo over my baby girl.

"No." My head hangs, and salty tears burn the imperceptible cuts on my mouth. "Don't let him have her. Oh, God. Please, no."

"It's okay. Daddy's here." Caleb says, bouncing Sarai in the cradle of his arms, his eyes tender.

"Officers, do you know who I am?" Caleb asks, his winning smile flashing white.

The three officers exchange looks before nodding.

This cannot be happening.

Defeat slumps my shoulders, and I go slack in the officer's arms.

"Caleb Bradley," one of them speaks up. "Sorry about the game tonight, man. Tough loss."

"Hey, you win some, you lose some." Caleb shrugs. "Then you know it's my rookie season. I really wanna get us in the playoffs."

"We barely missed 'em last year," one officer says, scowling. "I was so glad when we drafted you."

"It's been a good season so far." Caleb bends to kiss Sarai's nose, glancing up when my maternal growl rumbles in the quiet. "But it's been hard on me and my fiancée."

"I'm not your fiancée," I spit. "I'll *never* wear your ring, Caleb."

His eyes narrow at me, and the rage he's kept carefully checked slips its

148

chain for a second. It bares its teeth, and I know if he gets his hands on me, I'll suffer more than a slap across my mouth.

"Like I was saying, it's been hard on us," Caleb continues, a modicum of civility. "New baby. Rookie season. It's been a strain, and I think my fiancée just had a bad night." He suspends that statement in the tight circle of us and the cops, taking the time to look each of them in the eye. "But I think she and I can work it out at home."

His hard eyes penetrate mine. "Or you can take her in, and the baby can go home with me."

"No." I choke on my tears. I can't take my eyes off Sarai, whose little mouth is rooting, searching for my breast. She whines, her arms shooting up from the swaddling. Caleb catches her fingers, folding them into his mouth.

"You hungry, baby?" he asks, his voice gentle, yet still managing to grate on my nerves. "Let's get you out of here so Mommy can feed you."

"You sure, Mr. Bradley?" the first officer asks. "If we need to—"

"He's right," I interrupt, my hands burning with the need to snatch my daughter away from him, no matter what it takes or costs. "It's been a bad night. I didn't . . ." I swallow my pride to clear room for the lie. "I forgot to take my medication, like he said."

Caleb smiles at me indulgently.

"You see, officers," he says. "All a misunderstanding."

"Well, with something like an abduction accusation," the first officer says, discomfort creeping into his voice and expression even as he uncuffs me, "we still have to document the incident."

"Of course, document it." Caleb's stare mocks and warns me. "I understand, but we won't be having this kind of trouble again, will we, babe?"

I rub my wrists, crossing to Caleb immediately. I reach for Sarai, but he doesn't let her go. We hold each other's stare, a silent war of wills I'll have to wait for the right time to win.

Caleb finally releases Sarai. I clutch her to me, breathing in her sweet baby smell, burying my nose in her hair to hide my tears.

"I'll drive." Caleb opens the driver's side door.

"But what about your car?" I ask.

"Oh, he'll drive it home." Caleb nods toward his Ferrari a few feet away.

Ramone steps out of the car, circling around to the driver's side. Even in the darkness, his cold stare penetrates my clothes and leaves my skin clammy.

"Our bodyguard was the one who actually first noted Iris's erratic behavior at the game tonight," Caleb tells the officers, but his eyes are set on me. He's making sure I understand that Ramone is his ally in this ruse. "He was concerned days ago but wasn't sure he should say anything. He actually called social services."

I freeze in the process of buckling Sarai into her car seat, glancing over my shoulder to catch Caleb's stare.

"Of course, I've told him not to interfere that way again." Caleb's voice is chiding. "He thought he was doing what was best for Sarai, but it'll leave my fiancée some explaining to do."

This worsens by the second. Every lie Caleb has told is a straightjacket, hampering me, making me look like a madwoman.

How will I get out of this?

I climb into the car, watching through the windshield as the officers get Caleb to autograph their citation pads.

Once the cops are gone, Ramone and Caleb stand outside talking. Probably plotting how to best hold me hostage in that house while Caleb is on the road. I knew I felt a shift between us, but I had no idea how my life would be turned upside down.

In the midst of tonight's soap opera, the mundane intrudes. My breasts hurt so bad, tight with milk because I missed a feeding. Sarai stares up at me—hungry, alert, impatient. She pats my breast, a sure signal that I have about two seconds before she starts wailing.

I take her in, her face a tiny replica of mine: demanding and defenseless. My whole world swaddled in a blanket. She's happily suckling, and those feelings of resentment and confusion I had for her, for motherhood, in the beginning are completely foreign now. I barely remember my world when she wasn't the axis. The soft weight of her in my arms once felt like a burden. Now, she feels like a privilege I don't deserve. I'm willing to ride through hell on gasoline wheels for this little girl.

I look up and see the devil.

Caleb stands at the hood of the car, the stony lines of his face illuminated by the headlights, his eyes screaming obscenities. My stomach roils. This monster has been inside of me.

He opens the driver's side door, and in the car's interior light, his hair and golden skin appear almost angelic, but his eyes are demonic. His stare grows hungry and possessive as he watches me feed Sarai. My mind must like to torture me because it flashes back to the All-Star Game when I fed her while talking to August. Maybe in some parallel universe, I'm still in that room, soaking up his kindness and feeling sexy under the want of his stare.

I glance at Caleb's implacable profile, the cruel promise of his mouth and the tightening of his hands on the wheel, like he wishes it was my neck. We don't speak a word, but this won't go unpunished.

NINETEEN

IRIS

"It's not here," I mumble to the empty bedroom. I rifle through the random items in my bedside drawer, none of which are my journal. I was completely, embarrassingly transparent in that journal regarding my conflicted feelings about motherhood—the resentment of my pregnancy. So many dark, lonely days I turned to the blank pages to pour out my emotions.

And it's not here.

Did Caleb take my journal? I know how damning the turbulence of that season looks on paper. I'm ashamed to read it alone, much less have it exposed to someone else's judgment. In Caleb's hands, my most vulnerable moments are another weapon in his arsenal.

"Looking for something?" Caleb asks from the door.

I don't answer, but face him, coaxing the drawer closed with my knee. I watch him and wait.

"You shouldn't have done that, Iris." His voice sends shivers over my nerve endings. "You shouldn't have tried to leave me."

"You left me no choice," I sit on the edge of the bed, relieved to have Sarai fed and asleep while I deal with this—while I focus on how to untangle all these lies so I can get us away from him. "I told you what would happen if you hit me."

"I hit you because you insulted me." He tilts his head, coming to stand directly in front of me. "A dirty play, huh? You seem to have a soft spot for my old buddy August."

I don't respond, but wait for him to continue.

"I saw you looking at him," he whispers, chips of ice in his eyes. "And I saw him looking at you."

"No, you must have imagined it." I drop my glance to the hands folded in my lap. "I barely know him really, Caleb."

"You don't have to know him to want to fuck him, though, do you?"

My head snaps up. The rage prowling in his eyes is on a flimsy leash.

"But you don't get to fuck him," Caleb hisses. He jerks me close, palming the back of my head. He presses our noses and foreheads together, his breath fanning over my lips. "You only get to fuck me."

He reaches into his pocket and draws out a small silver pistol. I've never seen this side of him, and I've never seen this gun. I've been oblivious. It may cost my life.

He brings the gun to my temple. Fear is the calamity of my heartbeat behind my ribs. It's chaos in my veins, roaring in my ears and rushing to my head. Fear is a signal fire that puts my body on notice.

He uses the gun to tuck hair behind my ear. "I want you out of those clothes."

"God, Caleb, please no," I whisper. "Not like this."

"You think you have options? Choices?" His vicious laughter rumbles from his chest. "You and that pathetic journal have made all of this too easy."

"Where is it? I want my journal."

"And I wanted you out of those clothes twenty seconds ago." He nods to the jeans and T-shirt I wore to tonight's game. "That journal is just another page of my insurance policy with you. I said, clothes off."

With trembling fingers, I tug the shirt over my head, tossing it to the floor. I lift my legs just enough to slide my jeans down. My toes curl into the rug covering the hardwood floor.

"The underwear, too," he says, his voice dipping to a pant. A pulse ticks in his jaw. He's seen me without clothes more times than I can count, but when the bra falls away and the panties hit the floor, I'm violated by the stare of a stranger.

"Lie back," he rasps, his hooded glare lacerating my nakedness.

I grit my teeth, determined to resist, but Sarai sighs in her sleep over the baby monitor, a sound of innocence and contentment. I'd do anything to preserve that—to protect her from the bastard that is her father.

With my knees bent and my legs hanging over the edge of the bed, I lie back. He walks to the side and towers over me, his smile crafted from meanness and glee.

"We're going to negotiate new rules, you and me." He places the pistol against my lips. I whimper and begin trembling. Violence is poised to strike.

"Shhh." He leans down, brushing my hair back and gently, carefully pushing the pistol into my mouth, tapping my teeth.

A scream slices through my mind. I taste my fear—roll it around on my tongue like a tart mint. I wait for it to dissolve, but it never does. It slides down my throat whole, plunges into my chest and scrapes my ribs. It puddles in my belly, a sludge of dread. I dare not move. My eyes plead for mercy, but there's none in his eyes. They're just mirrors for his black soul.

There's a shadow on his soul.

Lo was right, and it's too late. If only I could go back and see things differently. Do things differently. Choose differently.

Oh, God. Please get me out of this. Please spare me for my baby.

"New rule number one." His eyes fix on my lips wrapped around the gun's muzzle. "You don't drive. Ramone will stay here with you when I'm on the road, and he'll take you anywhere you need to go. He'll make sure you always come home to me."

I'm having trouble swallowing with my lips open around the gun. Saliva pools in my mouth and runs from the corner to mix with the tears streaming down my cheeks.

"I would advise you not to bother Lotus with the details of our arrangement," Caleb continues. "I know what she does. Where she works. About her fourth-floor walk-up in Brooklyn. You saw what I did to August tonight. That's nothing compared to what I'd do to her. Anyone who tries to come between us, I'll dispose of."

For the first time, I'm glad Lotus and I are on the outs. I don't want her near the mess of my life. I can't handle anyone else being hurt because of me. I have to focus on Sarai. Worrying about anyone else's safety will only distract me.

"We understand each other?" he asks.

I nod with the smallest motion of my head, not wanting to jar the gun resting on my tongue.

"Good." He laughs harshly. "And I don't have to worry about your mother. We both know what a mercenary whore she is. I'm paying for her silence."

My eyes widen with an unspoken question.

"Yes, I've been paying her bills down in Atlanta," he confirms. "She has a much better apartment now. In Buckhead, no less. You know how many men she would have had to fuck to get that? I'm doing her a favor, and she's much too grateful to ask questions about how I'm treating you."

I squeeze my eyes shut, betrayal and shame for my mother burning a hole in my heart. He bends to whisper in my ear, slipping the gun free of my mouth and running it down my neck.

"I hope tonight has demonstrated that I hold all the cards." He circles my nipples with the muzzle and stops to dig it into my belly button. "If you try to leave me, I will at the very least gain partial custody of Sarai. You have no money, and whatever court-appointed lawyer you'll get will be no match for what I have—the best legal representation money can buy. Between that, your *Dear Diary* entries, and the 'concerning behavior' Ramone reported to social services, I think I'll have a pretty strong case."

He walks to the end of the bed, slides the pistol down to the juncture of my thighs, and my blood slams in protest against the skin at every pulse point.

"Add your exploits with the police tonight and you'll be lucky to even see her on weekends by the time I'm done with you."

He slides the gun another inch downward, nudging it against my pussy, separating the lips. My chest rises and falls with anxious breaths. Tears run over my cheeks and collect around my neck like a noose.

"But beyond custody of Sarai, and beyond your mother and Lotus and anything else I could use to keep you with me," he says, each word a brick in the fortress he's building around me, "the only thing you really need to understand is this."

He glances up from between my thighs, and if everything he's ever told me before was subterfuge and lies, I have no doubt that what he's about to say is the absolute truth. His eyes are finally honest. "If you ever try to leave me again, Iris, I will kill you."

A sob rattles my chest, and I bite my lip to contain it.

"Have you ever thought about the similarities between a gun and a dick?" he asks, pushing my knees open wider with his free hand.

"Please don't do this, Caleb," I beg, pressing my lips together against a moan.

"There's the obvious," he goes on. "You cock a gun. Get it. Dick. Cock?" His laugh is low and breathy, excited. He pushes the muzzle to my opening, exerting the slightest pressure.

"Oh, God, Caleb. Please, stop." A sob breaks my words up. "Pl-pl-please. Oh, God, please, Caleb."

With one hand he undoes his belt, the jangle of the buckle and the harshness of the falling zipper a knife cutting across my ears.

"With a gun, you have to consider safety," he says. "Just like sex. Not that I'll be using a condom tonight. Another new rule. I'll be fucking you raw from now on."

My eyes are closed, and everything blares on my senses. The fresh smell of his recent shower mixes with the scent of my terror. The rough muzzle biting into the sensitive tissue of my vagina. The sound of his pants slithering over his legs and hitting the floor.

"What a relief." He laughs. "No more holey condoms."

Anger slices through me. I open my eyes, waiting for him to continue, because I know he will.

"Yeah." He grins unabashedly. "I *may* have used a few condoms with holes, but we got Sarai, so it all worked out."

Lo was right. God, I've been such an idiot, trusting someone else with my body, with my future. And now I'm paying for my naivety.

"Sorry," he says with a laugh. "I took a little rabbit trail there. Back to the similarities. A gun discharges, and so does my dick."

He squeezes my thigh so tightly, I bite my lip to lock down a scream so I don't wake up Sarai.

"So, I ask you, Iris." He reaches up to grab my chin, tightening his fingers there until I meet his eyes. They're obsidian, hard and black with lust. "Choose. Do you want this cock or mine?"

He presses the gun deeper, not quite inside me, but deep enough, hard enough to leave abrasions on the most delicate part of me. My head lolls to the side, and I squeeze my eyes into complete darkness as I weep. Weep for my little girl, whose father is so evil. Weep for my innocence, squandered on a man worse than any of the ones my mother ever brought home. Weep for lost chances with a good man like August West, who will never have me now. I can't imagine anything beyond these walls. I can't think of anything other than the weapon between my legs.

"I asked you a question." Caleb's voice comes sharp and harsh, a cat o' nine tails, a whip dragging my flesh with its hooks. "Choose which cock you want, Iris."

If it weren't for the tiny sighs, the faint, steady infant snore coming through the baby monitor, I would beg him to shoot me. Shoot me right now instead of what is about to happen. But there is Sarai.

She makes the word I finally whisper not surrender, but survival. "Yours."

"I didn't hear you," he says. But the gun is already gone, and he lowers himself on top of me, his elbow on one side of my head and the gun on the other. His dick is hard against my entrance, a hammer poised to strike a nail. "This cock or mine?"

I open my eyes and look right at him. The cruel mouth, the lawless soul, the beauty God wasted on this animal. I want him to see my pain and the refusal I can't voice while he dangles violence over me. I want him to see the hatred in my eyes when he takes this from me. In this awful moment, it's the only brave thing I can do.

"Yours."

It starts as a sharp pain that dulls with every thrust. I'm dry and unready, and he is thick and aroused. He tunnels in and out of me, a raw passage for his lust. He's a ravenous beast, biting my nipples until I cry. He hurts me until I'm dizzy—he feeds on my whimpers. He stiffens, emptying a virulent stream into my body.

I want to hide behind my shame, behind my closed eyelids, but he jerks my chin and holds my stare long enough to make sure I know who's inside of me. He's rotten, and the golden façade is gone. He swipes at the wetness on my cheeks and shoves his thumb in my mouth so I taste my own tears.

Even after he rolls off and walks away, I still feel him. I fear I always will. His cum leaks out, a trickle of violence that scalds the vellum-thin skin inside my thighs. At the bathroom door, his eyes maraud my body, studying the bites and bruises. He looks at me like he's the conqueror and I am his scorched earth.

TWENTY

AUGUST

It's my first surgery.

I've been balling most of my life and this isn't my first injury, but it was my first time under the knife. The pain is being managed with medication, but I don't want to become too dependent. I take less than I should, and my leg hurts like hell. It's been three days, and I'm finally home. At my real home here in Maryland, not the empty condo in San Diego. If I have to rehab the entire off-season, I want to do it surrounded by the people I love and in the place that's most familiar to me.

We're at least six weeks away from physical therapy. This first chapter is all about keeping weight off the leg, letting time and titanium do the healing. That means being more sedentary than I have been since I could only crawl. It's driving me crazy and leaving me too much time to think. Too much time to dream.

I dreamt of Iris last night. We were by the water, surrounded by trees, and the sun was high. The sky was an explosion of color, vivid, vibrant just before sunset.

We were happy.

How can I dream about Iris when, in a roundabout way, she's the reason I'm here? I'm flat on my back, staring at the same spackled ceiling I fell asleep under when I was ten years old. And just like then, my mom stands at the door, ready to take care of me.

"You hungry?" she asks, walking in to fluff the pillows behind my head. "I can make those crab cakes you like so much."

"Nah." I shift my left leg on the bed and the right one on the small platform that elevates and stabilizes it.

"You need to eat," Jared says from the door. He was an athlete in high school and still carries traces of a baller's swagger, though it's usually hidden beneath a suit these days.

"Okay," I say, more to get my mother out of the room so I can talk to Jared than because I'm hungry. "Your famous crab cakes would be great, Mom."

Her face lights up. She's felt helpless over the last few days, like she wasn't doing enough. Laid up and barely able to leave this damn bed for the next few weeks, I feel helpless, too. I wish making me feel useful again was as easy.

I study the walls, still plastered with childhood heroes, the idols who shaped my game: Jordan, Magic, Kareem, Kobe. I've been staving off depression ever since I hit the floor, and the thought of Kobe Bryant and the Lakers makes me think of the first night I met Iris.

"What's the league saying about Caleb?" I ask Jared, balling my fists on the bed to contain my anger. "They rule it dirty?"

Jared grimaces, pulls a chair beside my bed, and flips it around to straddle. He rests his crossed arms on the back. "Everybody knows it was a dirty play," Jared says. "But his dad is a Hall of Famer, part-owner of a team, and a front office executive. That's a lot of power and influence. It'll always be hard to make shit stick to Caleb even in a shit storm."

"Are you kidding me?" I point to my leg. "I'm missing the end of this season and part of the next because of what he did. I knew he wasn't the saint everyone thinks he is, but even I didn't know how low he'd go."

"What's up with you and Caleb anyway?" Jared tips his head, his look probing. "I mean, I knew you were never fans of each other throughout college, but it seems to have gotten worse since you guys turned pro."

Jared is one of the best agents in sports. If we hadn't needed to keep our family connection on the low, there's no way I would have chosen Lloyd as my agent over him. Part of what makes Jared so good is his BS detector. He sees through bullshit excuses and lies from a mile away, but there's no way I'm telling him I jeopardized my career over a girl, much less one I barely know.

"Same old shit, I guess. Just higher stakes." I shrug. "We've been going at it for years. You know that."

"You sure that's all there is to it?" Jared asks. "He doesn't live far away from here. You rehabbing at home doesn't have anything to do with him, does it?"

Maybe subconsciously I did stay here with the hope of running into Iris, but I won't make it happen. If our paths are supposed to cross again, they will. I have other things I want to accomplish while I'm sidelined.

"We need to talk about Elevation." I'm hoping the abrupt change of subject will pull my stepbrother away from talk of Caleb. Thinking of her with him makes my head hurt worse than my leg does.

"Exactly what do we need to discuss?" Jared asks. "We're in year one of our five-year plan. Let's not get ahead of ourselves."

"I don't want to wait five years." I plow my fingers through the tangled hair that's longer than I typically wear it. "I have the capital. You have the expertise. Let's get it off the ground."

"We planned to wait until you had a few seasons under your belt." Jared rubs the five o'clock shadow covering his jaw. "A little more credibility and time to focus."

I gesture to my busted leg. "I don't anticipate having more time than I do right now, and you have enough credibility for both of us," I say. "You're a great agent with a stellar reputation. And you understand sports marketing. You can start signing clients now. I think having my name associated with the company at this stage *decreases* credibility. We want these athletes to take Elevation seriously. Some rookie ball player anywhere near the helm wouldn't reassure me. I'll be a silent partner for now."

"You may have a point," Jared admits. "If you're rehabbing here for the summer, where do I set up the office?"

"As far as I know, I'm still in San Diego, right?"

"Yeah, sure." Jared's face closes off, his agent's mask falling into place.

"Bruh, what aren't you telling me?" I ask.

"They're already talking about using a disabled player exception," Jared says. "They're eyeing mid-level free agents who can take your place until your rehab is done. Especially if it ends up being more like a year than eight months."

I drop my head into my hands. It's pretty standard to find a temporary replacement when a high-dollar contract player like me is injured, but I'm barely out of surgery and they're already doubting my comeback? Already working on a contingency?

I get it. That fall, this injury, reminded me of my own mortality. It shattered the illusion of invincibility that soaring through the air gives you. We may soar, but we land. Not always on our feet, and sometimes so awkwardly that our bones break.

"Well it sounds like I got something to prove," I finally say, flashing Jared a determined smile. "Dr. Clive projected at least eight months before I'm game-ready, right?"

"Yeah, at least eight months."

I nod decisively, smiling at the man who's been a brother to me, blood notwithstanding. "Then I'll do it in seven."

TWENTY ONE

IRIS

"I unequivocally deny ever doing harm of any kind to my daughter." My voice remains steady with truth, but my body trembles with outrage. "I would never."

The social services case worker, Ms. Darling, scribbles on her little pad, her brows knitted and her lips thinned. She practically vibrates suspicion and disapproval.

"Who accused me of this?" Of course, I know it was Ramone, but I want to hear her say it.

She looks at me from behind the glare of her glasses, sharp eyes taking in everything from my hair to my tennis shoes, and moving back over me like she wants to make sure she didn't miss anything.

"We maintain the anonymity of those who come forward to report suspected abuse," she says.

"That's not fair." I press my palms to my thighs.

"It is when you have the child's best interest at heart, which *we* do."

"So do I." I draw a deep breath. "I'm sure you can imagine as a parent who has never harmed my baby and would do anything to protect her, an accusation like this is really frustrating. Insulting, actually."

"Iris, let's just cooperate," Caleb says from the bottom of the stairwell. He has Sarai in his arms, and she blinks at me sleepily.

"We woke her from her nap for this," I tell Ms. Darling, my tone one-third apology and two-thirds accusation.

I shift on the couch, trying to get comfortable, searching for relief. I'm still raw and throbbing from Caleb's invasion last night. I thought he would hit me, but apparently, he believed a gun to my head and shoved between my legs was enough to keep me in line.

He was not wrong.

For now. At least until I can get my journal back and start demolishing this wall of lies he's trapped me in. My word against his isn't enough to get me out of this.

My chest goes tight at the sight of Sarai in Caleb's arms. I walk over and take her.

"Hey, princess." I smile into her sleepy eyes. "Did we wake you up?"

She gurgles happily, even though her eyes are sleep-hazed. She's such a happy baby, and I'm determined she'll stay that way.

Ms. Darling's face softens into that lady-putty women always melt into around Caleb. I get it. The shell is pretty impressive—six foot six inch, toned, tan, blond. The man is practically gilded. Not to mention those violet–blue eyes he's passed onto our daughter. When you get to the center, though—when you peel back the golden overlay—at his core he's nothing but a rotting side of meat. Spoiling and crawling with maggots. And I'm the lucky girl who gets to snuggle up to *that* every night.

"Mr. Bradley," Ms. Darling breathes, her eyes admiring. "Thank you for bringing her down."

"Please call me Caleb." He adds the megawatt smile. "We want to get to the bottom of why anyone would say something like this about us."

I roll my eyes. If I want to get to the bottom of anything, it's the lies he and Ramone told to bring this woman here in the first place.

"Well technically," Ms. Darling says, darting me a quick glance, "the complaint wasn't filed against you. Just your fiancée."

"I'm not his fiancée."

The words spew out before I think better of them. The glacial look in Caleb's eyes makes me wish I had kept my mouth shut, but my chin still tilts to a defiant angle.

"I'm sorry." She looks at MiMi's ring on my finger. "I thought—"

"No problem," Caleb cuts in, smooth as a knife through butter. "We're a family, the three of us. Natural mistake. What do you need to do? We want to cooperate fully."

I suppress a frustrated sigh. His false solicitousness frays my nerves.

"With older children," Ms. Darling says, "we interview them on their own, but since Sarai is a baby I'll just need to examine her."

"This is ridiculous," I mutter, fury bubbling under my skin. "I haven't done a thing to hurt her, and these accusations are completely unfounded."

"Of course they are, babe," Caleb says soothingly. "So we just get this over with. Ms. Darling is simply doing her job."

He reaches to brush the hair back from my shoulder, and I flinch. His eyes narrow, but the smile he offers is a thick pomade smoothed over his anger, slicking back his displeasure.

"May I see her?" Ms. Darling extends her arms, and it takes everything in me to hand Sarai over to her. I know she won't find any marks or bruises, but this process is humiliating. I'm adding it to the list of things I'll never forgive Caleb for.

Caleb and I watch as Ms. Darling lays Sarai on the couch and strips her clothes off, leaving her in only her diaper. Tears sting my eyes while she combs my baby girl's plump little arms and legs for marks I'm supposed to have left on her. The painful irony is that the real abuser is standing right beside me. Until I find that journal, Caleb's right. I don't trust our legal system not to award Caleb joint, if not full, custody after the tower of lies and circumstantial evidence he's stockpiled against me.

"I think everything is in order here." Ms. Darling slips Sarai's footed onesie back on. "I don't see any evidence of abuse."

"Of course you don't, because I would never," I snap.

Her brows lift at my sharp tone.

"I'm sorry. This is just all awful and disgusting. To think someone would accuse me of something like this, and we are . . . *I* am being subjected to this, is just a sore spot for me, as you can imagine."

"I'm sorry for any inconvenience," Ms. Darling says. "But when we receive a call like that, we have to make sure."

"Do you have any idea why someone would lie about this?" I demand, at least wanting her to consider someone is out to get me, to tarnish me. I wish I could spill Caleb's diabolical plan, but I have no proof and would only look like I was trying to deflect attention. I don't look at him, but I feel Caleb's stare boring into the side of my face as surely as the barrel of his gun did last night.

"I was just about to ask you the same thing," Ms. Darling says, a small frown knitting her brows. "Regardless, we'll stay in touch."

"Stay in touch?" My voice skips up a few octaves. "Why? You've seen that she's fine. Is this not over?"

"Just as a precaution, we'll schedule one more visit to ensure conditions remain consistent."

Dammit. I have enough to worry about without having to suffer through this useless farce again.

When Caleb walks her out, I'm already halfway up the stairs and in the nursery by the time I hear her car pulling away. It only takes a little humming, several walky-bounces, and a few minutes before Sarai's little eyes are drooping and she resumes her nap. I close the nursery door quietly and turn to go back downstairs, only to collide with a wall of muscle.

"Oh." Anxiety at being this close to him corsets my torso, making breathing difficult. "I didn't see you there."

He doesn't reply, but grabs my elbow roughly and herds me down the hall toward our bedroom. I'm tripping over my feet, trying to keep up. As soon as we're in the room, he closes the door.

"So this visit was a *sore spot* for you, huh?" he asks. "I'll give you a sore spot."

"Caleb, I—"

The back of Caleb's huge hand slaps the words from my mouth. I touch my lips, the sight of blood on my fingers transfixing me for only a second before I spring into action. I take off for the bathroom, but only make it a few steps before Caleb's arm, ungiving bone, tight sinew, and hardened muscle, hooks around my waist from behind, hauling me off my feet. He flings me to the bed so hard I almost bounce off. I sit up, determined to make it to safety, but his fist slams into my face. My teeth rattle, and agony blossoms over my jaw and cheekbone.

Now I understand why he didn't hit me last night. He knew Ms. Darling was coming and saved all this rage for after she left. His violence is not uncontrolled. It's a thing of cold calculation, which in some ways makes it even more dangerous.

"Caleb, please," I manage to say, though I can barely get the words past my swelling lips.

"Don't you ever defy me in front of other people again," he grits out, his expression made of stone, his eyes nearly black with rage.

His fist flies at me like a missile, but I duck and roll off the bed, landing in an undignified heap. I scramble to my feet, but he shoves me from behind, and I crash into the bedside table. It tips over, the lamp shattering against the wall. From the floor, I see him loosening his belt.

Oh God, no.

I raise my hands to protect my face from the leather strap hurtling through the air. It snaps against my wrist and fingers, cutting into the skin. Before I can process the first lash, several rain down on my arm, a deluge of terror that reddens my flesh with livid welts. In quick succession, the belt falls time and again, a wave that never ebbs, but just keeps coming, keeps crashing over me. The leather slashes into my back and my legs. The buckle nicks my knee, and I howl like a wounded animal, but there's no one to rescue me. I am the dumb lamb that wandered from the fold, and I've stumbled into the razor teeth of a hunter's trap.

"Oh, God. Caleb, please." Pain steals my breath, and my words barely make it out before another punch slams my head into the wall. The room spins and tilts, and the edges darken.

I slump against the wall, too disoriented to respond. The belt keeps falling, seeking any tender flesh it has overlooked, and I stop fighting the darkness because it's the only place I'll find mercy.

TWENTY TWO

IRIS

"Sarai!"

Her name cannons from my mouth, and I jerk up on the bed. Pain slices under my breasts. I grab at my midsection, disoriented for a moment. I know I've been unconscious, and the last thing I saw was that monster's face. My daughter's been alone with him for as long as I've been out.

I fling my legs over the side of the bed, wincing when my muscles scream in protest. I'm naked, and I have no idea how I got this way. My stomach whirs at the thought of what Caleb may have done to me. Welts, cuts, and bruises crisscross my bare legs and arms. Shame builds in my chest and burns my eyes. How did I let this happen? How did I become this battered woman? A sob shakes my chest, and pain ricochets through my rib cage.

"Careful," a deep voice says from the corner of the room. "Your ribs are probably bruised. There are painkillers by the bed."

The face is familiar, but my head is still fuzzy. I do my best to assemble the features into someone I recognize.

"Andrew?" I ask, my voice hoarse from my screams.

"Yeah." Caleb's cousin stands from a chair, and averts his eyes from my bruised, naked body. "You might want to cover up."

I snatch the bedsheet over my breasts. All my responses feel delayed as I drag pieces of this grisly puzzle in place.

"Sarai?" I ask. "Where is she?"

I hold my breath held while I wait.

"She's in the nursery. I checked on her a little bit ago. She was fine. I fed her one of the bottles from the fridge."

Relief is quickly followed by anger, fear, and trepidation.

"And Caleb? Where is he?" I ask.

Andrew's cheeks redden, and he clears his throat.

"He, uh, had a game." He grabs the bottle and a glass of water from the bedside table. "You'll need these for your ribs maybe the next few weeks."

I stare at the pills, afraid to take anything anyone in this house offers me.

"It's just naproxen," he says. "An anti-inflammatory painkiller."

"You're a doctor," I say dumbly, as if he doesn't know, but pieces of information are lining up in my head to make sense of why he's here and why he's so calm when it's obvious Caleb's beat the shit out of me.

"I'm still in med school." Andrew shakes two pills out of the bottle into his palm and offers them to me. "Remember?"

"Is this part of the Hippocratic Oath?" I pop the pills and gulp water, tearing up when the jerky movements hurt my jaw. "'Do no harm' actually means 'only aid and abet?'"

"I'm sorry, Iris." He shakes his head. "I've told him before—"

"He's done this before?" Horror widens my eyes and drops my mouth open. "Oh my God."

"I've . . . well, helped him before, yeah."

"You mean when he beat women, you came and patched them up?" I ask sarcastically. "Would have been good to know."

"I thought he had it under control." He runs his hands through hair only a shade darker than Caleb's. "This hasn't happened in a long time, and he loves you so much."

"Don't you dare say that ever again." Tears rise in my throat like floodwaters. I wait for them to recede before speaking. "He may deceive himself that this is love, but I won't play that game. He's sick, and so are you if you help him."

I stand in the middle of the bedroom and catch the first glimpse of myself in the wall mirror. The sheet knotted toga-style leaves my shoulders and arms exposed. Caleb's brutality has painted my skin in shades of black and red, of desolation and rage. My face . . .

A moan, loud and involuntary, falls out of me and bounces off the walls.

My cheeks are uneven, one monstrously swollen and the other nearly untouched. One eye is smeared with shadows left by Caleb's fist. A line of dried blood runs from the corner of my mouth down my neck and disappears beneath the fold of the sheet. I gently touch the swollen, bruised, puffy flesh.

I turn from the mirror to Andrew. "You have to help me."

He takes a step back, his expression withdrawing as surely as his body does. "I can't, Iris. I have painkillers, and—"

"Painkillers?" I sound hysterical, but I can't help it. "He raped me at gunpoint last night, Andrew, and he beat me today."

He squeezes his eyes shut, shaking his head. "I'm so sorry."

"He's blackmailing me," I say in a rush, praying that everything I reveal will somehow convince him he has to help me. "He stole my journal and will twist the things I wrote to get custody of Sarai if I try to leave. He had Ramone, that crazy bodyguard, report me to social services. He's cut off all my access to money. He says he'll kill me if I try to leave, Andrew, and I believe him." Tears flow freely while I rehash just how screwed over I am—how I've allowed Caleb to trap me.

"What about Lotus?" Andrew asks.

"He says he'll hurt her, too, if I involve her. He knows where she lives in New York." I swipe my hands over my wet cheeks. "No, just getting away from him won't solve my custody issue. His threats would catch up to me. I need something on him that will stick, to hurt him where it counts the way he's doing me."

"Caleb's good at threats," he says bitterly. "He deals in information."

"That's why you help him?" I ask. "He has something on you? That's why you can't help me?"

Andrew's lips compress. "I can get you more painkillers."

"I don't want painkillers!" I scream. "I want to not need them. I want to get out of here." I bury my face in my hands, slumping against the wall and allowing myself one moment of weakness. "I have to get Sarai out of here."

"I think things will get better," Andrew says. "He probably just lost it, what with August humiliating him like that."

"He didn't humiliate him," I counter. "He just played the game. Caleb let him get in his head, like he always does."

"I know you say he doesn't love you." Andrew holds up a staying hand when I open my mouth to argue. "But he's never felt like this about another woman."

"Oh, you mean abusive? Violent? Psychopathic? Wow. I feel so flattered."

"No, I mean you must be special to him. He's marrying you."

"We're not engaged," I auto-reply.

Andrew's brows bunch, and he tips his head toward my left hand. "Then what's that on your finger?"

I glance down and notice for the first time, my gris-gris ring from MiMi is gone.

In its place is the ten-carat diamond.

TWENTY THREE

AUGUST

Number thirty-three.

I lift my father's old basketball jersey out of the cardboard box, coughing a little from the dust. I've seen pictures of me as a toddler wearing this. It hung off my shoulders and dragged on the floor. Now, when I slip it over my head, it fits perfectly. At six foot seven inches, my dad was an inch taller than I am. His wingspan outreached mine and his feet were a size larger, but that's where I stop making comparisons. I leave that to the pundits and media who speculate about what he could have been and what I may achieve. He was cut down so young before he really had the chance to fulfill even a fraction of his promise.

I massage the soreness in my leg and wonder if I'll repeat history. The easy part of this recovery is over. I've been mostly off my feet for the eight weeks since surgery. I recently started upper-body work in a gym close by, just outside of Baltimore, and that is only the beginning. Months of grueling rehab lie ahead with no guarantee that I'll be a hundred percent at the end. Speed and agility, the ability to turn on a dime—those are trademarks of my game and are things this injury could compromise irreparably. Only time and the hardest work of my life will tell.

Fucking Caleb and his dirty play that wasn't ruled a dirty play. He's slithered his way out of consequences all his life. It's made him spoiled and cruel, but also clever enough to hide it. Me, he hates, so he did some underhanded shit that shoved me, at least temporarily, out of the way.

He'd never hurt them, though, right?

The more I've considered it, flat on my back and staring up at the ceiling, the less confident I am of Caleb's boundaries. God, if I had Iris, I'd treat her like a queen.

Can you miss someone you've never had?

Because I miss Iris. I can't even share that with anyone because they'd think I was a lunatic. Obsessed. Fixated.

I like to think of it as *certain*. Like when I'm in the zone, the game comes to me easily and I'm certain I'll make every shot before the ball even leaves my hands—that's how I feel about Iris. She's a shot that hasn't even left my hands, but I know will be nothing but net. I'm certain that if ever given the chance, it would be that way for us. Not that things would be easy all the time, but we'd just . . . click. We'd *belong*, something we've both needed for a long time. I felt hints of it the first night we met, and with each encounter, it's become clearer. It's quantified in breathless moments and skipped heartbeats. Nothing I can point to or prove, but it's real. I've only grown more sure that together, we could belong.

"What are you doing out here?" my mother asks from the open garage door. "I was looking all over the house for you. Your phone's been ringing off the hook all morning."

"Probably Lloyd." I grimace at the thought of another conversation with my agent. "He thinks he may be able to get me a good trade."

"Trade?" Mom's brows collapse into a frown. "Do the Waves wanna get rid of you because of the injury? Don't they know you'll be back stronger than ever? What's wrong with them?"

I wish everyone had a mother like mine who believed in them even when they weren't sure themselves.

"Lloyd's just looking at contingencies." I shrug and pull my father's jersey over my head and drop it back into the box. "The Waves are an expansion team, and this was their first season. Decker invested a lot in me. Me getting hurt my first year probably has them considering cutting their losses in case I don't come back as strong."

"Your first season ended with you as Rookie of the Year." Her eyes and smile are all pride. "They'd be fools to let you go."

"Maybe I'd be a fool to stay." I release a puff of air. "I could end up on a team that's championship caliber *now*. Maybe in the playoffs next season, playing for a ring. If Lloyd can make that happen, I'd be a fool to turn it down."

"You'll know what to do when you get to it. You'll know what's most important. I'm sure Jared will have opinions."

"Oh, always." I laugh. "And on everything."

She hands my phone to me. "You two still considering getting Elevation off the ground early?" she asks, poking through the box of memories.

"I want to. He's not sure, which means we probably will."

She chuckles, nodding and pulling out a photo album at the bottom of the box. "You *do* tend to get your way, August."

"Eventually. Sometimes." I pause at the look on her face as she flips through the album. It's love, and pain, and regret. "What's that you're looking at?"

She turns the album to show me a photo. It's a picture I've never seen. My mom, dad and I are standing on a basketball court with a packed stadium in the background, and my father is holding me, his arm wrapped around my mother. I've never thought we looked alike, but in this picture, I see echoes of my features in his.

"Wow," I say softly. "We actually do look a little alike."

"Of course you do." She brushes a fingertip over my father's face. "He's darker and his hair is coarser, but that bone structure. Same handsome face. Same mouth."

Her smile is wistful, and maybe slightly wicked. I'm sure she has memories of his mouth that I want to know nothing about. So much of what I know about my father has been through the media and old friends telling stories. There are things I never asked my mother that maybe only she knows.

"Was he a good man?" I ask, watching her face for the truth. I don't miss the bitter tilt of her lips settle into ruefulness.

"He was a great father." She looks up from the photo. "He loved you more than anything. He was so good to you."

"And to you?" I ask softly, prepared for whatever she answers. "What kind of husband was he?'

She hesitates, considering the picture again before looking in my eyes. "What kind of husband was he?" She tosses my question back before twisting her mouth into that rueful little curve. "A young, handsome one, with lots of money and time on the road."

"Like me then," I half-joke. "Sometimes I see so many parallels between us."

"You won't make the choices your father did when you're married, August. I'm not worried about that."

"Really?" I ask, thinking about all the ass I pulled in my rookie year. "Why not?"

"Because I raised you better than that." She winks and brushes her hands over my hair. "You just need to find the right girl."

Of course, my mind defaults to Iris—to the last time I saw her laughing with Sarai and bouncing her on her knee. Reminder. Another man's baby bouncing on her knee.

"Maybe I've found the right girl." I close the flaps of the box. "Maybe it's just a matter of timing."

It's hard for me to surprise my mother. She usually sees everything coming from a mile away, but her eyes stretch, and her mouth drops open.

"Do I know her?" she demands. "Is she in San Diego? How did you meet her? When can *I* meet her?"

"Uh, Mom." I hold up a hand to stay the tsunami of questions coming off her in waves. "It's not like that. I mean, it is. For me it is. I'd bring her to meet you right now if I could."

"She doesn't want to be with you?" She rests her fists on her hips, the Irish feistiness to match that red hair sparking in her eyes. "Does she have any idea what she's missing?"

"She doesn't care about my contract or the money or any of that stuff." Even though Iris is with Caleb, I know it's not because he has any of those things. And as soon as I figure out why she *is* with him, I'll convince her it's not enough. Not as much as I could give her.

"Those aren't the things I meant either," Mom says. "You're kind, and generous, and smart, and ambitious. I raised you to know how to treat a woman. She'd be lucky to have you."

"Thanks, Mom, though you might be just a little biased. I think you'd like her." My smile drops. "I mean, if she ever leaves her boyfriend."

"August, what?" Her eyes stretch. "Tell me."

"It's a long story."

She crosses her arms and sits on one of the nearby bins in the garage. "Do I look busy?"

I pull up a bin and tell her about that first night before the tournament, how Iris and I talked about any and everything; we shared our pasts, our families, our dreams, and hopes. I tell her how disappointed I was to realize Iris was dating Caleb. I leave out the part where I saw her naked breast at All-Star weekend, but I hit other highlights, ending with the last time I saw her, at the game before Caleb's dirty play.

"So you've only seen her a few times?" Mom asks. The consternation on her face gives me pause. She thinks I'm crazy. I know I am.

"But we talked for hours the first time," I say, hearing the defensiveness in my voice. "We talked about everything. I've never felt that connected to someone so quickly. And even at the All-Star game, it was like we just picked right back up." I toss my phone back and forth between my hands and shrug. "I know what you're thinking—it's some infatuation. Or maybe you think I just like her because she's Caleb's girl, right?"

"I knew Matt was the one after our first date." She chuckles at the startled look that must be on my face. "I did. We had exactly what you're talking about. That ease. That spark. It feels like you're the only two people in the world."

That first night in the bar, I didn't even notice the other customers leaving. I didn't notice the bartender cleaning up. I barely noticed the game ending.

"She absorbed me," I say, shaking my head. "I'd never felt that way about anyone else. When she told me she had a boyfriend, I felt like she was reading from the wrong script. Like that's not how this is supposed to go. How can it possibly go that way when I feel like this already?"

I roll my eyes, playing my words back in my own ears. "I sound like a chick."

"And what's wrong with sounding like a woman?" Mom's offended words chastise me.

"You know what I mean. Like all in my feelings. Desperate." I catch her sharp look. "Not saying that all women are desperate. I just mean I sound like I would do anything to be with her."

"Based on what you told me about her family history, maybe she needs someone who's willing to take an outrageous chance on her. It sounds like she hasn't had the easiest life and has seen a lot of bad in men."

"I don't get why she's still with that asshole." I run an agitated hand through the hair dipping over my eyes. "If you could have felt what was between us that night at the game. Neither one of us could look away. It's still there for me, and I know it's still there for her. I know how it sounds, but I'm not making this up."

"She has a child with this man, August. You said she was on bed rest and couldn't work. She probably has very little of her own. You never know what a mother has to do to do what's best for her child."

She grins.

"Even knowing I loved Matt, it was a long time before I let him fully into my life. I wanted to protect you. It hadn't been long since your father died, and you were so impressionable. I had to be careful about who I brought around you. I had to be careful about everything. It seems to me circumstances have made your Iris more vulnerable than she ever wanted to be."

My Iris.

It feels like all the stars and planets and the moon itself will have to align for her to be my Iris.

"I know you don't like the comparisons with your father," Mom interrupts my thoughts. "But there is one thing you inherited from him for sure."

"What's that?"

"Timing." Her smile turns fond, her eyes distant. "He'd hold the ball 'til the last possible second. I'm screaming from the bleachers for him to take the shot, but he'd just dribble and watch the clock, and at just the right moment, he'd take the shot."

"You're right." I laugh, because I remember watching tape of him when I was younger and thinking the same thing.

"As immature and impetuous as your father sometimes was off the court," Mom says, "on the court, he was a study in patience and vision. Seeing the right opportunity and taking the shot when it was time. He used to call it 'letting the game come to him.' Try that approach with Iris. Let the game come to you, and at the right time, take the shot."

My phone rings, startling us both. I grimace when I see Lloyd's name onscreen. I'm a grown-ass man. I need to take care of my career the same way I'm taking care of this leg, and that means talking to Lloyd. "I need to take this. I've been dodging my agent."

"Alright." She stands and dusts off her jeans. She drops a kiss on my unruly curls. "And at some point, you *will* get a haircut, right?"

"Rehab hair. This is why I don't let it grow." I sift my fingers through the thick curls flopping everywhere and answer Lloyd's call.

Lloyd takes forty-five minutes to tell me ten minutes' worth of information, so I'm chomping at the bit to get off the phone by the time he's bringing the conversation to a close.

"I'll email those contracts over for you to look at and sign," he says. "We need to get that commercial in the can. I suggested we not do it in your San Diego jersey, just to be safe."

"It's like that?" I ask, not sure if I'm excited or insulted that San Diego may be seriously considering trading me. At the start of the season it would have been what I wanted, but I had just started to feel like we were building something special.

"We'll see." Lloyd's voice is diplomatic and dissembling. "I like to have contingencies. No telling when that commercial will air or where you'll be by then. Oh, and did you speak to that Sylvia lady?"

"What Sylvia lady?" I'm only half listening, re-opening my dad's box and picking through it to make sure I didn't overlook anything significant.

"She called me this morning saying she's left several voicemails for you. Something about NBA charity stuff and you wanting to volunteer in Baltimore."

"Oh, yeah. I do. I have a ton of missed calls. I'll call her back."

"You start physical therapy next week, right?"

"Yeah. I mean, I've been doing some upper-body stuff but wasn't cleared for weight on the leg before. Now I am, so we'll go into beast mode next week."

"*Bleacher Report* approached me about documenting your road to recovery." I hear Lloyd's lips smacking in anticipation over the phone. "Like a web series or a special."

"Nah. I don't want to do the circus act, sympathy, look-at-him-go thing."

"It's a good idea to stay in the public eye. That next contract is mostly about how you do on the court, but it doesn't hurt if they know you can put butts in seats. And let's not forget you *were* Rookie of the Year, despite missing the last games of the regular season."

"That was probably a consolation prize," I say, resentment festering in my words. "They knew Caleb's play was dirty and didn't want to give it to him. Giving me the award was their silent protest since his daddy always finds a way to protect him."

"Well, it's certainly added to the public's interest in the two of you. It's turning into a Magic Johnson–Larry Bird kind of rivalry. Theirs started in college, too."

"Yeah, but they became friends, and Caleb and I never will."

"They really played it up. Did commercials together and everything."

I'm choking on my answer before it even comes out of my mouth. "The hell I'm doing a commercial with that motherfucker."

Total silence.

"So . . . I guess that's a definite no," he says.

"That's 'if you ever put me in the same room as that dude again, I'm firing your ass.' We legit don't like each other, Lloyd. It's not for the cameras or to hike ratings. The guy's a shitbag who jeopardized my career. Don't ask me to grin like a buffoon and drink Pepsi with him."

More total silence.

"Duly noted," Lloyd finally says. "Will you at least call Sylvia back?"

"Yeah. I'll do it right now."

I'm just eager to get off the phone with him. There are so many things Lloyd and I don't see eye to eye on. The more I think about it, the more I'm ready to turn things over to Jared. With us getting Elevation off the ground, it's the perfect time and ideal scenario: him managing my career as he convinces other athletes he can manage theirs.

I listen to the message Sylvia left. She invites me to do some talks for a week at the community center right outside of Baltimore where I played all the time growing up. It's exactly the kind of thing I'd hoped to do while I was rehabbing on this side of the country.

"Thank you for returning my call, Mr. West," Sylvia says when I dial her back.

"Please. Call me August. I'm sorry it took a minute. I've just started hitting the gym again and guess I hadn't paid attention to messages for a few days."

"No problem. Did you hear the opportunity I have in mind?"

"It's perfect," I say, thinking of all the times I got my ass handed to me at that community center. "I cut my teeth playing ball there. It's not far from my mom's, where I'm staying while I rehab. We're right outside of the city."

"Oh, good." Sylvia's warm voice comes from the other end. "I'll email you details, but basically it's a summer program, and we bring in someone different each week to inspire and encourage the kids. You'll talk for maybe thirty minutes or so."

"Sounds great." I pause for a second, hesitant to broach my awkward question. "Um, obviously I play for the Waves out in San Diego, not the Stingers, but this is my hometown, and I really want to contribute here, too. Will any other Stingers be involved?"

"Actually—"

"I'm fine working with anyone from the team," I cut in. "But Caleb Bradley and I aren't—"

"I'm familiar with the, shall we say, difficulties between the two of you."

"Good." I blow out a breath, relieved that I don't have to go into more detail to make my point.

"However," Sylvia says, "his fiancée, er, sorry . . . girlfriend will be one of the volunteers. Several of the players' partners are working at the center that week, but they—"

"Iris?" I stomp over whatever she was about to say, gripping the phone practically to the point of cracking. "Are you saying Iris DuPree will be there the same week?"

Crickets from the other line. Too eager?

"I mean, if that's what you're saying," I continue, deliberately dialing it down, "let's not mention it to Iris."

"Um . . . what?" Confusion and reluctance pile up in Sylvia's pause. "I won't lie—"

"Lie?" I laugh a little to put her at ease. "Who said anything about lying, Sylvia? I was thinking just so she doesn't feel awkward or maybe like she shouldn't come, considering how things have been between Caleb and me. I think it's great she's volunteering."

"If she asks, I'll have to tell her," she says a little stiffly.

"By all means. And if she doesn't ask . . ." I shrug like she can see me. "She'll find out when she gets there, and we'll help the community center, which is the ultimate goal, right?"

"Right, but I don't want any trouble."

"There won't be. Promise."

It's silent on the other end for a few moments, and I hope I've convinced her.

"Alright," she finally says, her voice still a little uncertain. "I guess we could leave it a surprise for everyone. That might add some excitement."

"Excitement. Exactly. Great idea. It'll be fine. I have no beef with Iris."

"Okay, well, I'll send that email of the topics we suggest. You can modify as you see fit."

"Thanks, Sylvia. I'm really looking forward to it."

Once I disconnect from Sylvia, I sit on the plastic bin alone. On instinct, I walk back over to the box of my father's things and pull out the jersey, slipping it over my head again.

"Perfect timing, huh?" I ask the empty garage. "Looks like the game is coming to me, Dad. We'll see if I get to take the shot."

TWENTY FOUR

IRIS

We've found a new normal, Caleb and me.

I've learned to negotiate the terrain of the hell in which I'm trapped. There is this strange balancing act of compliance and strategic resistance. Caleb is a sleeping volcano, always primed to erupt. I've learned his cycles. He's a pendulum that swings from Jekyll to Hyde. I try to anticipate his triggers as much as I can, but sometimes they don't follow the pattern they should.

He doesn't attack every day. In some ways, the unpredictability of it makes it even worse. He'll go weeks being perfectly well-behaved. He's still repulsive because I know what he's capable of, but he manages his behavior—and I manage to ignore it. And then something will set him off, a straw I didn't even know had landed on the camel's back. His steak is too rare. He's lost a game. His favorite show has been cancelled. There's no rhyme or reason to his viciousness.

"We're really looking forward to next week, Iris."

I glance up from my plate of chicken, mashed potatoes, and green beans, to the source of that statement.

Sylvia.

Sylvia's one of the eight or so people at our table. The Stingers are celebrating the end of a successful season with this dinner. They made it to the second round of the playoffs.

Whoop-dee-doo.

"I'm sorry." I bring Sylvia's face into focus. "What did you say about next week?"

"Yeah." Caleb slumps a little in his seat beside me, then leans back and rests his elbow on the back of my chair. "What's next week?"

He shifts to caress my neck under my hair. I force myself not to flinch at his touch. That infuriates him, seeing me flinch.

At least, it infuriates him when I do it in public.

When we're alone, it feeds him. It empowers him to see the fear he has carefully cultivated over the last few weeks thriving and growing inside of me. My fear is a plant he nurtures in the dark.

"Oh." Sylvia's dishwater blond eyebrows snap together. "The community center? Iris is scheduled to volunteer there next week."

Thank God.

Give me something. Something outside of that house and the open-air prison of my life with Caleb.

"I don't know if she'll still be able to do that," Caleb cuts in with a frown.

His hand at the curve of my neck probably looks like affection from the outside—like the hand of a rich, powerful man stroking his pet. He displays a possessiveness that might send a thrill of excitement through someone else. Most women have a bit of a crush on Caleb when they first meet him. They don't know him the way I do. Only I feel his fingers tighten. Only I know his hand at my neck is not love. It's a warning. It's a shackle.

Only I know the real Caleb, and it's a violent intimacy I wouldn't wish on anyone.

"Really? That's a shame." Sylvia flicks a glance between the two of us, like she's unsure where to direct her dismay. Instinctively, she knows that I have little say.

"It's all arranged, though," Sylvia continues . . . nervously? Yes, nervously. She doesn't *know* Caleb is a predator, but on some cellular level, maybe atavistically, her body knows, and it makes her nervous.

The heart speaks in whispers.

I heard too late.

"The kids are looking forward to seeing your family, even though you can't be there," she says. "We have signed jerseys and autographed photos for Iris to pass out, and we thought the kids could meet your daughter. You're one of the Stingers' star players. That would go a long way with them."

Sylvia looks to me like she expects me to advocate for myself. She has no idea that her request will earn me a slap or worse when I get home. Or maybe a hard pinch under the table. Caleb is usually careful with my face— with all the parts people see. Only when he knows he can keep me home long enough to heal does he hit my face. If I have my phone with me, he'll make sure I have no real evidence to display. And when I have real evidence of his brutality, my phone will go 'missing' for days. He and Ramone have my captivity down to a science.

"I'm away next week," Caleb says, picking up a glass of wine and taking a sip. He looks casual, but I'm so tuned into him now, to his moods, that I know there's nothing casual about him. He's tense at my side, a predator feeling threatened—like he might lose his prey if she gets out of her cage. "I'm away for the next two weeks actually, in China."

Basketball is exploding there, and the market is so ripe Caleb and his agent are exploring endorsement opportunities. Thank God Sarai has been sick and couldn't get the necessary shots. The pediatrician didn't clear her to travel, so I get two weeks without Caleb. Ramone will still be there, but Ramone doesn't hit me. Doesn't rape me. He just makes sure I never get away.

Complicit bastard.

"We knew you wouldn't be there, though." Sylvia frowns. "We could—"

"Iris is very particular about who watches Sarai," Caleb cuts in, sliding his thumb over my bare shoulder.

"Sarai is fine with the childcare provided for the event tonight, right?" Sylvia directs her question to me.

"Yes, of course. They seem awesome," I say. "And Sarai loves people. She loves to be out and interacting with other children."

Caleb doesn't look at me, but his displeasure nicks the surface of my composure.

"And there will be childcare at the community center for the players' wives and girlfriends' children," Sylvia says. "You're welcome to inspect the area and meet the workers, Iris. That is if you still want to do it?"

Shit.

Of course, I do, but it's not worth the fight. I pick and choose my battles, and this is not a battle I choose. I'm still searching for the best response when someone beats me to it.

"I think it's a great idea," Michael Cross says.

I hadn't spoken to the Stingers' president of basketball operations seated at our table all night, but now I'm really glad he's here.

"We could use some goodwill after all that talk of a dirty play with August West," he says sternly. "That cloud still hangs over the organization."

An awkward silence falls on the table, one with clearing throats and bodies shifting in straight-backed chairs. Not me. I remember what happened when I accused Caleb of hurting August on purpose. I'm quiet. I'm still, but August's name lands heavily on my ears. Even heavier on my heart.

"The league didn't fine me," Caleb says, his "I'm handsome and harmless" smile firmly in place. "Nothing was proven because it was an accident. Shit happens when you're on the court."

"Yeah, well, it's bad for the team's image. And West getting Rookie of the Year didn't help," Michael says, his eyes hard on Caleb.

What a night that was.

When August was named Rookie of the Year, I knew we would have a bad night. He actually doesn't bother me sexually very much—probably because he's getting it everywhere else. If I could send those women fruit baskets, I would. But that night, no one else would do. August wasn't there for him to take out his rage on, and I was the next best thing.

"Let's decorate that pretty face West seems to like so much," he'd grunted, ejaculating all over my face. His semen had flooded my mouth, blurred my vision, invaded my nose, and sunk into my pores.

"Iris, do you still want to do it?" Michael Cross's question jerks me back to the table, into the conversation. "*Would* you do it?"

All eyes on me.

I hazard a glance in Caleb's direction, but he's studying the wine in his glass. What am I supposed to say here?

I do want to do it. I need it. He and Ramone have me on lockdown every hour of the day. To draw a few breaths free of them? I won't have a better excuse than Caleb's boss practically ordering him to "let" me do it.

"Sure." I spread an easy smile around the table. "I'd love to help."

"Great," Michael Cross says, offering me a friendly smile. "Then it's settled." His eyes are a little stonier when they pass to Caleb. "That's okay with you, right, Caleb?"

"Of course." Caleb links his fingers with mine on the table, turning our hands so his albatross of a ring catches the light perfectly. "Iris will represent our family well."

"Oh, I just noticed your ring," Sylvia says, her eyes widening at the rock weighing down my finger. "I didn't realize . . . well . . . congratulations."

Her eyes rest covetously on the engagement ring during a chorus of well wishes from everyone at the table,

You can have him!

I want to scream it so that Sylvia and every woman in a thirty-mile radius knows I don't want Caleb and he's on the market. If you like being slapped around, blackmailed, entrapped, and held prisoner, he's your man.

Because he's certainly not mine.

Keeping up appearances *is* important to him. At Caleb's side, I'm a chandelier, lit and sparkling with artificial light. Tonight, he needs me to shine. Fortunately, Cross has taken away Caleb's choice in the matter.

How's that feel, Caleb? Having your choices taken away?

A few hours later, he taunts me with his silence in the car on the way home. If he started in on me as soon as we were alone, that would make sense. But no, he likes to keep me on my toes, so I'm a little mouse unsure of when the snake will strike.

It's not until I'm in the bathroom preparing for bed that he broaches the subject again. He approaches me from behind. In the mirror, his broad shoulders and naked chest come into view, the sculpted planes and muscled belly no temptation to me. I lift my eyes to meet his in the reflection, the serenity of my expression belied by my pounding heart. He's left me alone lately, probably because he knew the dinner was coming. And now, next week there's the community center. My face in the mirror is unmarked, and it will stay that way.

That's not true of my arms, banded with dark circles where his fingers have gripped, or of my back, bruised from his shoe. He's marked me in so many secret ways, I'm afraid that even when I escape, I'll never be rid of him.

But I will escape.

It's not enough to run, to get away from Caleb. Even if I run, his lies will hunt me down, and in the end, he'll have access to Sarai. For me, that's not winning. That's not freedom. And when Caleb says he'll kill me if I leave him, he means it. There's murder in his eyes, a yet-to-be-pulled trigger. I have to be smarter than that. Smarter than him. He trapped me, and I have to lay a trap for him. The timing has to be perfect. I may only get one shot.

"Don't do anything you'll regret next week," he says softly.

I wipe away my makeup, eyes set on my reflection in the mirror. I don't acknowledge him—a tiny rebellion. The only one I'm allowed.

"Did you hear me?" He grabs my arm in exactly the place that is already marked, drawing a wince and a sharp breath from me.

"I heard you." I look at him in the mirror and nod. "What would I do, Caleb? Run? I tried that, remember?"

"Just don't forget next week when you're at the community center." His hand wanders down my arm, slips around my waist, and creeps up to cup my breast. "I have so much on you, you'll be lucky to see Sarai on weekends."

"I'm well aware, Caleb." I tense under his hand, bitterness flavoring the words in my mouth. "Of what's at stake."

Ms. Darling called last week to make sure Sarai was still "safe." She said we were fine for now and shouldn't need any more home visits, but I need to find that journal and turn the tables on Caleb. He used the things most important to me against me—my family and my daughter. He knows I would die before I allowed him to have even joint custody of Sarai, having seen what he's capable of. He's schemed to be so many steps ahead of me before I realized I was even in the game.

"I can't believe Cross had the nerve to bring up West," Caleb says harshly, his fingers tightening on me. "That motherfucker stole Rookie of the Year from me."

He squeezes my nipple, and I draw a deep breath, breathing through the pain.

"West always wants what's mine," Caleb goes on, his eyes on me in the mirror, his mind on August. "He can't have you, though."

I nod jerkily, counting to ten to distract myself from the needles of agony piercing my breast. And then his hand is gone.

I lean weakly against the bathroom counter, hoping he walks away. I pray he leaves me alone, but like so many nights when I've prayed over the last few months, no one is listening.

He pushes the hem of my nightgown over my hips until cool air hits my thighs and butt. He shoves my panties down. They hit the floor, encircling my ankles like cuffs. He presses my back, forcing my chest to the bathroom counter. My cheek slams into the cold quartz.

"Caleb, please." I glance up to the mirror, searching his eyes for any sign of leniency. "Don't."

He doesn't answer but stares down at my ass, his look a mix of hunger, possessiveness, and malice. He digs his fingers into my hip, and I hear the pajama bottoms slide down his legs; feel the first press of his invasion.

I'm not religious. I'm not a high priestess. I'm not a believer in much of anything anymore. I can't buy into Lotus's superstitions or wrap my mind around MiMi's mysticism, but every time Caleb touches me, the same words come to my lips, an un-whispered prayer that echoes in the cavernous chamber of my heart.

God, deliver me from this.

Save me.

TWENTY FIVE

IRIS

"I'll be fine here by myself, Ramone."

He's in the driver's seat of the SUV I used to drive before Caleb took my license, and I'm in the back seat. The community center, sweet freedom—at least for two hours—is across the street.

"I'm coming with you." He undoes his seatbelt.

"No." Our eyes lock in the rearview mirror while I unsnap Sarai's car seat. "It's a community center for kids. It will look ridiculous for you to come in there with us. I'll meet you here when I'm done."

He eyes me with suspicion.

"Don't worry. I know I can't leave without being arrested for kidnapping," I say bitterly. "Or having social services show up at my door. Thanks for that, by the way."

Ramone doesn't look concerned that I know he lied to social services.

Anyone who'll stand by complicit while Caleb does the things he does to me can't have any shame.

"Two hours." He bounces a glance from the community center to his watch. "I'll be right here."

I make a run for it before he changes his mind. I set Sarai up in her stroller, grab her diaper bag, and barely close the door before I'm pushing her down the sidewalk. I'm determined to have some time without Ramone breathing down my neck. It's been even worse this week with Caleb in China. The watch dog is on high alert, and I'm sure he's under strict instructions to report any unusual behavior. Like the emergence of a backbone or will.

My life has been relatively tranquil with Caleb gone. I only have a few bruises in places no one will see. I'm relieved, for once, not to have injuries to cover up, besides the ones under my skin, around my heart. Those are the worst of all.

I reach the community center entrance. We're not quite in the hood, not quite in the suburbs. I know hood—I negotiated it the first twelve years of my life, and this ain't it. There's not a crackhead or prostitute in sight. The building has seen better days, but it's clean and in decent repair.

The young woman at the front desk looks up from her romance novel to offer me a pleasant smile.

"Hi." I give her a smile back. "I'm here for the basketball camp."

She inspects all my details. I dressed as unassumingly as possible, but after my pregnancy, Caleb "surprised" me with a whole new wardrobe. At the time I chided myself for not feeling more grateful, but now I recognize it as one more puppet string he pulled to exercise his control. My dark jeans are simple, but expensive. I only brought Sarai's diaper bag, but it's designer. Not to mention the albatross of a ring on my finger. With Caleb making such a big deal of it at the dinner, I dare not show up to volunteer without it. The ring and Sarai are his accessories, further presenting him as the ideal family man instead of the monster I know and hate.

"You a baller's wife, huh?" she asks, glancing at Sarai in the stroller.

"Um, girlfriend."

I know what people think when they see me: that I've got it made and Sarai is the meal ticket that sets me up for life, or at least until she's eighteen. They have no idea that under this silk blouse tucked into my designer jeans, bruises, black and blue and yellow, often splatter my ribs like ink blots—that on the regular, I taste my own blood. I'd trade with the poorest, with the homeless, with this young lady right here, just to be free of the tailless devil I sleep with every night.

"I heard I might be able to put my baby in daycare while I'm volunteering." I look around the small lobby curiously. "Could I see it?"

I definitely need to know what it's like before I leave Sarai there.

When we round the corner, an older woman, probably somebody's grandmother, makes her way over to the half-door, the bottom secured and the top open.

"Who's this little darling?" she asks, leaning out and smiling widely at Sarai. My daughter never meets a stranger and immediately begins blowing bubbles and waving her little starfish hands.

"Her name's Sarai." I pull her out of the stroller. "You have room for her?"

"Sure do." She opens the bottom half of the door and gestures for me to come in. "I'm Audrey."

The space designated for the daycare is small, but tidy and orderly, with just a few kids around Sarai's age crawling and toddling around. Changing tables line the perimeter of the room, and shelves stocked with books and toys dot the walls. The four other daycare workers range from about my age to Audrey's. All are either changing babies or playing with them on the floor or rocking them in the glider in the corner. It feels warm and safe. I can breathe easy for two hours.

Once I've checked Sarai in and taken the little pager they issued in case they needed me, I head back to the front desk. Two other women stand there, similarly attired in designer jeans, like me, but where I opted for flats, they wear stilettos. Their glamor quotient is definitely several notches above mine. No rings in sight.

"The kids will be going in that room down the hall on your left." The young desk attendant points in that direction. "They'll be in after they wrap up their morning activity. You can wait if you'd like."

Both women start down the hall without really acknowledging me, their heads bent together in whispers while they walk. When we reach the room and it's just the three of us, it's awkward for me to just stand here. I extend my hand to one of them. "Hey, I'm Iris."

They look at my hand for a few seconds before one and then the other shake it.

The second one grabs my left hand when she shakes my right.

"Oh, nice." She eyes my ring so long I wonder if she'll pull out a magnifying glass. "And she said you went to the nursery. You got the baby *and* the bling."

They exchange a meaningful look and then turn back to me with new respect in their eyes.

"You are #Goals, honey. Smart to get what you can while you can. You think a baller has a short run? Our shelf life is even less," one of them says. Flattering highlighted extensions fall past her shoulders, and she has a body that men must drool over. "I'm Sheila."

"Nice to meet you, Sheila," I reply with a smile that's not an open door, but not quite slammed in your face. It's . . . ajar. I'm ajar. Since Caleb showed his true colors, I find myself closing ranks around Sarai and me. I can't afford attachments or vulnerabilities or friendships. I don't know who to trust anymore. The last person I trust is myself because I didn't truly see Caleb until it was too late. Trusting the wrong person can destroy you.

"And I'm Torrie," the other woman, statuesque with skin smooth as whipped chocolate and a cap of dark curls, offers her hand, tipped with a metallic manicure.

"I think it's just the three of us today," Sheila says, pulling up a red plastic chair and gesturing for me to do the same. "Bonnie is 'sick' again." She air quotes sick.

Torrie leans close and speaks her next words sotto voce. "Her man plays for the Stingers, too, and she is always fly."

"But he beats her ass every chance he gets," Sheila finishes, her mouth tipped at one corner. "So when she's 'sick,' we know that's code for 'he got hold of her again.'"

I freeze in my chair, nausea starting in my belly and slowly crawling over my body, touching every inch of flesh and bone Caleb has terrorized. I keep my face a mask of mild curiosity, but my fingers clench in my palm, the nails cutting into the skin. It's been a few weeks since the last time Caleb really beat me, so other than the occasional easily hidden bruise or cut, you wouldn't look at me and know the hell I've lived through. Right now, though, I may as well be naked I feel so exposed.

"She won't ever leave," Torrie says, sitting down in the seat between us. "That money's too good."

Or maybe she's afraid he'll kill her.

"Girl, the first time a man hits me," Torrie says, lips twisted with disdain, "he's getting hit back. Slapped upside his head."

But what if he's a foot taller? A hundred pounds heavier? What if he has a gun?

"I don't know why she stays," Torrie continues. "But me and my kids would be out the door."

But could he bring them back? Could he take her children?

"She has kids?" I ask, not wanting to show too much interest.

"Girl, they have four kids," Sheila confirms. "Been together like seven years, since college."

"Maybe she's afraid he'll get custody or something," I offer.

"Not if he beats her!" Torrie's voice is indignant. "They won't give him the kids if he's abusive."

"They do," I counter quietly. "It happens all the time, especially if he's never abused the children and has no record. Lots of abusers get partial custody. Some even get to visit *at* the women's shelter she ran to. Our system fails women in lots of ways."

"Hmmmph. She's failing *herself*," Sheila says. "When somebody is beating the shit out of you, how hard is 'bye?'"

Sheila and Torrie share a cackling laugh and high-five over the joke, moving on to other juicy bits of gossip. Their conversation passes me by. I'm too busy processing what my life looks like from the outside. I know I'm not what people might assume—I'm not a mercenary, or a weak-willed woman afraid to leave her man, or even confused because I think Caleb loves me. Still, shame takes root in my heart. The same shame I feel when Andrew tends my cuts and scrapes the morning after. The same shame I feel when I see my puffy face in the mirror, one eye swollen shut. There's a rebel inside, but the girl he hits and kicks and rapes and scorns, the one biding her time and straining her eyes for a way out, she feels shame.

"Either of you know what we're doing today?" Torrie reaches for gum in her purse and offers us both a stick. "My man's in Germany scoping, so I needed something to do anyway."

"Today's the first day," Sheila says, popping the stick of gum into her mouth. "We'll pass out some jerseys and autographed photos. They'll want to get pictures, some with us, but mostly with the basketball player."

"Basketball player?" I ask. "I thought we were standing in for the basketball players."

"They found someone to come in to cover this week," Torrie says. "Not sure who. It'll be pretty laidback this first day. He'll work on a few fundamentals, some simple drills, and then some role model stuff."

"At least that's how it's gone before," Shelia adds.

Sylvia enters the room before I can probe further. She splits a smile between the three of us and greets us warmly.

"Thank you, ladies, for being here today." She eyes me nervously, maybe because of how much Caleb resisted me coming. "The kids are in for a real treat. One of the most popular players of the game today will be here all week."

"Who is it?" I ask idly, not really caring.

"It's me," a familiar voice reaches across the room and snares my full attention.

All the air leaves the room, leaves my lungs. My heart is a boom of thunder, and lightning streaks through my veins. Just like at the basketball game, and like every time I've seen him, I can't ignore him; I can't take my eyes off August West standing in the doorway.

I only allow myself a second of shock before the danger of this situation crystallizes as a stone in my belly. I have no idea what this will drive Caleb to do if he finds out. If Ramone sees, he's sure to tell.

Self-preservation has me on my feet. Wisdom has me brushing past August without looking him in the eye. Desperation has me doing what Caleb's lies and brutality keep me from doing every day.

I run.

TWENTY SIX

AUGUST

"Iris!" I call after her retreating back. She doesn't pause or even glance over her shoulder.

I'll be damned if she's leaving without at least talking to me. My legs are much longer than hers, so I ignore the pain and take two stretched steps to catch her.

"Hey." I take her elbow, firm, but gentle, and turn her to face me, one hand on her arm, one hand at her waist. "Iris, wait."

When I dip my head to line up our eyes, I don't think about the titanium pin holding the tendons and bones of my leg together. The dull ache in my knee and the long weeks I've been immobilized and frustrated—it all fades. I don't consider the months of grueling rehab ahead. I've been worried I won't be full strength when I return next season, maybe ever again, but right now I can't think beyond this mesmerizing moment. All those things pale and dry up, diminished by the woman in front of me. Even though I know Caleb did this because of her, right now it doesn't matter.

Just like at the Stingers game and at All-Star weekend, like the night we met, we don't look away. That thread that draws us in and close every time we're together shrinks the space separating us, even though we don't move an inch. A hundred missed moments and a thousand never-spoken words pass between us, and everything held rigid and tight in her body, in her face, softens as she leans closer.

The squeak of tennis shoes on the gym floor in the distance punctures the moment, and we both blink. I absorb the surroundings, which had folded into the background. She shakes her head and pulls away.

"Why are you here, August?" Iris asks. Her brown eyes, flecked with autumn, green and gold, seem darker than the last time I saw her. It's not the color. Something behind them. Something inside is darker. Dulled.

"I'm volunteering," I answer.

"And it's a coincidence? That we're volunteering here the same week?"

"Yeah, it is."

Her eyes search mine, seemingly not satisfied with my answer.

"Okay, I did know you'd be here," I admit, but speak quickly before she jumps to conclusions. "*But* I didn't arrange it. I told the league from the beginning I wanted to volunteer some locally, here where I grew up, not just in my team's town. My mom's house isn't far. I balled here all the time when I was a kid."

She studies me, the long lashes unblinking, before nodding. "I'll leave then."

She moves away, but I catch her, holding her in place. Eyes on my fingers around her wrist, she flinches and sucks in a sharp breath.

My hand looks huge wrapped around the delicate bones of her wrist.

I release her and step back.

"I'm sorry, Iris. Did I . . .damn, did I hurt you?"

I feel like some Incredible Hulk motherfucker who doesn't even know my own strength, grabbing her like that.

"No." She studies the ground for a moment, shaking her head and rubbing her wrist. "I . . .no. You didn't hurt me. I'm just tired, I guess, and on edge."

"All the more reason to do something you were looking forward to, right?" I ask. "Don't go. We aren't doing anything wrong."

She looks up and scoffs, her laugh humorless. "August, I can't do this."

"Do what?" I take a cautious step closer.

"This." Our eyes hold. Her voice comes husky and low. "I need to go."

I'm close enough to catch her scent and her warmth. I could do this all day. Just smell her. Touch her. Though we've only seen each other a few times, I've missed her. There's no one else I fall into so quickly, the conversation and banter and connection. The chemistry. I crave it again. Yes, I wanted to volunteer where I grew up, but right now, Iris is the reason I'm here.

"I bet you've been looking forward to volunteering, right?" I ask. "The last time we talked, you wanted some outlets."

"The last time we talked, I was suffering from post-partum depression and had no idea." She yields the smallest smile. "Until you suggested I talk to my doctor. Thank you, by the way."

"So you're feeling better?"

"Yeah, much better, but you're right. I was looking forward to volunteering." She shakes her head, resolve in the set of her mouth and chin. "There'll be other chances to help out, though."

"But this one's here now." I shake her wrist and tease her with a grin. "I promise I don't bite or have the cooties."

She rolls her eyes, her laugh soft and barely there, but an encouraging sign. Her glance drops to my leg and she sobers. "Does it still hurt? Your leg?"

I look down, too. I wear an Aircast under my jeans. I can walk carefully but have only recently been cleared to put weight on it.

"It's not bad." I shrug. "All part of the game."

She squeezes her eyes shut, pressing her lips tight. So tight I almost miss what she says next.

"He saw us, August."

I don't have to ask what she means. I know. I saw him seeing us at the game. And I saw the rage it caused before he made sure I felt it. "I know."

She raises startled eyes that fill with tears. "This happened because of me." She gestures toward my injured leg. "I'm so sorry. God, I feel so guilty."

"There's nothing to feel guilty about. It wasn't you. It was him."

"Right, and I don't want him hurting you again because of me." She steadies trembling lips into a firm line. "I don't want him hurting *anyone* because of me."

"Why are you with him, Iris?" I ask, confusion propelling the question out of me.

That something—that unfamiliar thing lurking behind her eyes slips a shadowy veil over her expression, and the truth goes into hiding.

"Things aren't always the way they seem. They aren't simple." She steps back until my hands fall away from her completely. "Nothing's simple."

"Then explain them to me. I can't believe, knowing he'd do something like this," I say, pointing to my leg, "that you would stay with him."

"Iris!" Sylvia calls from the end of the hall, her eyes darting between Iris and me. "Um, is everything okay?"

She's probably created all kinds of scenarios in her head by now about the relationship between Iris and me, especially since I asked her not to tell Iris I would be here. Seeing us together this way, she probably has more questions. I don't care, but I know Iris will.

"Everything's fine," Iris answers quickly, taking another step back. "I thought the daycare was paging me about my daughter, so I came to check.

She's okay, though."

She touches the pager I hadn't noticed on her hip. That's when I spot something else I hadn't noticed. A huge engagement ring.

Shit. I'm deluding myself. This thing I've been chasing in my dreams, this connection I even told my mom about, it's all in my head and all on my side. Her eyes follow mine to the ring on her finger.

"August," she whispers. "I can ex—"

"Guess I better get back in there, huh?" I cut over her harshly, addressing Sylvia.

"We *are* ready to start," Sylvia says uncertainly. "The kids are coming into the rec room now."

"Good." Without looking at Iris again, I head up the hall and into the rec room.

I'm an idiot. It's complicated? No, it's simple. She had his baby. She's wearing his ring. She's going to marry him. The sooner I get that through my thick skull, the better. I've lost enough pining over a girl who belongs to someone else. I've lost sleep and precious time.

I grimace at the pain arrowing up my leg from overuse today. I may have lost my career, my future, for something that doesn't exist. I'm going to shut down my disappointment and anger, board up my heart long enough to get through this talk, and then I'll put this fantasy away for good. I glance at the walls, plastered with motivational sayings and photos of famous role models. The community center has barely changed from when I balled here as a kid. The paint peels from the wall in places, and the hoops in the gym have seen better days. The best thing to dispose of a fantasy is a dose of reality, and this community will always remind you of what's real.

My family was middle class. My mom was a teacher and once my stepfather retired from the military, he was in sales. My home life was stable, but I was always trying to find my place. I felt like a cog that didn't fit in any wheel. A stray puzzle piece.

The best ballers in the city played pick-up games here. I wanted to be challenged and stretched, so I played here, too. I didn't expect to find lost pieces of myself on these courts; of the culture my father would have shared with me had he lived.

Basketball helped me find my place. Not number thirty-three, point guard, basketball champion, or All-American player. Those things aren't who I am. I'm more than that. This place helped *make* me more than that.

I compartmentalize, swallow the emotion seeing Iris's ring spurred in me, and look around the room, wall to wall with young faces—mostly black and brown. I remember what it was like to grow up here; the quest I was on, searching for my identity; feeling caught between worlds and comfortable nowhere. Many of these kids are struggling, too. Maybe not because they're biracial and wondering how to categorize themselves, but struggling to reconcile the harsh realities of their lives with the vastness of their dreams—with their impossible ambitions. I understand dreaming dreams that are too big and chasing a life that most never catch. Against all odds, I have that life and am living that dream.

"I'm not here to tell you how to become a professional basketball player," I start without preamble. "There are no guarantees, and most likely, none of you ever will make it to the NBA."

A few faces fall at this bit of reality, but I have their attention. With middle-schoolers, that's most of the battle. Iris walks in and takes a place at the back with the other two women here volunteering. Her sad eyes meet mine, but this time I look away. I'm not getting caught in that trap again.

"Even guys, *and girls*," I say with a smile at a few of the young ladies on the front row, "who have the talent don't always make the cut. Basketball is not the point. Dreaming is the point."

I risk the briefest glance in Iris's direction, and even with her shadowed eyes, she's the brightest, most beautiful thing I've ever seen.

"I know what it's like to want something you'll probably never have." Our eyes hold for the briefest moment before I tear mine away. "I understand the disappointment of someone saying you'll never be able to. Dream of something else. There are too many things that say you can't, so I'm here to say you can. Can what?"

I shrug, turning the corners of my mouth down. "Can whatever." I point to my leg. "How many of you saw the game when I went down?"

Hands go up. Sympathetic grimaces cross several faces.

"Yeah, it was tough. Something I worked for my whole life felt like it might be over in an instant. I've spent the time since my surgery reconciling myself to that possibility. What if basketball was over for me?"

I scan the rapt faces, finding an answering hunger and curiosity in so many.

"If that happens, I'm not gonna front like I wouldn't be messed up, because I would be." I pause for them to laugh, giving them a smile, too. "But I found my place here in this community center, at Saturday pick-up games, in summer league, and camps. This place, more than any other, taught me to reach for something more. I know things aren't always great at home. I know things don't always make sense at school. I even know that sometimes, you want to quit, because I wanted to a million times."

I slant them a wry grin. "Sometimes I still do, but I won't ever. This place taught me that. The counselors here and the students—the other dreamers." I point through the door and squint one eye. "My mom's house is about ten miles that way. This city is my home. I sat exactly where you're sitting years ago listening to someone tell me I could do whatever I wanted to do, even though my dream was unlikely."

I lift my leg a little, lift my jeans, making sure they can all see the Aircast. "I've decided I'm coming back stronger and faster than ever. I've decided I'll return sooner than everyone thinks I can and better than they expect me to be," I say. "While I was lying on my back with these pins in my leg and everyone speculating about my future, I decided that I wouldn't give up hope. Hope is the gap between what if and what is, but you have to fill that gap with a lot of hard work. And that's what we're going to talk about this week. Hope. Dreams. Work."

I glance at my watch and then to the pizzas Iris and the other two women are setting up at the back of the room. "I think your lunch is here. My time's up for today, but if you wanna talk, I'll be here for a few minutes while the food is being served."

I'm signing autographs and talking to the kids who gather around after my talk. I give them my full attention but sense Iris's eyes on me every once in a while. It's a heady feeling to be in the same room with her for this long, something I've wanted so I could test these sensations and see if they hold up under normal wear and tear. Now, it doesn't matter. Once she's another man's wife, these feelings aren't to hold up, but to be put down. And I'll start doing that today as ruthlessly as I'd approach an opponent on court. Only the opponent is me, because the stubborn part of me that never let me give up on my dream of playing in the NBA doesn't want me to give up on her either.

Sylvia and I are walking toward the exit, reviewing plans for the week. I'll talk, share some drills with those who play basketball, though I'm limited in what I can physically do, and participate in a beautification project in one of the rec rooms.

We're wrapping up when Iris calls my name.

She's walking toward us, her daughter on her hip. This isn't fair. *Both* of them? If you ever want a man to keep dreaming, give him a glimpse of what could be.

They could be mine.

A wave of misplaced possessiveness rolls through me. The thought of them returning to Caleb's house grinds my teeth together. The thought of

Iris in his bed is physically painful, clenching my gut. They're both Caleb's, and I covet them.

But one flash of that however-many-carat diamond on her finger reminds me how futile hope is.

When they reach us, Iris glances uncertainly from me to Sylvia and clears her throat.

"August, could I, um, speak to you before you go?" she asks, fixing her eyes on me and not straying to Sylvia.

"Sure," I say easily, like she and I talk every day. "See you tomorrow, Sylvia."

Sylvia interprets the comment as the dismissal it is and considers us speculatively before smiling, saying her goodbyes, and walking away.

"You need something?" I ask abruptly. "My ride's probably waiting."

She flinches at the impatience in my voice, and I feel like an asshole. Sarai wiggles on her hip and blinks at me with long, curly lashes. I bend until I'm level with Sarai and smile into her violet–blue eyes. I'll regret this, but the kid's as irresistible as her mother.

"She's gotten so big," I tell Iris but don't look away from the little girl staring back at me.

"Yeah." Iris laughs. Sarai's dark curls have grown longer since I last saw her, and Iris brushes them back from her face. "It's going too fast already."

Sarai reaches out and grabs a handful of my hair, pulling my face closer. It also brings me closer to Iris. I ignore the electric field our nearness creates and focus on Sarai. She drags her little hand over my eyes and nose, leaving a wet trail of exploration.

"Oh, God." Iris points to the wet patch I feel on my cheek. "She got you. I'm sorry."

When I allow myself to look at Iris again, the shadow is gone. Humor and affection light her eyes, for her daughter, maybe for me. If anything, she's more beautiful than the girl I met in the bar a few years ago. There's a strength, a maturity, a resolve—I don't know what has added dimension to what she was before, but it stirs a hunger in me. Not just to taste her body, but to know her heart. To read her mind and share her thoughts.

Fuck. I cannot make myself stop wanting this woman. And as Sarai flashes her little dimpled smile up at me, I want her in my life, too. I want too much. I want things I can't have, things that aren't mine, but that kid who showed up every Saturday before the community center doors opened, who was always the last to leave the court, he never learned to stop wanting impossible things.

The humor fades from Iris's eyes, the smile melts from her wide, sweet mouth, and she releases a ragged breath. She feels it, too. I don't have to ask if she does. Her widened eyes and stuttering breath, the answering jerk of awareness from her body to mine tell me. But too much stands between us: another man and the gaudy ring on her finger, circumstances I don't understand. We're separated by an incalculable distance, but she feels so close.

"I'm not engaged," she says softly, catching me off guard.

"What'd you say?" I glare at the ring on her left hand. "Then what does that ring mean?"

"Caleb asked me to marry him, but I haven't said yes." Her jaw flexes and her eyes ice over. "I don't plan to say yes, but he wants me to wear it for now—wants me to think about it."

"I don't get it." The more she reveals, the less I understand.

"I know, and I can't fully explain, but one day I will. I have to work this out on my own." She drops a kiss on Sarai's head resting on her shoulder. "Just know that she's the most important thing—securing Sarai's future is the most important thing."

"Securing her future? You mean money? Do you need money, because I can—"

"Please don't insult me. I'm not with Caleb for the money." A quick frown pleats her dark brows. "I mean, money is a factor, but not the way you might think."

If hope is the gap between what if and what is, her words, these few moments shorten that distance. I tentatively run a hand over Sarai's soft curls. She giggles and buries her head in Iris's shoulder, shyly peeking back out at me. God, these two could tie me in a knot with their hands behind their backs. Effortlessly.

"I better go." Iris looks at her watch, her eyes wide and panicked. "My ride's probably waiting, too."

"You didn't drive?" I walk beside her, holding the door open so she can pass ahead of me.

She glances across the street and up the sidewalk in the direction of a large black SUV. Her eyes go wide and she swallows, looking back to me.

"Don't walk with . . .You don't need to walk with us. We'll be fine. My ride's here."

She swings her head back to look at the SUV once more before flashing me a quick smile and wave.

"I gotta go," she repeats. "See you tomorrow."

Before I can reply, she dashes across the street. A huge body-builder looking guy steps out and helps her and Sarai into the back seat. He stares at me once they're inside, his presence like a threat—like a warning. He makes me want to snatch Iris and Sarai away from him. I stand there frozen, feeling helplessly protective until the red taillights disappear around the corner.

"Gus!"

I turn toward the only person who calls me that. Jared is parked a few feet away. I'm still not driving much, so he dropped me off.

I tap the hood of his low-slung sports car. "Dude, you're such a poser." I laugh and slide into the front seat, careful of my throbbing leg.

"You're just jealous of my whip," Jared replies.

"The fact that you used the word 'whip' in an actual conversation makes my point."

We share a grin, but Jared's ebbs as quickly as it appeared. "Was that who I think it was?" he asks, never one to pull punches. "Walking out with you? The chick with the kid?"

"Who?" I conveniently find something outside my window fascinating. "Was that who?"

"Cut the shit. That was Caleb's girlfriend, Iris DuPree, wasn't it?"

I swivel a curious look around to him. "How do you know Iris?"

"I interviewed her maybe two years ago for an internship," he says. "She's sharp."

"Yeah, she is. Why didn't you give her a job then?"

"Because at the end of the interview, she threw up all over me." Jared's grin is rueful. "She found out she was pregnant. I offered her a job, but by then she was on bed rest and couldn't work. I believe she was on bed rest almost the entire pregnancy."

Pregnant. Unable to work or earn money. Confined to the bed for months. No wonder she said she'd had hard choices to make. It sounds like she did the only thing she could do—stay with Caleb.

It infuriates me. She barely knew me. Of course, she wouldn't have turned to me, but I wish she had. I would have done anything to keep her free of him.

"Please tell me this hasn't all been about her. Tell me you didn't provoke Caleb and jeopardize your career, a thirty-million-dollar contract for some chick?"

"Some chick?" I lift one eyebrow. "You must not remember her if you think she's just some chick."

"I do remember her. I know how she looks." Jared shows his disgust in the scrunch of his brows. "You sound whipped. I assumed it was just pussy."

"Watch your mouth, Jared," I snap and point a warning finger at him.

"I didn't mean any disrespect, but damn. She lives with Caleb. They have a kid together. It's really inconvenient if you have a *thing* for her, Gus."

"We're friends." I rebuke him with a glare. "And don't call me Gus."

Jared knows I hate the childhood nickname and uses it to get on my nerves. I have enough on my nerves without adding him.

"So this dirty play was about Iris?" Jared asks. "I saw her at the game with her daughter."

"Yeah, I saw her, too."

"Doing rehab here in Maryland—that isn't about her, is it?" Jared shakes his head, not waiting for my answer. "And now you're conveniently volunteering with her."

I tip my head back into the soft leather of the headrest, answering with only a sigh.

Jared bangs a fist into the steering wheel. "Dammit, August. What part of 'keep the hell away from my girl' do you not understand? What's Caleb gonna have to break next for you to get the message?"

I snap narrowed eyes over to him. "I'd like to see that motherfucker try to break something else." I adjust my seat, leaning back, worn out from the few hours at the community center. "There's more going on than meets the eye. She's wearing his ring, but she tells me they're not engaged."

"Maybe she's playing you both. The only thing better than having one rich man strung out on you is having two."

"Shut the hell up. If you've met Iris, you know she's not like that."

"She seemed like a nice girl. Driven. Bright. Sharp. I wanted her on my team," Jared admits. "That doesn't mean she's not trouble."

"Well if she's trouble, it's trouble I want to get into," I tell him, defiance in the look I level at him from the passenger seat. "She made sure I knew she wasn't engaged for a reason. She doesn't want me to give up."

"But you should."

"But I won't." I shake my head. "You don't get it."

"What I *get* is that because of your preoccupation with Caleb's baby mama, your leg is broken, your career is up in the air, your team may trade your ass, and everything you've worked for your whole life is in jeopardy. For some pussy."

"It's not like that. She—"

"Oh, so you don't want to fuck her?"

Of course, I want to fuck her. What am I? A eunuch?

"Not *just* that." I try to stop it, but my lips twitch at the corners.

"It's not funny," Jared says, but when I look over at him, his lips are twitching, too. We both give in and chuckle.

It gets quiet while we zip through the familiar streets. So many Saturdays through the years he brought me to the community center in his beat-up Camry. We talked about my far-fetched dream of playing in the NBA. Of him managing the biggest names in sports. Of how we'd sit on top of the world together.

Now, we're in his Porsche. I'm a baller, a brand with one of the highest-selling jerseys in the league. One of the fattest contracts a rookie's ever gotten. And I'd risk it all for a girl? I know what he means, but I want more than basketball. I want a life beyond that. I'm not saying that life is with Iris, but I *am* saying I've never felt with anyone else what I feel with her, and I have to chase that as hard as I chased basketball. What I felt today, what I've felt every time I've been with her, it's real and it's special. It's worth chasing. If I don't try, I'll always wonder.

What if the thing that seems like an impossible dream is within my grasp?

TWENTY SEVEN

IRIS

I shouldn't have told HIM I WASN'T ENGAGED.

It's selfish and reckless to encourage August. At least until I get out from under Caleb. At some point, I know I'll have to ask someone for help, but it will be at the right time when I have the tools not only to escape from Caleb, but to *keep* him out of our lives. Until I have that, I should be so careful about every step I take, and indulging myself, my yearning for what I see in August's eyes and feel in his touch . . . It's anything but careful. If Caleb is capable of half the things I think he is, recklessness could get August hurt even more than he already has been.

But August's expression when he saw Caleb's ring . . . Devastation? Betrayal? Disappointment? Defeat? It was all those things on one handsome face. And maybe it was the defeat I hated most—the thought that he would give up on whatever it is that blooms between us like a flower, opening up a little more each time we're together.

I can stand back and objectively say it shouldn't feel this powerful, whatever is between us. We haven't spent that much time together, but from that first night, August felt like a milestone in my life. Like a turning point—like a hinge parts of my future swung on. And if he gives up, we'll never know what we could be when all the obstacles are gone. When Caleb doesn't stand between us.

"Two hours," Ramone says from the front seat, his stony stare a warning in the rearview mirror. "I'll be back in two hours."

It's unnecessary, Ramone's abrupt reminder that time at the community center is merely a furlough from my prison. I'm at the house every night alone, and it's bliss compared to how it is when Caleb's there. But I'm lonely, and I felt it most starkly last night after seeing August. Time with him resurrected my senses and summoned butterflies in my stomach I thought were long dead.

Without responding to Ramone, I climb out of the back seat and load Sarai into her stroller. I don't look at him once before I start across the street and enter the community center.

Ms. Audrey takes Sarai with a gentle smile, and Sarai is crawling around with the other babies before I'm even out of sight. The socialization is good for her. I wish there were more opportunities for that, but Caleb won't hear of it, much less pay for it. That would leave too many factors out of his control.

Torrie and Shelia are already in the rec room when I arrive. Today, I made a little more effort, wearing black wide-legged linen pants and a pink and black sleeveless top. My hair is down my back, freshly washed. My makeup is simple but heavier than it was yesterday. In other words, I *tried*. As much as I may not want to admit it, knowing August would be here today, I tried. It must be evident because Torrie and Shelia both raise their brows when I walk in.

"Mmmm-mmm-mmmph." Torrie flicks the large gold hoop in my ear. "Oh, you fancy, huh?"

Shelia looks up from the board games she's setting out for the kids to play when they return from the gym.

"Little upgrade, I see," Sheila adds. "Is this for us or for Mr. Rookie of the Year?"

I force a disdainful laugh. "August and I barely know each other." I make myself meet their eyes directly.

"Looked like you knew *something*," Torrie says, "the way he ran out of here after you, and y'all were all booed up."

Reckless. Careless. I have to do better today. "Nope. Nothing to it." I consider the table filled with games. "So are we playing games after August talks with them?"

"Oh, he's with them now in the gym overseeing some drills," Shelia says, looking at me slyly. "He'll probably leave after that so looks like you got all dressed up for nothing."

"I wouldn't call this dressed up . . ." Her words sink in, and disappointment follows. I don't even bother finishing my denial.

So I won't see August today. It's for the best.

I'm still convincing myself of that when the kids pour in, sweaty and laughing, from the gym. I put on a bright smile and serve the bagged lunches they'll eat before the games start.

I'm passing out Gatorades when a deep rumble of laughter raises the hairs on my arms. I snap my head around, searching for the source. August sits on one of the tables, one foot on the bench and his injured leg stretched out in its cast. He laughs at something with the kids clustered around him and throws his head back. His hair is longer than I've ever seen it, and with those dark, caramel-kissed curls, his skin, bronze melded with gold, and his teeth flashing white in the strong planes of his face, I literally cannot take my eyes

217

off him.

I'll give myself three seconds to look at him.

One.

Two.

And then he looks up, and our eyes hold. I'd love to pretend this is casual. Friends with a dash of attraction. Slightly forbidden, but mostly harmless. There's an undeniable truth, though, when my eyes connect with his. When our eyes meet, it isn't casual. He and I together are mayhem. When he looks at me, I can't pretend otherwise.

I turn away before Torrie and Shelia pay even closer attention, and walk over to the game table and pretend to arrange UNO and Monopoly and Taboo.

"You like board games?"

I jump at his question, dropping a deck of cards all over the floor and at August's feet.

"Ugh." I sink to my knees to gather them. "Such a klutz."

He squats awkwardly, scooping up cards.

"August, no! Your leg."

I grab his arm and carefully coax him upright, which brings our bodies almost flush. When he looks down at me, his stare mirrors the feelings, the desire pulsing through my body. That stare is hot and hungry and curious. It wonders how I taste. Asks how I'd feel crushed against him. It imagines a first kiss I'm not sure we'll ever have.

"You look pretty today." His words are polite enough, but the air between us is thick and carnal. One wrong word could slice right through it.

"Thank you. I . . ." I encounter Sylvia's inquiring eyes just beyond his shoulder. I turn my head and collide glances with Torrie and Shelia. "Why is everyone watching us?"

August casts a discreet look from the corner of his eye, and the dark line of his brows falls.

"I think they see the same thing Caleb saw at the game that night." He surreptitiously links our pinky fingers. "They see I can't stay away from you. That I don't want to."

"August." I reluctantly untangle our fingers, sweeping the room to see who might still be watching. Everyone seems to have found other things to occupy their attention, but we should separate. "I'm gonna go restock the drinks. I'll see you later."

He catches my elbow and bends to whisper in my ear, "Meet me on the basketball court once they start playing games."

I shake my head and scoot away as quickly as I can because that's the smart thing to do, but I already know I'll find a way.

We're cleaning up after lunch while the kids play games when Torrie broaches the subject I have no desire to discuss.

"So, you and August West," she says, pulling a bag from the trash can. "You know each other?"

I don't glance up from the sink of suds and the few dishes there were to wash.

"Not really." I give her my most innocent smile. "I mean, the way everyone else knows him. That he's a great player."

"You two should get on the same page." She laughs and shakes her head. "'Cause he's not even trying to fake it, and you're not very good at it."

My hands go still over the steamy water.

"I don't know what you mean." I look at her, clear-eyed, before I pick up a dish towel to dry the dishes.

"Oh, don't feel bad," she says "Not with his fine ass. His nose is wide open for you, girl. Stevie Wonder could see that."

"Wow. That's not exactly politically correct." I feel guilty for the giggle that slips past my lips despite the inappropriateness of her humor.

"I'm not very good at beating around the bush," she says, her expression going from uncertain to defiant to don't give a damn. "Get yours, Iris, because Caleb is definitely getting his."

The mere mention of Caleb's name runs my blood cold. He won't be back from China until next week, but I still feel the specter of him like an ill-intentioned ghost haunting me, dogging my every step.

"Look, guys talk." She grimaces. "At least, mine does—to me he does. He's not exactly your fiancé's biggest fan."

Neither am I.

I don't volunteer a word or even a breath that might stop her.

"He says people have no idea who Caleb really is." Torrie lays a hand over mine, and the smile she offers me is kind. Her fingers brush the very wrist that only a few weeks ago Caleb fractured. I've had so little kindness, so few gentle touches lately, that hers pricks tears behind my eyes.

"Don't feel guilty if you and August West have a . . . a moment this week." She gives me a direct look before going on. "At first, I thought you might be a little boogey, but you're alright. If it was me, I'd want someone to tell me so I'm telling you. He cheats on you left and right. Sticks his dick in anything that moves."

I know Caleb cheats, but for him to be so blatant that even the other girlfriends know is galling. It's not enough he humiliates me in private. He has to make a laughing stock of me publically, too. I don't give a damn if he cheats, but I'm nauseated over how he's exposed me. He rapes me at gunpoint and won't even use a condom. God, what might I have? An STD? Worse? Resentment and hatred boil under my skin.

"Excuse me." I toss the dish towel onto the linoleum counter and turn to leave. At the door, I look back over my shoulder to meet the sympathy in her eyes. "Thanks, Torrie."

She nods and turns away to finish dumping the trash. Rage and bitterness descend like a haze over me, and I'm stumbling down the hall. I tell myself I don't mean to wander into the gym, but that's a lie.

August shoots from several feet beyond the three-point line. He releases the ball, and it falls through the net.

"Show-off," I say softly from the gym door, but with only the two of us present, he hears.

A smile spreads slowly over his full lips and calm eyes the color of storm clouds.

"If I'm such a show-off . . ." He bounces the ball to me, and I catch it on reflex. ". . . come show me you can do better."

I dribble the ball to the center of the court, turning my back on him to release it. It swooshes through the net, and I face him, wearing a braggart's grin.

"Luck," he says, catching the ball when I bounce-pass it back to him. "You ever played HORSE?"

A disdainful breath is my only answer.

"Alright then." He laughs and tosses the ball back to me. "Ladies first."

For the next twenty minutes, he kicks my ass at HORSE so bad that by the end, I'm waving my arms in front of him when it's his turn to shoot. Anything so he won't keep making the shots.

"You don't guard in HORSE," he reminds me with a one-sided grin that has my heart double-dutching in my chest. "There's no defense."

"No defense, huh?" I ask. "No wonder you're so good at it."

"Ohhhh." He sticks an imaginary dagger in his heart. "Still busting my balls about playing D. I've gotten better. At least gimme that."

"There's always room for improvement." I laugh at the look on his face. He was the Rookie of the Year. His ego can withstand a little ball-busting.

He goes to shoot, and I grab his arm, making the ball fly wildly across the gym. I'm laughing, feeling freer than I have in months, maybe since before Sarai was born, when his hands land at my hips and he pulls me into him.

My smile vanishes. So does his. His broad palms burn through the thin material of my pants. My lungs feel shrunken because my breaths are so

221

shallow; quick, urgent pulls that lift my breasts against his broad chest. The air around us heats and caramelizes until it's thick and rich and sweet and dark—until I can almost taste it.

"I've been wearing this cast a long time," he whispers, inching his fingers up my neck and into my hair. "There's this one spot that itches so bad, but it's in a place that I can never quite reach."

With his eyes, he follows the line his thumb strokes down my neck, and every breath I draw tastes like him. The scent of him this close is inescapable, infiltrating. His body, hardened and towering over me, is all I can see. He bends to press our foreheads together.

"Have you ever had an itch you couldn't scratch?" he asks. The question hovers over my lips, and I shudder. His hands tighten on me, and our breaths clash between our open mouths.

I shake my head no, my eyes so heavy with desire, I want to close them, but I can't look away.

"It itches so bad, it starts to burn." His fingers spread over me, his hands so big he covers the space just under my breasts to my hips.

"That itch becomes the center of everything," August continues. "You can't focus on anything except the way it burns and that you can't reach it, can't touch it."

I lean into him, limp and seduced by his words, by the scorching intensity of this moment.

"You're my itch, Iris," he confesses. His breath labored, he tips up my chin, so I see the desperation in his eyes. "And if you don't step back right now, I have to scratch."

Do it.

The dare bounces around inside my head like the ball I'm supposed to be chasing. I want it—want his kiss hard against my lips, and his hands gentle and persuasive on my body, but I have too much to lose.

Sarai.

My life.

Everything.

And as alive as I feel, as on fire as I am for what his eyes promise, I can't risk it all. I can't risk any of it.

Wordlessly, I step back, staring at him for a few seconds before I turn to retrieve the ball, breaking the heated current flowing from me to him.

When I return, he's massaging his knee. Guilt stabs me. As if I haven't cost him enough already, I was this close to jeopardizing him even more. I dribble back to the center of the floor where he stands, watching me unsmilingly. I toss him the ball, which he catches, palms with one hand, and tucks under his arm.

"I should go," I say, but I don't head for the gym exit.

He steps closer, leaving a few inches between us.

"You probably should," he agrees, taking my wrist between his fingers and pulling me closer. "But you won't. Not yet. You have another twenty minutes before you have to pick up Sarai."

I don't speak, but remain quiet while we study one another. He brushes hair behind my ear, and it reminds me of how Caleb likes to do that with his pistol. I shiver at the memory of Caleb's cruelty. I shiver with the pleasure of August's touch.

"So how's Lotus?" he finally asks, attempting a segue to some kind of safe conversation. "Your cousin?"

I turn surprised eyes up to meet his. "You remember me telling you about her?"

His eyes caress my face. There's no other way to describe it, really. It's a look that kisses my cheeks and makes my lips tingle.

"Iris, I remember everything about the night we met."

I've had to barricade my spirit against Caleb's harshness. My only soft spot has been Sarai. I've reserved tenderness only for her, but August keeps . . . softening me. He keeps knocking on doors I want to keep locked. His words jangle on a ring of keys that persist in opening me up.

"Yeah. It was a great night." I blink and drop my eyes to the scuffed court floor. "It felt like I'd known you for years."

His finger under my chin tips my face back up so I have to look at him. "For me, too." He smiles and lowers his hand from my face, taking warmth and comfort with it. "So Lotus. How is she?"

"Well, I haven't really, um . . ." I stumble to talk about the person who's always been closer to me than any other. "That is to say, we haven't spoken in a long time."

"For real?" He frowns and studies my face. "I'm surprised. You talked about her so much that night. It sounded like you guys were inseparable."

"We were." I clear my throat. "We are, or at least I hope we will be again. We had a falling out. Disagreed about something. You know how it is."

I hope my shrug seems careless, but I care so much that there's a huge void in my heart where Lotus belongs. I can't wait until it's safe enough to bring her back into my space. Right now, my life isn't a safe place.

"We'll get back," I say. "It's not our first time being separated."

"Yeah, you said she lived with your great-grandmother when you moved to Atlanta, right?"

Even though he said he remembers everything from that night, I'm still surprised.

"Yeah, she stayed with MiMi."

I take the ball from him and shoot, doing a little victory dance when it goes in and tossing it back to him.

"Now who's showing off?" he asks with a grin. "So your MiMi. What's she like?"

"Well she's in her nineties." I pause, considering what I know, debating what to share and deciding I want to shock him. "She was a voodoo high priestess."

He freezes, the ball poised over his head to shoot, and gives me a disbelieving look. "A what? Did you say voodoo?"

I laugh at his dumbfounded expression.

"It's not like in the movies or anything. They were the most respected people in the community back in the day. Politicians and powerful people from all over the state came to them for advice and guidance." I shoot him a wry grin. "By the time I was born, she just made healing potions and did cleansing ceremonies, made gris-gris."

"What's a gris-gris? Or do I want to know?"

"It's like a talisman for protection." I twist Caleb's ring on my finger. "She gave Lotus and me rings years ago that were supposed to protect us."

He studies the engagement ring. "And where's yours?" he asks softly.

"Lost." I swallow the emotion burning my throat, the tears threatening to fall at the sudden sense of loss overtaking me. I've lost Lotus. I haven't spoken to my mother in months. My self-respect, my dignity, my independence—all stolen from me before I'd even realized Caleb was a thief. If I keep standing here thinking about all I've lost, I'll cry, so I change the subject and hope August lets me get away with it.

"I get my name from the bayou," I say with a slight smile. "Well, Mama told me that once. Who knows if it's true. She said MiMi's house is off the bayou, not far from the water, and all along the water's edge these flowers called Louisiana irises grow."

"She told you?" he asks. "You've never seen for yourself?"

I frown, feeling loss again, but for something I've never really had. "I haven't been. Not that I remember, at least." I grimace. "Mama took me when I was a baby so MiMi could see me, but that was it. MiMi visited us a few times in the city. Lotus knows her a lot better, since she lived with her."

"Iris, Lotus," he says with a smile. "I see a flower theme. Are you two a lot alike?"

My laugh is self-deprecating, scoffing at my own weakness compared to Lotus's fearlessness. "I wish." I take the ball and step behind the three-point line. "I'm nowhere near as strong as Lotus."

"You're probably stronger than you think." He raises a dark brow at the ball in my hands. "But not strong enough to make that three."

"Oh yeah? You think you're the only one who can make a long shot?"

I turn to the goal and train every bit of strength and focus I have into the ball in my hands and its trajectory to the goal. When I release it, I close my eyes and don't open them until I hear the "swoosh" of the net.

"I made it?" I ask with an incredulous laugh.

"You didn't even look? Yeah, you made it. How can you not look?"

"Woohooo!" I lift my arms Rocky-style and face him. "Am I ready for the pros?"

The look he gives me alternates between affection and indulgence. "You can be on my team."

"Oh." I lob a smile up at him, much too close to flirting. "And what position will I play on your team?"

His smile melts a little around the edges, and his eyes lose some of their humor. "At the five-spot," he says softly.

The five-spot? His position is the point guard, or the one-spot. Shooting guard is the two. The three is small forward, and the four is power forward. The five is . . .

"Center," he says, linking our fingers and toying with the hair hanging on my shoulder. "If you were mine, Iris, there would be no doubt what position you'd hold in my life. You'd be center. I'd play you at the five."

I want to laugh. I want to cry. I want to sing hallelujah that a man like this exists and that I know him. A deep-seeded longing springs up inside of me, and I'm not sure when I'll be able to give in to it. I long to let him hold me. To let myself hold him, have him. I drop my forehead to his chest and take in his scent and the intoxicating nearness of him. He strokes my hair, and I feel his lips ghost the top of my head.

The door swinging open startles us apart. Sylvia stands at the gym entrance, looking between us before settling on me.

"Sorry to, um, interrupt," she says. "But there's a man looking for you, Iris. Quite insistently actually. He—"

She stops when Ramone appears at her side, as unyielding and intimidating as a brick wall. Panic rushes the air from my body and pounds the blood in my ears.

"I have to go." I take two steps toward the door, but August's hand gently restrains me.

"Who is that guy?" he demands.

I can practically feel Ramone's narrow gaze lasered in on August's hand touching me. Damning information for his report to Caleb, no doubt. This is only making things worse. What an idiot I've been, playing games in here with August and forgetting that I live in a war zone. That I'm fighting for my life, and Sarai's.

"He's my driver, August." I jerk my arm away and walk swiftly across the gym floor, not looking back.

When I reach the door, Ramone stares at August for a few seconds before following me into the hall. I run to the daycare to get Sarai.

I'm pushing the stroller to the exit when August appears. His confusion, displeasure, and concern are all soldered together into one stare that burns holes in my back. I don't acknowledge him, but walk past with my baby and my watchdog. I walk past with indifference, as if we didn't just share the best afternoon I've had in as long as I can remember—as if he hadn't gotten past the guard I'd erected around my heart for my own protection.

I don't even say goodbye.

TWENTY EIGHT

AUGUST

It doesn't make sense. Yesterday was like the first night Iris and I met all over again—laughing, teasing, opening up. The attraction sometimes lurking just beneath the skin of our conversation, sometimes shivering across its surface. And then Muscle Head showed up, and she shut down and rushed from the building without a word.

And today? Still no words. She hasn't looked at me. Hasn't spoken or even acknowledged that I exist.

By all rights, I shouldn't even be here for the community center beautification project. Sylvia told me I wasn't needed. The students are painting the rec room, and Torrie, Shelia, and Iris are helping. Iris paints a wall across the room and wears dark denim overalls and Chuck Taylors. Her hair is in a messy bun, and the work lends a glow to the soft curve of her cheeks. She looks like a little girl.

She bends, stretching the denim across the fullness of her ass.

Maybe not a little girl.

I'm a guy. I can't be expected to ignore how good her ass looks in those jeans. But it's not the most important thing. We only have two days left, and after spending even the little time with her that I've had, I know things can't go back to the way they were. Us having no contact. Her living with Caleb, sleeping with Caleb. Her staying with Caleb is not an option anymore, and I need to hear her say that, promise that. I need her to explain what the problem is, so I can fix it.

How hard can it be to leave him? How complicated can it be to choose me over him? To throw his damn ring in his face and walk away?

She said she wasn't with him for the money. Or not the way I might think, whatever the hell that means.

And I believe that. I may not know everything about her, but she's no gold digger.

I know she sees him clearly. She said herself it was a dirty play.

She says she's not marrying him, but she's wearing his ring.

What the fuck is going on?

I'm not leaving today without answers. I won't get them with her avoiding me, so I walk over to the wall the three women are painting.

"Iris, can I talk to you for a minute?" I pitch my voice low so we don't draw more attention than I already do here.

She jumps like a bullet whizzed past her ear instead of a whisper. A wide, quick glance is all she offers before training her eyes back on the wall.

"I'm really trying to get this wall done," she says. "I . . . um, maybe later."

I sneak a look at Torrie and Shelia. They roll their painting pins over the wall, but they're watching us.

"It'll only take a few minutes." I cover her hand to stop the rolling motion, and she looks at me with a frown. "Please."

Her eyes dart from Shelia and Torrie to Sylvia in the corner before she sighs and places the paint roller in the pan at her feet. Wordlessly, she heads toward the door, not checking to see if I'm behind her. Of course, I am.

In the hall, she leans against the wall and folds her arms, still not looking at me. "What do you need to talk abo—"

Her words disintegrate when I grab her hand and pull her behind me down the hall and around the corner.

"What are you doing?" Her voice climbs an octave, and she tries to wriggle free. "I can't do this. I need to get back in there."

We reach a utility closet. Fortunately, the knob turns easily, and the door swings open. I gently shove her inside and follow, turning on the light. I lean my back against the door and fold my arms across my chest. We aren't leaving until I get some answers. Not the cryptic ones she's been giving me, but the straight kind that tell me what the hell is actually going on.

"I need to get back, August." She reaches around me for the knob, but I shift so my back covers it. Her irritated eyes latch onto mine. "This isn't funny. You have to let me out."

"No, you have to talk to me. You've been avoiding me ever since that goon showed up yesterday." I take her arm, extended toward the knob, and pull her into me. The whisper of our bodies together, that simple contact, even through our clothes, is a match lit in gasoline-soaked air. It's a sweet singe—a rapid-burning brush fire spreading across my whole body, consuming everything in its path—my reservations, my good sense, and my patience.

"You feel that, Iris." I bend to float my words over her ear, rustling the fine strands of hair escaping around her neck. "Please tell me you feel this, too. Tell me I'm not fooling myself that we'll be good together."

A sigh mists her pouty lips. Lashes, thick and midnight-dark, hide her eyes from me. Defeat marks the slumped line of her shoulders.

"You're not fooling yourself," she admits, her voice shaking.

"I know I'm not." My hand slides over her arm, and her skin prickles with goosebumps. I stroke her palm with my fingertips, and she inhales sharply. Her lips tremble. Slowly, I twist the ring, working it off her finger and slipping it into the front pocket of her overalls.

"What are you doing?" She breathes the question, her eyelids heavy over the cloudy passion hazing her eyes.

I frame her face, tracing the striking framework of high, sculpted cheekbones.

"I'll be damned if you'll be wearing his ring the first time I kiss you."

I stroke her lips with my thumbs until her mouth falls open on a needy gasp. I dip so our mouths are mere inches apart, our ragged breaths twining in the tight space. My fingers spear into her hair, my palm cupping the base of her skull.

"I should have done this the night we met," I whisper into her mouth, my head spinning from breathing her air. "It should have been me, Iris."

Her eyes squeeze shut and a tear slides over her cheek. "I know." She bites her lip and nods. "It should've been you."

I outline the bow of her lip with my tongue, and we share our first moan. My hand slides under the overalls, caressing her back through the fitted cotton T-shirt. Tracing the curve of her hip and sliding down to touch the small of her back, I press her into me. She must feel my dick, swollen against her. I can't hide it. I've wanted her too long and too badly.

I capture the fullness of her bottom lip between mine and suck hard and greedily. God, she's so sweet. My dreams, fantasies, everything I imagined is ashes beside the sweetness of this mouth, the taut, rounded curves of this body. She tilts her head and returns the favor, suckling my bottom lip.

"Fuck, Iris." I bend my knees, both hands sliding down to her ass. "I haven't been able to look anywhere else all day. Only at you."

Her hands map the muscles in my arms and chest, her eyes closed as if she's reading my body by Braille. She tips up on her toes, her fingers burrowing into my hair. With my arms under her butt, I lift her off the floor, closing the gap between our heights, and nibble around her mouth.

"Open for me," I rasp over her lips. I won't take anything from her. Every kiss, every touch, has to be freely given so I know she's with me and she wants this. I need to know that even with Caleb's ring nestled in her pocket, she wants *me*.

She leans in, her mouth open and seeking and eager, but I hold back a little, slowing it down, savoring our first kiss. I lick gently into her mouth, skating my tongue across her teeth, lashing the sweet, slick walls of her jaw.

"August, oh God." Her arms circle my neck and she wraps her legs around my waist. "Dammit, kiss me."

And I lose it. Every scrap of restraint it's taken for me to stand by and watch her with him evaporates. This kiss is now years past due, and I'm desperate for it. So desperate I turn her against the closet wall and dive into her mouth, a dying man on his last gasp. My hands filter through the silky mass of loosened hair spilling around her shoulders. Our tongues wrap and wrestle, tangled in the wet heat of our mouths. I'm sucking her tongue and licking the roof of her mouth, my teeth biting, my lips begging.

"Oh, God. Oh, God," she whispers over and over, a prayer between kisses. "Don't stop. August, don't stop."

I run my nose back and forth along her neck, and then my lips ghost the satiny skin. With broad strokes of my tongue and greedy pulls of my mouth, I make love to the delicate tendon in her throat until she whimpers. My lips wander over the fragile slash of her collarbone. I fumble with the buttons on her overalls. Every button I undo, undoes me. The front flap falls, and her nipples show through the tight T-shirt, straining and budded. I step back, and her legs drop from my waist. She stands and, mindful of my leg, I sink to my knees in front of her. My palms flatten at her back, drawing her closer, drawing her down to me. She looks at me, her mouth open, panting her anticipation. I suckle one tight nipple through her T-shirt, through her bra, never releasing our stare. The intimacy of our eyes locked together while I roll her nipple over my tongue is almost unbearable. It hardens my dick, and penetrates my bones, and arrests my heart.

Her head falls back, and her fingers slide through my hair in rhythm with my mouth drawing on her breast. Her tiny gasps punctuate the air grown sultry with our kisses.

"Iris." My fingers wait on the last button at her hips holding the denim in place. "Can I?"

"August, you're gonna get me . . ." She doesn't finish that thought but traps her bottom lip between her teeth and nods.

When the overalls slide to the floor, I realize I've only seen her legs once, in that short skirt the night of the NCAA Championship. She's thicker now, after having Sarai. God, I love it. Her legs are long and toned and shapely, and her hips and ass curve dramatically from the narrowness of her waist.

"You're perfect." I nudge her T-shirt up with my nose, dipping my tongue into her belly button and leaving kisses above the waistband of her panties.

There's a mark, almost like a smudge on the otherwise unblemished skin. I thumb it gently and look up at her.

"What happened here?" I ask, concern pulling my brows together.

"Nothing." Her gaze drifts to the side before meeting mine again, and I must have imagined the flash of panic, because she's composed when she looks back to me. "I was just moving a few heavy things and got nicked by one. It was over a week ago, so it's fading. No big deal."

I caress the mark again and place my lips there, brushing my tongue back and forth over the stretch of silky skin at her waist. God, how many nights did I wonder how she would taste? How her skin would feel under my lips? Now I know she tastes like heaven and feels likes satin.

"What are you doing?" she asks, her breath growing ragged.

I look up to catch her heavy-lidded stare and smile. "Kissing it better."

Something flickers over her expression. I can't identify it, but it looks like longing. Like the longing that wracks me right now also tears at her.

Her fingers dig into my scalp. She bends to kiss along my hairline, angling my head and trailing her lips over my eyelashes, my nose, my cheekbones.

"I'm tired of resisting you," she whispers.

"Then stop." I slip my thumbs into the waistband of her panties, tugging until the curve of her hipbones and the arch of her ass are visible. "Don't."

I slide her panties down. They pool inside the overalls around her ankles. Her pussy is bare, the lips plump and wet. I smell how much she wants me. I'm drunk on this scent, reeling with this sensation, mesmerized by the sight of her. I run my nose along her pubic bone and slide lower. I separate the lips, open her up to reveal her clit, glistening and plump like a cherry. "Jesus, Iris."

I pull it between my lips and feel her response like a shock wave running from her core and through her limbs. My fingers stretch her open wider, my whole mouth gaped wide and covering as much of her pussy as I can, and I'm consumed with the taste and texture of her most intimate parts. She steps fully out of the overalls and panties, leaving only her T-shirt, and I pull her legs onto my shoulders, leaning her back into the wall for support so I can feast sloppily, my chin, lips, and nose dampened with the nectar dripping from her body.

Urgently, I grip her ass and press her legs as wide as they'll go on my shoulders. Thoroughly, my tongue sweeps from bottom to top, not missing a drop. I suck the lips, bite her clit, eat her out like a man devouring his first meal. And all the while, she rocks into my face, her hips a metronome for our lust, her hands caging my skull, timing her grunts with the bobbing of my head between her legs.

"August." My name rides her breath. "Oh, God. So good. So good."

Her legs tighten around my head and tremble on my shoulders. I glance up to see her go stiff, her back arching, her mouth open on a silent scream, tears trickling down her face. And if I never see another woman come, that's fine with me. If I could just watch this one in the eye of her storm, in this crisis of her pleasure, it would be enough. God, for the rest of my life, it would be enough. The look on her face is wondrous, as if she's suspended between realities, has wandered into a fantasy and is drowning in this rapture.

She's coming down, the frantic thrusts melting into a languorous roll of her hips. Her eyes heavy-lidded, her limbs limp, her smile slow and sated. Her fingers comb through my messy curls, and she rubs her thumbs over my lips with the casual possessiveness of a lover even though I haven't been inside her yet. Sex is a formality. One I want very badly, but true intimacy we already have. It shimmers in the air around us, and I've never felt more content.

Heavy footsteps stomp down the hall outside the door, and a deep voice, tight with anger, rumbles beyond the closet. Iris jerks at the sound, one leg sliding off my shoulder.

"What was . . . who . . .?" Her panic-stretched eyes lock with mine. "I think I heard Caleb."

"Nah, he's still in China, right?"

I roll my palm over the tight curve of her thigh. Even hearing his name after what we shared feels wrong. She can't go back to him. She needs to explain all the mystery and walk away from him. I know it has something to do with Sarai, but no judge would award him full custody. He's an asshole, but I guess even he's entitled to see his child. We can work out the details, but Iris can't be part of that package anymore.

"Iris, can we talk about what just happened?"

"I have to go." She stands, scrambling to pull up her panties and fasten the overalls. She hastily pulls the ring from the front pocket and slips it back onto her finger.

Hell, no.

"Wait." I pull myself up, wincing at the sharp pain in my knee and taking her carefully by the shoulders. "Are you going back to him? After that? You . . . you can't."

"August." She clenches her eyes shut and runs a trembling hand over her loosened hair. "I have to. You don't understand."

"No, I don't." I snap, my forehead crumpling into a frown. "Explain it to me."

"I can't. Not right now." She looks at the door and back to me. "I think I heard him, August. I have to go."

Anger and frustration burn twin trails of acid in my belly.

"Whatever," I bite out. "I'm sure you're being paranoid, but do what you think you need to do."

I step aside and wrench open the closet door. And outside in the hall, standing there like he just ascended from hell, stands Caleb, his eyes a murderous blue as they slide from me to the woman we both want.

TWENTY NINE

IRIS

If looks could kill . . .

That's how the saying goes. Caleb doesn't have to leave it to a look. I've seen what he can do with his hands. I know the sting of his belt, his shoe, or whatever is at his disposal. If we were alone right now I think he'd find a way to kill me with a Q-tip.

But we're not alone. August stands behind me and Sarai is ahead, blinking sleepily at me from her father's shoulder.

"What a surprise," Caleb drawls, his eyes icy. "You just can't stay away, can you, West?"

August isn't touching me, but the very air stiffens. These two men hate each other. I'm only part of their mutual abhorrence, but I'm the part standing between them right now.

"Back so soon?" August's words come easy, but there's a tripwire running under his words, waiting for Caleb to take one wrong step. "That's a shame."

"When the cat's away, huh?" A smirk distorts the firm line of Caleb's mouth for just a second, but soon it flattens back into a hard line. "Iris, let's go."

He doesn't wait to see if I'll follow when he walks away with my baby girl. He knows I will. She looks at me over his shoulder. Her cotton-candy pink mouth wobbles, and her little chubby arms reach back toward me. She must have just awakened from a nap. She always wants me right away.

I've almost caught them when I'm pulled up short by my arm.

"Iris." August stares down at me, his frown fierce and puzzled. "Don't go with him."

I tug free of his gentle grip. It's the last gentle thing I'll have for a while, but I can't linger. Caleb has my daughter, and I'll be lucky if social services isn't getting another anonymous tip after this debacle. I'll be lucky if he hasn't already laid more traps and snares for me. I need to be a step ahead of him, but I've fallen behind. Surrendering to my weak desires today, I've fallen behind again.

"I'm not going with him." I beg with my eyes, with my hand spread on his chest, with my heart—I beg for him to understand. I beg him with everything but my words. "I'm going with *her*. Sarai is my priority, August. She has to be."

"Of course, Sarai should be your priority," August says. "But I . . . you said I wasn't fooling myself. That I wasn't imagining . . ." He grimaces and tunnels long fingers through his hair—hair I clawed at and disheveled moments ago during my orgasm. It's been so long since I came. So long since Caleb took the time to please me, to cherish me. August made me feel wanted, but not in the way Caleb wants me. Not tainted with selfishness. Not twisted with cruelty or stained with obsession. August gave me something brief and glorious, and I don't know if I'll ever have it again. If I walk out that door, I may never have it again.

"You aren't fooling yourself," I say. "It's not that we wouldn't be good together. Our timing's bad."

I hold August's hand between both of mine, wishing I could confess everything.

What would I say?

Caleb blackmailed me? Lied on me?

He beats me? Rapes me?

He holds me hostage in plain sight?

August wouldn't understand. He'd tell me to run. He'd say leave, but getting away is not enough. As long as Caleb has any claim to Sarai, getting away is not being truly free.

I glance over my shoulder, but Caleb's out of sight.

I tip up on my toes and kiss August's cheek. He reaches for my waist, but I step back, already aching for a touch I never should have allowed myself. It only makes this harder.

"I have to go." Tears burn my eyes. "Goodbye, August."

I turn and run from the community center, praying Caleb didn't leave. I spot Ramone immediately, standing on the sidewalk, the jailor to my prisoner, his eyes insolent. I walk past him with my head held high and climb into the back seat.

I don't know what I expected—probably a slap across the face as soon as I sat beside Caleb—but I'm met with eerie silence. It persists, the minutes stretching out on a torture rack while we leave the city and head toward my palatial prison. Sarai drowses in her car seat until sleep takes her again.

"Caleb, I can explain," I venture softly.

The look he levels on me is a guillotine, falling and slicing through any excuse I could offer, any lie. He knows the truth, and there's no way I'll avoid paying for it. Wanting August West is a high crime to Caleb. It's treason.

Off with my head.

When we pull up in front of the house, I unsnap Sarai and walk her swiftly inside and up to the nursery. I lay her down in her crib and linger there. My mind races over possible escape routes, but as usual, there are none. None that actually solve my problem.

"Meet me in the bedroom, Iris," he says from the door. "Stop dawdling. We need to talk."

Talk.

I know better.

Once in the bedroom, my eyes rove the corners and surfaces for a possible weapon. I've resisted before. It usually makes it worse for me, but tonight I can't imagine just taking it. That's usually when he brings out the pistol, against which I have no defense.

"Strip."

That one word is the slap I was anticipating. I hesitate, unsure how to play this. He sighs impatiently and pulls the pistol from his pocket, holding it up.

"Why does it always have to come to this, Iris?"

"Don't ask me to pretend this is normal, Caleb," I say harshly. "You raping me at gunpoint is not normal, and I won't pretend it is."

"I bet West wouldn't need a gun, would he?" His eyes narrow. "I said strip, you low-class swamp whore."

He tries to demean me with his words, but I don't feel it anymore. His words are a dog with no bite. They have no teeth with me.

But who needs teeth when you have fangs?

With unhurried movements, he unbuckles his belt.

Eyes trained on the pistol, I unsnap my overalls, dropping them to the floor and pulling the T-shirt over my head. I undo my bra and take off my panties.

"Bring those to me."

I freeze, staring at him in disbelief.

"I said bring me the panties, Iris." False calm is a needle threading his words.

I walk over to him and he snatches them from me, squeezing them in his fist.

"Wet," he growls.

Oh my God.

"Your panties are soaked." He carves a barbarous smile into his face. "Were you thinking of me?"

I shake my head, a denial springing to my lips. "I didn't . . . it wasn't—"

"Biiiiitch!" he roars, spittle ejaculating from his mouth. "Don't lie to me."

The walls seem to tremble, and so do I. The air goes subzero, freezing my blood. His fury emerges, fully formed and dangerous. Instead of shoving me onto the bed and taking me fast and rough like he usually would, he sits down on the edge, one hand clutching the panties, the other gripping the pistol.

"Come here," he says more quietly, but with no less threat.

I stand in front of him, naked and determined not to show fear. A callus has formed over my dignity and my self-respect. I barely feel them anymore. They're casualties of my survival and of my eventual escape.

"Make me believe you want me, Iris. Ride me."

My eyes fly to his, stunned and stupefied. I can't. I don't even remember what it feels like to want Caleb.

"I . . . well, I—"

"Kiss me," he says softly, almost persuasively. Like he cares, but I've played this game enough to know his gentleness is always a trick card.

I gulp down my disgust and lean tentatively to place my mouth over his. I nearly gag when his tongue sweeps against mine, rough and thorough like he's scrubbing the taste of August from my mouth. It's a nasty mimicry of the perfect passion I felt not even an hour ago. His hand snakes out to clamp around my throat, barely squeezing, but exerting enough pressure to remind me he could snap my windpipe if he pleased.

"I said ride me."

Every command is more confusing than the last. He pulls me by the throat to his lap, spreading my thighs over his. He doesn't wait for me to position myself but snatches me up and slams me down onto his dick. The air whooshes out of me when he spears up into my tightness. He grips my hip painfully, coaxing me into a rhythm I can't find. He pulls me flush to his body, crushing my breasts to his chest and shoving the pistol into my side.

"You're still wet. You came for him, didn't you?" he snarls. "When was the last time you were this wet for me?"

Fear ripples over my body. This could be the night he kills me. He reaches for my throat, fingers tightening until there's no air.

I grasp desperately for the manacle at my neck. Black spots speckle my vision, and cotton fills my head. Just when I think I'll pass out, he releases my throat.

"Did he touch you here?" Fury strains his voice to the point of snapping. "In your pussy, Iris? *My* pussy?"

"Stop." I choke on the word and the nausea filling my throat the longer he fills me. "Please stop."

"I'll stop." He lifts me off his lap and shoves me onto the bed behind him. "You asked for it."

Relief floods me, my body releasing the fear that held my muscles tight. All I want is a shower. I'm sure there will be repercussions when I least expect it, but maybe not tonight.

No sooner has the thought formed than Caleb rises over me and flips me onto my stomach. A prickle of foreboding tickles my consciousness. "Caleb, what are you—"

"You think I'll follow behind West?" he growls.

"You aren't," I say, desperate and struggling to loosen his hold. "We didn't, Caleb."

"So I'm a fool now?" A laugh, void of humor, whips the air. "I'll just go somewhere he hasn't been."

I can't submit to this. I squirm loose and spring off the bed, sprinting toward the bathroom, but I'm no match for Caleb's long arms and legs, for the lightning speed of his well-conditioned athlete's body. He's at the door ahead of me, blocking my way, laughing in my face. I turn to flee in the other direction.

His arm snakes around my waist and he lifts me from the floor, tossing me back onto the bed. His hold feels bionic when he jerks me to all fours, and I buck my back into his chest, trying to dislodge him. My arms flail wildly. I claw at his thigh and feel his skin curl under my fingernails. I slap any part of him I can reach, until the cold steel of that pistol at the base of my skull petrifies my fight.

"How dare you let him touch what's mine?" he growls behind me, jerking my hair painfully.

Tears crawl from my eyes and over my cheeks. His large hand slams between my shoulder blades and he grasps my hip, lining himself up with my ass.

"Please don't," I beg unashamedly, fisting the sheet. "God, Caleb, don't do this."

It's not like in the movies where the woman wrestles for minutes, and you keep thinking there's a chance she'll get away, undefiled. That someone intervenes just in time to save her.

No, it's not like that for me.

With one brutal thrust, Caleb invades a place no one has ever been. He's hinted at it, threatened it, but never taken me this way.

There's no lubrication. No preparation. No warning.

Just dry agony.

The pain steals my breath. It snatches my words. I can't even scream for a moment. It's that dizzying hurt that muzzles you, silences you completely. Every part of you is focused on surviving that injury, and you can't spare the energy to even speak.

I feel tissues tearing as he knifes into me repeatedly, a sharpened weapon wielded mercilessly. Tears roll unchecked into my mouth. My words dissolve into a pleading litany, pathetic syllables that spill out of me while he grunts and moans and pistons, a tireless machine. I don't even know how long he goes. I feel wetness between my legs and know it's blood. My elbows slide from under me, my chest collapsing to the bed.

"Fuck, stay still," he rasps. "It's not all in."

Oh, God. There can't be more, but he shoves himself in farther, and I scrape the very bottom of my soul for the scream that rips through the bedroom. I pray for numbness, but I feel every thrust, like a burning poker ravaging me.

"Please stop. Please. Please," I beg, my voice scratchy, my heart racing, my body wretched.

But Caleb is lost in a paroxysm of wicked pleasure, coming long and loud inside my raw, stretched entrance.

Once he has milked himself empty, he slaps my ass almost affectionately and pulls out. The relief is immediate, but the pain lingers. He flops onto the bed beside me, releasing a long exhale.

I lie completely still, a woman mauled and afraid the predator could return. I play dead, except I'm not sure I'm pretending. Some part of me has withdrawn—is curled up in a tomb begging for death. Welcoming the end with open arms.

Caleb strokes a finger over the faint bruising August caressed and soothed. "You always do stupid things that make me have to hurt you," he says. "Why do you do that when I love you more than anything, Iris?" He sounds genuinely perplexed and sincerely irritated.

I'm dealing with a madman.

I turn my head in slow inches until my eyes settle on his handsome face. "Fuck you, Caleb."

His expression freezes, eyes narrow, and his lips flatten. "You stupid bitch. You're such a masochist, aren't you?"

I've been careful all these months. Plotting. Looking for just the right moment, just the right time. But caution's gone, and though provoking him might ultimately hurt me more, I look for a way to hurt him. After what he just did, I want to hurt him back.

I gingerly scoot to the head of the bed, wincing at the discomfort between my legs and the pain of his invasion. I dispassionately note the streak of blood on the sheets. I know it's mine, but I feel no fear, no connection to it.

"I never answered your question," I say quietly.

"What question?" He bends his brows into a perplexed frown.

"You know." I deliberately look at him and smile. "You asked if I came for him."

A tornado touches down on his face, his brows. Lightning strikes over stormy eyes.

"I did." My voice is soft, but my eyes meet his unwaveringly. "It was the best orgasm of my life, Caleb. In a closet with August West. What are you going to do? Break his other leg? Break my leg? Keep breaking everything around you like a spoiled little boy smashing his toys?"

He lunges for me, his teeth bared, and his fist drawn back to strike. But I'm drawn back, too. I grab the bedside lamp, jerking it so the cord wrenches from the wall.

I smash it against his head. Pain and shock skitter over his face, quickly followed by fury. He touches the line of blood skating from his hairline, bemusedly rubbing the wetness between his fingers. I know the shock of seeing your blood drawn from a blow you didn't see coming.

"You have a death wish," he bellows, reaching for me. As quickly as my soreness will allow, I run-hobble to the door. I get it open, not caring that I'm naked. I have to run. After all these weeks of waiting and watching, I've chosen the worst time to fight back. The worst time to run. When there's no escape route. No plan.

No chance.

His booted foot slams into my back, the momentum sending me forward and skidding across the marble floor, chafing the bare skin of my stomach. I rise only as far as my elbows. I try to drag myself up, but that boot connects with my ribs, forcing all the air from my body. Doubled over, I'm shocked when maniacal laughter unspools from my belly. I flip onto my back, meeting his rage head on and with a bedlam smile.

"Now what? The pistol?" I taunt. "That's the only way you can keep me under your control, right? The big man with the gun? You pitiful coward."

"A gun?" His own demented grin cracks the polished surface of his face, and we are two witless loons in a death match. "I could kill you with my bare hands."

With blood smeared on my thighs, bruises blooming on my ribs like African violets, and a new defiance boiling in my bones, I look up through a tangled curtain of hair and say the most reckless words of my life. "Then fight me like a man."

And he does.

I was there when the levees broke.

Though I was safe in my ward when the monster lost all restraint and unleashed watery havoc on New Orleans, I lived in the city.

I later saw the devastation left in the wake of the beastly storm. We frantically gathered our things, fled our home for higher ground. My family left to survive.

There were those who stayed too long. Remained when they should have fled.

They did not live to regret it.

In this torrent, this chaos of cruelty, I realize I've made the same mistake. I've remained when I should have fled. Now, I witness the exact moment when this monster loses all restraint. And his fury, his rage rushes at me like a wall of water. Like a gale-force wind, he blows over me, and I am the devastation left in his wake. His fist and his open palm are untiring anvils that bruise my flesh and crack my bones. His fury is swift and efficient, a mesmerizing brutality of syncopated slaps and perfectly spaced blows.

The mind is a master strategist, knowing instinctively when to advance and when to withdraw. My mind is a haven when the pain is beyond bearing. With no escape in sight, I seek the only freedom left to me—my thoughts, my dreams, and my memories. I remember a magical night under the stars, under a streetlight on the eve of greatness. A night filled with laughter and confidences, pregnant with promise. And I see him so clearly, my prince, asking for a kiss.

Sometimes, we stand at a juncture on which our path, our very life can turn. A fork in the road. Sometimes the heart speaks in whispers, and by the time we hear, by the time we listen, it's too late and we don't know. We don't know that we should have turned right instead of left. Chosen one instead of the other. But now, in the retreat of my mind, I know.

And I kiss him.

In my dreams I choose him, my prince, instead of the fraud. In this parallel universe, at this second-chance juncture, I turn right instead of choosing wrong . . . and there, only there, we are together.

But that's not my universe, not the one I chose. So the world goes black, in a galaxy of pain and brutality, and I see stars. A flash of brilliance. A light I should have acknowledged long ago.

As the stars dim and the darkness encroaches, I understand I'm like those in my ward who stayed too long, assuming their survival. I fear that I, like them, will not live to regret it.

THIRTY

IRIS

Light creeps in through one cracked lid. With my awareness comes not only light, but pain. It's universal, all over, seeming to leave no part of my body untouched. Even my nails ache, but I have to press through this. Caleb's never hurt Sarai, but he's never hurt me this badly before, either.

I have to get up.

"Ramone, you did good." Caleb's voice comes from the hall. "You showed real loyalty alerting me so quickly about West."

At the sound of his voice just outside the door, my beaten muscles tense involuntarily, trained to brace for a blow.

"Thank you, sir," Ramone answers stoically, his voice pitched low and gruff.

"You'll find a bonus already wired to your account," Caleb says. "I have a flight to catch. Leaving China early threw a few things off. My agent needs me in New York tonight. I'll be back tomorrow, though."

Fury percolates in my pores. Oddly, no fear. I'm done with fear, and I'm done waiting.

The stars and moon have aligned. The circumstances are right, and today *I* will strike.

The door swings open, and I go limp, close my eyes, and play possum one last time for the hunter.

I'd know Caleb's footfalls anywhere. The sound of him approaching has struck terror in me many times. His steps are heavy and deliberate. He wants you to know he's coming, but to feel helpless. His steps say *you can run, but you can't hide.*

I'll always catch you.

His expensive cologne wafts over my face. Even with my eyes closed, I know he's standing over me, assessing the worth of his prize.

"Why did you do it?" he asks, voice tortured. "Why did you let him touch you? Why did you make me hurt you?"

The toughened bend of his knuckle brushes the hair away from my face, skimming a tender spot. I suppress the urge to wince, still feigning sleep.

"Andrew will be here soon to . . ." Caleb pauses in his one-sided conversation to clear his throat. For the first time, I wonder if he feels any real guilt when he hurts me. If in the husk where this psychopath's heart used to be, occasionally there is a Lazarus sign—a reflexive heartbeat.

"Andrew will be here to take care of you," he finishes. "I'll be back tomorrow night, baby. I know you'll be mad, but we'll get past this. We've been through so much together." His rough chuckle pricks my skin with porcupine needles. "Maybe you'll have good news when I come back. I keep hoping for another baby."

My gag reflex almost gives me away. The thought of his seed planted in me again roils my stomach, and the thought of his daughter in the next room is the only thing that has me holding on. The kiss he leaves on my forehead slithers over my flesh.

The most welcome sound is his retreating footsteps. My relief, the sound of his car pulling away.

It usually takes hours for me to move after a beating half this brutal, but I don't have hours. There's only now. This beating, timed with Caleb's trip, is the perfect opportunity. I've had these things before, but what I've been missing is help. Today, though, I'll ask for it. Ignoring the protest of my ribs with every breath, I force myself to sit up, to roll out of bed, wrapping myself in the sheet.

The debris of our fight litters the floor. A shattered lamp and glass from broken picture frames. There's a crack in the wall in the shape of my defeat— the shape of my body slammed into the plaster.

I fought back.

It was my worst beating at Caleb's hands, but I pray it was also the last.

I make my way gingerly over to Sarai's diaper bag in the corner of the room. I search the small pockets, almost weeping with relief when I find my cell phone, still where I stowed it yesterday. Footsteps approach in the hall. I clutch the diaper bag to my chest just as the door eases open.

Andrew and I stare at each other. From the horror on his face, I can only imagine how I look.

"God, Iris." Pity dulls his eyes. "I'm sorry. Let's get you taken care of."

"No." I expel the word with force.

"What do you mean 'no?'" He shifts his medical bag from one hand to the other. "We need to get you patched up."

"Patched up?" Disdain saturates the air between us. "Is that what you think I want? For you to patch me up so he can beat me again? Until one day he kills me? Because one day he will, Andrew. If I stay, he'll kill me. He almost did last night."

His glance roams my face, my battered features testifying on my behalf. Telling him I'm right.

I walk toward him, pain marking every step. I death-grip Sarai's diaper bag with one hand and the sheet with the other. Once I'm standing right in front of him, where he can't escape what I'm sure is the bruised, cut, and swollen topography of my face, I speak.

"I need your help."

The doors slam shut on his expression the way they do every time I plead with him.

"I can't." He shakes his head and averts his gaze. "You know I can't."

"All I need is your cooperation, not your assistance," I say desperately. "Just don't stop me. Don't shout when I run." I pause, letting my simple request sink in before the biggest ask. "Don't treat me."

He looks up sharply, narrow-eyed and curious.

"You have friends who could examine me, right?" I ask.

"No, Iris. I don't."

"A doctor who can document this and all the things that have been done to me. I need X-rays, and tests, and . . ." I swallow shame, embarrassment, guilt—all the artificial things that have held me back from asking for help in the past. "A rape kit."

He squeezes his eyes shut and pinches the bridge of his nose.

"I may know someone," he finally admits. "But I can't get you out of here. Ramone is downstairs on guard as usual. I don't put it past him to shoot you in the back if you try to run."

"I have a plan." I pull my cell phone from the diaper bag. "Let me worry about Ramone."

"You know Caleb monitors that phone," Andrew says quickly. "He'll intercept any message you send."

"I know." I type one word in and press send. "If he bothers to look, this message won't make any sense to him."

I stare at the word in all caps on my screen, hoping it's enough of a distress signal to bring in my cavalry.

HOPSCOTCH.

251

THIRTY
ONE

IRIS

There's a ruckus downstairs just a few hours later, and it's the most blessed sound I've ever heard. The proverbial music to my ears.

"Get the hell out of my way or I'm calling the cops and every news station I can get here. You want shit at your front door? 'Cause I can bring shit to your front door."

"This is private property," Ramone's deep voice rumbles up to me.

"Yeah, and my cousin lives on this private property," Lotus fires back. "If I don't see her in the next thirty seconds, whatever is going on here will be on every major broadcast tonight. Test me."

I don't give him a chance to test her. That kind of exposure would work against my plan. I open the bedroom door and step onto the landing. Two pairs of eyes climb the stairs until they reach me with Sarai on my hip.

"Oh, my God, Iris." Outrage, incredulity, and fury war in Lotus's voice and on her face.

By now I've looked in the mirror and know what she sees. I'm not so much Iris as a black-eyed Susan. My face is the canvas of an abstract painting with eyes distorted and mismatched, one bigger than the other. I'm splashed with wild streaks of black and magenta and scarlet. My lips are split and triple-sized. A many-colored bruise blossoms on my forehead and flowers into my hairline. My other parts haven't fared much better. My body is a patchwork of violence.

And it's all the evidence I need.

"Lotus." Her name releases from me like a held breath. There is still so much ahead, and my plan must be perfectly executed to the last detail for me to truly escape, not just today, but for good.

I look to Ramone standing beside her. Panic widens his eyes, and he immediately starts dialing.

"Call him, please," I say, starting down the steps, holding Sarai close and carrying a small bag with only our most essential things. "Tell him I'm gone."

"You aren't going anywhere," Ramon snaps, his brows jerked together.

"Try and stop us." Lotus climbs the last few steps to meet me halfway. She takes Sarai and buries her face in the baby-scented curls for a second before grabbing my hand. Linked at our hands, linked at our hearts again, we rush down the staircase and across the foyer.

When we reach the door, Ramone's hand snakes out to grab my arm, but I force myself to stand straight.

"Get your hands off me." I meet his eyes with no hesitation. "Or we call the cops right now, and I tell them everything. Think you're the only one who can lie to the authorities? I'll say you've been beating and raping me, too. You want to go down with Caleb? Does your loyalty really stretch that far?"

His hand drops, and his throat bobs with a gulp.

Lotus and I open the door and walk swiftly through. A green Volkswagen

Beetle sits out front, parked haphazardly in the circular driveway.

"You got a new car?" I ask. This banal question is all I can manage. Let's talk about the easy things we've missed, not about the purgatory I've been trapped in.

"No, I don't even own a car. I borrowed a friend's as soon as I got your message." Tears flood Lotus's eyes and she sniffs, swiping under her running nose, even as she climbs in. "What the hell, Bo? How did this even . . . happen? What's going on?"

I ignore her questions, my heart battering my chest cavity with the promise of escape so close. I climb in the back, because I don't even have a car seat for Sarai. I'm leaving it behind with all the other things Caleb bought. A small portion of our possessions is in the duffle bag, along with a little fistful of cash Andrew gave me and the little I've been able to hide and hoard over time. I pull the seat belt across us both and spend a few seconds hating myself for not trusting Lo sooner—for letting my shame and resentment and our petty disagreement come between us. I hate myself for not taking the risk and reaching out. Letting that minutiae stand between her and me, and between me and freedom, for too long.

I'll make up for it now. I'll pull back the curtain and show her my scars. "Just drive, Lo, and I'll tell you everything."

THIRTY TWO

IRIS

"What will it take to make this go away?" Caleb's father asks, closing the folder on the conference room table in front of him.

Caleb shifts in his seat, the muscle in his jaw ticking and barely checked rage rolling off the tightly held muscles of his body. I look at him until he looks up and returns my stare unblinkingly, unflinchingly and without an ounce of remorse.

"This doesn't go away," I answer, my eyes never leaving Caleb's face. "Ever."

"Then what are we doing here?" Caleb stands abruptly, the chair scraping across the hardwood floor. I chose neutral ground for the meeting I called with Caleb, his father, and his agent at the hotel where my credit card was denied that first night when I tried to escape. I hope Caleb appreciates the irony.

"Sit down, Caleb," Mr. Bradley says, his voice flinty. "And shut your fucking mouth. You're lucky she's even offering us terms."

Mr. Bradley's cold eyes turn to me again, the same shade of blue arrogance as Caleb's.

"I assume there *are* terms?" he asks me, one brow lifted and his hand already drawing a check book from his pocket.

Ah, he came prepared.

"You can put that away." I nod to the check book. "I don't want your money. I don't want anything from you or your son, except my freedom and my daughter."

"No," Caleb snarls. "You're not leaving, and you won't take my daughter from me."

"You sadistic bastard, I've already left." I lean forward, fixing my eyes on the piece of shit who fathered my child. "She's my daughter, and we'll go wherever I say." I hold up my copy of the folder they have. "Unless you want the NBA, all your fans, sponsors, and the entire world to know their golden boy is an abusive monster."

Maury, Caleb's agent, closes the folder containing photo after photo, from every angle, of the bruises and swollen places aching under my clothes even now, two days later. The pictures, the rape kit, documentation of previous injuries – all of it tells the story I've hidden for months until I had as much damning evidence on Caleb as he fabricated about me. Maury pushes the folder away on the table like a plate of rotten meat.

"Shit, Caleb," he mutters. "How could you do this?"

Maury looks at me for the first time, wincing when he encounters the evidence of Caleb's brutality stamped into my face. The only sympathy I'll find in this room lies in his eyes.

"I'm sorry this happened to you, Iris," he says softly, swallowing deeply. "What do you want? How's this gonna go?"

I draw in a fortifying breath, ignoring the heat of Caleb's glare. "As you see, the injuries I suffered only two days ago have been documented by a physician." I steady my voice even though the humiliation of exposing what happened nearly chokes me. "X-rays and a complete examination also show evidence of past injuries never properly attended." With one look, I fire a shot across the table at Caleb. "Tests also found evidence of rape." I use the word deliberately, lest Caleb or anyone else think there was anything consensual about what happened to me.

"Rape?" Maury asks, his indignation emerging again. "What the hell? Damn you, Caleb. I'll turn you in myself."

"Oh, no." I shake my head decisively. "Other athletes outed as abusers are fined and miss a few games, only to be back on the court, back on the field in a few weeks. I'm not trusting my life, my daughter's life to a system that favors men just like Caleb. I've seen the so-called consequences we have for domestic abuse, and I need more than that."

Cracks in the system are tailor-made and just the right size for men like Caleb to slip through. Caleb's fame and money only tip the already-tilted scales even more in his favor. I've seen it too often to leave this to chance.

"No," I continue. "You'll comply with everything I ask or all the gory details come out. Endorsements gone, NBA career over, and at least a few years of your life behind bars."

"Just get to the point," Mr. Bradley says. "What do you want?"

My daughter. My innocence back. My tattered illusions repaired. My dreams restored.

My second chance with August.

All of it feels improbable, so I ask for the things I know I can get using the evidence splayed on the conference room table.

"I want my freedom." I shift steady eyes to Caleb. "You don't follow us. You don't try to find us. You waive paternal rights, and you leave us alone."

A disbelieving laugh sputters from Caleb's lips. "You stupid bitch," he spits. "You think I'll give my daughter to you?"

"Did you bring the journal and my ring like I asked?" I ignore his insults and his arrogance. "Because I want those, too."

He sobers fast, thinning his lips and icing his eyes over in the way that used to strike terror in me, but no longer can.

"Caleb," Maury says sharply. "Give them to her."

For a second it looks like he won't, but his father snaps his fingers, and I know I've won at least this battle. Caleb pulls out the journal and slides it across the table so hard it skids off the edge and falls to the floor. Before I can squat to get it, Maury is there, picking it up and offering it to me with an apologetic look.

"My client's an asshole," he murmurs.

"Obviously, you don't have to tell me that," I say, accepting the journal. "And my great-grandmother's ring?"

"I have no idea where your backwoods jewelry is," Caleb drawls, contempt frosting his smile. "What use do I have for that cheap shit?"

I know he's lying, but the ring is a small casualty in this war, considering all I'm gaining today. Considering all I've lost.

"Fine. My journal and my freedom will do," I say, locking eyes with him.

"That's it?" Caleb slouches in his seat. "And I don't ever get to see my daughter again?"

Everything in me screams *hell no*, but having stripped him of his parental rights, I make the only concession I can. "When she's older, and if you've completed anger management therapy to my satisfaction, then I'll consider supervised visits."

"To *your* satisfaction?" He rolls his eyes and sucks his teeth. "We'll see about that."

"Caleb, shut your fucking mouth," his father snaps. "Iris, I understand. I'll have paperwork drawn up reflecting your . . . demands."

The hesitation on his face seems out of place. He's always sure, but uncertainty is as clear as the pride he pushes aside to ask his next question.

"Maybe you could . . ." He clears his throat, an uncharacteristic pause from a man who always sounds sure. ". . . consider allowing my wife and me to see Sarai when the time is right? She is our only granddaughter, after all."

I toughen the soft parcels of my heart, giving no ground. Anyone I have contact with is someone Caleb can use to find me before I'm ready to be found. Phone calls, letters, messages—they're all bread crumbs Caleb would sniff out and follow if his obsession overpowered his sense of self-preservation.

"I'll consider that later," I reply. "But right now, I need to put distance between me and everything to do with your son, including you."

"This is ridiculous," Caleb says under his breath.

"That's fair . . ." Mr. Bradley's expression hardens into granite, his negotiating face. "Now for *our* terms."

I knew this was coming, and I'm prepared. I simply nod for him to go on.

"You sign an NDA that you'll never speak of this and never release the contents of this file, as long as Caleb complies with your requests," he says. "And I mean speak of it to *no one*. Ever. Violation of that nullifies everything else and restores Caleb's parental rights."

I meet Caleb's eyes, and for a second, I think he wants me to violate it—to give him an excuse to break the leash I'm imposing and come after me, take Sarai. Hurt me again.

"I can do that," I agree.

"And I can write a check for a generous amount to get you settled." Mr. Bradley pulls out his dreaded checkbook again.

"No." I'm not yielding on this. "I don't want your money. I don't want to take anything from your family into our new life. As matter of fact, I have something for *you*, Caleb."

I reach into the front pocket of my jeans, remove the engagement ring

Caleb forced on me, and slide it across the table with such force it skips across the hard surface and lands on the floor, repaying his earlier disrespect.

Caleb's cheeks mottle with emotion. The corners of his eyes tighten.

"Yours, I believe." I rub at my ring finger as if it's contaminated.

Mr. Bradley slips the checkbook back into the inside pocket of his jacket. "We'll draw up the papers tomorrow, and—"

"I want the papers today." I gather my things and the tiny scraps of self-respect I've recovered and turn toward the door. "Instructions for delivery are in the folder. I'm leaving town tomorrow."

"Where are you going?" Caleb demands. "Where are you taking Sarai?"

"You heard the terms, Caleb," Maury interrupts. "If you don't want to lose everything and find yourself in a well-earned prison cell, you don't get to know, and you don't get to follow. Regardless, you'll need to find yourself a new agent."

Maury grimaces, taking in the gruesome images of my pummeled face and body. "Iris, are you sure you don't want to press charges? He shouldn't get away scot-free."

A bitter laugh precedes my answer. "I press charges and what? He gets a slap on the wrist? Probation? A year for what he's done by the time his lawyers whittle it down? And *still* can get joint custody of my daughter?"

I glare at Caleb before going on. He blanks his expression, looking deliberately bored, like I'm wasting his time.

"Should I live looking over my shoulder, waiting for him to decide he wants me back?" I continue. "Or wants me dead? Is that the justice you want me to seek? No, thank you. I'll make my own justice. It's not perfect and it may run out one day, but it's the best I can do right now for Sarai and me."

I shake my head. "I've taken the things from him that matter most: access to me and my child. Forgive me for being more concerned about our freedom than whether or not he is 'scot-free.' The only thing he wants to do more than hurt me is to protect himself."

"Well then let's get on with it," Maury says, standing and extending his arm for me to precede him through the door.

I'm walking out when Caleb snatches me by the arm, his touch setting off an alarm system in my body, red lights flashing, sirens blaring, and sprinklers spitting water. Shackled to him again, protest roars through me.

"Get your hands off me," I ground out.

Maury pushes against his chest, but Caleb won't let go, his fingers tightening painfully over my bruises.

"Iris, don't leave me." Desperation fills his eyes and some sick kind of sorrow, but no regret. "I . . ." His gaze dips to Maury's face and then to his father, who stands by, disgust and disappointment marking his expression.

"I need you, baby," he whispers. And I know it's true. He needs something to control, to manipulate, to toy with when the pressure is too much, but I'm not his punching bag. I'm not his anything anymore.

"Get your fucking hands off me." I jerk at my arm, but he refuses to let go. "Or the deal is off and your precious endorsements and your career—they'll all be over."

For a moment, just a flash, maybe a trick of the light, I think he'll refuse. It looks like holding onto me means more to him than all I hoped he held more dear, but then the frigid calculation, the ruthless cannibal who ate my heart and nibbled on my soul, shuts off all emotion. The monster is back.

"You stupid whore." He laughs, releasing my arm and sliding his fists in the pockets of his pants. "Like you can do better."

A smirk tickles the corner of my mouth, and I can't resist thrusting a sword through the one spot where I know he's weak.

"Oh, you and I both know I can do much better, Caleb." Butter wouldn't melt in my mouth when I smile.

Seeing the smirk fall apart on his face is small comfort, but any comfort is better than nothing. I won't be seeking out August anytime soon. I can't. Not feeling stained and smudged and shamed the way I do. Rationally, I know what happened to me was not my fault, but shame doesn't reason.

Where I'll go, I don't know yet. Caleb's a demon constrained to hell with chains of gossamer. It's a fragile exile I'm making for myself, but I'll take it and run for shelter while I can. And if he breaks free, I'll run again, maybe for my life.

I slip on oversized sunglasses and a hat to cover my bruises, looking like a *Lifetime* movie cliché, I'm sure.

In the lobby, Lo holds Sarai in her lap. She looks chic, her long braids tucked into a snood. She wears skinny jeans, a leather blazer, and ballet flats. Caleb rushes past me, headed for Sarai. Before I can put myself between them, Lo points a slim finger at Caleb and squints one eye, as if she's peering through a telescope. I wonder if she still sees the shadow on his soul because I may not have seen it then, but I can attest that it's there. There's latent power in her eyes, in the strong, slender arrow of her arm aimed at him.

"You'll have to pay," Lo says.

Caleb breaks stride, like her voice sprouted tentacles that slithered through the air and locked around his ankles. Something ominous hangs around Lo, and goosebumps pepper my skin.

"What the hell are you talking about?" he mumbles but doesn't step closer.

A knowing grin blooms on Lo's pretty face, and she opens her fist, revealing her gris-gris ring.

"These are your days." She blows over the ring, eyes clinging to his face. "Scattered, and lost, and falling to the ground like dust."

"Are you threatening me?" he asks, only half-laughing. I bet if I peeled his sleeve back, his arms would be covered in gooseflesh, too.

"No. A threat you see coming." The smile drops from Lo's face. "It's not a threat. It's *real* justice, and by the time it reaches you, it'll be too late."

Caleb pales under his tan, but while he stands there, no doubt considering the cryptic message Lo delivered, I rush past him and scoop Sarai into my arms. He approaches, but Lo interjects herself.

"Walk while you can, Caleb," she says, her words in a lower register that sounds laced with danger.

With one frustrated look at me and Sarai, he moves on. The breath trapped in my lungs releases in a rush. His father and Maury emerge from the conference room, their heads bent together. They glance at me, and I don't know if it's pity or respect in Maury's eyes, but I'll take either as long as it means he executes the papers and keeps Caleb away from me.

"So what now?" Lo asks.

"What was that all about?" I ignore her question.

"What was what all about?"

"Um, the powerful voodoo priestess act."

"I don't act," Lo says with a humorless curve to her full lips. "I am."

Twilight Zone.

"Where will you go?" Lotus asks, redirecting me, distracting me.

"I need to go somewhere far from Caleb," I answer in a rush. "Somewhere he doesn't know about and can't get to. I need some time without him in my life at all. Time to heal, I guess, because right now I just feel so . . ."

I can't articulate how I feel. Hurt, but numb. Lost. What do I do now? Next? Where should I go? I have to find my place.

Center.

I'd play you at the five. If you were mine, you'd be at the center of my life.

August's words filter through tiny gaps in the barbed-wire fence surrounding my heart. That could be my place. Instinctively, I know August *would* put me at the center, but one could argue I was Caleb's center, too. A dark, twisted center with the sides closing in and choking, but the center nonetheless. What if I've misjudged August as badly as I misjudged Caleb?

Hell, as badly as I misjudged *myself?*

I need time to find my place in this world without anyone else at the helm. As much as I feel for August, I need to stand on my own. I need to do what's best for my daughter and savor life and freedom and everything we almost lost.

"I know where you need to go," Lo says as we step outside the hotel and onto the sidewalk.

"Where?"

Lo hooks her arm around my neck like she did when we were kids.

Hopscotch.

Gratitude overtakes me, and I blink tears away. She came. I called, and Lo came. She hasn't condemned me or called me a fool for not calling sooner. The closeness between us didn't fade when she moved to the bayou. It didn't wash away when Katrina came, and I moved and Lo stayed. And it didn't budge when Caleb came between us. Not really. The closeness never moved. I did. I hid behind my anger and shame, and now it's all exposed. The light breathes grace on me.

"It's so obvious where you should go," Lo says.

"If it's so obvious, then why don't you enlighten me?"

Lo kisses Sarai's forehead and then mine. I swear when she looks up, I feel a hot, sultry breeze tease my hair, hear the distant sound of jazz, and taste a harvest of rich flavors on my tongue.

"Where you belong, Iris," Lo insists softly, "is home."

THIRTY THREE

AUGUST

"Did she say anything else?" I ask, carefully molding my mouth into a normal-looking, I'm-not-a-stalker smile. "Tell me again what Iris said."

Sylvia sends me a long-suffering look over the clipboard pressed to her chest. The same look she's been giving me the last few days. When Iris didn't show the day after Caleb came, I was worried but didn't have a way to reach her. I started bugging Sylvia then, and have been bugging her ever since, but it's only today that she has any answers.

"She called to apologize for missing the last two days of camp but said she had to leave town unexpectedly and wouldn't be back."

"It was her?" I demand. "Or was it Caleb delivering the message?"

"Like I told you the first three times you asked, it was Iris," she says impatiently.

My harmless smile slips a millimeter. That was not the answer I wanted to hear.

"Isn't that unusual?" I lean against the wall in the community center hall, my attempt at looking casual. "I mean, Iris shows up every day to volunteer and then just calls to say she's leaving town and won't be back. Are you concerned?"

"No." Sylvia knits her brows. "Why would I be concerned? Concerned how?"

"Well, that she's okay." I rein my frustration, remembering how Caleb swept in and ruined everything. The rage in his eyes.

"The woman had a bodyguard." Sylvia's wry smile does nothing to ease my concern.

"Yeah, well the bodyguard's creepy as fuck," I say bluntly, abandoning any semblance of calm. "And Caleb looked . . ."

Unhinged. Enraged. Dangerous.

The thought of him hurting Iris somehow is driving me crazy. Why did I not get her damn number . . . *again*?

"Look, I've seen where she lives," Sylvia says, her voice dry and void of sympathy. "I've seen the car she drives, her ring, her clothes. She was being very well taken care of, let me tell you."

"What the *hell* does that have to do with her safety?" I demand, through gritted teeth.

"Safety?" Sylvia asks with a wry smile. "Really, August? You think Caleb did what? Hit her? Hurt her? He can be arrogant, high-handed, but he's crazy about her. If anything, I feel sorry for him if she's left. He's probably devastated."

Someone up the hall calls Sylvia's name, and she turns away from me briefly to answer before giving me her attention once more. "I have to go," she says, sighing heavily. "Thank you for helping us. The kids loved it."

"Yeah, I loved working with them, too." It's the truth, but right now I can't focus on it.

"She's gone, but she's fine, August." Sylvia pats my arm as if I'm a cat who should drink the milk set in front of me and leans in to whisper, "There are lots of other girls out there."

After delivering that humiliating pearl of wisdom, Sylvia scoots down the hall without a backward glance.

Outside, I spot Jared parked on the street. When I ease into the passenger seat, he watches me warily . . . wearily? Maybe both. He's handling me with caution *and* also tired of my ass.

"No answers?" He taps his thumbs against the leather-wrapped steering wheel.

"The wrong answers." I shake my head, still trying to make sense of it. "Sylvia says Iris called to say she was leaving town and wouldn't be back."

"Well then that's that," Jared says. "Hooters for lunch?"

"Dude, this is serious."

"Maybe she's left Caleb. Isn't that what you wanted?"

It's only half of what I wanted. I also wanted her to come to me. And Sylvia may be satisfied with this incomplete picture, but I'm not. I won't be until I hear it from someone who *does* know what the hell is going on.

I flop my head back against the seat and side-eye Jared. "I need a favor."

"No."

"You don't even know what I'm gonna ask."

"Oh, I don't?" He shoots me a look that is both disgusted with me and satisfied with himself. "Then why'd I already call the Stingers' training facility to see if Caleb's scheduled to work out today?"

I grin and pull on my seat belt. "This is why I keep you around."

"And because I chauffeur your ass everywhere." He pulls away from the curb and glances at my leg. "At least temporarily. How's the leg?"

"Good." It's actually hurting like a motherfucker today, but I don't want any lip from Jared about me overdoing it. I need my brother right now, not an agent.

"I'm taking you because I knew you wouldn't rest until you got some answers," Jared says, looking away from the interstate only long enough to catch my eyes. "But don't get into shit with him, Gus."

"I'm not," I say defensively. "I'm just gonna make sure Iris is okay."

"Oh, yeah. That won't infuriate him at all."

"Ask me how many fucks I got for that," I snap. "Sylvia made Iris seem like some gold-digger who should just be happy she has a roof over her head."

"Well . . ." Jared shrugs. "I mean, he did take care of her."

I boil in scorching silence. Is Caleb some kind of warlock? Does he cast a spell so everyone misses what a complete asshole he is? He just skates through life without consequences. I saw it while we were growing up over and over. Son of a bitch breaks my fucking leg in front of the whole world, and he doesn't even get fined.

And I'm not just saying that because he has Iris and Sarai.

Had Iris and Sarai. Maybe.

"In and out," Jared says, breaking into my hostile thoughts.

"Huh?" I look over at him questioningly. "What'd you say?"

"We're here." He points through the window to the building where the Stingers train. "Find him, ask your questions, and get out. No fights. No scenes, bro."

"I really hate it when you call me 'bro,'" I say, matter-of-factly.

"I know. Why do you think I do it?" He studies me closely, the little bit of humor on his face fading. "You need me to come with you?"

"No, I needed a chauffeur, not a chaperone," I say, climbing carefully out of the car. "Be right back."

It doesn't take me long to find Caleb. He's pressing weights, spotted by a tall, lean man wearing a Stingers T-shirt. The guy looks up, his eyes widening when his eyes lock on me. Everyone in the league knows how bad the blood is between Caleb and me.

"Hey, you can't be in here bec—"

I wedge myself between the trainer and the bench where Caleb is lying down. I grab the bar from Caleb's hands and place it on his neck enough to cause discomfort but keeping the full weight from pressing down.

I bend over so he sees me upside down.

"I'm only asking you once, Caleb," I say calmly, while his eyes bug and he starts to turn red. "Where is she?"

"He can't breathe!" the trainer guy says, sputtering and pointing.

"That's kind of the point." I nod to the exit. "Get out. We got shit to settle. I promise he'll still be in one piece as long as he cooperates."

Caleb manages to shake his head, his eyes latched onto the trainer dude's as he puffs air and claws at the bar I hold over his throat.

"I said, get out!" I yell at the indecisive trainer. He's still looking back over his shoulder until he disappears through the exit.

I lift the bar just enough for Caleb to breathe and talk, but not enough that I can't drop the full weight on his throat if he doesn't give me what I want: answers.

"Fuck you," he hisses, the blood vessels sprouting around his eyes.

"Wrong answer." I drop the bar a little more, and he immediately starts gasping again. "I will break your fucking windpipe, Caleb, so I suggest you answer the question I already told you I *would not ask twice*."

I lift the bar an inch, and his arms fly up, trying to dislodge me. I can hear Jared now if I actually fight this dude with my leg in its current state. Not to mention the insurance the San Diego Waves have on my body. I'm pretty sure there's not a brawl clause in the multi-million-dollar policy. I step away and let him breathe while I compose himself.

"Answer the question," I snap.

"What business is it of yours?" he rasps, sitting up and grabbing his water bottle to guzzle.

"I'm making it my business. Iris didn't show up at the center, but Sylvia says she called to say she wouldn't be coming back."

He pauses mid-sip, narrowing his eyes at me. "Really concerned about finding another man's girl, huh?"

"Not here for games, dude. Tell me what's going on."

He stands, mopping the sweat from his face with a nearby towel. "What is 'going on' is that she's gone." Bitterness corrupts the line of his mouth. "Iris left. Didn't take her phone, so good luck calling it."

I've seen Caleb with Iris—the way his eyes track her every move like he might miss something if he looks away. He would not just let her go. He's as obsessed with her as I am.

Almost.

"Left and went where?" I persist, irritation pinching the muscles in my face.

"No idea," he mutters, watching me down the length of his water bottle while he gulps. "She wouldn't tell me."

"And Sarai? You don't know where your own daughter is? How to reach her? Them?"

Caleb turns away from me, shrugging while he sorts through the items in his duffle bag. He's avoiding looking at me. This is some shit, but I can't get to the truth. It's like a puzzle with all the pieces on the table, but I can't see how they fit together. I know I'm missing something. There's a question I should ask or something I don't know, and somehow, he's hiding from me. Caleb is covering his ass, I'm sure, but why would she go along with him all this time? And he's fine with her just leaving him?

Leaving him.

"You two broke up?" I ask, keeping my voice steady.

The way to Iris is actually clear for the first time since we met. He throws a piercing look over his shoulder at me, his smirk a forced lift of his lips when his eyes don't smile at all.

"We're not together anymore," he replies. "But she doesn't want to be found by anyone." He turns to face me now and crosses his arm over his chest. "And that includes you, West. Did you think because she gave you a few minutes in the closet you meant something to her? You didn't."

A practiced smirk lifts one corner of his mouth.

"She has my money and my kid, so I guess she doesn't need me anymore." He shakes his head. "Who would've thought I'd let some swamp whore from Louisiana trap me? I suspect that Creole bitch even gave it up to my bodyguard while I was gone."

I lunge for him, ignoring the twitch in my knee and slam him to the wall, then pin him by the throat.

"You're a liar," I grit out, tightening my fingers around his neck. "Say it again and I'll break more than a leg, you entitled son of a bitch. You're not good enough to touch her."

"But I did touch her." A demon's smile teases the corners of his mouth. "Oh, I've touched her everywhere you've never gotten to. Fucked her in all the ways you've only dreamt about, and to top it all off? She had my baby."

He cocks a brow, regaining his arrogance by the second. I hate his handsome face, his blond hair and blue eyes and tan skin. I hate everything outwardly appealing about him because inside he's crawling with worms.

"Write her off, West," he says. "She's gone. She got what she needed, and now she's gone."

Iris is not like that. I know she's not, but why didn't she try to get in touch with me? If she's gone . . . after what happened in the closet? Would she just leave without even saying goodbye? Without telling me how to find her? Was I that wrong about what we had? Maybe I've been misreading this woman since the night we met. I just knew that what I felt, she was feeling, too.

You're not fooling yourself.

She told me that. Her whispered words spark again in my memory, and

271

all the feelings, the sensations, the perfection of those moments in the closet with her flood my mind. I wasn't fooling myself. I don't know everything that's going on, but there's one thing I hold onto even as I exit the training facility and Jared and I pull out of the parking lot.

I'll see her again.

That thread that connects us, glowing neon, it's still there. I may not be able to see it, but I *feel* it. It's still wrapped around me.

Wherever Iris is, I hope it's wrapped around her, too.

HALF TIME

"She remembered who she was
and the game changed."

LALAH DELIA

THIRTY FOUR

IRIS

MiMi says she was tutored by the bayou, by the Mississippi itself. She says that river is the blood meandering through Louisiana's veins, and it casts a spell on all who love it.

I don't know that I ever *loved* Louisiana. I never knew this Louisiana. I lived in the Ninth. On the bayou, a thick carpet of green grass squishes between my bare toes; in the city there was concrete under my feet, cracked and unforgiving.

An arch of cypress trees shelters the path from MiMi's small house down to the river, but in my neighborhood growing up, power lines crisscrossed the sky like electric spaghetti. No, I didn't love the Lower Ninth, but I think I'm falling for the bayou.

There are so many differences between the city and St. Martine. Being here the last year, I understand why Lo saw living with our great-grandmother as a blessing.

How she must have laughed when I claimed to know MiMi as well as she does. What a ridiculous notion. When we showed up on her modest doorstep, I barely recognized her. I don't know exactly how old she is, but traces of great beauty still remain on her face, even past ninety years old. She has fewer wrinkles than she should, her skin carrying the patina of age, shined to a high polish.

And her eyes—those eyes can see your soul in the dark.

Lo hadn't told her much about my circumstances, except that I needed to come home. But when I stood on the front porch and the blue door to MiMi's green house swung open, her eyes probed mine in the dim porch light. That omniscient gaze sliced through the humid, heavy air, narrowing and softening with every new thing she read in my soul and dug out of my heart.

Her thin arms drew me close, and she whispered to me in French. I didn't understand what she said. I didn't need to. The power of her voice, the life in her words, winnowed to the bottomless pit where I hid my hurt. Before I knew it, my pain and disillusionment, my disappointment and regret, poured out of me into the silver braid hanging over her shoulder.

"Maman?"

Sarai's sweet voice startles me and forces me to turn away from the bayou. She's learning more words every day, half of them French, because people speak that here more than anything else, and the rest of them English, because that's all I know to teach her.

"Hi, princess." I bend and scoop her up. "Did you walk down here by yourself?"

She nods, bobbing the pigtails I scooped her dark curls into.

"Eat." She clumps her fingertips together and presses them to her lips, making the sign.

"Time to eat?" I ask, waiting for another nod. "What's MiMi got for dinner? Wanna find out?"

The patch from MiMi's to the river's edge is short, safe, and well-worn. This arch of trees provides the coolest spot for miles, and I find myself down here every chance I get. In the summer, humidity is the sultry breath of the south. I've given up on taming my hair since the moist air coaxes it into tight coils that hang down my back and around my shoulders. There's a freedom to it.

Caleb liked my hair straight. He wanted everything a certain way. Wanted *me* a certain way. With distance and time, I realize I probably initially gave in to many of his preferences to make up for the fact that I just didn't love him. Didn't. Couldn't. I'm not sure I ever did. If I hadn't gotten pregnant, Caleb probably would have been "that guy" I dated in college who ended up in the NBA. Maybe we would have had a long-distance relationship for a little while that eventually ran out of steam and followed a path to a natural end.

But I did get pregnant, and everything changed.

I barely recognize the woman I've become, so different from that girl, fresh from college, driven to achieve whatever she set her mind to.

"*Affame?*" MiMi asks, lifting the top from a pot on the stove and smiling through a cloud of steam.

"Yes, starving." I grab three plates from the hutch against the wall, silverware, and three of the linen napkins MiMi still eats with each night. At two years old, Sarai can barely reach the table, but she strains up on her little toes to set the forks down by each plate. She's mature for her age. Bright. Observant. And so beautiful.

"*Etouffe!*" she says when we sit down to eat, her smile pegged with baby teeth.

"Grits," I correct gently. I raise my spoon to taste and close my eyes to savor. "And shrimp. So good, MiMi. Mine never turn out this good."

She has taken up my culinary education, which my mother never really bothered to do.

We eat in relative silence for the first few moments, but that won't last. At MiMi's age, her mind still races with questions, and her curiosity makes for lively conversation.

"You like Jerome, eh?" MiMi's silver brows lift and fall suggestively over mischievous eyes. "He likes you so much, he may start delivering the mail on Sunday soon."

"Oh my God." My cheeks flush with embarrassment, and not from the heat in the non-air-conditioned house. "He's our mailman, MiMi, so I like him fine as far as mail goes, but nothing else." I attempt a stern tone, but my lips twitch at the corners and so do hers.

"You are beautiful, young." MiMi narrows one eye at me before taking a bite. "You have needs."

"I have *needs*?" I cock a dubious brow. "So . . . Jerome, the only man I see on a consistent basis, qualifies to meet these supposed needs of mine because he delivers our mail on time?"

There's nothing like MiMi's laugh. It starts as a cackle then swells to a guffaw, the sound booming from her small body and floating through the air like bubbles that settle around you and pop with energy. It's the kind of laugh that invites you to join in.

"Besides," I say when our laughter fades and we turn our attention back to dinner. "I don't know if I do have those needs. I'm satisfied with a good meal and my princess." I lean over to kiss Sarai's silky mop of curls.

"You buried your needs with your pain," MiMi says, her voice sobering and her eyes probing. "But they are still there."

"Are they?" My index finger makes a circuit around the porcelain rim of my bowl. "Maybe once, but . . ."

I shrug and hope she'll leave it alone. I have aches and scars from my life with Caleb, some visible and some hidden from the naked eye. This body kept all my secrets. My shame took sanctuary in its crevices and cracks. I'm not sure this body's capable of pleasure anymore.

"Tell me," she persists. "Your boyfriend, he hurt you, yes?"

The scorching summer's day and boiling soup in the kitchen make the air like a wool blanket around my shoulders, hot and heavy, but I still shiver. Caleb is far away and has never so much as sent a text to the pre-paid phone only Lo knows about. He doesn't have my number, and I don't think he knows to search here, but I find myself on alert.

Some people are afraid a gator will crawl out of the swamp and emerge as a threat. My nightmares star a different predator. I dream Caleb will rise out of the bayou some day and eat me whole, and next time I won't be able to pry his jaws open and escape.

"He took from you." MiMi says it like she knows for sure. She probably does. "He took, and you think you'll never want a man again."

I glance self-consciously at Sarai, but she is too young and oblivious, chewing on crusty bread with her little teeth and eating the grapes I put on her plate.

There was a man I wanted once, but if he knew all that'd happened to me . . . God, the thought of August finding out about Caleb and all that he did. I touch my neck. The idea of wanting a man again is hard to swallow when I still feel Caleb's hand at my throat. Only it's not his hand cutting off my breath, choking me. It's shame.

My spoon drops, clattering in the bowl. I'm shaken by my memories, so visceral that after a year, I still feel Caleb shoving inside me like a battering ram. The sting of his belt buckle biting into my hip is still fresh. Yesterday's regrets make today's sorrows.

"You'll want again." MiMi covers my hand with her weathered one, the ringed fingers squeezing mine. "You need to be cleansed."

She's right. I'm dirty. How could I not be after that animal was inside me? After he subdued me like a rabbit he only left alive for sport? Even so,

279

I don't put much stock into the rituals MiMi thinks will make a difference.

"Meet me in the back after her bath." She nods to Sarai, whose long, drowsy blinks send shadows on her cheeks.

After bath with bubbles in MiMi's claw-foot tub, Sarai insists on a story. She loves fairytales, and I don't have the heart to tell her that sometimes Prince Charming turns out to be an abusive asshole like her father, and sometimes his kisses bust your lips. When her lashes flicker and her breath slows into sleep, I turn off the lights in the small bedroom we share. Funny. We lived in a mansion, and every day I felt caged, claustrophobic. Now we live in a four-room house out in the middle of nowhere. We share a bedroom whose walls I can practically touch with each hand when I spread my arms, yet the sense of freedom is like none I've ever known.

I push back the curtain, studying MiMi's "back room" with interest. I've seen people enter distraught and leave clutching their newfound peace and a mason jar or bottle of something from MiMi's shelf of solutions. I don't understand all that MiMi does—the potions people from town come to buy, the rituals she performs in the back of the house behind a curtain. I don't know all that she does, but I believe every word she says.

She lights the last in a line of candles on a table against the wall, glancing up to find me paused on the threshold.

"Come," she says. Even her voice is different here. Brusque, but not stern. Soft, yet impersonal. Gentle and firm.

She has work to do.

Work on me that I'm not sure I'm ready for. Once I climb on that table, I don't know what will come next. Delaying, I browse the bottles crammed onto shelves lining the wall, a restless tactile exploration with my fingertips. I hesitate over a bottle with an unfamiliar symbol.

"Don't touch that one," MiMi says with her back turned to me.

How did she . . .?

I've stopped asking questions. There's an omniscience to my great-grandmother. Some days, when her shoulders droop and her bustling steps slow to a shuffle, I wonder if she's tired of knowing all the things she's learned. If maybe soon, she'll weary of living in a world that no longer holds mystery and set off for a new adventure.

She's bent, looking for something under the table. Still nervous, I ease open a drawer, surprised to find a pocket knife. The handle is curved and ornate. It's delicate, designed for smaller hands. I pick it up, caressing the jeweled button that opens it. I press, and with a snap, it unfurls a sharp, wicked length of blade.

"Touch a lady's knife," MiMi says, some humor sprinkled in her words, "you better be prepared to use it."

I glance up, then catch the slight smile on her lips and return it. The simple connection spreads warmth over me as effectively as a physical embrace. MiMi communicates more with fewer words than anyone I've ever known. It feels like we learn as much about each other in glances, touches, and smiles as we do with the things we say.

"I was surprised to find it," I admit, replacing the knife and closing the drawer.

"Well, a woman in this world has to keep her wits about her and her weapons at hand." MiMi measures me from head to toe with a glance. She gestures for me to climb on the table. My nerves stretch so tight I'm sure I'll tear in half.

"You must breathe," MiMi whispers. Her words float above me, shrouded in the candles' aromatic smoke. Below, my body's held by a cloud of pillows. I should feel safe, secure, settled, yet I feel exposed. I'm so vulnerable, I close my eyes and cover my heart with my hands.

"Hands down," MiMi commands gently.

Lowering my hands, I lock eyes with my great-grandmother and draw in deep, scented breaths.

"Breathe out." Her eyes never leave mine as the breath pushes past my lips, and the longer she looks into my soul, the sadder her gaze becomes, shimmering with tears. "Oh, *ma petite.*"

Can she see? See past the fragile façade I've erected to cover the ruins? Can she see that last night and all the nights before? How he ravaged me? Does she know that I feel plundered, like a picked-over battlefield littered with dead bodies? That some days I am dead, and that Sarai, taking care of her, is the only thing forcing me through the motions of life? When MiMi looks in my eyes, does she see?

Her hands pass through the air above, covering me in scented breezes. Her words migrate from Spain, from France and West Africa, all the places that made us and mix in our blood, in our heritage. The syllables fall from her lips, foreign and familiar, as tossed and varied as the gumbo she taught me to prepare.

"Breathe out the lies," she says. "That it was your fault. That you failed. That you are what he said you were."

When her words sink in, when they drill down to my core, a sob explodes, detonating through my belly and chest, and blasting open a wall of deceit I didn't know was there. Tears leak from the corners of my eyes, and I'm so damned tired of tasting my tears. The image of Caleb pressing his thumb into my mouth that first night, soaked with my tears, flashes through my mind. The night his wicked trap caught me.

"Breathe in truth." Her hands are busy in the air over me, slicing through lies. "You are pure. You are enough. You are strong." She leans closer, her whisper as sharp and fierce as the knife in her drawer. "He can't hurt you."

My shoulders shake and my head tips back, emotion stretching me wide, arching my back, elongating my neck, and wrenching my mouth open in a wail, a warrior cry. And in a smoky room filled with shadows, those parts of me Caleb scattered, I reconvene. All the pieces he splintered, I mend. And everything he stole from me like a petty thief, those things, *every single one of them*, I repossess.

"Yes." MiMi's affirmation infuses the air with power. "Strength. Dignity. Courage. All these things belong to you. Take them back. Your soul is yours. Your heart is yours. Your *body* is yours. Yours to keep and yours to share."

Yours to keep and yours to share.

The words summon a memory I haven't allowed myself in months. Breathing in and out, I indulge in thoughts of August. His carved profile and soft, full lips. His thundercloud eyes and gentle hands. A body of granite covered in taut, velvet skin. The urgent want smoldering between us. His hunger so palpable, I felt it stroking me everywhere. His tongue delving inside, seeking, giving.

"Oh, God." A gasp transports me, and my eyes drop closed until we are alone again, he and I. Back in that closet, the door shut, sealed off from the world. Our mouths meld and our breaths tangle, and I can't gather enough of him on my tongue, can't reach enough of his body. I press into him until our bones touch, until our souls kiss, until every part of me, from the inside out, I've shared with him.

And I break.

I break like a storm on the Mississippi River, a relief from the cloying weight of summer heat. I'm a deluge, drowning my doubts and washing away my fears. I stiffen with a catharsis so spiritual and sensual, so pure and carnal, that for a moment, I'm not of this world. I'm above its cares, outside of its confines, divorced from my body and untethered from the earth.

"Breathe in," MiMi says softly. "Breathe out."

Her words slowly reel me back, returning me to the small room behind the curtain. They ground me in a fresh sphere with a lightened body and spirit.

"What was that?" My breath comes in pants and my hands shake. "What did you do?"

At first I think she'll only answer with a smile and an otherworldly light in her eyes, but she reaches back to answer my question from before.

"These," she says, waving her hand at the bottles on the shelves, "don't tell me what you need. They don't tell me what to do. You do that. You, ma petite, you needed the truth. I gave it to you."

I'm still not sure what she actually means.

I sit up carefully, expecting my head to spin, but the room is steady and I'm not weak-limbed.

"A few moments with the truth don't chase away the lies forever," she says, pushing back the sweat-dampened hair clinging to my face. "Lies don't give up easily. You'll have to remind yourself and heal yourself over and over, every time they come."

"You mean I need to talk to a therapist?" I ask. I've thought of that and probably will at some point.

"Yes." Her smile is that of a younger woman, knowing, teasing. "And sleep naked sometimes. Soon, you'll want again."

We share a husky laugh. Recalling August's kiss, I wonder if she's right. I slide off the bed and touch my bare feet to the floor, reaching for her.

"Thank you, MiMi." I blink at my tears with my head tucked into her long, silver braid. "I feel so weak sometimes, and you make me feel strong."

"Struggle does not make you weak," she whispers back. "Struggling against those who hold us is what makes us, over time, stronger than they are. Strong enough to fight back. Strong enough to win."

That night, with the soft sounds of crickets and swamp creatures drifting through my window, I sleep better than I have in months. I sleep so deeply that by the time I wake up, the sun is higher and brighter than usual. I reach out and find the space beside me empty.

"Sarai!" I bolt up, my breath caged and flapping in my chest. I fumble through the sheets, stumbling out of bed and into the narrow hall.

My daughter's sweet voice drifts back to me from MiMi's room. My smile comes full and wide. I'm so glad we've had this time with my great-grandmother; the experiences I missed as a child, Sarai will be able to treasure.

"Wake up," she cajoles in that sing-song voice she uses to stir me on mornings when it's hard for me to rise. MiMi usually beats the sun up and, at more than ninety years old, is making coffee and cooking eggs and bacon before I'm awake. Last night must have worn her out, too. I lean my shoulder into the doorjamb, running my eyes over MiMi's small bedroom, stuffed with furniture too big for the space and photos, many black and white, crowding the walls. The room is set to burst, a larger-than-life woman squeezed between the walls.

Sarai sits beside MiMi, rubbing her little palm over the silver hair loosened on the pillow. Her eyes, the darkest parts of blue and violet, consider me solemnly. My gaze drifts to MiMi, who stares back at me, eyes unblinking and void of life. I rush to the bed, grabbing her hand. It's cold and stiff. At her wrist, there is no rhythm.

"Shhhh," Sarai whispers, one finger to her rosebud mouth. "MiMi's sleep, Mama."

"No, baby." I shake my head and let the first tear fall. "She's not asleep."

THIRTY FIVE

AUGUST

In the grand scheme of life, one year is a drop in the bucket. When you're looking for someone, wondering if they'll call or when they'll come back, a year feels like forever.

Sylvia said it. Caleb told me that Iris left, but I still keep thinking maybe she'll call or contact me. Caleb's been seen with other chicks, living his life, so I assume he told the truth and they really aren't together anymore. His girlfriend has left, and I'm the one who can't move on.

"You should fuck."

I glance up from the report I'm studying at lunch with Jared. Our server, who overheard his comment, blushes and stretches her eyes.

"Um . . . did you need anything else?" she asks, sliding a look between Jared and me.

"We're good for now," I tell her, forcing a smile. "You can bring the check."

"Sorry," Jared says, but he doesn't look repentant as she walks away. "Her overhearing it doesn't make it any less true. I've never known you to be this . . . grumpy."

"I'm not grumpy. You make me sound like an eighty-year-old man."

"You have the sex life of an eighty-year-old man." He sips his wine. "Hell, I'd be grumpy if I didn't get any ass for a year."

"I'm not you." I flip through the report, hoping to divert his attention back to business. "These second-quarter numbers look good. Elevation's doing even better than we hoped it would."

"Yeah, they look great. Don't change the subject."

"The subject is none of your business. Speaking of business, let's talk about it."

"Okay." Jared tears a bread stick into little pieces over his plate. "Did you talk to Pippa about signing on?"

"I did. She's interested."

"In fucking you."

I tilt my head and blank my face, exasperated.

"Are you saying she doesn't want to?" Jared asks. "She would have already signed if you'd give her what she wants. She practically spelled it out in the sand when she visited the office last week."

One advantage of living and setting up our agency in San Diego is an office only a pebble's throw from the beach. It's worked for us, wining and dining clients oceanside. Well, I don't wine and dine. I'm still a silent partner but have recently started persuading high-profile athletes that since I now trust Elevation with my representation, they should, too.

"What are you now?" I smirk and pour water from the carafe on the table. "My pimp?"

Jared's expression loses most of its humor. "If you need me to be." He sighs. "She may not ever contact you, Gus. You should move on."

Does he think I don't know that? That I want to be in this limbo where I think Iris *might* come back? I'm not an eighty-year-old man, and there is nothing wrong with my sex drive. I simply have no outlet. The only person I want is gone. The obvious solution is to want someone else, but my heart and my dick don't see it that way.

"I do have something we need to discuss." Jared narrows his eyes, assessing. "I need to put on my agent hat for a minute."

"What's up?" I ask.

"Deck called." The look Jared angles at me holds excitement and speculation. "You won't believe this, but the Waves are open to a trade."

The glass in my hand stops midair halfway to my mouth. I set it down with a thump on the table.

My contract isn't up for another two years. I'd resigned myself to spending the first five years of my NBA career on a losing team and just distinguishing myself on the court so I'd get good looks from other teams when it was time to go.

"You shitting me?" I ask.

"Nope." Jared grins like a buccaneer. He's a hard-ass negotiator and probably relishes the prospect. "They know they could get a few quality players from Houston for you."

"Houston?" My mouth drops open. Houston is in the playoffs again this year, as we speak. They might even take it all. "Houston wants me?"

"Bad." He leans forward, elbows on the table. "They're focused on the playoffs right now, of course, but some of the front-office execs reached out on the sly. They're looking ahead."

A disturbing thought occurs to me. "So are the Waves open to this because they don't think I'll be back a hundred percent?"

Rehab was long and grueling, and by the time I could get back on court, I'd lost almost all of my second season. Playing those last couple of months was more a test for the upcoming season than anything else, seeing if I still had my strength and explosiveness off the dribble. My distance-shooting hasn't been affected. Jag had me shooting from anywhere on court seated in a wheelchair from the early days of rehab.

"No, they aren't worried that you won't be back full-steam," Jared assures. He knows that would bother me—the brass thinking I couldn't perform anymore. "If anything, it's the opposite. Everyone saw how good you looked out there at the end of last season. If they want to build, to add some key pieces to the roster, you're their most valuable asset to get them."

"Huh." I lean back in my seat and consider leaving Deck and Jag. Even Glad and I have become friends.

Winning has always been the most important thing in my life. I'll never get used to losing, but I was getting used to those guys. We were just starting to feel like a real team.

"Did you say 'huh?'" Jared asks, a frown snapping his brows together. "'Cause I don't speak grunt. You want me to move forward or not? And if you say 'not,' you're a fool."

He's right. If I'm stuck in this place, mired in too-few memories of Iris and the little time we had together, something in my life should be moving forward. Why not my career?

"Yeah." I smile at the rosy-cheeked waitress and accept the bill. "Let's see where it goes."

And if it takes me to Houston, I'm closer to a championship than I thought I would be for years. That should make me happy. And it does. I can't be ungrateful. A percentage of a percentage of people live the way I do, have the things I have, but something's still missing. I don't have to ask what.

I know what it is. I know *who* it is.

I just don't know where to find her.

THIRTY SIX

IRIS

D eath has a way of uniting or dividing. Families come together and draw comfort from each other or fight about wills and the things that have kept them apart. It can go either way.

Even with the funeral over and everyone gone home, and MiMi's small refrigerator stuffed with Tupperware and leftovers, I'm not sure what her death will do to our family. Lo hasn't seen her mother or spoken to her in years. She avoided Aunt May even at the funeral and shows no sign of breaking the silence. I can't blame her. What Aunt May did was unacceptable, even more so to me now that I have a child of my own. I could never choose a man over her, much less accept his word as truth when my daughter accused him of wrong. But that's what Aunt May did, and I'm afraid Lo will never forgive her.

And then there's my mother.

Her beauty hasn't faded. She had me so young she's barely forty. Heads still swivel when she walks past. Her body is a trail of winding curves—breasts and hips and butt and thighs. My father diluted my skin color, but hers is a flawless mixture of darkened honey and caramel, and her hair, slightly coarser than mine, is an unrelieved fall of black to her waist. She's the most beautiful woman I've ever seen.

And she could never get over herself enough to find out if she had anything else to offer.

"It's been a long time since I was back home," she says, glancing around the tiny kitchen before her eyes settle on me. "You should have told me you were here. If I'd known you were so close, I would have—"

"Told Caleb?" I cut in over whatever lie she was poised to tell. "I know. That's why I didn't tell you."

"I have no idea what you mean." She touches her throat. From years of observation, I know it's her tell. She can look you dead in the eyes, a picture of innocence, while she tries to sell you a goldmine on the bayou, but she can't keep that hand off her throat.

"What I *mean* is that I know about the apartment in Buckhead." I wipe down the counter, cleaning because I can't think what else to do while navigating this awkward conversation with my mother. "He still paying your way, Mama? Caleb told me he had you well under control."

"Control?" She snaps a brow up, gentile disdain perfected. "No such thing."

"Did you know?" I toss the rag, sopping wet, into the sink, giving up on any semblance of cleaning. Considering the NDA, I won't ask her explicitly, but I can read her. I need to know if she sold me out. "You were so thrilled about all that 'security' that came with having his baby, you never considered what it was costing *me*."

Her eyes flicker, but not with surprise. Did she *know*? Or at least suspect? "I really don't know what you mean," she says.

But her hand is at her throat.

Tears sting my eyes, but I won't let them fall. Lo and I won the lottery with MiMi, but our mothers are a pair of snake eyes.

"You 'bout ready, Sil?" Aunt May asks from the kitchen doorway. She meets my eyes with difficulty. "Great service, Iris. You did MiMi proud."

"Your daughter planned most of it," I reply, my voice a quiet accusation with a million *how could yous* puckering beneath the surface.

She stiffens, tilting her chin, a picture of defiance and grace. She and my mother are almost mirror images of one another separated by just a couple of years. They've always been close, covered for one another, chosen one another even over their own children.

"Where is Lo?" she asks. "I . . . we didn't get to talk."

"Is that a new development?" I ask, sarcasm thick in the air and in my voice. "I seem to remember her not speaking to you for the last decade."

Her full lips tighten, the delicately chiseled jaw clenching. She tosses her head, the cloud of dark hair settling around her shoulders.

"Tell her *I* wanted to try," she says.

"I will tell her no such thing, because if you really wanted to try, you know she's down at the river and you'd walk down there until she listened and forgave you." I release a cynical laugh. "But you don't want to do that, do you?" I lean back against the counter, my arms folded across my chest. "Or at some point since that night you chose him over her, you would have actually tried."

"What has gotten into you, Iris?" my mother demands, indignantly. "You never used to be so . . . You weren't like this before."

"Right," I say with cold calm. "I never was, thanks to the two of you. Thank God Lo and I have MiMi's blood to make up for your failings."

"Let's go, Priscilla," Aunt May snaps. "We don't have to stay here for this kind of treatment."

"Now *that* I understand," I deadpan. "Not accepting abuse or taking anybody's shit. Again, lessons I didn't learn from you."

"When you are ready to be reasonable," my mother spits with rare gracelessness, "call me."

"If you can do me one favor, Mama," I say to their slim, outraged backs as they head for the door. "The next time Caleb calls, don't tell him that I'm here."

She looks over her shoulder, and for once she can't dissemble the truth in her eyes. *Lucky guess.*

"If not for me," I say softly, "then for the sake of your granddaughter, don't tell him anything."

Without another word, she nods, and the screen door slams shut behind them.

I slump against the sink, relief and anxiety warring inside me. If all goes according to plan, I have nothing to worry about. If I've calculated properly, and I think I have, Caleb cares too much about his father's opinion, his sponsors' approval, and his precious NBA career to jeopardize it all chasing me.

But what if I'm wrong? What if one day, the sick obsession that drove him to hatch elaborate schemes and engage in manipulation to keep me is stronger than his desire for all those things?

I chuck that into the pile of shit I can't control. There's a much larger pile of things I can control, starting with what I want to do next. There's a part of me that wants to remain here, just Sarai and me, hiding from the world, safe from danger. But I know it can't be forever. Sarai is too bright not to be in preschool soon. Too curious to only have this small patch of the world to explore. Too social not to have friends.

I follow the path to the river, that swathe of shade and grass overseen by a cypress canvas. Every step brings my grief, carefully stowed away today in a church full of strangers, closer to the surface. Today, the slight breeze whispering through the Spanish moss overseeing the river is a swaying

293

lament for MiMi.

Lo and Sarai sit several feet from the riverbank, and Sarai holds a Louisiana iris. *My namesake.*

It makes me smile and remember the day with August in the gym when he asked about my name. An ache, separate from my grief, spreads across me. I miss him. I want him, but I have no idea what to do about it.

"They're gone?" Lo asks, not turning, facing the river.

She's so like MiMi. Now that I've spent time with our great-grandmother, her influence on Lo is clear. I envy that.

"Yeah." I pull up beside her on the bank. "They're gone. Your mother—"

"Don't." Lo's voice is iced coffee. Dark. Cold with a bitter edge. "I buried my mother today."

I nod, not denying it.

"I wish I'd known MiMi longer," I venture, keeping one eye on Sarai and one eye on the river. It's not inconceivable that a gator could crawl up on the riverbank or that a snake could slither out of the thick greenery. The bayou is a calculated risk, benefits and dangers constantly on a scale.

"You knew her when you needed to," Lo says, her voice showing no emotion but her face a ravaged canvas, painted with tears. "So did I."

I slip my hand into hers, and silently, we squeeze. United again. I can't imagine I let Caleb come between us. That's a lie. I let my shame, my embarrassment, and maybe even my jealousy come between us.

"I'm sorry, Lo," I confess. "I think I was jealous of you."

"What?" Lo turns startled eyes to me. "When? How could you ever be jealous of me?"

I shrug, my shoulders weighted with self-consciousness and late summer heat. "When you confronted me about letting Caleb control me, I was frustrated. Maybe I regretted my choices." I pause, assembling my words into the right order. "I resented my life, how small it had become. You were running off to New York to work for a famous fashion designer in an atelier, whatever the hell that is. Meanwhile, I was mashing baby food and wearing yoga pants every day."

Lo's husky laugh charms the sun out from behind a cloud, and the last flare of sunlight illuminates the regal bones of her face.

"You? Jealous of me?" She shakes her head, the long braids caressing the curve of her neck. "That's ironic since I've been jealous of you most of my life."

"What?" I snap my head around to study her fully but don't release her hand. "No way."

"Oh, yes way." She throws me a teasing look, even through damp eyelashes. "Don't worry. I have since realized the fullness of my own fabulousness."

I laugh, mouth closed, the humor coming as short nasal puffs of funny air.

"Growing up, I loved you, but I wanted so much that you had," she says. "I hate what happened to me, but it was good I moved away from you and our mothers."

I'm curious but also hurt to hear this.

"I can think of a dozen reasons why living here was better than living with them, but why did you need to get away from me?"

"You'll think it's silly in that way that girls who never have to think about these things think it's silly," she says, her smile self-deprecating, her eyes knowing.

"Tell me anyway."

"I was dark." She lifts her braids. "My hair was coarse. I was the odd egg in our little nest, and everyone knew it."

"What the hell do you mean?" I demand.

"You don't think about it, but our mothers look exactly alike. Your father was white." With her free hand, she tosses a few blades of grass into the river. "They were light and you were even lighter, but my dad was black, and I look different."

It reminds me of August telling me how displaced he felt sometimes. The irony of me feeling like I didn't belong because I was "too white" and Lo being jealous because she was "too dark" strikes me as funny, and I release a giggle.

"That's funny to you?" Lo asks, one side of her full mouth tilted.

"It's just . . . I never felt like I fit in our neighborhood because I looked so different, and the girls always said I was stuck up and thought I was better than them. I really just wanted to fit. I just wanted to look like everyone else."

"And I just wanted to look like you." Lo twists her mouth to the side. "When I came here, MiMi sniffed that shit out right away."

A movement in my peripheral vision catches my eye. "No, Sarai."

I pull my hand free of Lo's and walk to the water's edge, retrieving my little adventurer. I plop down on the grass, careless of the black dress I wore to the funeral, and sit my daughter between my legs. Lo settles in a puddle of black linen beside me, stretching her legs out on the grass.

"MiMi knew that even beyond the hurt of what Mama had done, choosing that motherfucker over me," Lo says with dispassion, "that there was another hurt under it all. Mama choosing him only reinforced that I wasn't good enough. Maybe she didn't love me as much as she would have if I'd been . . . different."

Memories of Aunt May complaining about Lo's hair come to mind. She'd say she didn't know what to do "with hair like this." When Lo learned to press her own hair, Aunt May and my mother would complain about the "smell of burning hair" in the house. A hundred little thoughts come to me like pinpricks, piercing my ignorant bliss.

"I'm so sorry," I whisper. "I hope I never made you feel that way, Lo."

"No, not you." She reaches for my hand again and smiles. "You were my hopscotch, Bo. I knew you didn't feel that way."

"Did MiMi do one of her cleansing ceremonies to fix you, too?" I only half-laugh because I'm still not sure what that was or what it did, but I know

I'm changed somehow.

"It wasn't that simple," Lo says. "It never is. No, she told me about a boy she loved when she was young. When he came to the house, her mother said he failed the paper-bag test."

"What is a paper-bag test?"

"You have to remember it was New Orleans, years ago," Lo offers. "Our family was filled with quadroons and octoroons and a whole bunch of words for almost white. So when she came home with a brown brother, her mother broke out the paper bag. They would hold a paper bag against your skin, and if you were darker than the paper bag, you didn't pass the test."

"That's awful. Oh my God."

"Yeah, and MiMi regretted letting him go. He ended up marrying a friend of hers. He treated her like a queen, and they lived a happy life not a block from where he asked MiMi to marry him." Lo blinks at tears, her lips tightening. "She told me that she missed out on him because of a stupid paper bag," Lo says. "And anyone who misses out on me would be as foolish as she had been and that they would live to regret it."

I glance down at my daughter, with her skin lighter than mine and her eyes of blue–violet, and I swear to myself that no one will ever make her feel out of place or question her identity. It may not be a promise I can completely keep, but I'll try.

"Anyway, enough reminiscing." Lo looks at me, clear-eyed and probing. "It's the future we need to discuss."

I watch the sun dipping into the long, watery line of horizon, like a cookie diving into milk. "It's getting dark." I stand, brushing my dress off and bending to pick up Sarai.

"Listen to me." Lo grabs my wrist, looking up from her plot on the riverbank. "You can't stay here, Bo."

I swallow a quick retort, a defense. Even though these were my very own thoughts before I came to the river, I resist the idea of leaving. "What if it's not . . ." I gulp sudden trepidation, ". . . safe to leave? What if Caleb comes after us?"

"You've done all you can to keep him from doing that." Lo squeezes my wrist gently until I meet her eyes. "The leash is tight around his neck, but it's also tight around yours. Think about all you gave up. Get it back."

Take them back. Your soul is yours. Your heart is yours. Your body is yours. Yours to keep and yours to share.

MiMi's incantation circles my thoughts.

"The dreams you had. Your ambitions," Lo continues, in unknowing chorus with MiMi's voice in my head. "Reclaim them."

"But Sarai needs—"

"Sarai needs to see what we never saw," Lo says dryly. "Let her see her mother pursuing her dreams. Let her see you standing on your own two feet."

"I will need the money," I murmur. The little bit of cash Andrew smuggled to me when I left will run low eventually, even though our expenses have been next to nothing out here.

"You need more than money. Girl, you need a life." Lo stands, too, taking Sarai from me.

"Do you remember any of your Louisiana geography?" Lo asks.

"Um, that would be a no." I laugh. "I mean, the basics, yeah."

"Did you ever learn about deltaic switching?"

"No idea," I tell her, frowning and searching my memory.

"I don't remember all the details, but the long and short of it is that the Mississippi River searches for a shorter route to the sea. It makes these deposits of silt and sand over time to get there faster." Lo shrugs. "Think of it like geographical evolution. Well, the bayou was one of the points of deltaic switching, and over time, about every thousand years or so, it literally changes its course."

"Wow." I'm not sure what else to say. "What does that mean, though?"

"It means that this very spot where we're standing right now was powerful enough to be a part of that—to help set the new course for the freaking Mississippi River." She starts walking back up the shaded path to the house, but looks over her shoulder, locking our eyes.

"Take a few minutes and think about that," she says. "Don't let Caleb define the rest of your life. Change your course."

I take more than a few minutes after she walks away. I stand there until the sun disappears, and the night spreads the sky with black velvet and studs it with stars. I know I should go in. I'm never this close to the river when it's dark, but tonight, there's no fear of gators or snakes or whatever the swamp could use against me. Tonight, the crickets whisper Lo's words back to me.

Change your course.

And in the lapping water, I hear MiMi's voice, too.

Breathe in. Breathe out.

I draw a deep, bracing breath, strength in my lungs and pulsing through my blood. I breathe out my fears, releasing my reservations and all that could hold me back. And then I feel it. The power that changed a river's course floods my veins, and I rise inside, so high I assume a new form, a new shape. A new course.

I rush down the path back to the house, stumbling occasionally in the dark. And it'll be that way sometimes, running this course, stumbling. All that I've been through, all that is to come, none of it is easy. There is no quick fix, but tonight, I feel powerful enough to forge ahead.

Before I lose the nerve, I dig around in my purse until I find it. A small white card, bent, stained, and nearly forgotten, that may lead to big plans. May lead to my future. To my new course.

With shaking fingers, I dial.

THIRTY SEVEN

AUGUST

"We need to talk."

Good things rarely come when Jared says that to me.

I lie back on the couch in his office, my legs crossed at the ankles, my feet propped up on the armrest.

"What's there to talk about?" I toss a mini basketball up in the air, catching it with one hand. "Pippa's signing, right?"

"Yeah, I think so." Jared walks around his desk, sitting on the edge so he's facing me. "She hasn't signed the contracts yet, but we're close."

"And I didn't even have to fuck her." I toss him a grin. "Aren't you glad to hear my virtue is still intact? It's called integrity."

"It's called a wasted opportunity, if you ask me," he drawls.

"That's why I don't ask you about anything other than contracts and money." I toss the ball up in the air again, watching its spinning descent before catching it. "Speaking of money and contracts, we all set for the Houston trade?"

I still can't believe it. I'm getting out of basketball no man's land, and being shipped to the holy land. Houston went far in the playoffs this season, falling just a few games short of the championship. They'll get even further next year with the addition of a few key pieces—me being key.

"Yeah. I have the contracts." Jared hesitates, sliding his hands into the pockets of his expensively tailored slacks. "You're sure you want to do this, right?"

"For real?" I eject a disbelieving laugh. "I mean, I'll miss Decker and Jag and Kenan and all the guys, but it's business, and we're all getting something out of it."

The Waves will get three great players they can continue to build their team with, in exchange for me. And I will get the chance to play for a truly contending team, in line for a championship.

Along with forty-five million dollars.

Did I forget to mention that?

I didn't want to ask for that much, but Jared is a hard-ass and believed we could get it. Never will I complain about more zeroes.

Jared clears his throat, sighing and then looking at me.

"What? They're bucking on the money now?" I toss the basketball once more, catch it and drop it to the floor, sitting up, slumping into the leather cushions.

"Nah, nothing like that." Reluctance is smeared all over Jared's face. "We agree that this is the best decision, right?"

"Of course." I frown, crossing one ankle over my knee. "Why you keep asking me that?"

"I got a call last week." He looks up from the floor, and I brace myself for whatever bomb he's about to drop. "From Iris."

Hiro-fucking-shima.

That's the level bomb he just dropped on me.

"*My* Iris?" My question shoots out like bullet.

"Well . . ." Jared dips his head from one side to the other. "That's up for debate."

"This is not the time to play games with me." I stand, anticipation humming through my blood, breathing life into parts I didn't know were dormant. "Did she say where she is? Where she's been?"

Jared heaves a huge sigh, like he might regret this. "No, and I got the distinct impression she didn't want to," he says. "She was more concerned about the future." He fixes his eyes on me and then rolls them. "She called about a job."

"A job?" I fire back. "With you?"

"Yeah."

"Here?"

"Yeah."

"And you gave her one, right? You said, 'Yeah, I'll find a job for you if I have to because my brother will peel my skin back if I don't.' Did the conversation go something like that?"

"I still don't think she realizes we're related, so you didn't come up, but yes, I offered her a job. An entry-level job."

"Entry level?" I flop my arms up and let them fall to my sides. "Is that supposed to entice her?"

"I wasn't trying to *entice* her," he replies. "She's a sharp girl, smart and ambitious, but that doesn't change the fact that she's never worked in the industry beyond college. I told her I was no longer with Richter, but that I had my own agency now in San Diego."

"*We* have our own agency," I correct. "And? This entry-level position, is she accepting it?"

He tosses his eyes up to the ceiling, dropping his head and running his hand through his thick hair. "Yeah, she accepted."

"Holy shit." I start pacing, my arms and legs conduits for all the nervous energy zipping through me. "After more than a year, she's coming back into my life. She'll be right here in . . ."

My words die a quick and painful death. Iris will be in San Diego, and I'll be in Houston with my championship ring and my forty-five million dollars.

"We *did* just agree that Houston is the right basketball decision, Gus," Jared reminds me. "Don't do anything rash."

"Yeah, it's the right basketball decision, but I'll retire from basketball at what? Thirty-five? Thirty-six years old? And the rest of my life will be ahead of me. I'll spend more of my future off court than on. Basketball isn't my whole life."

"Isn't it?" Jared gestures around the luxurious office. "Aren't we building Elevation around your credibility as a professional athlete?"

"If the last year has shown me anything," I say softly, "it's that I need more than ball to make me happy." I take a deep breath, struggling to slow my heartbeat. She's not even in the room, not even in the state yet, and she's got me twisted.

"When does she start?" I ask.

"Three weeks."

"And would the Waves be open to me staying?" I hold my breath while I wait. If the Waves would rather leverage me to get other players than keep me, I don't have much choice in the matter.

"The front office would probably be thrilled to keep building around you. I know Deck would." Jared shakes his head and rubs the back of his neck. "But I'm begging you not to make a hasty decision you'll regret."

I know about regret. I regret not getting her phone number the first night we met. I regret not trying harder to make her see what a jackass Caleb was. I regret not kissing her sooner—not figuring out a way to make her mine. I regret not being the father of her first child.

But with the same instinct I had that night at the bar, the one that told me she would be important to me, that we would be right together, I know I won't regret this.

"Kill the deal."

"Gus." Jared lowers his face to his hands and speaks through his fingers. "Don't do this. You don't even know if she'll want a relationship with you."

Is he right? No. He can't be, not when I remember the ease Iris and I shared every time we were together. Confessions, hopes, dreams, fears, insecurities pouring out of us. I've never felt that connected to anyone else. And the way that kiss in the closet still scorches my memory and gives me a hard-on. God, I'll never forget how she tastes—sweet and tangy.

A rich fantasy pours over my senses, the smell of her when my face was buried between her legs. The silky skin inside her thighs kissing my cheeks. My mouth, hungry and sloppy, feasting at her core. My face wet with her arousal. Her fingers digging in my hair. That strip of golden skin above her panties. Fuck, her beaded nipples through that T-shirt.

"Kill the deal," I say hoarsely, heading toward Jared's office door. I'm gonna need to rub this one out in the restroom. I won't even make it home.

"August, you know this is a long shot, right?" he reasons one last time, though the resignation in his eyes tells me he understands it's futile to try to dissuade me from this course.

"A long shot?" I ask, pausing at the door to give him a cocky grin. "Last I heard, I'm pretty good at those."

THIRTY EIGHT

IRIS

I have first-day jitters. Or maybe these are new-life jitters. New-*course* jitters.

When I dug out Jared Foster's business card, who would have thought I'd be here a month later, in the offices of his new agency, Elevation? Yes, I'm entry level, but it's a small company looking for motivated people who want to make things happen.

That's me, I remind myself.

"Here she is," Jared says when he strides into the small conference room where the receptionist instructed me to wait. "Elevation's newest employee."

"Hi." I stretch my hand out to him, shaking firmly, even though I have to stop myself from flinging my arms around his neck for giving me this opportunity. "So good to see you again."

What are the odds?

Me living in San Diego.

And August moving to Texas, if the reports of his trade are correct.

I never got his number, but if I want to find him, I might be able to. Jared may even have connections with his agent.

I force myself to focus and not think about August, which has been hard ever since I landed last week. We are in the same state, in the same city, though both are bigger than any I've ever lived in before.

"You settled into your new place?" Jared asks, sitting on the edge of the conference room table with his arms folded.

"Yeah, I'll have to thank your assistant for helping me find it." I widen my eyes and grin. "I'd heard San Diego was so expensive, but I found a great place that I can actually afford and childcare for Sarai."

"Yeah, how about that?" Jared scratches behind his ear like a dog searching for a flea before clearing his throat. "We, um, just recently started the daycare for our staff."

"I was so surprised an organization as young as Elevation already has on-site childcare."

"Yeah." He lifts his brows, a sardonic turn to his mobile mouth. "No one was more surprised than me. My, uh, partner insisted on it for the, um, parents."

"I dropped Sarai off a few minutes ago." I press my palm to my heart through my silk dress. "It's my first time being apart from her, so the on-site daycare is perfect. And so affordable. They said it will be deducted from my check, and I'll never even see it."

"Yeah," he says with a wry grin. "It'll be like it's not even being taken out."

I force myself to stop gushing about how smoothly things have gone. He doesn't want to hear all of this. I'm sure he's here to lay out my responsibilities. I cannot wait to dive back into this industry—to do the thing I've wanted to do since high school.

"We'll talk about the job and all the details in a little bit," Jared says, as if he's reading my mind. "But there's someone from, um, human resources . . .

kind of, who needs to meet with you first."

"Oh, sure." That makes sense. Probably to review benefits and sign paperwork.

"I'll check in with you later." Jared stands, prompting me to stand, too. "They'll be right in."

"Okay." I sit once he leaves and smooth my palms over the slim-fitting dress Lo made me wear.

Right on time, my phone buzzes with her face onscreen. I glance over my shoulder at the door, taking the chance that I can make this quick before human resources arrives.

"Make this quick, Lo," I say. "HR will be here any minute with paperwork and stuff."

"I will. Sorry. I wasn't even sure what time it was there." She chuckles over the sound of a sewing machine in the background. "I'm on button-duty today. Sewing ten billion buttons onto this dress for next week's show."

"Paris?" I shoot a covert look at the door.

"Milan." She pops a bubble with her gum over the phone. "Sorry. It's all I've got to eat in here. These models are like robots. Seriously. They don't require food to operate."

I snicker, forgetting my nervousness for a moment.

"I was wondering if I can come visit when I get back?" Lo asks, still popping her gum.

"Oh, God, yes, Lo." I release a pent-up breath. "I'm still settling in, getting to know the city. Come explore it with us."

"I won't be able to stay long," she says, "but I've realized how much I missed you when . . ." Her voice trails off. We don't discuss my time with Caleb. He hasn't contacted me, and I refuse to put my life on hold another second fearing that he might.

Footsteps are approaching, and I practically drop the phone. "I gotta go, Lo."

"Okay, but how does Sarai like her new daycare?" she asks in a rush. "I miss my baby. I know she misses me."

"Yeah, terribly. We'll FaceTime tonight. Gotta go."

I disconnect just as the conference room door opens behind me. I'm about to turn around when a flower is placed on the table at my elbow.

Not just any flower. A gorgeous Louisiana iris in full bloom.

My heart gallops in my chest like a herd of wild thoroughbreds. A premonition prickles my skin, and there's an uprising of the fine hairs on the back of my neck. My body knows before I do, but I'm still speechless when I zing a glance over my shoulder.

I meet those thundercloud eyes under lashes as thick and curly as I remember. Every detail of his face, his hair, his body, is the same, only better. There are so many things he'll want me to explain—so many things I want to tell him, but right now his name is all I can manage.

"August?"

THIRTY
NINE

AUGUST

I passed on forty-five million dollars and probably a championship title.

You'd think that would be the first thing I thought about when I woke up this morning, since I can still hear Jared's damn voice screeching in my head.

Nope.

This moment. This moment right here is the first thing I've thought about every morning for the last three weeks. I had so many ideas about the way it could go, but I thought the flower was my best bet. It would remind her that, though we haven't ever been a couple, we have a history and an undeniable connection. That every time we've been together, we've gone deeper and known each other better. There *is* an August and Iris, and I'm ready to go all in on it. I'm sure that by the end of my life, I, like most people, will have a stack of regrets and "wish I hads," but Iris DuPree won't be one of them. Even if things don't ultimately go the way I'd like them to, I won't regret trying.

She's too worth it.

"August?"

Shock and pleasure and confusion march across her expressive face in quick succession. She stands, the Louisiana iris held between her fingers, and I get my first full look at her in more than a year.

Sweet Jesus.

My eyes rove her from head to toe, taking in every minute detail. Except for the night we met, her hair has always been straight, but it's not today. It's longer, untamed waves flowing down her back and almost reaching her elbows. Thick, dark coils cling possessively to the silky curve of her throat and to her arms, touching all the places I hope to claim. Those eyes, flecked with autumn—amber, gold and green—startle me with their clarity under a dense sweep of sooty lashes and brows. Her skin has this glow. She's always been beautiful, but there's some new dimension to her. I can't put my finger on it, but it adds this layer of irresistibility, and I clench my fists so I won't reach for her.

My eyes drop to her mouth. It's too soon to kiss her. There are explanations and questions and details. There's all of that shit, but really, I want to set it all aside and just devour her mouth. I want to suck those lips between mine, plunge my tongue down her throat, and lick around until I've sampled every hot, slick inch of her.

I hazard a glance below her neck.

Holyyyyyyy shit.

Iris has one of those bodies. She's one of those women men recall in perfect detail years after they've seen her. Even a glimpse would burn an impression into your memory. But to stop there is to literally skim the surface because under the fineness of her skin and the unflawed shape of her lives an opulence of spirit—a richness of strength you could overlook if you let her beauty distract you.

"August?" she asks for the second time.

I don't know. Maybe she's said my name five times, six. Maybe she's snapped her fingers in my face. I'm so damn wide open for this woman, I've lost track of time and space just taking her in after so long.

"Yeah." I smile down at her. "Hey."

"Hey?" She shakes her head and presses a hand to her forehead as if that will help things make sense. "You're not from human resources."

"Uh, no. Not exactly."

"Not at all." She swallows, her dark brows pinched together. "I'm glad to see you, but—"

"I'm glad to see you, too," I pounce on the positive. "You look . . . amazing, Iris."

She blinks at me owlishly. If you're a goddess-like owl, that is. "I'm glad to see you, *but* really confused," she finishes. "What's going on?"

"Well, Jared and I are brothers," I say. "Stepbrothers, actually."

"I don't understand." She takes a shallow breath. "Go on."

"I didn't realize you two even knew each other until the day before you disappeared." I leave my last word dangling in the air. You know. In case she wants to elaborate on where she's been for the past damn year or so and tell me why she never showed up again.

She tilts her chin up, silently telling me she's the one demanding explanations right now.

"Yeah, so, the day before you *disappeared*," I resume, "Jared picked me up from the community center and saw you. That's when we pieced together how we both knew you."

I smile, knowing there is more to say, but really just kind of losing my train of thought. We're finally in the same room when I didn't know if I'd ever see her again.

"And now I work here?" she asks, her brows lifted. "Isn't there a lot you're leaving out?"

"Isn't there a lot *you're* leaving out?" I ask right back. "Like why you wore Caleb's ring, but said you weren't engaged? Or how we kissed and I ate you out and you came in the closet, but then I never heard from you? Couldn't find you anywhere? Are there some details you might want to share?"

It's only in the silence tightening around us that I realize that underneath my rampant desire to fuck Iris, to hold her possibly for the rest of my life and never let her go, I'm also a little pissed. Well, now we both know.

"You first." A muscle flexes along the delicate line of her jaw. "Why am I here, August?" She clasps her hands together in front of her, her eyes fixed on the Louisiana iris cupped in her palms.

"Is there even a job?" she asks.

"Of course there's a job. I'm a silent partner in Elevation. Jared and I never advertised our connection and decided he wouldn't be my agent when I first came to the league, but we dreamed about this company for a long time." I shrug and go on. "We were gonna wait, but my injury put everything in perspective and made me realize just how short this career can be. So we started it last year."

"You own Elevation?"

"Part-owner, yeah. Jared handles all the business stuff. I'm just kind of our poster child to make other high-profile athletes want to work with us."

"But Elevation is yours." Her dark lashes flutter in quick blinks, and she bites the corner of her mouth. "Is that what you want me to be? Yours? I'm just here . . . for you?"

My first instinct is to bang my chest and say damn right she's mine, but then I realize she doesn't mean it in an *I find cavemen sexy* kind of way.

"Not like that." I blow out an uneasy laugh.

When she looks back up, I hate the hurt and disappointment darkening her eyes, detracting from that glow she wore when I first saw her. And now I get it. That glow, it was pride—in herself.

When I graduated from college, I went to the NBA just months later, received a ridiculous amount of money, set up my home here in San Diego, became a brand, racked up endorsements, and now I have one of the highest-selling jerseys in the league.

She never had that.

Not the money or the fame of any of that shit. Most people never get that—that independence.

After college, Iris was pregnant and on bed rest, unable to earn money, then responsible for a baby, dependent on Caleb, and living in his house, guarded and kept. That's the way she probably thought of it. The night we met she said she never wanted to be like her mother, a woman *kept* by men. On some level, she probably thinks that's what she was.

The idea that she was standing on her own, making her own way, it made her glow.

And she thinks I've taken that from her.

"It all makes sense now." She huffs a disparaging breath. "I'm such an idiot. I knew I shouldn't have been able to afford a house in that neighborhood."

Oh hell.

"You know I called on the house for rent next door. Just for shits and giggles, to see how much of a bargain I got." Her laugh goes sour and cynical. "It was three times what I pay. That's you, too? You did that?"

"Iris, let me explain."

"And the daycare. You can explain that, too, right? How Elevation just happened to start on-site daycare for their employees when Jared hired me?"

I'm silent. I thought I was being awesome. I thought it would make her happy not to have to leave Sarai miles away. I wanted to make this easy for her, but somehow I've screwed it all up.

I have to make this right, to explain and drive out the disappointment clouding her eyes.

I breach the invisible wall of tension separating us by cupping her chin, tilting her face up so she can see the truth when I tell her. I'd do anything to restore that glow, that pride in herself that made her even more beautiful than I've ever seen her. "Iris, no." My thumb strokes over one high cheekbone. "I can explain about the house and the daycare. I can explain everything."

"I should be flattered you made up a job for me, huh?" Her eyes shimmer with unshed tears. "Men always seem to find good use for me, don't they? What are my responsibilities exactly? Blow jobs under desks, quickies in the copy room? When do I start?" She drops to her knees in front of me and touches my belt. "Now?" Bitterness sets the lushness of her mouth into a hard line. "Or maybe you'd like to see the goods first?"

I'm stunned as she fumbles at the buttons holding her dress together, her fingers shaking as she undoes the top one and then another. The curve of her breasts swell over a black satin cup. I hate that my breath quickens and my dick stiffens at seeing even that much of her.

"I thought you'd like that," she whispers, a tear splashing onto her hand.

"Stop, Iris," I grit out. "It's not supposed to be like this."

"Like what?" Her fingers keep slipping buttons out of holes, revealing the taut line of her waist, the exaggerated curve from waist to hip. She's so finely crafted, but I'd hate for her to think that's all I want from her.

I go to my knees, still much taller than her, but at least now we're on the same level. I quickly re-button her dress, ignoring the silky skin my knuckles brush over along the way. I cup her jaw and press our foreheads together. I gentle my grip on her, my displeasure and frustration softening when I feel her under my hands.

"You did this. I promise," I say. "Jared had already given you the job before he even told me you called him."

She opens her mouth to speak, but I rest my index finger over her lips. I have to get this out.

"When he told me about the job he'd already offered you . . ." I pause, making sure she hears it was a done deal before I was involved. "I admit, I was excited."

Slight understatement.

"I wanted things to go well for you," I continue, reluctantly dropping my finger from her mouth. "San Diego is one of the most expensive cities in the country. With an entry-level position, you wouldn't have been able to afford the neighborhood you're in. I wanted you and Sarai safe and in a good spot. I don't expect or want anything in return. I haven't set you up like a mistress or something."

"It feels like it," she says, but some of the tightness eases from her neck and shoulders.

"I don't even own that house. One of the guys from the team dabbles in real estate on the side. It's one of his properties. When he heard an Elevation employee, a single mom, needed a place, he knocked the rent down."

The air begins loosening between us, and I risk taking her hand.

"And the daycare." I shrug. "I don't have a good excuse for that except . . . I wanted you to have Sarai close, but in Jared's last employee survey, several moms indicated on-site daycare would be helpful. It's not just for you. There *were* other kids there when you dropped Sarai off, right?"

Iris nods, searching my eyes for several seconds. "So there is a job?" she finally asks. "A real job? That phone interview Jared put me through wasn't just him going through the motions for his brother's girlfriend?"

Girlfriend?

Calm down.

She doesn't mean it like that.

She isn't saying . . . shit. Who am I kidding?

"Girlfriend?" I can't resist asking. "Are you gonna be my girl, Iris?"

I'm still cupping her face, and her thick hair is falling across my fingers. She smells like paradise, and I'm not sure I can do this—can make it out of this room without kissing her. Without lifting her onto the conference room table, shoving that dress over her legs, and eating the hell out of her pussy. Because that's pretty much all I can think about now that we're this close. It's like I haven't had a meal since the last time I had her, and my mouth is watering imagining that clit, those lips, her juices. Her coming for me—coming in my mouth, dripping down my chin.

"I need to take it slow, August," she whispers.

Slow.

That would be in direct contrast to my right-now fantasy. I struggle to command my body. I haven't had sex in a really long time. Jared was right. I need to fuck, but the only girl I want is telling me she needs to go slow. And though my body is raging and burning and yearning to bury every inch I *got* inside of her, slow we will go.

"We can do that," I tell her. "However long it takes."

My voice sounds even. You'd never know there's a rocket in my pants ready for lift-off. Rehabbing my leg, getting back on the court in less than a year, coming back stronger—that took Herculean effort. If I can be that disciplined for a *game*, I can control myself for Iris. I've waited for her, and I'll wait some more until she says we've waited long enough.

"I wasn't prepared for this," she says, her voice almost an apology. "For any of this. I thought . . . I know I've been out of the loop, but last I heard you were being traded to Houston. I didn't even know you'd be living in the same city."

That's when an awful thought occurs to me. Have I had things *that* wrong?

"So did you accept the job *because* you thought I'd be gone?" Disappointment and embarrassment drive me to my feet. I miss her warmth immediately, but maybe I need to get used to the idea that she moved here because she thought I was leaving.

"Wow. Now I feel like a fool." My laugh is a three-dollar bill. Fake. Counterfeit. "I didn't even think . . . yeah, I guess I didn't think this all the way through. I assumed you felt . . ."

I swallow down the emotion burning my throat. Jared's voice comes back to haunt me—his warning that I would regret staying with the Waves if things with Iris didn't pan out. The flower I brought her lies on the floor by her knees, and that's how I feel. Clipped at the stem. Discarded.

"I did." She stands, her head only coming to the middle of my chest. "I do . . . feel it, I mean."

She reaches for my hand, winding her fingers through mine and looking at me the way I imagined she would, a mixture of possibility and want and hope in her eyes. "I feel it, too, August. I always have," she says softly, tucking her full bottom lip into her mouth for a second before going on. "I've just . . . been through a lot, I guess, and I'm still sorting some things out."

Been through a lot? What the fuck does that mean? What's she been through? Who hurt her? Caleb? That dude is dead if I find out he hurt her.

"What does that mean?" I ask, hoping my voice sounds more civilized than I feel. "What have you been through, Iris?"

I feel it immediately, the wall erected between us. Her eyes go distant, looking inside herself. "I can't . . . I mean . . ." Her eyes beg, and I'm willing to do whatever she wants. To give her whatever she needs. "Can we just not talk about that right now?"

Frustration strangles me for a second, but I force myself to calm down. She'll tell me eventually who I need to maim.

What happened to her?

I nod, twisting our fingers tighter, letting her know I'm not going anywhere.

"Oh." She shakes her head, confusion back on her face. "Wait. So what happened with the Houston deal? Last I heard, it was all but done."

Do I tell her the truth? If I tell her what I did, all that I gave up on the off chance she'd be with me, that's a lot of pressure. On her. On me. On this relationship, once it becomes an actual relationship with dates and daily conversations like normal couples have, and sex . . .

Shit. I'm probably gonna break my dick jerking off so hard before I leave this building.

"August?" she asks again. "What happened with the Houston deal?"

Sneaking around trying to help her, not being completely upfront got us off to a rocky start. I won't risk that again being anything less than honest.

"When Jared told me you were moving here, I passed on the deal." My words fall into this chasm of stunned silence. She rears back as if I've struck her. Her fingers start loosening from mine, but I don't let her go.

"No." I squeeze her hand gently, lifting my other hand to cup her face. "Listen to me."

"August, that contract was forty . . ." She draws a deep breath before charging on. "Like, forty million dollars."

"Forty-five, but what's a few million here and there?" I joke.

"But what about the team?" She asks, ignoring my attempt at humor. "Houston made the finals this year."

"Yeah." I stamp down the fear that I'll never win a championship, never have a ring, the holy grail I've pursued most of my life.

"That team is primed for a championship," she reminds me unnecessarily. "Maybe even next season."

"Iris, I'm well aware."

"But it makes no sense. I don't understand."

Here's my chance to get it right. My chance to make sure she knows that, though I've been chasing a ball up a court all my life, with this I'm not playing games.

Take the shot.

"Your dreams and ambitions got swallowed up when you had to follow Caleb," I say, holding her eyes with mine. "I want you to know there's someone who will follow *you*."

She blinks several times, and I can only hope my words are sinking in.

"But you can't . . . I'm not . . ." She falters and tries again. "August, Houston is your best shot at winning a ring."

"You're right." I loosen my fingers from hers so I can hold her face between both hands. "Going to Houston is my best shot at winning a ring."

"Then why would you—"

"But staying here," I cut in, caressing the fullness of her bottom lip with my thumb. "Staying is my best shot at winning you."

FORTY

IRIS

"What the hell is wrong with you?"

It's not the first time Lo has asked me this question, and it certainly won't be the last.

"Don't start, Lo," I mumble, stretched out on my stomach on the living room floor, coloring with Sarai.

"Now tell me again what he said?" she asks, knowing good and damn well what August said. I've told her the last four times she's asked.

"He said Houston is his best shot at winning a championship," I repeat, stripping all the emotion from my voice but swooning all over again inside, "but staying here is his best shot at winning me."

"Damn, he's good." Lo gathers a fistful of popcorn. "The last thing I would be telling that man is that I want to go *slow*."

I don't answer but keep my head down and focus on coloring in the lines.

"More like, let's go right now." She squints at the television mounted on the wall. "Now, which number is he?"

I glance up from the *Frozen* coloring book to the television broadcasting the Waves game. The players' backs are turned into the huddle for a time-out.

"He's number thirty-three. It was his dad's number, too."

"Now his dad was a brother or what?"

"Yeah, his dad was black. His mother's white. His father actually played in the NBA, too. He died in a car accident his second season."

"Oh, man. That's rough."

We both glance at the television when the crowd cheers. August just made a three-pointer. He high-fives his teammates.

I could be there. In the month we've been in San Diego, August has offered Sarai and me tickets, but we've never gone. They're still in pre-season, though, and this is an exhibition game. The regular season doesn't start until the end of this month, and I promise myself I'll go to some of those games despite the public scrutiny that will inevitably follow if I'm associated with Caleb's biggest rival.

"I'm glad he's having a good game." I smile, because I know he'll text me after and ask if I watched, and what I thought, and how'd he do.

"Hmmmmmmmm. Look at all that curly hair." Lo slides a sly glance from the television to me, watching for a response.

I glance up again, and my heart triple times. August stands at the free-throw line. Of course, he makes the shot. He's a ninety percent free-throw shooter.

"He does have great hair," I admit neutrally. It's shorter than when I saw him in Baltimore, when it clung to my fingers like hungry silk, but he was rehabbing then.

"That man is fine," Lo says. "He could get it."

My head snaps up and my eyes shoot venom.

"There we go!" Lo points to my face and laughs. "About damn time. I'm just trying to gauge if you're feeling him or not."

Oh, I'm feeling him. I'm feeling . . . *everything*, and it scares me to death.

"So he's okay with you taking things slow?" Lo probes further.

"Yeah." An involuntary smile tugs at my lips, and I drop my crayon. "You know he has a Louisiana iris at my desk every morning when I get to work?"

"Well, he's rich. He can afford to have it delivered."

"Nope." I shake my head and suspect I may look dreamy. "On the way to his early morning workouts, he delivers it himself. He even leaves handwritten notes."

"What do the notes say?"

I shrug, biting my bottom lip and caressing the blue–gray crayon that matches his eyes almost exactly.

"Simple things like *I hope you have a good day*." I giggle and feel my cheeks heat up. "Or *you're the prettiest girl I've ever seen*."

Are we still going slow?

I'd play you at the five.

I can't wait for our next kiss. Remember our first?

Our first kiss ended with his head between my legs and my best orgasm to date. In a closet, no less. What could August accomplish with a bed?

"We talk about everything," I continue with a smile. "Work, life, ball. It's so easy, so natural for us."

Lotus sits up on the couch, leaning forward and pressing her elbows to her knees.

"He sounds like a great guy. He's fine as hell."

"He loves Sarai," I add with a smile. "Every time he's in the Elevation building he goes by to see her, even if it's just for a few minutes. She can't say his full name, so she calls him Gus. He hates it, but he won't make her stop."

"You've already fallen for him," Lo says softly.

Groaning, I flip onto my back, the coloring book abandoned. Of course, I've fallen for him. I'm not an idiot. I started falling for him the day we met, and I haven't stopped falling since.

"That doesn't change how I need to handle this," I tell Lo, my eyes fixed to the beamed ceiling in our small house. It's in a great neighborhood, but our place is small—just the right size for Sarai and me. A tiny square of grass serves as our backyard, and we have a lemon tree that scents the air when we sit outside. There's a second-hand . . . okay, third- or fourth-hand car in the driveway, purchased with a little bit of the money MiMi left for Lo and me to split. It's not much, but it's all mine.

"When I told you to change your course," Lo says, bringing me back, her eyes and voice matched for seriousness, "I didn't just mean find a job. There's a life out there, girl. You are not just somebody's mama."

"And I'm not just somebody's woman either," I say curtly. "Believe me. I've been that."

"Don't let Caleb win, Bo."

Since Lo helped me escape and already knows what happened, she's really my only outlet to speak freely about it. That NDA keeps me locked down, but it's also the agreement that gave me my freedom.

"I'm not letting him win." I sit, finding her eyes and looking at her straight. "I just have reservations."

"About August?"

I shrug, not sure where my reservations stem from, but sure that I have them.

"It's hard to trust again," I admit. "I missed all the signs with Caleb. The jealousy and possessiveness. Pressing for deeper commitment than I was ready for. Isolating me from the people I care about. When you're *that* wrong about someone, it makes you cautious."

"And that's it?" Lotus presses.

"I also worry about what Caleb will think—what he'll do."

"Excuse me?" Lo's face wears full-coverage indignation. "What's that sombitch got to do with anything?"

"He hates August. Hell, August hates Caleb, too." I plow a nervous hand through my hair. "You know it was Caleb's dirty play that broke August's leg two seasons ago, right? He did that on purpose, Lo. And he told me he'd do worse if I got involved with August."

"He can't do a thing to either of you now."

"That's easy to say when it's not you," I say bitterly. "You have no idea."

"So now we gonna compare rape stories?" Lo asks softly. "Is that it?"

"Oh, God. No." I rush to the couch to sit and grab her hand. "I didn't mean it that way. I know you know how it feels to be violated. I just meant . . ." How do I make her understand the depths to which Caleb sank to control me?

"Caleb is crazy. Like truly crazy." I close my eyes against a torrent of nightmarish memories. "The things I'm holding over him only work if he cares about his career and his endorsements and everything else more than he cares about . . ." I don't want to make my fears more real by voicing them.

"More than he cares about you?" Lo finishes for me.

"Yeah." I hesitate before going on. "He was obsessed with me. I know that sounds self-absorbed or conceited or something, but it's true."

"I've seen his crazy, Bo. You don't have to convince me."

"He threatened to hurt August again if I didn't stay away from him. He threatened to hurt you, too."

"Me?" Lo touches her chest. "The hell. I'd like to see him try."

"I told you before he knew your address by heart. Knew your schedule and where you worked in New York. I didn't even know that."

"I know." Lo's thick brows converge above the outrage in her eyes. "I just hate that he used me against you.

The walls feel like they're closing in on me even discussing the invisible but very real chains Caleb used to hold onto me.

"Everyone who meant anything to me, he used against me, and he'd do it again and worse if he got the chance." I shake my head. "Seeing me and

August together—I just hope it doesn't push him over the edge. That's part of my hesitation, too."

"You can't live your life in fear of him, though."

"Sometimes it's the fear that keeps you alive, Lo. I learned a lot from this experience. I learned that people are really cavalier with other people's lives."

"What's that mean?"

"They tell women to 'just leave', and they say 'you're so weak to stay.'" My words tumble out of me faster than I can process. "Yes, there are women who stay too long. Yes, there are women who accept abuse, confused that somehow it's still love. That wasn't me, but I knew that if I tried to leave and failed, he would kill me."

Lo stares at me in silence for a few moments. I can tell she thinks I'm being melodramatic, and I have to make her understand.

"Seventy percent of domestic-abuse homicides occur when the woman tries to leave. That means that when a lot of these motherfuckers say 'I'll kill you if you leave me,' they mean it." A sob catches in my throat, but I shove it back down, determined to have my say with a strong, unwavering voice. "Imagine if I'd left and he got partial custody of Sarai. That monster having my daughter on the weekends? Never."

"That wouldn't have happened," Lo says, but she sounds less certain than she did when we first began.

"Oh, yes, it would have. He's rich, famous, has the best lawyers money can buy, and no prior offenses. Sports, especially at his level, is so insular, and they protect their own. I've seen it for myself. Behind every woman who comes out telling her story, there's a line of officers, staff, coaches, and people who should have helped, who knew and did nothing."

Hurt, outrage, and fury throw a tantrum inside of me. I pause to draw a calming breath before going on. "He wouldn't have gotten more than a slap on the wrist, and that's *if* anyone believed me."

I gather my hair back from my face and link my hands behind my neck. It's an impractical justice, a woman having to share custody with the man who tried to kill her because his parental rights should be protected.

"People have no idea what some women go through behind closed doors or what keeps them there." I shake my head. "That was me, living a lie and getting beaten up by the truth until I found my way out. And I don't know if I'll ever really get over it."

"You will." Lo tucks a lock of hair behind my ear, and I flinch.

"See?" My laugh comes out slightly hysterical. "He used to do that. He'd push my hair behind my ear so gently, but with his gun."

"Shit, Bo," Lo says, anger and horror taking up arms in her expression.

"You know I still sleep curled at the edge of the bed because it's the only way I can. I didn't want our bodies touching while we slept." Tears clog my throat, and a few escape my eyes no matter how much I will myself not to cry. "I didn't want him that close when I was asleep, but he wouldn't let me sleep anywhere else."

"You need to talk to someone, babe," Lo says.

"I am, actually. I do. I've been talking to a counselor at a women's shelter here in the city, but can a therapist strip my mind of the memories? Of the nightmares? Sometimes I wake up thinking there's a gun between my legs."

"What the hell?"

"Yeah, he liked to put a gun to my vagina and make me choose between that and his dick."

"That bastard." Lo's eyes harden, and her full lips thin. "Don't worry. His is coming. His days are numbered."

Lo has removed her braids and wears her hair's natural texture in a close cap of curls dyed platinum that contrasts starkly with her complexion. She looks so different, but the same light that burned in her eyes when she confronted Caleb ignites now.

"Lo, what does that—"

"Mommy, potty," Sarai says. She stands and crosses one little foot over the other.

God, she's adorable. I'm not biased.

"Potty training," I mutter, standing and taking Sarai by the hand and heading for the bathroom. "We'll be back."

Sarai's all done and washing her hands when Lo yells from the front room. "Bo, you said August's number thirty-three, right?"

The concern in her voice propels my heartbeat, and I rush back into the living room just in time to see a replay in slow-motion.

August and his teammate Kenan, the one they call Glad, go up for the rebound at the same time. Kenan is huge, a little taller than August. He's several inches wider and thicker.

His elbow slams into August's forehead at full force. With dread building in my belly, I watch August fall to the hardwood and stay there unconscious for several seconds.

"Oh my God, get up." My insides knot. "Please, baby, get up."

I don't even question the endearment when it slips naturally out of my heart and past my lips. I've been fooling myself, guarding my heart with a porous shield, and August slipped right in.

His eyes open groggily and he tries to sit up, but his hand starts shaking violently, and he collapses back to the floor.

I cover my mouth and ball my fist up over my heart.

"He's gonna be okay," Lo assures me. "Look. He's getting up."

Correction. Kenan is pulling him up, and someone is walking him off the floor. He gives a little wave to the crowd and stumbles into the tunnel.

They show the play over and over again, and every time, I hurt a little more. I think about everything I told Lo, and it's all true. I am afraid of how Caleb will respond when he finds out about August and me. The fears

I hoped to leave behind still wake me at night drenched in a cold sweat. Seeing August go down like that, though, and not knowing how bad it is puts everything in perspective. Every day that we're living, breathing, and in good health is a blessing, not promised. Understanding that, seeing him get hurt, makes me realize that I don't want to go slow after all.

Not anymore.

FORTY ONE

AUGUST

D*amn,* my head hurts.

That's what happens when Jolly the Big Ass Giant elbows you in the head.

My own teammate sidelined me. Not that it was Kenan's fault. We were both going after the rebound and collided. He feels like shit and will probably come by as soon as the game is over. I'd love to be gone before then, but it's not happening. "Concussion" is never anybody's favorite word. I don't need to be in the hospital, but I get it. When your whole body's insured and a team pays you millions, they tend to take precautions. That doesn't mean I'm not ready to go home.

I check my phone. No calls from Iris. Maybe she doesn't know. Maybe she wasn't watching the game. Or maybe she and Lotus, who's visiting from New York, took Sarai to that park up the street. My finger is poised over her contact when the nurse pokes her head in.

"Sorry to disturb you, Mr. West."

"No problem." I force a smile. "What's up?"

"You have a visitor," she says with a grin. "A pretty brunette."

My heartbeat picks up, but I try not to look all overeager and shit. "Please send her in."

I adjust the bed to a sitting position as the door eases open and a dark head peeks in. But the hair isn't long and hanging in thick coils. It's a bone-straight bob, and her golden skin glows from her afternoon tennis practice.

"Pippa," I say, my tone flat and disappointed even to my own ears. "Come on in."

"Don't sound so happy to see me." Pippa walks in and sits on the bed beside me.

"Sorry." I rearrange my features into a pleased expression, though my face feels like wax. "Just the concussion probably."

"I know." She takes my hand and scoots a little closer on the hospital bed. "I saw."

"I didn't realize you were here in San Diego." I want to pull my hand back, but I'll give her a few minutes. We *are* friends.

"I was meeting with the team at Elevation." She smiles brightly. "I'm signing."

"That's awesome." I squeeze her hand. "Jared and company will take care of you."

"And what about you?" Her voice drops, taking on a husky tone. "Will you take care of me, too?"

"*Uh . . .*" Is there a diplomatic way to say hell no?

"I'm here for the rest of the week. Maybe we can get together before I leave."

"*Uh . . .*" I *must* have a concussion because I haven't said more than "uh' in the last two minutes. "Sure. Why not?" In my head, I hear Jared pimping me out at least for drinks until we have her signature on the dotted line.

She leans closer so her blouse droops, and I see the curve of her breasts. Don't get me wrong—Pippa's got a great body. She's one of the top tennis players in the world. And the sex was good, but her light floral scent is all wrong. Her hair is jet black, missing the burnished streaks. Her lips are thin, not full and pouty and pink. She's beautiful and just right for someone, but she's not Iris. So she's not right for me.

The door opens again, and another dark head peers around the corner. This is the one I was hoping for.

"Iris." Everything brightens—the room, my voice, my smile, and I feel Pippa's regard sharpen on my face. "Come on in."

"Oh, I . . ." She flicks a glance between Pippa and me, darting down to our clasped hands on the hospital bed. "I didn't mean to interrupt."

I snatch my hand from Pippa, and she looks at me, wearing hurt on her face. I haven't given Pippa any reason to think we'll be anything again. I need to be kind, but clear that we are not happening.

"You're not interrupting." I gesture to the other side of the bed. "Come on and sit down."

She walks over to the bed with dragging steps, glancing at Pippa's expensive clothes and the shiny diamond studs in her ears. Pippa is gorgeous. Of Asian descent, her dark hair falls straight to frame the high slant of her cheekbones. She's beautiful, but she's not my Iris.

Yes, I think of her as mine. I will have no trouble telling her so once we get past "slow." Hell, I'm hers, too, whenever she wants to claim me. Over the last few weeks, though we haven't even kissed, we've been building something.

I guess? I think? I hope?

"Sorry. Blame my rudeness on the concussion." I gesture to the curious girl beside me. "Pippa Kim, this is Iris DuPree. Pippa's signing with Elevation, and Iris works with our team."

"Oh, that's wonderful, Ms. Kim," Iris says, her enthusiasm genuine. She really does love her job. "If you two were discussing—"

"Nope," I cut in because if I know Iris, and I'm glad to say that I do now, she's about to leave. And I can't let that happen. "We were done, right, Pip?"

Displeasure passes over her face like a cloud, quickly hidden. "I guess we are," she mutters, rising and grabbing her purse. "I'll still be in town this week. I'll call you about getting together."

You just had to say that, huh?

"Sure." My smile is stiff and my voice curt. "See you later."

As soon as the door swings closed behind Pippa, I reach for Iris.

"Hey, you." I bring the back of her hand to my lips. "How's tricks?"

She studies me for long seconds, her inspection thorough. "Forget tricks," she says, her voice subdued. "How are *you*?"

"Were you worried about me?" I tease, rubbing my nose over the palm of her hand and smiling when she shivers.

"Of, course I was worr . . ." She heaves a deep breath and blows it out, running her free hand through the wild hair that's erupted into waves and curls. "God, August."

A tear slides over her cheek, and I feel like a royal asshole. My head may hurt, but I can still lift someone as small as Iris, so I do, dragging her to sit up against the pillows in the bed beside me. I tuck her under my arm and lower my forehead to hers. We've covered a lot of ground since she moved here a month ago. She said slow, and I added consistent. The Louisiana irises every morning. Daily text messages. Lunch together whenever my schedule allows. We've been seeing how we fit into each other's lives. After years of seeing each other so sporadically, it's good to set a normal pattern.

If I ever wondered if I was simply infatuated with the idea of Iris and the reality wouldn't live up to my expectations, I know now she doesn't just match to my fantasies. She's so much better. As hard as it's been, I haven't tried to kiss her. Don't want to rush her. I've honored her request for slow, and now when I see how she watches me, I believe it's paying off.

"Hey, I'm okay." I work my fingers into the thick hair spilling around her neck.

"You're sure?" Her breath is cool and minty, but my lips burn. "I saw you fall and . . . I'm just glad you're okay." Another tear streaks down her cheek. I brush it away with my knuckle and push the tangle of hair from her face.

"I'm glad you're here." I leave a few kisses along her hairline. "Thanks for coming."

"I had to." She watches me from beneath lowered lashes for a few seconds before clearing her throat. "It was nice of Pippa to come by, too."

"It really was," I agree.

"She's even prettier in real life."

"She really is."

"And so talented." She pushes a skein of hair behind her shoulder. "I guess you guys have a lot in common."

I'm struck by the irony of Iris being jealous of Pippa when Pippa stormed out moments ago, clearly aware Iris is the one I want.

"Iris." I lift her chin until she meets my eyes. "Is there something you want to ask me about Pippa?"

"No, I . . . no, I—"

"Do you wanna know if I fucked her? Because I did, but that was a long time ago."

Her eyes widen and then drop to her fingers twisting in her lap.

"I was with a lot of people then," I confess. "Because I was trying my damnedest to forget you were with him."

Her head snaps up, and we look at each other.

"You can ask me whatever you want, Iris, about anyone." I run my nose along her cheek, listening for the hitch of her breath at the charged contact of my skin on hers.

She turns her head, and a centimeter, not even a fully drawn breath, separates our mouths. She sinks her teeth into her bottom lip and reaches up to touch my face, her fingertips wandering over my cheeks and painting a stripe down my nose. Her thumbnail outlines my lips, and I crave her touch on me everywhere. I lean into her, brushing our noses together once, twice, again.

"What are you doing?" she asks with a breathy laugh.

"Eskimo kisses," I whisper, spreading my fingers to span her waist. "I'm scared to do the real thing. To kiss you."

She rubs my nose back, her eyes never leaving mine, her lips just shy of a kiss.

"Why are you scared to kiss me?" she asks.

"Because the last time I kissed you," I say, biting my lip, wanting to bite hers, "you disappeared."

She leans back a little, but I don't let it last. I bring her back into my side until our thighs press together and the curve of her breast tortures me.

"Please don't pull away from me." I trace one dark eyebrow, studying the striking framework of her face. "Where'd you go, Iris?"

Her lips part, then slam shut, then part again before she finally speaks. "Louisiana." She closes her eyes. "I went to my great-grandmother's, but I didn't want anyone to know."

Why the secrecy? Was she in some kind of trouble? "Tell me what happened. What's going on? Did Caleb—"

"I can't talk to you about him," she interrupts abruptly, opening her eyes to hold mine. "Don't ask me about my life with him, August."

"Nothing?" I press my back into the pillow to get a clearer look at her. "But I need to know if—"

"I signed an NDA." A hard swallow flexes her slim throat. "Okay? So when I say I can't talk about things with him, I mean I can't. Breaking that jeopardizes sole custody of Sarai. Please don't ask me."

Can I move forward without understanding what happened in the past?

I have a million questions about her and Caleb, but I doubt her answers would actually satisfy me. I want to know if she ever loved him. I want to know if he was really her first, her only lover. The thought of her giving him that honor when he's such an asshole scratches the inside of my brain.

"If you can't," she says after a few moments of silence, "then I understand." She searches my face, her eyes anxious, and clutches her T-shirt in her fist.

"I used to think of you with him," I admit. My laugh is bitter between us. "Of you . . ."

Fucking him.

Even now, the thought of him inside of her, of him getting her pregnant, watching her grow with Sarai, staking that claim on her that I can't ever erase or usurp—it's an asylum in my mind. My thoughts go crazy, and I draw a deep breath to stem the insanity.

"I can't change the past, August." Slowly, one finger at a time, she unclenches the shirt fisted at her waist and reaches for my hand. "But we can talk about the future, if you want."

If I want?

If I fucking want?

I've never wanted anything more.

"Iris, once we start this, I can't go back." I'm a fool for giving her time to reconsider, but we have enough regrets. "Are you sure?"

"Yeah, but I . . ." She lowers her lashes, hides her eyes. "Things with Caleb were . . . I haven't been with anyone since . . ."

I really don't want to talk about him, but whatever this macho ego shit is I got going on, I need to set it aside so she feels she can talk to me about anything.

"Hey, look at me." I tilt her chin, catch her eyes. "We said slow. That's on everything. Physically. Emotionally. Whatever you need. You set the pace, okay?" I drop my hands to my sides.

"Okay." Mischief lifts some of the seriousness from her eyes. "So if I say I'm ready for our next kiss, would that be alright?"

"Is that a real question?"

We laugh, and my heart thumps while I wait for her to make a move. I said she could set the pace. Now to keep my hands to myself until she lets me know how this should go.

Her hands are gentle on my face, and for a few moments, she just looks at me, and then, eyes still locked with mine, she takes my bottom lip between hers. There's something uncertain in her gaze when she tilts her head and deepens the kiss with the first pass of her tongue over my teeth. It's an exploration, a tentative touch that singes my lips and ripples from the point of contact to the tips of my fingers.

It may be the sweetest moment of my life.

I grip the sheets, pressing my back deeper into the pillows, fighting the urge to pull her closer, tighter. Fighting the urge to do what I'm conditioned to do. Take over. I'm the floor general. I run the team. This is foreign, putting the ball in someone else's hands. It goes against everything in me to let someone else call the plays, but I'll do it. God, I think for Iris I'd do anything.

She stares at me while our mouths meld, cling, open, and the intimacy swells between us the longer we watch each other. The longer we taste each other. With every second, the more I have, the more I want. She pulls away just long enough to glance at the sheet knotted in my fists. With a smile, she sifts her fingers into my hair.

"August," she whispers, "you can touch me."

I've been waiting for permission, but now I'm the one who's tentative. It's crazy. We've kissed before. Hell, in that closet, we did a lot more than that. But there's something more fragile about her this time. I'm a big guy. I'm sometimes clumsy and not always careful. Whatever is fragile about her,

I'd rather die than break.

"It's okay," she says softly. "Touch me how you want."

My hands glide over her waist, slipping under her T-shirt and learning the exquisite craftsmanship of her ribcage, the flare of her hip. My lips wander down her cheek and dot kisses over her chin, jaw, neck, every inch of fine-grained skin I can get to. She's the most intoxicating champagne. I sip. I drink. I slurp. I gulp her until I can't remember the taste of another woman— there's only ever been her scent and her hair and her shape. She is singular, obliterating every kiss that came before her, eliminating the possibility of anyone else ever tasting this good.

She ducks her head, recapturing my lips, angling her mouth, as hungry for it as I am. Her lips are greedy. Her tongue matches mine, velvety stroke for velvety stroke. I'm panting, almost choking on need. Knowing she wants this as much as I do drives it higher. It's wet and hot and urgent. Every kiss stokes the craving that's been brewing between us since our first moment in that bar.

She presses closer, whimpering under my hands and crawling onto my lap, straddling me. The smallest movement of her hips rolling over me stills us both. I'm only wearing a thin hospital gown, so she has to feel how hard I am. I thrust up, and she drops her head into the cove of my neck and shoulder, her breath a heat wave on my skin. Our hips move in concert, each of us seeking traction, relief. She sits up, capturing my eyes and rocking into me, the rhythm of her body steady and deep. Her eyelids droop, and her mouth falls open on a quiet moan.

"Oh, God, August." Her brows pinch together and she bites her lip, rolling over me, dropping her head back until her neck is elongated. I lick the stretch of satin from her jaw to her collarbone. I nudge the neck of her T-shirt aside, licking the tops of her breasts. I insert my tongue, dipping in to taste her cleavage.

A knock on the door startles us. She's still scrambling off my lap and I'm reaching for a blanket to cover my erection when the door swings open.

Fucking Kenan.

First, he elbows my head.

Now, he blocks my cock.

With his jet-black brows lifted, Kenan tips his mouth in a knowing half-grin.

"I'm pretty sure that's not part of the concussion protocol," he says. "If so, you can elbow *me* in the head."

"Jackass." I grin, still panting, and run my fingers through my hair. "You come to finish me off?"

His smile evaporates, and he steps farther into the room. They don't call him Gladiator for nothing. At nearly six-eight, with wide shoulders and a broad chest and just about zero body fat, I'm glad we're on the same team.

"Bruh, I'm sorry." He crosses over to the bed, glancing speculatively at Iris.

"Kenan, this is Iris." I grab her wrist so she doesn't leave the bed just because he's here. "Iris, this is the man responsible for my concussion."

"I know," she says smiling faintly, her cheeks still rose-gold with embarrassment. "I saw. Nice to meet you."

"Likewise," he says, not trying to hide his curiosity. "You look so familiar."

Iris stiffens at my side and tugs harder until her wrist is free. "Maybe I've just got one of those faces," she murmurs, her smile stiff and plastic.

Her text alert sounds, and she frowns down at her phone.

"Everything okay?" I ask.

"Yeah. It's just Lo asking me to translate something Sarai is saying. Sometimes I'm the only one who understands her."

"She's at home?"

"No, they actually came with me. They're in the waiting room." She rolls her eyes. "Lo thought I was too upset to drive."

"Were you?" I tug on one coil resting on her shoulder. She looks from me to Kenan, her smile tight at the corners.

"I'd love to see Sarai and to finally meet Lo," I say, sparing her having to answer in front of Kenan. "Give her the room number."

"You'll love Lo, and she can't wait to meet you." She types out the text, sinking her teeth into a smile. "I'll warn you in advance. There's never any telling what will come out of her mouth."

"Lo?" Kenan asks, one brow cocked.

"My cousin." Iris stands, and I miss her already.

The door opens and Sarai darts across the room to her mother, throwing her arms around Iris's knees as if they've been separated fifteen years instead of fifteen minutes. With it being just the two of them for the last year, she probably got really attached.

Sarai peeks out from behind Iris's knees to look at me, her lips curving up to match the huge grin I'm giving her.

"Hi, Sarai," I say, wishing she felt comfortable enough already to give me a hug, too.

"Gus," she whispers.

Iris snorts, laughing at the nickname I told her I hate. There's still time to retrain Sarai, but right now she could call me Attila the Hun and I wouldn't care.

Iris's cousin enters the room at a more measured pace.

The first thing I notice about Lotus DuPree is how much she and Iris look alike. There *are* marked differences. Her skin is a few shades darker but no less smooth. Her hair is coarser but still curly, cut close and died platinum blond. She's slimmer than Iris, a little shorter, but she looks like a model. Not in her stature, but with an effortless kind of grace. Over a wife-beater, she wears a fitted multi-colored silk kimono jacket. Dark jeans mold the lean line of her legs. The tiniest hoop adorns the keen curve of her left nostril.

Beyond her obvious attractiveness, there's something about her that highjacks your attention. Even with no expression, Lo's face seems animated. The expressive brows and wide, mobile mouth speak on her behalf without her uttering a word. She's as hard to look away from as Iris, but for different reasons.

Iris said they come from a long line of voodoo high priestesses. I see it in Lotus. A regalness—a mystery and an aura, like she knows your thoughts before you think them and is fully capable of changing your mind.

Kenan can't seem to look away. His eyes follow her path from the door to the bedside.

"Nice to meet you, August," she says, extending her hand.

Where Iris's voice is sweet and husky, Lotus's voice emerges low, commanding, and with an inherent sensuality that would have many men under her spell immediately.

Is that what's happened to Kenan?

He still hasn't said a word, and, as far as I can tell, he hasn't looked anywhere else since Lotus walked in the room.

"Glad we finally get to meet," I tell her, smiling. "Iris has been talking about you since the night we met."

"Well, we're even because your name may have come up a time or two today," she says, smiling and ignoring the glare Iris shoots her way. "Or maybe twelve times. I stopped counting."

A chuckle rumbles through my chest, and I grab Iris's hand to squeeze.

"And this is Kenan, the teammate who put me here in the first place." I gesture toward the giant beside me, who dwarfs both women considerably. Standing on opposite sides of my bed, Lotus and Kenan exchange looks, neither smiling. Lotus narrows her eyes on him as if she's seeing beyond the sinew and muscle and bone to the parts Kenan hides from everyone, maybe even from himself.

"Nice to meet you," Kenan says, clearing his throat and breaking the silence between them.

"Yeah." Lotus slides her glance away from him. She turns to Iris. "She's getting whiny. I think she's hungry."

"Yeah." Iris glances at her watch and grimaces. "It's about that time. She hasn't eaten since lunch." She steps a little closer to the bed, still holding my hand. "I better get going."

"Of course." I agree, even though what I really want to say is *not yet*.

"When are you getting out of here?" she asks softly.

"Should be tomorrow. I'll call you when I'm leaving."

"Do you need a ride or anything?" she asks.

"I got him," Kenan says. "It's the least I can do."

I shoot him a disgusted look. First the cock blocking. Now this?

Iris intercepts my look and chuckles softly. We share a look as intimate as a touch. I know she wants to be careful about how Sarai sees her, what she sees her doing.

"Okay," Iris says, picking Sarai up and walking toward the door. "Call me."

With one last furtive glance at Kenan, Lotus says her goodbyes, too.

There's a thick silence once they leave. Their mingled scents still linger. Their presence was so strong, I can practically see an impression of them left in the air.

I turn my attention to Kenan, prepared to shoot the shit for a few minutes, maybe tease him a little more about hospitalizing me, when I realize he's still staring at the door Lotus just passed through.

He turns on me and voices the question in his eyes. "Who the hell was that?"

FORTY TWO

IRIS

August: You up?

The text message lights the phone on my pillow, and I shake myself awake. The Waves flew back tonight from an extended road trip. August hasn't been home in more than a week. I told him to call me whenever he landed, and I'm glad he's reaching out. They lost three of the four away games, and the media coverage has been brutal, much of it centering around August, his lucrative contract, and if he'll deliver on the promise of his rookie season. There's even been speculation that he's not the same since his injury.

Me: I'm up. You wanna talk?

August: I'm at your front door. Is that okay?

My heart somersaults, aerobic, quickening my breath. The upper-hand corner of my phone shows it's midnight.

I want to see him. I glance down at my breasts, my nipples piqued under cotton sheets.

MiMi suggested I sleep naked, and she was right. There's a sensuality to having my bare body caressed by the soft cotton.

I wasn't sure how I'd feel being intimate with someone the first time since that last awful night with Caleb. For a long time, I felt no desire, but that kiss in the hospital room proved that desire was simply dormant and not gone for good, if it's the right person.

August is the right person.

Me: Yeah! I'm on my way.

I grab a robe Lo sent me from her designer's collection. The silk slides over my arms and kisses the sensitive tips of my breasts. August and I have kissed some since that time in the hospital room, but we've mostly kept it casual. I guess we're dating, even though with his schedule so crazy and me not having anyone to watch Sarai, we haven't actually gone anywhere. It seems strange, but finally right.

I make sure Sarai's bedroom door is pulled closed and then rush to let August in. The porch light streaks amber through his dark, misbehaving curls. Fatigue draws lines at his mouth and paints shadows under his eyes. I'm thrilled that by all rights, he should want to go straight home, but after a week away and a lengthy flight, he's come to see me.

"Hey." My smile up at him is wide and holds nothing back.

"Hi." He walks past me when I step aside, but instead of continuing to the living room, he turns me to the door, bends to align our lips. He pulls my bottom lip inside his mouth, sucking lightly and then intensifying the pressure until my knees are putty. His hand at my waist tightens, and he slowly straightens to his full height, pulling me with him until only the very tips of my toes brush the floor. I wrap my arms fully around his neck, angling my head and widening my mouth to accommodate the aggressive thrust of his tongue. When his hands drift from my waist to cup my ass, I moan into the kiss.

"August," I gasp, resting my forehead against his chin. His labored breaths pant into my hair, and he's hard and huge against my belly. If we don't slow down, there'll be no going back.

Would that be so bad?

I think I'm ready. There's no doubt in my mind I want him, but sometimes my body flashes back and freezes up. I don't want that to happen—don't want to explain when there's already so much he wants to know that I can't tell him.

"Are you hungry?" I whisper.

He squeezes my ass in one hand and explores my back with long strokes with the other. "Starving." His eyes run over my face, down my body, suggesting another appetite. "What's on the menu?"

Me?

"Gumbo?" I offer as a half-question. "MiMi's recipe."

The way he looks at me, as if he'd be inside me already if he could, it softens into affection. He sets me on my feet and tucks my hair behind my ear, settling a kiss between my eyebrows.

I didn't flinch!

He tucked my hair behind my ear and I didn't flinch.

I'm inordinately pleased with myself while he conks out in the living room and I heat up a bowl of gumbo for him. I lean a shoulder into the archway leading from the kitchen and steal a moment to watch him.

He's on the floor, his back to the couch and his long legs stretched out in front of him. His head flops back, eyes closed and hands linked over the tight, muscled plane of his abs.

"You wanna eat right there?" I ask, hesitant to disturb him.

His eyes open and he sits up straight, resting his arm on the coffee table. "You sure it's okay?"

"So nice of you to be concerned about ruining my flea market table." I laugh. "But yeah. I eat there all the time to watch TV or whatever."

"Okay." He smiles and runs a hand over his messy hair. "Thanks."

I head back to the kitchen to grab his meal, then return and set a glass of water and his bowl on the coffee table. "Unless you want wine?"

"Nah. I don't drink much during the season."

He spoons the first steaming bite into his mouth, groaning appreciatively and looking at me.

"This is delicious." He takes another bite, shaking his head. "Be careful or I'll be demanding this all the time."

"You're not very demanding." A sad smile touches my lips. I know what a demanding man is like, and August is the opposite. If anything, he's constantly looking for ways to help, to make things easier for me.

"Did you watch the game?" he asks, his full lips tightening and his eyes on his bowl.

"Of course." I settle onto the couch and tuck my legs under me, careful to keep the robe closed. "I saw it."

He closes his eyes and frowns. "I hate for you to see me lose," he admits softly. "And we're losing so much."

"You shouldn't have lost tonight," I snap, indignation ramrodding my spine. "That ref needs glasses and a lobotomy. All those shit calls in the last five minutes." I growl, banging a fist on my leg. "And the foul he called on you in the third quarter? Are you *fucking* kidding me with that shit? I wanted to come through the television and strangle him with his whistle. I mean, really? You barely touched that guy."

I'm fuming so much, I don't notice at first that he's watching me with a wide smile. "What?" I frown at him and cross my arms under my breasts.

"You."

"What about me?"

"One, you cuss like a sailor when you watch basketball," he says. "Two,

I love how you're so outraged on my behalf. I thought you saved all that for your precious Lakers."

We share a smile, and I go back to that first night we met in the bar.

"Well they have to share me with the Waves now." I sober. "I am sorry, though. I know you hate losing."

"Fuck." The hard line of his jaw sharpens. "And of course, everyone's saying it's my fault."

"Which is ridiculous! It's a team sport."

"Yeah, but I'm the franchise player. When a team is paying as much as the Waves pay me, when they build their team around you, the expectations are higher." He shrugs and grimaces. "This kind of scrutiny comes with the territory," he says. "Thank God for Kenan. He's so much more mature than the rest of us. He's been doing this a long time and knows what it takes to win. He's the real leader in our locker room."

"I'm sorry about the losing streak." I sift my fingers through the silky curls at my knee while he sits on the floor. He leans his head back into my touch, a deep breath lifting his shoulders and swelling his broad chest.

"That feels great," he says huskily. "Don't stop."

It feels great to me, too—touching him, breathing in the scent unique to his hair and skin and whatever molecules combine to make August. I want all of them wrapped around me. I shift on the couch, feeling myself growing wet at the juncture of my thighs the longer I touch him.

I clear my throat hoping to say something that will make my horniness feel less awkward. "Your hair is getting so long."

What am I even talking about right now? Should we discuss the weather, too?

He turns his head to peer up at me. "You said you like it longer, right?" he asks, almost uncertain, which August rarely is.

Now I really don't know what we're talking about.

"I said that?" My fingers tunnel through his thick hair, from his neck where it's shorter and straight to the crown of his head where it lengthens into amber-streaked sable curls.

"Yeah. That week in Baltimore," he reminds me, his voice soft.

My hands go still in his hair as his meaning sinks in.

"Are you saying . . ." I swallow and try again, unfolding my legs from under me and setting my feet on the floor. "You're growing your hair out because I said I liked it longer? For me?"

He flips his body so that he's facing the couch, still sitting on the floor, angling a grin up at me.

"Let me get this straight," he says. "You were completely unimpressed when I turned down forty-five million dollars to live in the same city as you, but you're kinda blown away that I'm growing my hair out?"

When he puts it like that, I feel like an idiot. We both laugh, our eyes tangled in affection and something more—something that neither of us acknowledges, but it fills the air around us.

"I wasn't unimpressed," I say, teasing him with a look. "But you do kinda blow me away."

He watches me, taking in all my details, starting at the hair casually knotted on my head and the silky robe, then my bare feet. He grabs one foot and kisses the arch.

"August!" I snatch my foot back, laughing and trying to ignore the feeling simmering low in my belly. "Don't kiss my foot."

"I'll kiss your foot if I want to." He grabs my other foot and kisses the arch, this time lingering, then running his nose up my leg. It's hard to swallow, and I'm struggling to breathe. With his eyes closed, he feathers kisses up my bare thigh. He lifts my leg just enough to gently suck at the flesh behind my knee.

"Ah, August." Pleasure arrows through me, and I press my back into the sofa.

"You're sensitive there," he says, his voice husky. "What about here?"

Open-mouthed kisses climb the inside of one thigh while his hands minister to my other leg, stroking, kneading my calf. I stare at his mouth drawing on a muscle in my thigh, an erotic suction that ripples shockwaves to my core. The sound of it, his lips and teeth and tongue working in tandem to mark me, leaves me a trembling mess.

August lifts his head, catching my dazed eyes with his. "Are you naked under this robe, Iris?" His voice is a hope and a prayer, and he makes me feel divine. Worshipped.

I nod, gulping down my anticipation, the nerves over what happens next.

August groans and drops his forehead to my thigh, still stinging and wet from his mouth. "You're killing me, babe."

"I was asleep when you texted, and—"

"You sleep naked?" His palms skid along the outside of my thighs through the silk, heating me up even more. "Shit, Iris."

He draws the panels of the robe together over my legs, concealing me from view, and drops a chaste kiss on my thigh before standing up. "I should go." He looks around. "What'd I do with my keys?"

"Why are you . . .?" I stand, too. Barefoot, I rise no higher than the middle of his chest. "You're leaving?"

He studies me and squeezes the back of his neck. "Keeping it one hundred here, Iris. You said you needed to take this slow, and I don't want to make you feel . . . I don't know. Pressured." His broad palm cups my chin, and he caresses my lips with his fingers. "I want this so badly." He shakes his head. "But I've waited a really long time for you, and my out-of-control libido isn't fucking that up."

He starts to pull away, but I place my hand over his on my face.

"What if I like your out-of-control libido?" One step forward narrows the space between us.

"Iris, don't . . ." He bites his bottom lip and knuckles my cheekbone. "I'm gonna go."

When I thought of this moment, the moment when I'd have sex again, I thought there would be trepidation. Terror. That the memory of what Caleb did to me that last night, and all the nights before, would shadow my intimacy with someone else.

But it's not the pain of that night on my mind. I'm not remembering his hostile takeover of my body at all. I'm navigating these seas for the first time—waves of want I've never ridden. My body is a stranger to me, an imposter wearing my skin, but disguised in new urges.

"Would you like to see me, August?" I rub the silk ties of the belt between my fingers.

"What?" Shock and hunger vie on his face. "What do you mean?"

Instead of talking, since that seems to be getting me nowhere, I slowly untie the belt and let the silk glide over my shoulders and puddle at my feet.

His sharply indrawn breath and the ravenous way his eyes eat at me lick fire under my skin. I reach up to the hair knotted on my head, releasing it so it cascades in heavy coils around my shoulders and down my back.

Power surges through me. The power to render such a huge, beautiful man speechless with the gravity of my robe falling to the ground. With his first sight of me, naked and ready and strong. I have the power to determine when I share myself and when I will withhold.

Your body is yours. Yours to keep and yours to share.

"I want to be with you, August." I step so close my nipples brush against his T-shirt. He hasn't moved—hasn't touched me or said a word. His Adam's apple bobs in his throat with a deep swallow. "I choose you."

"Are you sure?" His voice scrapes, scratchy and barely audible. "Because once we start . . ."

"I don't want to stop." I walk past him, my body buzzing from the heat of his eyes on my back, my legs, and my ass. I head toward the bedroom, turning to see if he'll follow. "I'm sure."

I expected some other response. I didn't think I'd have to persuade him. Maybe I miscalculated. I'm considering running back, grabbing my robe and yelling April Fool's in October—anything to retract my offer. But then large, warm hands span my waist from behind, and the cotton of his sweatpants brushes my legs as he matches my steps. In my bedroom, I turn to face him, reaching around to lock my door. It brings my naked body into contact with his fully clothed one.

"Sarai stumbles into my bedroom sometimes," I whisper, gulping at the sudden nerves assailing me.

Only minutes ago, I felt like a sensual, adventurous creature. Now, I'm starting to just feel exposed and relatively inexperienced compared to all the women he's been with.

He doesn't respond to my statement but leans down to capture my lips, swirling his tongue inside my mouth. Driving one hand into my hair, he sends his other hand to my waist and down to cup the globe of my ass.

"I'm struggling here, Iris," he says against my lips, his breath picking up. "I want to give you time to change your mind, but with you like this . . ." He catalogues every nuance of my body, starting at my toes and working his way up until he meets my eyes.

"You're the most beautiful thing I've ever seen." There's passion, desire in his eyes, but also rampant emotion. And I realize I'm not just sharing myself with him. He wants to share himself with me, too, and my mind eases. Any leftover doubts and residual fears fade.

I go down on my knees in front of him, slipping my hands into his sweatpants and working them down narrow hips and over powerful thighs. I lick my lips at the sight of his erection tenting his briefs.

"Babe, you don't have to . . ." He draws his brows together. "What are you doing?"

I know he doesn't mean that literally. He's probably lost count of how many blow jobs he's gotten over the course of his life. Hell, even just over the course of his career.

He won't lose count of this one. This one, he'll never forget. Not because I'm better than those other women, but because I want him more. There's no way they had this with him, what started between us that night and has only grown since.

"What am I doing? Making you feel like a winner," I say, trapping his eyes with mine and taking the tip into my mouth.

"Holy . . ." His breath stutters, and he slumps against my bedroom door. "Babe."

I lick the rigid length of him, my tongue wrapping around warm steel. He plunges his hand into my hair, commanding my mouth to take him deeper. For a second, I freeze, thinking of all the times Caleb forced me to do this at gunpoint. How he liked to make me choke and drool—how he invented ways to debase me. Before fear can take root, I look up, and it's still August. The look on his face is not sick pleasure, but awe.

"You make me feel so good," he says huskily. "There's never been anyone like you, Iris. There never will be."

With every encouraging word, I take another inch. I roll his balls in my hands, emboldened by the sounds of his pleasure. Even when he becomes the aggressor, holding my head still, pumping between my lips, growling and tugging my head back, I don't forget who's fucking my mouth. I don't lose track of this moment—of its scope. Its breadth. It's one of the biggest moments of my life, and there's only room for the two of us. There's no room for anyone else. Not Caleb. Not even the naysayers who'll accuse me of being a gold-digger who hops from player to player. No one else intrudes.

It's just me and the man I love.

FORTY THREE

AUGUST

I come in spectacular fashion. Iris sucks it all down, flattening her small hand around my ass, clutching me as close as she can get me. Her eyes are molten, the pupils golden and nebulous. I've seen her eyes change colors, oscillating through every shade of brown and green, but right now they're almost gold. She glows with the satisfaction of pleasing me, licking her swollen lips, rubbing them back and forth over my still-wet tip.

Desire resurges, overtaking me like a hurricane. I pull her to her feet and lift her. She wraps her legs around my waist, and her forehead drops to rest against mine as I walk us to the bed. Our breaths meet, a sultry congress between our mouths. I lay her down like she might break, but I already know I'm gonna fuck her like she's indestructible.

How can I not?

Dark hair streams behind her, and I study her for long minutes, determined not to rush this. She's small. Her shoulders are slim, her breasts full, her waist narrow, and her hips flared. A master craftsman took his time with the dips and lines of her body, ensuring symmetry. He exaggerated her curves, balancing them to perfection.

With one knee, I nudge her leg to the side. Taking my cue, she silently opens both wide.

"I want to look at you." I glance between her legs, waiting for her subtle nod. I push her legs up until her knees are bent and she's completely exposed to me. A self-conscious laugh slips past her lips.

"August." She covers her face, hiding her eyes. "Are you just gonna stare at it all night?"

"Definitely not." With my hand under her ass, I guide her up to me and swipe my tongue through her wet folds. Her taste, her smell, the silky heat of her saturates my senses. I press my palms inside her thighs, widening her even more until that bud buried between her lips plumps and rises, begging to be sucked, bitten, consumed. I comply, giving her clit the complete and undivided attention it deserves, while one hand slides up her torso to twist and pluck her nipple.

"Oh my God." Her hips buck into my face. Her back arches. Inch by inch, her body loses control, loses inhibition. When I probe her entrance, rolling my tongue tight enough to slip into the small opening, her hands claw into my hair and rake over my shoulders. God, she's wild. She presses the arch of her foot on my shoulder, urging my face deeper between her legs. She grinds against my lips, and I love every hot, juicy second of it.

Her orgasm is an infinite refrain of whimpers and moans, a keening sound set loose in her throat. She unravels before my eyes, liquefying right into my hands, her lips moving in a soundless, sensual prayer.

She's limp and sated. She got hers. She took it, and I love that. I shower her shoulders and breasts with kisses like she's the only girl in the world, because for me she is. I glide my fingers over her clit, inserting one, two, three fingers until she's fucking my hand so hard, the headboard knocks the wall. She wrestles with her passion, pinning it down and then bucking wildly when it flips her and regains control. I love her wanton and disorderly.

I suckle at one breast and continue working between her thighs. Her eyes glaze over. Her mouth slackens with unrelenting pleasure. I lick the underside of her breast, my open mouth kissing the curve.

"Oh, God, August," she says hoarsely. "Now. Please now."

I get up to grab my sweatpants and pull a condom from my wallet. It's on before I even make it to the bed. Her eyes fix hungrily on my cock. I pump it lightly, as much for me as for her.

"It's all yours, Iris." I settle between her hips and thighs, relishing this last moment of mystery when I haven't known this part of her. The moment before a miracle of intimacy, when we merge and for those moments, become one.

I plan to ease in, take my time, but as soon as my cock gets that first taste, I surrender to a force that is almost centripetal, drawing me in deeper. I plunge into the tight clutch of her body. She folds around me as I enter. When I withdraw, there's a reluctant letting go. With every thrust, she takes more of me. Her body is the call, and mine is the response.

"Holy shit, Iris," I groan into her neck.

I've never had anything like this. Not just her pussy, though the tight, wet grip of her is the best I've ever had. No, I've never *felt* anything like this. Like my soul is being turned inside out. Does she feel this, too? I rear up on my elbows to watch the answering passion play across her face. I dip to kiss her, and the contact ignites a scorching intercourse of lips and teeth. We're mouths clashing, hips colliding, and hearts pounding in tandem, in sync. This feeling is sorcery. Her touch is a spell, and Iris? She's my witch.

She goes first, her hands shaking as she cups my face, her head tipping back into the pillow, the elegant line of her neck straining and exposed. I rut unrelentingly, pounding between her legs, gripping her thigh tightly, holding onto her for dear life because I'm coming apart. Splintering. Parts of me peel away, falling at her feet.

"Don't stop," she whispers. "More, August. I didn't know it could be . . . I had no idea. Oh, God, I had no idea."

The awe in her words and in her eyes undoes me. I grip her neck, nipping at her lips and muttering words of worship into the untamed spill of her hair.

I empty myself of all I was before and take whatever she has to give. There's a newness when our eyes meet—wonder in the laughter we share while I hold her. We don't speak, but there's eloquence in our fingertips, in our hands as we touch and explore. Our bodies commune, confess.

I don't have to say the words.

She knows I'm hers.

FORTY FOUR

IRIS

"Okay if I move that one here," I say, shifting a number on my spreadsheet, "then I could put that over here."

I move fifty dollars from the column marked electric bill and squint at the bottom line like it might have grown bigger when I look back.

Nope. Still a tiny amount of money to live on after the bills are all paid. Paid-ish.

I'll call on the water bill to see if I can get an extension.

I'm still doing the dollar shuffle at my makeshift desk, also known as the dining room table, when a pair of huge hands slides under my arms to cup my breasts through my T-shirt. My nipples instantly pebble beneath the cotton, and my breath constricts. August's thumbs tease the tips of my breasts, and he sucks at the curve of my neck.

"Come back to bed, Iris," he says huskily. "You know I have to leave soon and I *reeeeeeally* need to fuck you again."

The words stroke a finger along my clit.

This man.

I had no idea—no earthly idea sex could be so addictive and satisfying and transformational. Every time August is inside me, I feel different afterwards. Like we're swapping atoms—I'm taking some of him and giving so much of me.

I used to think Lo was being silly when she said I settled for sex with Caleb because I had nothing to compare it to. Boy, was I wrong. I want to write letters to *Cosmo* about my experience. Diary of the Previously Underwhelmed.

Maybe *that* could make me a little change on the side . . .

"Okay," August whispers. "Don't make me pull out all the stops."

"Is that a metaphor for your dick?" I laugh when he twists my nipples.

Also, I may leak a little.

"My dick doesn't need a metaphor to know how awesome it is. It's a literal dick, and I will literally pull it out whenever you want. It's at your service." He laughs at his own joke into my shoulder. "No, I meant the oral. That seems to always get you."

August has a talented tongue, and it's in league with his teeth and lips to drive me crazy every time we make love.

#Keeper.

Some things, like brain-bursting orgasms, never get old.

Despite the temptation, I ignore him and keep moving my little—and I do mean little—numbers around. I need to figure this out before the day begins.

"Are you seriously passing up sex for this spreadsheet?" August groans into my hair. "You know I have to leave soon."

He never stays all night. That first night we made love—was it only two weeks ago? That night we agreed that for now, he would be gone before Sarai woke up. Seeing men walk in and out of my mother's life made me feel insecure. I hated getting attached to some man I just knew I wanted to be my daddy and have him leave. Then, the next one would come, and the cycle started again.

Not that I anticipate August going anywhere anytime soon, but that's part of my hardwiring I'm just not ready to let go of.

"Are you coming willingly?" he whispers, instigating a battle of butterflies in my belly. "Or do I need to throw you over my shoulder?"

"You wouldn't dare." I look up from my laptop, momentarily distracted by the rungs of muscles in his abs and the sinewy slash at his hip where his sweatpants hang low over the shape of him already semi-erect.

"See something you like?" He grins and flexes his pecs. "'Cause I do."

Before I can respond, he pulls the hem of my T-shirt over my head, plunging me into semi-darkness. I'm quietly screeching so I don't wake Sarai, when I feel the first hard, wet pull on my nipple. Needless to say, my arms drop limply to my sides and I lean back. August spreads my thighs and, on his knees I presume since I can't see, settles between them, his lips never leaving my right nipple. He employs his other hand on my left. My head falls back, my breath coming fast, hot and humid into the T-shirt covering my face. He finally relinquishes my nipple, and the air cools my damp breast. I'm tugging the shirt from over my head, ready to re-focus, when I feel him mouthing me through my panties.

"Lord, please," I beg, blindly thrusting my fingers into his messy curls.

"Answering your prayers down here," August mumbles into my thigh, his stubble a welcome abrasion. He tugs my panties aside to lick and suck and groan into my pussy. "I could do this all day."

It does not take all day.

I stuff my fist into my mouth to muffle the sounds fighting their way out. Bliss spirals from my core and explodes over my limbs, my extremities, my nooks and crannies. My head goes galactic, a black sky awash with stars. For just a moment, I seem to float outside of time and space. I come back to my body in inches and seconds, surprised to find my heels digging into August's back, my fingers buried in his hair and my thighs bracketing his handsome face.

"Hi." He grins up at me unabashedly, his mouth shiny and wet. "Welcome back."

I answer with a husky laugh and a shake of my head.

"You distracted me," I slur, sex-drunk. "Now it'll take me forever to finish."

"I'd say you 'finished' in record time." He ducks when I swing my hand lightly at his head. "Now about me finishing."

My eyes flick to the flashing cursor, awaiting my executive decision on the electric bill.

"Babe, come on." He licks the inside of my thigh. "When I go on the road next week, you're gonna miss my loving."

"Do you think I don't know that's an old Lou Rawls song?" I ask, carefully lowering my legs from his shoulders and turning back to the laptop so I can move more money around.

"What do you know about Lou Rawls?" he asks skeptically.

"Dude, I grew up in the Ninth Ward," I say with a touch of NOLA pride. "We took R&B classes."

For a moment, he looks uncertain. Like he wonders if it really was that hood. I mean . . . it was, but we didn't actually take the classes. It was a much more informal education of the OGs blasting classics while we played outside in the streets.

"Seriously. Come back to bed." He picks me up, ignoring my yelp, and sits down with me on his lap. "I don't even need to get off. We'll just cuddle before I have to leave."

"Every time you say we'll just cuddle, we actually end up screwing anyway."

"And that's a problem?" he asks, lifting my hair and sucking along the curve from my neck to my shoulder. I shiver but refuse to get up, refocusing on the bills, some of which are already past due. If I don't get this figured out, Sarai and I may come home to the water turned off.

"Okay. Be like that." He blows out a long-suffering breath, sitting forward and pressing his chest against my back, patting out a rhythm on my bare legs. "What are you doing anyway?"

"Robbing Peter to pay Paul." I tilt my head to calculate if I'm breaking even yet.

"Is that another joke?" His hands go still mid-tap against a thigh.

"If you're asking if my utility company is actually named Peter, then no."

"But you're joking, right?" He shifts forward so he can see my profile. "You don't need money, do you?"

"No." I shrug, wanting him to drop it. "Things are just a little tight this month."

"Money should never be tight for you." With my eyes trained on the screen, I don't see his frown, but I *feel* it.

"I'm a single mom living paycheck to paycheck in one of America's most expensive cites. Just living the dream. Of course things get tight sometimes."

"Iris, if you need money, you can tell me."

My fingers pause over the keys and dread slicks the lining of my stomach like an oil spill. I really don't want to go there with him. "I'll keep that in mind." I accidentally bump my little mound of bills and bend to retrieve them from the floor. When I sit back up, August is leaning forward, squinting at the screen.

"Seriously?" He turns aggravated eyes on me. "*That's* how much you make each month? Like everything?"

My hackles rise at his tone and the implication that what I make isn't enough. "It's good money, August."

"No, it's crap money, Iris." He shakes his head, his expression resolute. "I'll talk to Jared about bumping it up."

"You will do no such thing, August West." I jump to my feet, outrage humming through me. "I don't want more than any other entry-level employee."

"You're my girl, Iris."

"Yeah, I am, so all the more reason for you to respect my wishes." I fold my top lip against my bottom one. "Things are just a little tight because I want to take this online sports marketing certification Jared recommended."

"Well if Jared recommends it, Jared needs to pay for it."

"For everyone?" I roll my eyes. "Stop being—"

"What? Concerned?" he cuts in. "I'm your boyfriend. Of course, I'm concerned."

The word "boyfriend" floats in the air like a feather, and I chart its course. We've been so happy the last few weeks. Things have been amazing, but we're on the verge of our first fight, and we both know it.

"Boyfriend, yes." I prop on the edge of the dining room table. "Sugar Daddy, no. I need to stand on my own feet, August. Please don't make this a big deal."

"I think it is a big deal if you need something and don't feel like you can ask me for help." He scoots to the edge of the seat so I'm within reach and rests his hands at my hips. "Baby, not sure if you heard, but I make a lot of money."

"Good for you," I say. "You make yours. I'll make mine."

"Are we not in a relationship?" His eyes, the color of a pending storm, search my face. "Did I misunderstand what we're doing here?"

"Of course we're in a relationship, August." I run a hand over the tension in my neck and brush a dark swathe of bed-hair back from his face.

"And aren't you there for me? When I lose a game? When you cook for me? When I need *your* help?"

"Picking up your mail when you're on a road trip is nothing."

"Yeah. Nothing. Like this little list of bills is nothing to me." He gestures to my laptop. "Iris, do you have any idea how much money I make? Not the contract. That's a drop in the bucket. The shoes. The video games. The endorsements. Baby, I can take care of your bills."

Some wound I thought healed, scabbed over, smarts. Everything in me resists taking money from him.

"It's bad enough you're driving that piece-of-shit car," he continues.

"My car is not a piece of shit," I counter, my voice turning brittle. "It runs perfectly fine and gets me where I need to go."

"But I could get you something really nice, dependable, and never even miss the money."

"Yeah, Caleb bought me a beautiful Mercedes," I say bitterly, taking a few steps away. "But I found out fast that all of his gifts had strings attached."

"What the actual fuck, Iris?" His voice rumbles in the space I've put between us. "Are you comparing me to him? What we have to what you had with him?"

"No, I—"

"Are we only going to talk about him when it's convenient for you to bring up and use against me in an argument?" he demands, his voice cooling off. "That's kind of unfair since I have no context for what he did, how he behaved, or what happened. Since you won't tell me shit, ever."

"We've talked about this." I draw a calming breath, wanting to keep this from venturing into dangerous territory. "I signed an NDA."

"Whatever. Or maybe you just don't want me to know what happened."

He's partially right on that score. Why would I want him to know how Caleb ground me to dust? That I allowed that? No matter the reasons or the circumstances, he caged me like an animal, and now that I'm out, I don't want to revisit my captivity.

"I just need to do this for myself," I say more softly. "I don't want to owe anyone."

"Owe?" He runs his hands over his face and pushes out a frustrated breath.

"If I ever give you a car . . . correction *when* I give you a car, because when that thing you're driving dies, I *will* give you a car . . ." He closes the space between us and gathers both my hands in his against his chest. "When I give you something, it's yours. You'll own it, and no one can take it away from you. Not even me." He bends to whisper in my ear, "The same way you own my heart, Iris. Outright."

It's the closest we've come to saying the words, but something holds me back. I'll never forget the night when I first tried to leave Caleb—the humiliation at the hotel. The credit cards denied. Seeing those flashing blue lights, being pulled over by the cops and accused of stealing the car, of kidnapping my own daughter. I'd thought Caleb and I had built something together, but it turned out he was working alone and setting a trap. I trusted someone else with my welfare, and they used it against me in the most unimaginable ways. I don't know that I'll ever be able to trust my and Sarai's security to someone else again, even someone I love and who loves me.

The silence stretching out after August's subtle declaration grows cool and awkward. I don't know what to say. If I press past my fears and tell him what I feel for him, what I really feel, will he use it against me? Deep down I know August isn't Caleb, but some pain goes deeper than what we know. It fundamentally changes who we are and how we live, and it's beyond the reach of reason.

"Mommy."

August and I both turn to see Sarai, her dark hair ruffled and little fists twisting in her eyes. I walk over and pick her up.

"Morning, baby." I breathe in her little girl freshness.

"Gus," she says firmly, stretching her little arms toward him. He glances up at me, silently asking if it's okay. I don't like her waking up with a man in my house. I don't want to confuse her, but I know there's a bond forming between them. I don't want to take that away. I offer a terse nod.

"Hey, princess," he says softly, scooping her up and pressing his forehead to hers. "What are you doing up?"

She doesn't answer but burrows her head into his neck, already blinking drowsily and halfway back to sleep. Watching his tall frame travel back up the hall with her head resting on his shoulder twists my heart. I want to believe it, but it all feels too good to be true. August feels too good to be true, like Caleb did once. That boy who brought me coffee every day for weeks, wooing me, listening to me, and treating me kindly, he seemed too good to be true. But Caleb's good wasn't true. He was a cruel fraud—a mistake I made that may chase me for the rest of my life.

I finish with the bills, noting the calls I need to make for extensions until my next paycheck. Closing the laptop, I check the time to see if I can grab a few winks before I have to be up for work. If August is still down to cuddle, I'm here for that.

But when he re-enters the living room, he's dressed in his San Diego Waves sweatshirt, a baseball cap, and his tennis shoes. Keys jingle in his hands.

"I'm gonna go." His eyes rove around the room like he's checking for anything he may have left, but his glance skids over me. "I need to meet my trainer soon."

I know his schedule. He has plenty of time.

"August, I—"

"Just . . . it's okay, Iris." He walks toward the door, stopping only to drop a kiss on the top of my head. "Let's talk later when we're both . . ." He shakes his head, pulling his cap lower over his hair. "Let's just talk later."

The door closes behind him.

FORTY FIVE

IRIS

The client Jared asked me to follow up with decided not to sign. I received an email reminding me that the money for the online sports certification is due today, and I don't have it. The daycare called me out of a meeting because Sarai bit some kid. I had to review a fifty-page contract Jared needed "like yesterday" . . . in five minutes.

It's a day from hell, and it's not even noon yet.

My email alert dings, distracting me from the branding strategy Jared asked me to tweak for a soccer player who recently signed. I open the email from human resources, and my blood pressure soars. I'm up and charging down the hall, knocking on Jared's office door before I give myself time to cool off.

"Iris, hey," he says, glancing up from his laptop. "Come on in."

"Can I ask you . . ." My words falter. "Did August . . ." Shit. I know he did this, but it sounds ridiculous saying it aloud, and if I'm wrong, it will make things awkward between my boss and me.

"The email from human resources," I start again. "It said all entry-level employees are receiving a raise, effective immediately. That our next check will reflect the increase."

"Yes." Jared sits back from his desk and links his hands on top of his head. "What about it?"

"Did August do that?" I rush the question before I change my mind. "For me, I mean?"

"I'm not in the habit of discussing high-level financial and human resources decisions with our entry-level employees."

"Of course." Embarrassment heats my cheeks and twists my insides. "I'm sorry I bothered you."

I back out of the door, but his voice stops me.

"Iris," he says. "Wait a second."

I force myself to meet his eyes.

"I've never seen my brother like this about anyone." He rests his elbows on the desk. "Not just since you've come here, but even before, when you were still with Caleb."

"Oh, well, I—"

"Don't hurt him."

I search the stern expression on his face. "Me?" I touch my chest. "Hurt *him*?"

"When he asked me about increasing the entry-level pay at five o'clock this morning," he says, pausing to give me a pointed look, "thanks to you both for that, by the way. Because who needs more than five hours of sleep?"

"I'm so sorry."

"When he called," Jared continues, blasting past my apology, "he seemed to think it was going to piss you off but said it was the only way to help you, and he won't stand by watching you struggle."

Tears spring to my eyes. How much did that cost him? Or this company? I said I didn't want anything all the other entry-level employees didn't have, and he gave them all raises so I'd feel better about accepting his help? Would a man who secretly meant me harm do that?

No. And it's no secret August loves me.

There are many things that may always have to remain a secret between us, but how I feel about him shouldn't be one of them.

FORTY SIX

AUGUST

"Good run," Kenan says, slamming his locker closed. "You're getting better, Rook."

"I'm pretty sure a player in his third season," I say, closing my locker, too, "is no longer considered a rookie."

"It's got such a ring to it, though." Kenan's deep chuckle rumbling in that massive chest of his coaxes a grin to my lips.

"Why were you in a shitty mood today, West?" Valdez, the back-up point guard, asks. I suspect he resents me at least a little. He's been in the league for a decade and probably doesn't appreciate playing behind me.

Oh, well. It's like that sometimes.

"It's a chick, huh?" Valdez asks with a taunting grin. "That tennis player? Pippa Lee?"

"I doubt Iris would appreciate that." Kenan laughs and hefts his duffle bag on his shoulder.

"Iris?" Valdez's eyebrows rise dramatically. "I heard Caleb Bradley's baby's mama, Iris DuPree, lives here now. You don't mean *that* Iris?"

My teeth clench. I already know this conversation's gonna go to shit if he starts with Caleb. I just look at him and walk past, deciding it's better not to respond. Iris won't even tell me half of what happened with Caleb. I'm certainly not discussing their relationship with this motherfucker, and there's even less of a chance I want to discuss *our* relationship with him.

"Wasn't trying to start nothing, Rook," Valdez says behind me.

I ignore the name. Kenan teasing me that way is one thing. He and I have an understanding. I'm the face of the team, but he is the heart of it. His maturity and accomplishments have earned my respect, and he leads so well from behind. This dude—not so much.

"I'd be careful if I were you is all I'm saying," Valdez persists. "She already trapped one baller. Now she's fucking you. Better wrap it up or you'll be paying for some pussy for the rest of your life. Not worth it, no matter how good it might be."

His voice, his words behind me pause meaningfully.

"And I've seen her," he continues. "That looks like some good pussy."

I turn before I even realize it. His T-shirt is bunched in my fist. His face only inches from mine.

"You crossed the line, motherfucker," I grit out. "You ever talk about her like that again, you're gone."

"What the—"

"Don't act like it can't happen." I drop him but don't step back. "You are here at my discretion, Valdez. One word to Deck and you'll be traded, cut, whatever I say, and you know it."

"You son of a—"

"Your game is adequate, *at best*, on a good night," I snap. "You're lucky to be drawing base pay, but if you ever talk about Iris again, you won't even have that. Not here."

Resentment and bitterness twist his features. "Glad, tell this kid he better back up."

Kenan shrugs, adjusting the strap of his duffle as he stands by the locker room exit.

"If he doesn't follow through on the threat," Kenan says, "I will. You don't talk about a teammate's girl like that. That's how you get your shit messed up." He cocks one dark brow. "And it's the quickest way to ruin a team's chemistry. *That* I can't have. Not in this locker room."

Kenan would know. He's still haunted by his ex's affair with a teammate on his last squad. Valdez glances between the two of us, muttering and scowling, before stomping out of the locker room.

"Thanks for having my back," I mumble, my hands stinging with the need to punch a hole through that son of a bitch.

"Nothing to it." Kenan pauses. "But he might have a point. Chicks can make you believe anything when your dick is in their mouth."

I wheel on him, angry words queued up and ready to slice.

"You better learn how to handle your shit better than that, Rook," Kenan says calmly. He walks down the hall toward the exit, and I follow him. "If you can't even take it from me, I'd hate to see you when we play Caleb and the Stingers on Thanksgiving Day."

My anger ebbs as I realize he's testing me, and I'm failing.

"You think there won't be speculation when people find out you're dating Caleb's girl?"

"She's not his girl." *She's mine.*

"She had his kid. I assume he's still in their lives and supporting them financially."

"He's not." The opposite actually, which I still don't understand and Iris still won't tell me. We reach the exit and head toward the parking lot of the training facility.

"For real?" He turns his lips down at the corners. "What's that about?"

"I don't know. She . . ."

Iris's piece-of-shit car, the one we argued about this morning, is parked beside my truck. She's leaning against the hood, watching us walk up.

"Speak of the devil," Kenan says under his breath, then speaks loud enough for her to hear. "Hey, Iris. Good to see you again."

"Hi, Kenan." She glances between the two of us quickly, biting her lip when she meets my eyes. "Hey, August."

"When's your cousin coming back in town?" Kenan asks before I can speak.

Iris and I both turn shocked looks on him. Since his wife showed her ass cheating on him and is putting him through hell in custody court, Kenan is notoriously gun-shy when it comes to women. I mean, I'm sure he's getting ass somewhere. A baller bouncing from city to city—that's not hard to do. But for him to ask about a girl? A *real* girl? Unusual.

"Um, you mean Lotus?" Iris asks, just to make sure.

"Yeah, I think that was her name." He shrugs as if he's not sure, except Kenan is always sure of everything.

"I guess . . . I'll probably see her at Thanksgiving."

"Cool," he says with a nod.

"Should I, um, I don't know," Iris says, "tell her you said hi?"

"No." He looks at her strangely. "Why would you do that?"

Iris and I exchange a look, and I give a subtle shake of my head, telling her not to try and figure out Kenan.

"I'll see you on the plane tomorrow, Rook," Kenan says, walking toward his truck. "Don't be late."

Once he's gone, Iris and I stare down at the same patch of concrete. I assume she found out about the raise and is here to rip me a new one. What-the-hell-ever. There's no way I'll stand back and watch her struggle raising Sarai by herself on that measly paycheck.

"I got a raise today," she finally says softly.

"Oh yeah?" I drop my duffle bag to the ground and cross my arms over my chest. "That's nice."

"It was more than nice." She looks up, a slight smile on her face. "It was kind. It was more than I deserved after I was so ungracious."

I hope she doesn't expect me to stop her.

"Thank you, August." She reaches for my hand and holds my eyes with hers. "I'm sorry I was so hard to help."

"So is Jared." I laugh, but he really was ready to disembowel me when I called demanding a raise for all the entry levels.

The laughter fades, and we're back to awkward. I wanted Iris for years and thought if I ever got my shot, we'd never run out of things to say. I don't want to say the wrong thing, something that would drive a wedge between us. We had our first fight, but I've never been happier than I am with her.

"August, Caleb was . . ." She stops herself and looks off to the side, avoiding my eyes.

I'm on high alert. We never talk about him. That's a blessing and a curse because even hearing her say his name drives me a little crazy.

"What about him?" My voice is about as pleasant as rat poison. I should fix that, but I can't. When she doesn't talk about him, I have questions. When she does, I'm a jealous prick.

"Nothing Caleb ever gave me was truly mine," she says, biting her bottom lip. I want to gather her in my arms, but she's stiff, and I sense she won't continue if I touch her.

"He used everything against me to control me." When she looks up at me, her eyes hold a million secrets, and I want to know every one of them.

"I know you signed an NDA," I start.

"I did."

"But," I continue, "it feels like you and Caleb have these secrets that I know nothing about. All this stuff I'm not in on, and I hate it."

She twists the line of her mouth into a hard curve. "The only thing Caleb and I have together is Sarai," she says. "And I do everything I can to keep him away from her." She squeezes my hand and takes another step closer. "I want nothing from him, August, except to be left alone. I promise you that." She studies my face for a few seconds. "Do you believe me?"

"Yeah. I do." I rub the ends of the braid hanging over her shoulder between my fingers. "You won't find me complaining about Caleb not being in our lives."

I should be careful. I don't want to scare Iris off by making her think I expect her to share her life with me. To share her daughter with me. To move in with me soon. To marry me someday.

Though these are all the things I expect.

I just need to give her time to get used to them. I have to learn to temper my responses. I think I freak her out with the intensity of my feelings. I mean, I did once hit on her while she was breastfeeding.

That's not intense at all.

"You said something this morning." She's back to studying the concrete.

"We said a lot of things this morning." I draw and release a quick breath. "Which thing are we talking about?"

"You said I own your heart outright."

In the tiny shred of silence that follows her words, I don't know if I want to take it back or say it again in a hundred different ways.

"I'm sorry I didn't . . ." She swallows and looks up at me, an apology in her eyes. "Well, that I didn't respond or say anything back."

"You don't have to say anything. I get it."

"No, you don't get it." She shakes her head, an impish smile curving her lips. "I should have said that I'd play you at the five."

My blood is fizzing, like someone dropped an Alka Seltzer in my veins. Little pops and tiny explosions occur under my skin while I wait for her to continue. Iris and I have had too few moments alone together over the years, and that day in the gym playing HORSE was one of my favorites. Second, of course, to that kiss in the closet. I know what I meant when *I* said that. My heart goes loud and hard like a bass drum in my chest to think she might mean the same.

"I never realized how cryptic that was," I say, tucking a few escaping tendrils of hair behind her ear. "Until right now when I'm trying to figure out if you mean what I think you do."

She reaches up, framing my face between her hands, and I've never seen her more earnest. "I don't want to be cryptic," she says. "I'll just say it so there's no doubt."

She folds her lips in and closes her eyes, taking a deep breath as if she's preparing to jump out of a plane. "I love you, August."

I doubt the world actually stops, because based on the laws of physics or whatever governs the Earth's axis, that isn't possible. That's how it feels, though, when she says those words. Like all of creation has tuned in to hear this—a universal pause to acknowledge possibly the greatest moment of my life. Not winning the NCAA Championship or being drafted by the Waves. Not being Rookie of the Year. And when I finally win my ring, it won't even compare. None of those things are as monumental as the words coming out of this beautiful little angel-witch who cast a spell on me the first time I saw her, one that has never worn off.

"I didn't quite hear you," I say, staring at the top of her head.

Her eyes pop open and then narrow. She smacks my chest, a wide grin stretching her mouth. "Just for that, I take it back."

"Oh, yeah? It's like that?" I ask laughingly. "How you just gonna take it back?"

I pick her up, ignoring her laughing screeches, and deposit her on the hood of her car, standing between her spread legs. Our breaths hitch, part exertion, part passion. My thumbs discreetly trace the underside of her breasts, and her lashes drop over the desire growing in her eyes. Glancing around the empty parking lot, she slowly slides her hand down to the front of my sweatpants and grabs my dick through the thick cotton. I squeeze my eyes closed tight against a rush of carnal pleasure. I dip to take her mouth with mine, entangling our tongues. We shelter urgent touches between our bodies.

A door slams across the parking lot, and we look up to find one of the trainers getting out of his car, trying to pretend he doesn't see us just about fucking on the hood of Iris's car.

I clear my throat, looking up to find Iris's eyes laughing back at me. We sober simultaneously. I'll never forget this moment when I understood, truly understood, that the basketball and the money and the fame, they're all great. Those words she just said to me, though, eclipse everything else.

"I can't remember if I said I love you, too." I look up at the sky, as if I'm trying to recall.

"You didn't actually," she says.

I cup her chin, bringing her close and kissing her slowly, tasting her love, those words still resting on her tongue.

"I love you," I say against her lips, kissing down her chin and behind her ear and any place I can get to that won't get us arrested for indecent exposure.

"We made a memory on the hood of my car," she says, her eyes wide and pleased. "See? It's not so bad."

My smile drops, and I shake my head.

"No, babe. This car's still a piece of shit."

FORTY SEVEN

IRIS

I've got a bad feeling about today, even though it's Thanksgiving and I want everything to be perfect.

The last time I watched a Waves–Stingers game, August ended up with a broken leg, and within twenty-four hours I'd been raped and beaten unconscious.

But what's there to worry about?

I can't help but feel I'm tempting fate sitting here out in the open, like a tree in the middle of a lightning storm. In this scenario, I'm the tree. The thing that finally feels solid, has put down roots and is flourishing. Caleb is the lightning—always violent and ready to strike.

A sinkhole has been deepening in my stomach ever since August's mother invited me for Thanksgiving dinner. The game is Waves versus Stingers in August's hometown, so of course we're here watching the game, minus Jared who's skiing in Vail. Matt, August's stepfather got called into the office for an emergency, but should be home in time to eat. I definitely wanted to accept his mother's invitation to dinner, and I didn't want to have to explain my hesitation about attending the game. I can't without divulging more than I should. And maybe . . . just maybe I'm getting tired of living my life in shadows cast by Caleb.

"You okay, Iris?"

Susan Foster, August's mother, studies me with some concern. She's probably called my name several times with no response.

I tune back in to our surroundings. It's pre-game, and we're a few seats behind the Waves' bench. Apparently, Susan always sits in the stands, and it would have been doubly awkward explaining that the first time we meet, I wanted to sit apart from her in a box.

The last time I was in this building I sat behind the Stingers' bench. Sarai sat on my lap, just like she is now, but she was only a few months old. I have to keep reminding myself that Ramone isn't watching over me—that I won't go home with Caleb tonight and wake up tomorrow with bruises.

"Sorry." I give her a smile that I hope reassures her. "Just thinking about Lo and hoping she makes it in okay."

Lo is flying in from New York for Thanksgiving dinner with us at Mrs. Foster's. She would have been here sooner if work hadn't held her up in Prague.

"She'll make it in just fine." Mrs. Foster pats my hand and smiles kindly. "We'll have dinner ready and all she'll have to do is sit down to eat."

"Thank you for inviting her. For inviting Sarai and me, too."

"I've been wanting to meet you for a very long time, Iris."

"You have?" I turn to her, surprise temporarily overshadowing my anxiety.

"August told me all about you long ago."

"*Long* ago?" I shake my head and laugh as lightly as I can with a boulder sitting on my chest. "I don't understand."

"Well, he didn't give me all the details," she says hastily, her blue eyes teasing. "But he did say he thought he had found the right girl. This was when he stayed home for rehab."

It would have been around the time we saw each other that week at the community center.

August and I didn't see each other much until I moved to San Diego. What was it about me that struck him so powerfully? That made him think I might be the one after only a few encounters? Probably the same thing that urged my thoughts back to that first night we met time and time again—the thought of that night as the fork in the road, and of him as the path I should have chosen.

"I don't know what to say," I finally respond, my cheeks hot.

"I'm just glad it worked out. I'm glad to meet the girl who stole my son's heart." Mrs. Foster says. "And I couldn't be happier."

Neither could I.

The moment I've been dreading lands on me with crushing force. When Caleb's team takes the floor for the pre-game shootaround, every nerve in my body screams for me to run. My internal alarm system warns me of danger. My muscles tense to the point of pain. I'm braced for a confrontation of wills, but when Caleb looks up into the stands and sees me, he smiles. He's at the opposite end of the floor. There's so much distance between us—I should feel safe. But I could never feel safe with him in the same building. Some days I don't feel safe knowing he's on the same planet.

All of his teammates go through the pre-game warm-up, but he just stands and stares. His smile grows wider the longer I stare back. He shifts his glance to Sarai in my lap, and the smile falls away. His eyes, when they return to me, promise retribution. That one day, he'll make me pay.

"Iris!" August calls from just beyond the bench, down on the floor.

As soon as I see him, my body relaxes. The tension dissipates. At the other end of the court is my dark past—a nightmare I barely survived. My future stands in front of me. And it's so bright. *August* is so bright. We share a smile before he starts his pre-game shootaround and joins his team.

He asked if I was sure I wanted to come today. He doesn't know everything that happened with Caleb. In the grand scheme of things, he knows almost nothing, but he knew today would be difficult for me. I'm so damn tired of running, though. For a long time, I was Caleb's marionette, but he doesn't pull the strings anymore. My boyfriend's mother wanted to meet me; wanted to meet my daughter; wanted to sit beside her son's girlfriend and watch him play on Thanksgiving. Maybe I'll regret it, but right now, I'm glad that at least I tried.

At halftime, the game is tied. If the Waves don't win any other game this season, I pray they win this one. The speculation has been rampant leading up to this rematch between the two teams, specifically between August and Caleb. It resurrected talk of Caleb's dirty play.

Everyone knows Caleb and I have a child together—that I lived with him during his rookie season. And anyone who didn't know I was with August will figure it out now. I'm sitting with his mother. I know some of his teammates have wondered about it, and I'm sure some of them have talked. There's already some nasty speculation. People will say I'm out to trap August the way I "trapped" Caleb.

God, if only they knew what a trap Caleb set for me.

"Would you have preferred we sit in a box?" Mrs. Foster asks, her eyes astute.

"It's just . . ." I laugh, a false sound if I ever heard one. "This may fuel more talk about me being with August after Caleb. Some have said it's August's revenge for Caleb's dirty play. They say I'm a . . ."

I don't even want to voice the things people say about me.

Whore. Opportunist. Gold-digger. Trick. Groupie. Thirsty. Trap chick.

Don't google yourself if you don't want to know what people actually think. They freely express it from the anonymity of their laptops and behind the mask of their avatars.

"You know the truth," Mrs. Foster says, patting my hand. "And so does August. He doesn't care what they say, and neither should you."

I force myself to relax, running my hands up and down Sarai's arms. She's playing the piano on her iPad and wearing her headphones. She's gotten so big and probably wouldn't even recognize her father if she saw him.

"Gus!" Sarai screams, jarring me back to the action.

August is on the free-throw line, and I'm so afraid Sarai's scream might break his concentration, I cover her mouth.

"Shhhh," I say in her ear. "August needs to focus, baby."

She puts her index finger to her mouth, her eyes wide, and looks up at me.

"Fo-cus," she whispers.

I laugh and tap her nose. When I look up, August is peering over the time-out huddle observing us. He smiles, and of course, Sarai chooses that moment to scream "Gus" again. She blows him a kiss, and he flashes a quick grin at her, pressing his palm to his lips to blow a kiss back. His eyes, though, fix on me, and contentment, pleasure, and the closest thing to joy I can imagine all flow through me like the Mississippi, wide and powerful. My eyes water and my nose burns. The emotion grows so dense between us, even separated by half an arena.

"*I love you,*" he mouths, the look in his eyes warm and so certain.

I nod, press a hand to my lips, and discreetly return his blown kiss. He crooks a smile and returns his attention to the huddle.

I experience a sharp sensation, like a needle pricking my flesh. When I glance over at the Stingers' bench, I meet Caleb's barbed stare. Malevolence festers in his eyes, and his hands tighten into fists at his side. Menace surrounds him, as much a constant companion as Ramone had ever been.

It's a dark déjà vu of the last time we found ourselves in this place, but the tables have been turned. There's always been an inescapable awareness between August and me. Caleb saw it then, and he sees it now. The day I met August, I stepped into a force field, setting something into motion that was in some ways my fault, and in other ways, out of my control. That defiance rises up in me, and I don't care if Caleb sees it. He can't do anything to me now without taking himself down, too. In a mockery of the special moment I just shared with August, he blows me a kiss.

"Is he going to be a problem, Iris?" Mrs. Foster asks from beside me.

Startled, I give her my full attention. She's still looking in Caleb's direction but waits for my response.

"No. I . . ." I've only ever talked openly with Lo about the details of what happened to me, but I wish I could share everything with August's mother and her kind eyes. "He was a problem, but it's been handled."

"August loves you very much," she says, looking at me and smiling at Sarai. "And your daughter, too. He talks about you both all the time now."

"He does?"

"I'm sure you know you're the most important thing in his life."

I'd play you at the five.

I don't answer, but wait for her to go on, because I know there is more.

"That man broke my son's leg over you," she says, holding up her hand when I start to apologize. "It's not your fault. It's only his fault, but even knowing how complicated your situation was, August still wanted you. He'd hate me butting in, but he is *my* important thing, and I want to know your intentions."

"My intentions?" A laugh, rich and full, escapes my lips. "You want to know my intentions toward August?"

She yields a small smile and caresses Sarai's hair.

"I have no illusions about my son. I know he's been a bit of a player, on court and off." She waggles her eyebrows suggestively. "But I know he's deeply in love with you and has been for some time." Our humor fades, but the kindness in her eyes remains. "So yes, I'm asking you, not if you love him, because it's obvious you do. I'm wondering if you'll be able to marry him when he asks you."

Marry.

For most girls, it means June weddings and flowers—hopes and dreams fulfilled.

It doesn't mean that to me anymore. It means a trap. It means a man has access to my life, to my daughter, that he could, at his discretion, abuse.

"I haven't asked August about it," she says softly. "And I know he is probably just so glad to finally have you that he isn't pressing it, but I have to wonder—a man cruel enough to break someone's leg over the woman he wants, well . . . he could be that cruel to the *woman* he wants, too. Am I right?"

Irrationally, I glance up at the jumbotron. I've been taken by surprise more than once, finding myself, unsuspecting, onscreen. If my face were onscreen now, I fear everyone would know what had happened with Caleb and me—a vignette playing out in vivid black-and-blue-bruised technicolor for everyone to see. They'd know what I'd survived. And as much as I know it wasn't my fault, shame spreads, leaving no part of me clean. I'm sullied by Caleb's touch, my heart and soul covered in invisible smudges.

"Legally, I can't talk about most of the things I experienced with Sarai's father," I tell her, my voice hushed and conscious of any perked-up ears around me. "But I'll say that getting away from him is the best thing that could have happened for us."

"And August knows this?"

"August knows that I love him and only him." This should be awkward, but after so many things I haven't been able to say, to tell anyone anything feels good.

"Can I tell you something?"

When I nod, she goes on with a smile.

"My son is the most competitive person I've ever met, second only to his father. He doesn't know how to give up. Eventually, the Waves, if he stays with them, will win a championship because August will *have* to. He doesn't know how to settle, and he won't settle with you."

Her words should make my heart float, but instead it sinks like a stone because as much as I love August, and God, I do, I don't know what I'll say if he ever asks me to marry him. Sharing my life, my money, my home, and my security with *any* man scares me to death. I've seen a man whom I thought loved me and would never do anything to hurt me pull back the mask and show me his true nature after I was in his trap. I don't know that I can risk that for me or Sarai ever again.

I go through the rest of the game in a daze, barely registering the action on court, except to note that, as usual, Caleb and August provoke one another to perform even better than they usually would. They both have exceptional games, but August always seems to manage a win against Caleb. Thank you, God, because that is a loss I wouldn't want him having to process over Thanksgiving dinner.

Susan and I are entering the private underground parking lot to wait for August, when I sense danger.

I look up, and Caleb is right there, a few feet away. His dark sweater and slacks throw that golden hair into relief. He looks like something sent down from the sun.

Only I know he's something dispatched by Hell.

With a cocky grin, he moves in for the kill. He can probably smell my fear, so I smooth my face to neutral. I lift my chin and meet his eyes squarely. He can't attack me in the open, and I refuse to show the terror that's being pumped into my heart, carried by my blood.

He looks from Sarai on my hip to August's mother. "Good to see you again, Mrs. Foster. It's been years, but you look beautiful as always."

I forget the history Caleb and August have pre-dating me. They've known each other longer than they've known me.

Mrs. Foster isn't one for phonies. She doesn't answer him but stares with hard eyes at Caleb until he shrugs.

Sarai looks at Caleb, fascinated. She reaches out to touch his nose and his lips. I want to run with her in the other direction—to get her as far away from him as possible. I know what it's like to be deceived by the angelic shell. You never suspect that beneath it beats the heart of a demon until it's too late.

Caleb tries to capture her little fingers, but I angle my hip away so her hand falls out of his reach.

"You're so pretty, Sarai," he says to her but looks at me. "You have your daddy's eyes. Do you remember me?"

Thumb in her mouth and tugging on her ear, Sarai shakes her head.

Caleb glares at me and grabs a lock of her hair, rubbing it between his fingers. "I'm your daddy."

I take several steps back, putting more distance between them.

"Daddy," Sarai whispers, violet–blue eyes locked with violet–blue.

"Mrs. Foster, would you take Sarai to the car?" I ask abruptly, watching the interplay between father and daughter with dread. Sarai is bright and curious and has the memory of an elephant.

"Are you sure, Iris?" Mrs. Foster asks.

I pass Sarai to her and fabricate a smile. "I'll be fine," I assure her. "Caleb and I need to talk."

"But Iris, maybe you should wait for—"

"No, now's fine." I nod toward the black SUV a few feet away. "I'll come in a little bit."

She splits a concerned look between Caleb and me but turns with Sarai and goes to the car.

"Alone at last." Caleb touches my hair, sifting it through his fingers. "I prefer your hair straight, but you do look beautiful."

I pull away, scooping my hair with one hand and tucking it behind my back and out of his reach. "What do you want, Caleb?"

His smile, his eyes—everything about him is lascivious as he studies me, my face, my breasts, lingering at the juncture of my thighs and down my legs.

"I want what's mine." He leans forward to whisper in my ear, "Do you honestly think you can leave me, Iris, and never come back? Do you think you can take my daughter from me and not pay for it?"

The fine hairs on my body lift. My heart pounds and my muscles brace. My body is an uprising, prepared for anything.

In a flash, his hand shackles my wrist, gripping to the point of pain. "How dare you fuck him?" he hisses. "And flaunt him in front of me on my home court? Let him watch my daughter grow up when I can't?"

His tongue darts out and licks behind my ear, and the saliva freezes and dries on my skin, repulsing me.

"I wish I could fuck you right now in front of everyone." He laughs. "Wouldn't August love to see how we do it?" He steps so close his dick pokes my belly. "Only you do this to me, Iris." He swallows, the hardness in his eyes fading to that sick desperation he covers with hubris. "Come back home. I miss you. I'll be better this time. I promise. I—"

His breath stalls in his chest. He glances down between us, where MiMi's jeweled knife glints in the dim parking lot. The wicked tip is pressed to Caleb's dick.

A woman in this world has to keep her wits about her and her weapons at hand.

"You never gave me much satisfaction." I smile serenely. "So I have no use for this dick. If you do, I suggest you let me go right now, or I will cut it off and leave you bleeding out like the sick animal you are."

"Iris, let's be—" He stops when I press it deeper into him. "Fuck, baby."

"I'm not your baby. I'm not your girl. I'm not even your baby's mama because as far as I'm concerned, Sarai's not yours." I glance down to my wrist still cuffed by his huge hand. "Let me go, Caleb, or I take one of those hairy balls."

His hand falls away, but his eyes assault me.

"I used to resent you for making me do all those things at gunpoint," I say. "But now I realize that's how the game is played when you know someone doesn't love you, and you always knew that, didn't you, Caleb? You knew I didn't love you before I knew it myself. That's why you held on so tight."

"One of these days, Iris . . ." His smile is possessed, mad, and it makes me shiver.

I put more distance between us and discreetly slip the knife back into my purse.

"It better be soon because, according to Lo," I say, blowing over my palm the way she did that day, "your days are numbered."

The closest thing I've ever seen to fear enters his eyes. If I didn't know before, I know now. Lo is definitely more badass than I am. I hold a knife to Caleb's dick and he barely looks nervous. I remind him of Lotus's words, and he's scared.

"Iris, you ready?"

It comes from behind us. August walks up, dressed similarly to Caleb in a dark sweater and slacks. That's where the similarities end. Caleb is bright as eighteen-carat gold, but tarnished and counterfeit. August is dark, towering over me like a wall providing shelter. He steps into the spot beside me and takes my hand. With his eyes never leaving Caleb's face, he leans down to drop a kiss in my hair.

"You need something, Caleb?" he asks tonelessly.

"You have no idea," Caleb replies, his eyes cold and glinting, focused on me.

"I'm going to say this once." August doesn't release my hand, but steps into Caleb's space until their shoes practically touch. "Iris and Sarai are under my protection, and if you bother them, you're bothering me."

The words settle among the three of us.

"And I'll do more than just break your leg, Caleb," he says softly. "You don't get to see them unless Iris says so."

"You're so wrapped around her little finger." Caleb laughs cruelly. "She has you pussy whipped."

"She does," August replies pleasantly, allowing a smile. "Jealous?"

Caleb's smile drops. "Just remember I had that pussy first."

"Then you know what a lucky man I am to have Iris for the rest of my life." August laughs. "This is one instance where I'd rather be last than first. You had your shot. You screwed it up. I'm what they call in basketball . . . a closer. A finisher."

The faux ease evaporates, and August's face freezes over. "This is the only warning you get, Caleb. The next time I find you trying to intimidate my girl, you won't be playing ball for a long time." He tilts his head, his narrowed eyes cutting through the tension-thickened air. "And I won't bother disguising it as a dirty play."

They stare at one another for long seconds stretched and thinned by their mutual malice. I know how clever and insidious Caleb is. Even seeing August close to him for a few minutes makes me nervous. Caleb carries a miasma of evil, and I'm choking on it. I want everyone I care about as far away from him as quickly as possible.

"August." I tug on his hand. "Baby, let's go."

Caleb's eyes flash to me. I didn't mean to provoke him by using the endearment, but I don't care if he knows that what I withheld from him, I give freely to August. He finally slides his hands into his pockets and walks away, whistling.

I expel a breath held so long I'm dizzy. While facing Caleb, my bravado was high and my knife was drawn, but with him gone, my knees shake and I lean limply into August. He rubs my arms, linking our fingers with one hand and cupping my face with the other.

"What was that?" he asks, a frown creasing his brow. "You're trembling. Iris, what the hell is going on?"

One day I'll have to tell him. I'd hoped I would never have to and that I could use the NDA as my excuse. It's really the shame, the embarrassment, and the horror that I don't want to share with him. I don't want him to know that those things happened to me and that the woman he loves is such damaged goods. I'll have to swear him to secrecy, and he'll have to promise not to go after Caleb, which I don't know if he'll be able to do. My thoughts swirl and tangle.

"I'll tell you everything soon, okay?" I rest my forehead against his chest. "Just not today. Can we just go to your mom's and enjoy Thanksgiving dinner?" I lift my head and piece together a grin. "And celebrate your win? Can we do that?"

His expression doesn't change or soften when I tease him, but he finally blows out a tired breath, running his hands through his hair. "You will tell me everything soon?" he asks. "Because I'm gonna lose my shit if I walk up on him like that with you again. What the fuck? He's creeping hard, and—"

"Yes. I'll tell you soon, but not yet." I close my eyes and press my lips tight against the tears, the emotion that if I uncork, I won't be able to stop. "Promise."

He bends until our lips are level and takes mine between his, and the day, the scrutiny, the fear, the anxiety—it's all eclipsed by this. By his lips, sweet and urgent and hungry over mine. By his devotion.

"I just need . . ." I let the words rest on his lips. *Time? Space? Grace? Understanding? Patience?* "You," I breathe into our kiss, angling my mouth to take more of him, to take as much of him as my lips can hold. "I just need you."

"You have me." He straightens and looks over to the car where his mother watches us through the window. "Wow. My mom is watching us make out."

"I'm so embarrassed," I groan into my hands. I don't know how much of the interplay she could see with Caleb either, but after our conversation in the stands, I think I care less about that.

"She probably suspected that we make out when I told her we were staying in a hotel tonight."

"We're what?" I'd assumed we'd stay at his mother's.

"Lotus is gonna keep Sarai," he says. "And you and I are gonna spend the whole night together."

The mom in me immediately wants to protest. No one else should have to look after my daughter. I should be able to do it, but August's had to leave before the sun came up every time we were together.

I'm going to give this to myself. Give this to us.

I lean my head on his shoulder as we approach the car and his mother's knowing grin. "That sounds marvelous, baby."

FORTY EIGHT

IRIS

What was I thinking?

My reflection in the mirror mocks me. August and I get a night on our own in a billion-star hotel. One night when he doesn't have to leave. Instead of lingerie to tempt him, I'm wearing a basketball jersey. I mean, it's *his* jersey, but still. It's not as sexy on me as it is on him.

I fluff my hair around my shoulders and over my arms, crossing one foot over the other like Sarai does when she has to pee.

"Well, all your crap is in the other room," I tell the girl in the mirror. "So you gotta go out there at some point."

I need this. Today's game was stressful. Seeing Caleb was a nightmare. Dinner with August's family was great, but the anticipation of tonight hung over me the whole time. The prelude of covert touches under the table, stolen kisses in the hallway, long looks charged with promise—it's drawn my nerves tight and has me poised on a fine edge. The Stingers' game was the end of a road trip, so August hasn't been home, and we haven't been together in days.

Lo is the only person I trust with Sarai overnight, and with them safely up the hall, I can relax completely.

When I enter the bedroom, I don't even take in the white and gold furnishings, the thick pile carpet, the stunning view of the city. The only thing I notice about the huge bed is the man sitting at the foot of it.

August showered shortly before I did, and he's hasn't bothered dressing. He's always a luxury for the senses. August naked, the muscles in his stomach stacked, his skin beaded with moisture, his hair a chaos of messy curls? That's a matter of irresistibility.

I make it my business to know sports stats, so I know August's wingspan, but that's not the same as seeing his shoulders stretched wide, a horizon of muscle and bone and bronzed flesh. I know his vertical, how high he can jump from standing, but that's a flat number. It tells you nothing about the legs of a man six inches over six feet, long and lean with chiseled flanks and thighs, or the calves carved from clay, hardened and burnished in the sun. He's a shooter. He's one of the best the league has ever seen and deadly from behind the arch. But I know those arms, carved and sculpted, as a haven, and those "handles", his hands, the safe place where I leave my heart.

His eyes widen on me, a heated scan of my body. "Damn, Iris."

I cross over to him, and he tugs me to stand between his legs. His cock, hard and stiff and hot, brushes against my skin. My toes curl into the carpet and my fingers curl into the dark silk of his hair. He palms my shoulders and strokes down my arms. There's reverence in the hands tracing the shape of my hips through his jersey.

"I should have worn something sexy," I say in a rush. "Like a negligee or—"

"Just stop." His laugh comes out, a wisp of smoke. "Seeing you wear my number is like a wet dream wrapped in a hand job."

He outlines his number, thirty-three, emblazoned over my chest with one finger. When he pinches and rolls my nipples, the cartilage in my knees goes to goo. I grab his shoulders, smooth and velvet, to keep me on my feet. His hands wander over my legs, creeping under the hem of the jersey to cup my bare butt, squeezing until his fingers meet at the crack of my ass. With his eyes locked with mine, he spreads my cheeks and runs one thick finger along that secret, sensitive ridge. Like he's pulled a lever, moisture leaks from my body, dampening my thighs.

Stealthily, one hand slips between my legs, and for a few moments he just caresses my lips. My breath grows jagged. I'm a moaning, shameless girl spreading her legs, silently begging him to touch me *there*. To open me up, invade, and own this pussy.

August teases me until his fingers are soaked with my body's wet, begging offering, with the supplication leaking down my thighs. My nails sink into his flesh, demanding more.

He doesn't look away and neither do I, when his mouth, steamy and insistent, possesses one breast through the jersey. He finally spreads me and taps my clit.

"Oh." I wilt against him, weak and gasping, resting my forehead on his. "August."

His thumb strokes me, repeating the caress and stealing more breath with every pass. He pulls one leg on either side to frame his muscled thighs until I'm splayed over him, cool air whispering over the wet, hot pleat of me.

"I wanna fuck you in my jersey, wearing my number." He tongues the length of my neck. "Ride me, Iris."

Just those words said just that way—I'm frozen in the moment. Preserved in a block of ice. For a second, my body shuts down. Cools. Stalls. Those words haunt me.

Another man commanded me to ride him. He told me to make him believe I wanted him, but I couldn't. I didn't. His cruelty stole my passion and turned me cold.

"Iris?" August's frown, the concern on his face, in his voice, remind me where I am. "Baby, you okay?"

I blink down at him dumbly, swallowing my tears, eating my memories whole and digesting a nightmare from long ago. I nod, my lips a cold, wobbly curve.

"Kiss me," he whispers, his eyes so tender, so intent.

I remember a magical night under the stars, under a streetlight on the eve of greatness. A night filled with laughter and confidences, pregnant with promise. And I see him so clearly, my prince, asking for a kiss.

And I do.

I kiss him like the world might end tonight because I'll never take this for granted. Not his kindness, when I've known cruelty all too well. Not his tenderness, when I've been handled roughly in the past. Not his love, when I've been possessed and owned and mistreated.

He thaws me with his kiss, my prince, and I melt into him. We're chest to chest, with August's number crushed between us. I take his cock in my hand, aligning our bodies, and two become one in a carnal slide of flesh. I anchor myself by my elbows hooked around his neck, and we kiss until I'm dizzy and our breaths tangle in a cloud of bliss. Under the jersey, his palm spans my back, digging into the naked flesh as our hips lock and roll and grind. My body clenches around him, and we pray, we curse, we moan, we mate like our bodies were made for this moment.

Ours is a love that reimagines—that peels back the sky at high noon searching for the stars, collecting them like shells in a bucket. We bathe in stardust, drink from the Milky Way, and dance on the moon. We pierce the firmament, peer into infinity, and tread on time and space. There is no before. There is no after. Now gives birth to forever. This moment may die, but this love never will. Time is not a line. It's a circle, and we, August and Iris, we stand at the center.

"Have you seen *Sliding Doors*?" I ask, pressing my back into the rigid wall of August's torso.

It's dark and I'm only a few minutes past an orgasm that left my brain like an old floppy disk wiped clean.

"The movie?" His hands move in my hair.

"Yeah, *Sliding Doors*."

"Kate Winslet?"

"No, Gwyneth Paltrow."

"Is that the movie where her mother-in-law tries to kill her?"

"No, that's *Hush*."

"Why do you know so much about Gwyneth Paltrow?" he teases, pinching my sides and making me squeal. "It's weird."

"It's not w . . . okay. So in *Sliding Doors*, this lady—"

"Gwyneth Paltrow."

"Oh, my god. Yes," I agree, laughing into the pillow both our heads rest on. "Gwyneth Paltrow."

"I'm just clarifying."

"So she drops this earring in the lift."

"A what? A lift?"

"It's London. Lift. Elevator. Same thing."

"So she drops an earring in the *lift*."

I hear his grin in the dark and wait a beat to let my silence warn him.

"Okay, okay." He laughs into my hair. "I'll stop."

I elbow him in the stomach. He "omphs", and I go on.

"Well she drops the earring and the story branches off into these two different scenarios." My good humor dissolves like sugar in vinegar. "With these two different men."

August doesn't laugh either, but finds my hand and links our fingers under the overstuffed weight of the duvet. He waits for my next words.

"I used to think of the night we met all the time." I bite my lip and blink back unexpected tears. "You wanted to kiss me outside the bar."

"And you told me you had a boyfriend." His voice has grown sober, too.

"When I was . . ."

Beaten. Bruised. Threatened. Violated.

". . . unhappy, I would imagine that I kissed you that night." I squeeze my eyes shut, wishing I could erase the wasted years between then and now. "I would imagine that I chose you, and that one choice changed everything."

He's quiet. I won't tell him everything. I won't tell him much at all, but it will be the truth.

"It was like there was this parallel universe where I made the right choice, and we were happy." I struggle to release the words that acknowledge my error. "But I would always wake up, and you weren't there. Caleb was."

"In this alternative universe," he says softly, caressing the webbing between my fingers, "was Sarai mine?"

I hesitate, not sure what he wants me to say, so again I choose the truth. I nod. He drops his head to my nape and leaves a long breath there.

"Then we were there together, because that's what kept me going when you were with him." He rolls me onto my back, pressing his forearm by my head into the pillow. "Not that it had already happened, but that it still *could*." He brushes the hair back from my face, peering down at me in the darkness like it's the light of day and he can see me clearly. "It *has* happened, Iris." He brings our clasped hands to his lips. "That's not an alternative universe. That's our life, baby."

I almost don't want to smile—like my happiness might shatter this illusion, and I'll wake up curled at the edge of the bed, staring down the barrel of Caleb's pistol. But I won't. Tomorrow I'll wake up in August's arms, and my past, my memories, Caleb – can't rob me of that.

"Can I tell you something?" August's voice anchors me in this dream, extends it a little longer.

"Of course."

"I want to wake up this way every morning," he says, hope lifting his words. "And I want our kids to bust through the door and jump in bed with us."

Tears gather at the corners of my eyes and silently stripe my cheeks. There was once a girl brave enough to want those things, but she was crushed and ground to dust. I don't know if I could find her again if I tried.

"And I'll make pancakes," he continues, his enthusiasm growing. "And I can teach them to shoot, or not. They don't have to play basketball. I don't care. I just want them to be ours. Yours and mine."

He strokes his thumb over that finger on my left hand, which once held a ring of protection and once held a ring of bondage. The tears won't stop because I'm not ready to put a ring on that finger. As much as I love August, that's a step, a risk I'm not ready to take. Not even for him. Not yet.

I'm braced for the question, trying to figure out how to tell the man I love no.

"If I were to ask you tonight, Iris, would you say yes?"

He already knows. I hear the resignation, the disappointment in his voice, and I wish I could surprise him. I can't yet.

But I will.

I lived in hell, and my way back is a journey. I survived a nightmare, escaped a monster, and I faced him down today. I may not be able to tell August yes tonight, but one day I will.

"I'm sorry, August." I shake my head helplessly and brush at the tears. "I-I can't say yes yet."

"I know, baby." He tightens his arm around my waist and tucks his chin into the curve of my neck. "That's why I'm not asking."

FORTY NINE

AUGUST

"Good game, Rook," Kenan says as we get off the bus.

"You, too." I grin at him, lowering my duffle bag to the ground while we talk. "We've put together a little winning streak here lately."

"Little bit." Kenan's stern face yields a smile. "Next year we'll be a plus five hundred team."

"You think?" He and I start toward the hotel entrance.

"If Deck and the front office play their cards right in the draft this summer and get us some more key pieces, hell yeah. We're doing well for an expansion team."

"Yeah, we're starting to gel. Tonight was great." I grimace. "Minus the snow. The last place I want to be is stranded in Denver an extra night because of weather."

"You called Iris to let her know?"

"About to. Once we get settled in the room, I will."

"How's her cousin?"

I stop in the hotel lobby and stare him down. "Do you want Iris to put in a good word for you with Lo or something?"

"What?" He looks at me like I have two heads and an extra nose. "Why would you think that?"

"Obviously because you keep asking about her."

"Has . . . she ever asked about me?"

I've never seen Kenan "Gladiator" Ross tentative, but the expression on his face is probably about as close as he'll ever come.

"Never," I answer unhesitatingly, my lips stretching into a smile.

Kenan rolls his eyes and gives me a middle-finger salute.

"August, hey." Decker walks over to us from the front desk, a file in his hand. "Can I talk to you for a second?"

"Sure." I fist-pound Kenan before he walks toward the elevator. "What's up, Deck?"

"Come sit." He gestures to a nook just off the bank of elevators.

It's late and I have no idea what this is about, but I hope he makes it quick. I want to call Iris as soon as we're done since she's expecting me tonight.

"Um, I just got off the phone with Avery," he says, watching me closely.

"Cool." Now I really don't know where this is going. "How's she doing?"

"Good." Decker hesitates and then goes on. "How much do you know about Iris's relationship with Caleb?"

Predictably, my hackles rise. The hackles on my hackles rise.

"I know it's over." Even I hear the tension in my voice.

"Calm your ass down, West." Deck's lips tighten around the words. "I'm just trying to figure out if you know . . ." A sigh heaves his heavily muscled shoulders.

"Know what, Deck?" I ask impatiently. "Dude, spit it out."

"There was a file delivered anonymously to Avery today at the station," Deck says, the words dragging over his lips.

"Okay. What kind of file?"

"This one." He slides it across the table to me but places his hand on top so I can't open it. "It's a file of pictures. Um, pictures of Iris."

My hand knots into a fist on my leg. "*My* Iris?"

"Yeah." Sympathy fills his eyes. "Your Iris."

"Like . . . naked pictures?" I try to keep my brain contained in my skull. "Give me the file, Deck."

"Not naked." He keeps his hand over the file and blows out an extended breath. "Pictures of her beaten pretty badly. And some medical records that detail . . . a pattern of abuse."

"Abuse?" The word, ugly and harsh, shouldn't even be in the same sentence as her name. "Like when she was young? Like someone touched her or . . ."

"No, not when she was young. More, um, recent." His look offers sympathy. "You didn't know?"

Decker and I stare at each other. I know what's in that file. Maybe I've known all along and didn't want to accept that it could have happened to her. Too many things that didn't add up suddenly stand in perfectly straight columns and equal a horrific sum.

"Caleb?" The name is strangled in my throat. "Are you saying Caleb hurt her? He put his hands on her?" I stab the file on the table with my index finger, rage pistoning through my body. "Is that what's in here?" I grit out. "That motherfucker hurt my girl?"

"Yes." He lifts his hand from the file. "Before you look at this, consider something. Iris probably had her reasons for not telling you."

"She said she signed an NDA. That was the only way she could guarantee sole custody of Sarai."

"Yeah, well that makes sense." He draws a deep breath and expels it. "Considering what's in it, she probably never wanted it to come to light anyway. I need to tell you something else."

"What else?" I stand and pace in tight circles, driving my hands into my hair. "What is it, Deck?"

"August, he . . . he raped her pretty brutally."

God, no.

I stop, stock still, turning only my head in careful inches to make sure I heard him right.

"He . . .he raped her?" My voice can't make it past a whisper. "Caleb?"

I honestly can't remember the last time I cried, really cried, but tears burn my eyes and blur my vision. My chest feels concave, like it collapsed on itself and is crushing my heart. My hands tremble when I link them behind my neck. I'm holding on—to my sanity, to my composure—but everything's slipping through my fingers.

"Fuck!" I scream it so loud, conversations in the lobby stop, and all eyes turn to me. I don't care. I'm spiraling, thinking of that son of a bitch violating Iris. Of him abusing her. Beating her. I kick the table, and it spins a few feet into the path of a couple walking to the elevators. I turn to the wall and punch it, denting the lobby wallpaper. Denting my hand. My knuckles swell and redden immediately.

"August, stop it." Deck grabs my arm, his frown stern. "We don't have time for tantrums."

"Tantrum?" I croak, my voice like sandpaper. "If someone raped Avery, someone beat her, what would you do?"

He goes quiet, a flare of violence in his eyes. "I'd want to kill them."

"Right. Then let me go find Caleb."

"But I hope I'd have at least one friend who would stop me," he says.

401

"Look, Caleb's going to get his. That file didn't just go to Avery's station. It went to every major station."

"Shit." I drag my hands over my face. "This'll be a media circus."

"Yeah. You might want to sort through all your feelings later and worry about Iris right now. I think Avery was one of the first to get it, but there'll be reporters and TV cameras at Iris's door very soon, if not already."

"I can't . . ." I pull my phone out to check the time. "How much time you think we've got?"

"It's late on the east coast," he says. "That helps, but we may want to get her out of there and get some PR on this. You can best believe Donald Bradley is already lawyered up and has his spin machine hard at work."

"Fuck him," I spit. "What are the odds he didn't already know about this? Caleb doesn't piss without him signing off on it."

"I've already got our PR team working on it." Deck glances at his phone when it dings with an email alert. "Matter of fact, this is from them. I sent the file over as soon as Avery told me so they could vet it and figure out a statement since the public knows about you guys now."

If I'd gone to Houston, I'd have forty-five million dollars, and maybe I'd even be on my way to a ring, but I wouldn't have Deck—someone who's truly a friend and looking out for me.

"Thanks, Deck. I . . ." Emotion clogs my throat. "I just . . . Iris? God, she's the sweetest thing in the world. And she's . . . she's so small. How could he . . ."

Deck hooks an elbow around my neck and brings me in close.

"Hey," he says gruffly, pulling back and placing his hands on my shoulders. "We'll work through all of that. I promise you he's gonna get his, August."

"You sure about that, Deck?" I ask bitterly. "Did he 'get his' when he broke my leg? No, his daddy and the powers that be protected him. And you and I both know how it is—how there's a different set of rules for

402

athletes. How we close ranks and protect our own. Consequences aren't ever guaranteed. I'm not having it this time. I'm telling you, if he gets out of this, I'll kill him myself."

"Keep your voice down," Decker says through clenched teeth. "You don't get to be a hothead. You hear me? You got a bright future that most guys would give anything to have. And you got a girl most guys would give anything to have. Would you sitting behind bars make this go away? Would it take away what happened to her? Is that gonna help her raise her kid?"

I'm quiet because I know the right answers, and I can't make myself say them. My rage needs an outlet, and I don't know one more deserving than Caleb.

I want my dad.

The thought comes from nowhere and doesn't even make sense. Who even knows if he'd have the right words to say. Despite having so little time with him, he always comes to mind in trouble or triumph. It strikes me how important a father is, and Caleb, that sorry, degenerate asshole, is Sarai's.

He can't have any part of her. He can't be in her life. He can't touch her.

"Okay." I nod at Deck to let him know my head is in the game. "I got it. You talk to the team. I'll call Iris. I need to get her out of there."

"Car's on the way," Deck says.

"What?" I do a double-take. "What car?"

"Already got a car on the way to her house ready to take her to the airport. Team plane will take her and Sarai wherever you say."

My shoulders slump with gratitude and a tiny measure of relief. I don't have my dad, but I do have Deck.

"Thank you," I tell him. "God, thanks, Deck, but redirect the car. She and Sarai are at my place. She was cooking dinner for us there."

I pause, dreading the call I need to make.

"She's been so happy, Deck," I say. "We've been so happy, and now this shit—"

"This shit will pass." He starts toward the elevator and says over his shoulder, "Call your girl so we can take care of her."

Take care of her.

I didn't do that. I let her down. How did I miss this?

Was he beating her when I saw her at the All-Star Game? I know I didn't see her often then, but from the first night we met, I've always felt so connected to her. How could I not have known? Why would she not tell me?

It doesn't matter. I know now, and she needs me more than ever.

FIFTY

IRIS

"Weather delay?" I look at the food in various stages of preparation in August's kitchen, a veritable Louisiana feast. Etouffe, shrimp, beans and rice, and bread pudding. MiMi would be proud.

"It's okay," I tell August, my phone pressed between my shoulder and ear as I measure whiskey sauce for the bread pudding. "The food will keep. It'll be here tomorrow. You *will* be home tomorrow, right?" Forget the food. I just miss him.

"You got me all Lou Rawls over here," I joke, waiting for him to laugh back. There's just silence on the other end.

"'You're Gonna Miss My Loving'?" I sing a little part of it . . . badly. "Remember?"

"Yeah, I . . . I remember," August finally says, his voice sounding as if it's passing through a cheese grater. "Babe, there's something I need to tell you. We don't have much time."

I tilt my head up to hold the phone properly. "Don't have much time?

Why?" I ask. "August, you sound weird. What's going on?"

"Decker came to me a few minutes ago and told me . . ." He clears his throat. "He told me that Avery received a file at work today."

"Avery, his girlfriend? The sports anchor?"

"Yeah. It was a file about . . . baby, it was a file about you."

I drop the measuring cup, and shards of glass litter the floor.

"A file?" My breath is choppy. Blood surges in my veins like the Mississippi primed to overflow. "What kind of file?"

The question is superfluous. I already know. I'm as shattered inside as the glass at my feet realizing that the world will know what happened to me. What was done to me.

That August knows.

"It's pictures of you," he says, swallowing so hard I hear it over the phone. I hear the anguish in his voice before he says the words. "Beaten, Iris. He beat you?"

He beat me? No, I beat *him* at his own game. I escaped. I got away.

I survived!

But all anyone will see is a victim. Not Iris, but the black-eyed Susan in those pictures with her lips split open and her jaw swollen twice its normal size. All they'll say is *he beat you? You let him beat you? You stayed?*

Weak.

Fool.

And they'll have no idea who I am.

"August, I wanted to tell you." I say, pressing down my shame. "I signed an NDA."

"You could have told me, though. Iris, you should have—"

"Excuse me, but I don't need a lecture from anyone on what I should have done." I fight back tears of hurt and anger. Not at him. At Caleb, and whomever leaked this, and at the whole world. "My situation was complicated beyond what you can imagine. If I had just left Caleb, he would have gotten joint custody of Sarai, and that was never going to happen. I would die to prevent that from happening."

I almost did.

"We'll talk about that later," he says. "I'm not mad at you. God, do you think I'm mad at *you*? For not telling me? No, baby. I'm mad at myself for not seeing it. For not . . . I'm furious at him for . . ." He pulls in a fortifying breath and goes on more calmly. "Right now, we need to get you out of there. Avery isn't the only one who got this file. Every major news station has it."

My knees buckle as the scope of my humiliation comes into full view. I grip the counter and raise a shaking hand to my mouth. "What? Oh, God."

"A car's on the way to my place," August says, and I hear the deliberate calm of his voice trying to soothe me. "Grab a few things for you and Sarai, and the car will take you to the airport. Wherever you want to go."

Spanish moss. The Mississippi River flowing through my veins.

MiMi left Lo and me her tiny house on the bayou. We haven't sorted through what we want to do, so it's just sitting there empty, waiting.

"I want to go to Louisiana," I say. "Not many know about MiMi's place, that I'm connected to it."

"Okay. The Waves have a plane that'll take you there."

"And you?" I don't want to sound pitiful, but I need him so badly. I never wanted to be dependent on a man again, but it's too late. Our hearts are interdependent, and when mine is aching, it needs him. Wants him. *I* want him.

"I'm coming to you, of course." He growls over the phone. "God, I'd be there by now if it weren't for this damn snow in Denver. As soon as I can get a flight out of here, I'll come. Just text me the address."

"Okay." My heartbeat slows just a little.

"A driver will take you to the airport, and a guy from the security team will go with you to the house."

My blood congeals. "No," I croak. "No. I don't want that. I don't want a bodyguard or security or . . . no. Just you, August."

"Iris, there's no way in hell I'm letting you and Sarai go to the middle of nowhere by yourselves during this shit storm," he snaps.

"That's right. You're not *letting* me do anything," I snap right back. "I'm *telling* you that I'm not having some strange man staying with me and my daughter. End of story."

"But Iris—"

"Did you read the file?" I ask abruptly.

We're separated by miles and an ocean's worth of silence floating between us.

"No," he finally replies. "You wanted to tell me yourself, and I know you hate your story, your life being out of your control. That everyone else gets to judge and interpret you. At least with me, I want you to be able to tell your story yourself. That's how I want to hear it."

My prince.

He sees me. He knows me. He loves me, and I thank God for a second chance.

"Thank you for that, August," I say, gulping back tears. "Caleb's bodyguard kept me in that house. Made sure I could never leave. He stood by while Caleb beat and raped me."

The word rises from hell and climbs up my throat, burning and sulfurous in my lungs.

"I was . . . I was raped by Caleb on a . . . on a regular basis at gunpoint." I pause for the softly uttered expletive from the other end. It all rushes back so vividly that my scalp stings when I think of Caleb jerking me by the hair.

"Iris, God." I managed to hold back *my* tears, but I hear them in his voice—the agony for me. "Baby, I want to be with you right now."

"I know. I want that, too. Tonight?" I ask hopefully. "You think you'll make it there tonight?"

"If I have to drive a bus to the nearest city that can get me a flight out, I will. I promise."

"Just no bodyguard. Please," I whisper. "I know it's silly to you, but—"

"No bodyguard," he agrees, still reluctantly. "The driver will drop you guys off at the house. You'll only be there a few hours without me, and I'll see you tonight."

I turn off all the food and abandon everything. I know this feeling. I remember my family running, chased by a pending storm. The panic, the hysteria. The terror. I feel it all riding to the airport and flying to Louisiana. Thank God for Sarai. Occupying her, soothing her on the plane, feeding her when she's hungry—the business of motherhood helps take my mind off the storm whirring around me, picking up strength with every person who sees that file. I'm not googling or surfing the web. I don't want to know what's going on. When the time comes, I'll speak.

It's only when we are inside and the driver is on his way back to the main road that I really stop to think. To take myself off autopilot and process the implications of the file coming out. Was someone out to get Caleb? It wouldn't surprise me, of course. Surely, I'm not the only one he's been cruel to. August knew he was a jackass. Andrew knew. Andrew helped me with the medical reports.

Andrew?

Caleb had something on Andrew to keep him under his thumb. Was this Andrew's revenge?

If so, thanks a lot, buddy.

Sarai is bathed and in her nightgown of choice, a San Diego Waves T-shirt, and I'm wearing one of August's button-ups I grabbed from his place when my phone rings.

"Story, Mommy," Sarai says plaintively, holding up her copy of *Goodnight Moon*.

"Mommy will read. Just hold on." I run into the kitchen where I left my phone, making sure to check the caller ID before I answer.

"Lo, hey. Thanks for calling back so quickly."

"Of course, girl." Sympathy and anger mix in her voice. "I wish I could be there. I'm stuck here in New York 'til the weekend. How did this happen?"

"I have no idea. A copy of the file was delivered to Avery Hughes. She's dating Mack Decker, one of the Waves front-office execs, and she gave him a heads-up."

"Are you okay?" Concern softens Lo's usual brashness. "You know you have nothing to be ashamed of."

"Yeah, I know." My laugh sounds hollow. "But everyone's going to judge me anyway. Make assumptions. Presume to know. I never wanted this to come out. It was purely a threat to keep Caleb out of our lives." I flop onto MiMi's flower-patterned couch. "Man, this is an ugly couch."

"What?" Lo laughs. "The one in the living room?"

"Yeah. It's like one of those gators in the bayou threw up a garden."

"Yeah, it's bad," she says, and we share a laugh that dies at the same time. "I miss MiMi so much."

"She was amazing." I swipe at the corners of my eyes, surprised by the tears. "I wish I'd had more time with her."

"You had the time you were supposed to have. I believe we go where we're supposed to go when we're supposed to and that people are in our lives when they're supposed to be."

"What if they never should have been in your life at all?" I bite my lip. "I wish I'd never met Caleb."

"He's an asshole, but your experience with him taught you a lot about yourself and made you stronger than anyone I know."

"Yeah, right," I scoff, picking at a faded flower on the upholstery.

"Listen to me, Bo." Lo's firm voice gets my attention. "The struggle made you stronger. Lesson learned. Move on and show the world what a survivor looks like."

"I just feel haunted by my mistakes," I whisper, clenching my eyes closed. "And like everyone will see me as weak."

"Weak?" Lo scoffs. "Fuck 'em. If they haven't walked in your shoes, haven't had to fight for their lives and for their kid's life, haven't had to survive what you survived, and lived to tell it, they have no room to judge."

"Lo." I can't manage anything more.

"You have Sarai. You have August. You have me. You had MiMi," she says vehemently. "One person in your life was an asshole, and you evicted him as soon as you could. I'm proud of you."

The words spread over me like salve, and I can't speak because of the emotion choking me—because of how much that means.

"I guess August is losing his mind," Lo says after a few seconds of silence, shifting the subject.

"Pretty much." I shove my fingers through my tangled hair and sniff. "He was trying really hard to stay calm for my sake, but 'lose your shit' was all in his voice."

"He loves you."

"Yeah, he does." I smile wider. "I love him, too."

"You sound a lot better than I thought you would."

"I feel better." I shrug. "It's like, yes, I hate that people will know, and I don't know what this will mean for Caleb—his career, endorsements, and all that stuff. He's so insulated by his money and his father's power. I don't think this alone will take him down. I'm more concerned about him pursuing custody of Sarai at some point."

My phone signals an incoming call.

"Hey, this is August," I say hastily. "I'll call you back."

I click over and settle back on the ugly couch. "August, hey."

"Hey." He sounds tired. "I'm on my way."

"You're on the plane?" I ask, my voice and my heart lifting.

"Even better. Flight just landed, and I'm in the car. According to navigation, I should be there in like two hours."

"Thank you, August." Some of the tightness in my chest loosens knowing he's coming.

"Babe, don't thank me. There's nowhere else I want to be."

"Wait." I sit up, frowning, mentally collating dates and information. "Don't you have a game in San Diego tomorrow night? What time is your flight back out?"

"I'm not flying back tomorrow." He blows out a weary breath. "I told Deck I needed to take a day, and he agreed. I'm skipping the game."

"To be . . . to be here with me?"

"I told you if you were ever mine, I'd play you at the five." The sound of a smile breaks through his voice. "You're the center, Iris."

I don't answer but absorb his promise to me. His devotion to me.

"And we need to talk," he continues before hesitating. "Maybe you need to talk to someone soon? A counselor or something."

"I have a counselor," I answer softly.

"You do? When do you see a counselor? How did I not know that?"

"I plugged in with a counseling service for survivors at a local women's shelter in San Diego." I clear my throat. "I have a lot of baggage to sort through."

"Can I come?" he asks. "Like talk to them and ask how I should handle things? Or how I can support you? I just . . . I wanna kill him, Iris."

"I knew you would and that you'd have to see him all the time for games, events, whatever. That's why I—"

"Mommy!" Sarai yells from the other room.

"Let me go see what she wants."

"Tell her . . . *Gus* loves her," he says, begrudging the nickname.

"She'll grow out of it." I grin, because he legitimately hates it. "Maybe."

"Jared hasn't."

"I know, but Jared—"

"Mommy!" Sarai calls again.

"Go. You're being summoned," he says. "I love you. I'll see you soon."

Sarai is sitting up in bed when I enter the room we used to share. Her eyes are wide, her lashes wet, rounded arms with their dimpled elbows stretched up to me.

I sit down on the bed and pull her close, brushing down her hair, which now reaches the middle of her back. She's growing up so fast. I can barely remember the time when I resented having her, didn't want her. Now she's everything to me, and I want time to slow so I have as much of it with her as possible.

"What's wrong, princess?"

"I . . . I saw a monster," she whispers, her voice trembling. She's shaking in my arms.

I draw back and study her face. Real fear darkens the blue of her eyes.

"Bad dream?" I kiss her forehead and rub her back. "Wanna tell me about it? What did the monster look like?"

Her eyes fix over my shoulder, and she stares unblinkingly for a few seconds before answering, "Daddy."

Panic vacuums the breath from my chest, and before I can ask what she means, a sound behind me turns me to ice.

"Hello, princess."

I whip my head around. Caleb leans against the doorjamb with his arms folded over his chest.

I've never seen him look so disheveled. His jeans and shirt are wrinkled. Shadows and bags lurk under his eyes. For once, the gold is tarnished.

I stand up and position my body in front of Sarai.

"Caleb." I smooth my voice, kneading out the lumps of fear and anxiety. "What are you doing here?"

His grin is diabolical, mocking my attempt to protect our daughter. "You mean you weren't expecting me?" he asks, a dark stream of laughter running through his voice.

Maybe I was. On some level, I knew that without the restraints I imposed on him, Caleb would come after me, but I didn't think he'd find me here.

He's proven me wrong.

"Did you think I didn't always know where my girls were?" he asks, his voice a cloaked threat. "I had eyes on you from the time you left the hotel 'til you arrived here that first night."

He steps deeper into the room, and every step he takes closer to Sarai's bed, a screw turns in my spine until I'm a taut wire ready to snap. I don't want to make sudden moves or fight in here. If I can just get him out of this room. . .

"Sarai, you remember me?" He reaches around me to touch her hair.

Sarai nods and says, "Daddy."

"That's right," Caleb says, looking pleased. "I'm your daddy. How would you like it if you and Mommy could come live with me?"

My throat implodes, trapping a scream inside. I dig my nails painfully into my palms, but that's good. The pain keeps me sharp and aware.

"I wanna live with Gus," Sarai says, clear as day.

I close my eyes, my head dropping forward, because I think my daughter may have just sentenced me to die.

"Gus?" Caleb asks, a frown pinching his dark gold brows together. And then his eyes latch onto the San Diego Waves T-shirt she's wearing to bed. "Is that right?"

The words are stones hurled at the bed, but she doesn't realize it and answers honestly, nodding.

"Let's go talk in the living room, Caleb," I urge him, forcing myself to touch his arm and tug. "Sarai was having a bad dream but needs to sleep."

Their dark violet–blue eyes hold for long seconds. Sarai, perversely, looks more alert than she has all day, not like it's time for sleep at all.

Finally, Caleb walks into the hall. I turn the lock on Sarai's door and pray she doesn't figure out how to get out. Whatever happens in the next few moments, I don't want her to see it. I have to know she's safe, or I won't be able to fully focus on getting out of this alive.

My mind is on spin cycle, whirring with possible weapons, escape routes, distractions—anything to hold him off until August arrives. I decide on redirection—stalling him by pretending he didn't come here to kill me.

"I didn't release that file, Caleb." I gesture for him to sit on the couch while I take the seat a few feet away. He cocks one brow, asking if we are really going to play this game, but shrugs like he has all the time in the world to remind me how much he likes hurting me.

"I know that." He sits back on the ugly couch, spreading his long arms across the back. "Andrew did. Bastard."

"What did you have on him?"

He looks surprised for a moment before shrugging. "He accidentally gave his girlfriend in college too much of some drug he was experimenting with, and she died."

"What? Oh my God."

"I handled it for him," Caleb says. "But, of course, he owed me. Idiot confessed and ratted me out."

"I'm sorry." I assemble my features into concern. "Has there been much backlash?"

Maybe it was the wrong thing to ask. The adrenaline coursing through me is muddling my thoughts and has my fight-or flight instinct in overdrive. There is no "sit down for banal chatter with your predator" instinct, but that's the route I take because in a physical fight with Caleb, I'd have no chance.

Taking flight from him, I'd have no chance.

The longer I delay a physical confrontation, the closer August comes.

"Backlash?" He barks out a laugh like the rabid dog he is. "I've been cut from the Stingers, lost all my endorsements in a matter of hours, and my father has basically disowned me."

"Your father?" I ask, shocked because Mr. Bradley has always navigated any rough waters for Caleb.

"Too damning, I guess." Caleb shakes his head. "The league is taking a very hard line on this, and my father can't be seen on the wrong side of it. Probably making me an example."

"I'm so sorry," I lie.

"Sorry?" he spits, sitting forward suddenly and shrinking the space separating us. "This is your fault."

"No. I kept my end of the bargain."

My mind hums like a machine, thinking on overdrive of a plan to escape as I watch his skin mottle, his eyes narrow, and his fists open and close, like he's itching for something to pummel.

"So you did," he admits. "But unfortunately for you, all of my . . . incentives, shall we say, for letting you go and leaving you alone . . ." His handsome faces creases with a half-grin. "Are gone."

I don't know if he moves first or if I do. I don't know if the predator and prey are somehow psychically linked and we move in harmony, but it becomes a hunting party. He's the hound and I'm the rabbit. I rush past him to the kitchen. Heavy, rapid steps eat up the floor behind me.

If I can just get to my purse on the counter.

It's in sight when he circles my waist from behind and lifts me off the ground. My arms windmill and I flail, kicking at his legs, a dervish of flying, fighting limbs. He hurls me to the floor. I skid across the linoleum and land in front of the sink. I'm scrambling to my knees when he grabs a fistful of my hair and rams my head into the cabinet.

I haven't felt this kind of pain in a long time, but you never forget it—the hurt that blossoms from one single spot and infects your whole body. The room tilts, and blood runs into my eyes.

"Caleb, please." I force my tongue to move. "I can explain."

"Explain!" he screams, squatting so his breath blows over my face. "Can you explain why you fucked him, Iris?"

Oh, God.

He wipes the blood from my face tenderly but then grips my jaw in one large hand until I'm afraid it will crack.

"And you gave my daughter to him," he hisses.

"No, I—"

The back of his hand sends my head swiveling on my neck, a flower on a fragile stem. The swelling has already started. My forehead and my cheek throb to the familiar beat of my racing pulse. He touches my thigh, just below August's shirt. I scuttle away from his touch, but he drags me back by my ankle, quickly pinning me to the floor and planting himself between my thighs. He gathers my wrists in one large hand.

"I've missed you, Iris." He breathes the words into my neck, his dick pressing through my panties. I squirm my hips, trying to dislodge him.

"No. Caleb." My breath heaves with fruitless exertion. "Don't."

"Is that what you say to West?" he screams in my ear. "Do you say don't to West, Iris?"

"Mommy!" Sarai's voice reaches us from behind the locked bedroom door.

"It's okay, baby," I call back, fighting the tears that would make her more anxious. "We're playing a game, okay? Mommy will be there soon."

"Is that what you think?" he asks. "That we'll just go back to business as usual? After this?"

"If you get help," I say in as reasonable a tone as I can manage with a man determined to take me by force, "you can see her. You can be part of her life. You may get back on the Stingers. Your dad'll come around. There's no telling what your father can accomplish."

"And you'd come home?" he asks, his eyes almost sad, his mouth a wistful line drawn through the middle of his madness.

What do I say?

"Maybe," I lie. "If you get the help you need, we could see, Caleb."

His grip on my wrist relaxes just a little, just enough. I pounce. I shove him with all my strength. His bulk shifts. I surge to my feet and dive for my purse on the counter. It's barely out of reach when he catches me, pressing my stomach painfully into the counter's sharp edge.

"I'm done talking," he rasps into my hair. One hand loosens his belt while his thickly muscled arm circles me, pinning my arms to my sides. His hand fumbles under my shirt, and I hear my panties rip.

"No!" I screech and struggle and fight with every ounce of resistance I have.

Sobs shake my shoulders, and my head droops forward helplessly. He's nudging, hard and aroused, when he shifts and tries to get in. I wiggle one arm loose just enough for me to turn, and the edge of the counter digs into my back. I slap at his head and punch wildly. His fingers, thick and long and strong, manacle my neck, squeezing mercilessly, not budging even when I claw at them, desperate for air. My vision darkens and the stars come out, bright pins of light penetrating the velvet blanket falling over my eyes. With the last of my consciousness, I stretch to my purse, drag it toward me. I pull out MiMi's jeweled knife. Angling down, I thrust blindly, sinking the blade into flesh.

He howls, jumping back to grab his leg gushing blood. I stumble past him out of the kitchen, gasping for breath, massaging my throat, tripping across the floor. If I can just get him outside, away from Sarai.

I'm almost at the front door when a sound fires behind me. Pain explodes in my shoulder with atomic force, sending me to my knees. I clutch my shoulder, blood running through my fingers.

He shot me.

In all those months he held me against my will with that gun, he never actually shot me.

He means to kill me.

"It's useless to run, Iris." He drags his injured leg behind him and over to the wall where I slump, so disoriented with pain, I can barely move.

"I never wanted to hurt you, baby." He pushes my hair back with the barrel of the gun, making me shudder. "I only wanted to love you, but you messed that up."

A bitter laugh cracks my lips. "You lying piece of shit," I whisper. "I can't even count all the ways you've hurt me."

I don't wait for him to answer, but go on, ignoring the seething crater in my shoulder.

"I have a cracked tooth." I tap a molar on the side. "Right here. I lost twenty percent of the hearing in my right ear when you busted my eardrum. You fractured my wrist, and it never healed properly. It aches all the time."

I ache all the time.

"You've done nothing but hurt me." Tears and blood from my head wound mingle on my face.

August.

His name whispers through my thoughts. I say a silent prayer that Sarai will make it through this, that August will take care of her. That he and Lo will make sure she doesn't forget me. Sorrow, wide and deep, swallows me, for all the lost moments with her and August I'll never have. My stolen second chance.

"New rules," Caleb says, pushing the gun into my side. "We either live together, or we don't live at all. Those are the rules. I do have one gift for you, though."

He pulls something small from the pocket of his jeans, opening his hand to reveal MiMi's gris-gris ring. It glints against his palm, so unassuming, so powerful.

I know I can't actually hear her voice, but the sight of the ring MiMi crafted to protect me brings her words, spoken to me in this very house, back to mind.

You are pure. You are enough. You are strong.

He can't hurt you.

Strong enough to fight back. Strong enough to win.

Strength. Dignity. Courage. All these things belong to you. Take them back.

"I only wanted us to be together," Caleb says, his sorrow, his madness and ruthlessness twisting in his voice. "And one way or another, we will be. It all ends tonight."

The hell it does.

His rules. His dictatorship. His *girl*. For too long, he's acted like he owned me, but I'm not his. He doesn't get the last word. It's my life. My body. My spirit.

Yours to keep and yours to share.

There is a reservoir in my soul. A pool of strength, lying in wait. Like MiMi's Mississippi, it surges through my veins, cleansing me, renewing me, imbuing me with the power of a thousand priestesses. Lending me ancient courage born a thousand years before.

I slam my fist into his injured leg, scrambling out of the way when he grabs at the wound. I push against him, shifting our bodies until the gun flies from his hand. We both dive for it, blood leaking from my shoulder and gushing from his leg. Our hands wrap around the barrel and the handle. He presses me to the floor, and we fight and fumble until our fingers overlap on the trigger, the gun wedged between our bellies. It's him or me.

Or maybe it's both of us, because together we pull the trigger.

FIFTY ONE

AUGUST

Every horror movie on the bayou I've ever seen comes to mind while I drive the long road to MiMi's place. "Secluded" was the word Iris used. That's a daytime word. At night, "scary as hell" seems more appropriate.

When I finally pull into the driveway, the rental car is the first thing I see. Iris was adamant that security not stay. I can't even think about her reasons without nearly busting a blood vessel. Caleb has so much to answer for, and I plan to personally see to it that he does. Not his money, or his family's power, or the rug we like to sweep shit under will save him this time.

The car makes no sense, and the closer I get to the house, my duffle bag in tow, the more cautious I become. The door is cracked open, an eerie invitation to come inside.

The house is so tiny, making the scene in the front room unavoidable. It's the first thing I see, and I'm sure it will haunt me until I die.

"Iris." I say her name out loud, but I don't hear it. I don't hear anything. The words are muffled. I'm underwater and drowning, burning lungs, weighted limbs, struggling to the top, fighting for air.

My Iris.

Lying in a pool of blood—still. And that monster on top of her—still. There's so much blood, and I can't tell where he ends and she begins, and whose blood is coming from where. For a second, I'm immobile at the door, trapped in a tragic snapshot, but then all the sounds rush in and I'm in motion, desperate and frenzied. I push the dead weight of Caleb's body aside.

"Shit. Shit. Shit."

Iris lies on the floor, wearing one of my shirts. It's shoved up past the top of her thighs. Blood blossoms across her torso, dousing the shirt from belly to shoulder.

"Iris?" I touch her arm, gentle and hesitant and desperate. "Baby?"

I search for signs of life. I don't breathe while my heart waits to know if it's irreparably broken.

When her eyes slowly open, it's daybreak. It's dawn. This moment puts everything in perspective because despite all the things I have, if Iris is gone, I've got nothing.

"August!" She tries to sit up, and I scoot my body under her so her head can rest on my knee. "Sarai. Where is she?"

My heart seizes when I don't see Sarai. Did he do something to her? But then a sound from the back of the house filters into my consciousness, insistent, but faint.

"I hear her in the back. She's calling you."

Iris releases a long breath out and nods. "I locked her room. She must still be in there," she rasps, her voice hoarse. She squints, focusing on the prone man a few feet away. "Is he dead?"

Her lips tremble. She's shaking in my arms. Her cheekbone is swollen, and blood streaks down her face. Black marks stripe her throat.

God, I hope he's dead.

"I . . . baby, I don't know," I say. "I need to call nine-one-one. There's so much blood."

"Not my blood." She grimaces and lifts her hand, painstakingly slow, to touch her shoulder. "Some of it is. He shot me in the shoulder."

Motherfucker.

I squeeze my forehead and claw my hair to keep myself focused on her and not tearing his arms out of their sockets. The desire to kill him is an ache in my bones. It makes my heart contract.

"He's shot, though," she says weakly. "We fought, and I shot him." Pride sparks in her eyes, dulled to brown.

"You did good, Iris." I run a shaky palm over her hair, and my fingers come away red and sticky with blood. "Jesus, baby. Are you sure you're—"

"Is he dead?" she cuts in, her grip on my arm tight. Her eyes are wide, urgent. "I need to know, August. He won't ever leave me alone. Do you hear? He'll kill me. And Sarai will—"

I press my finger to her lips, staunching the panic rising in her voice. "I'll check."

"Now." Tears leak from the corners of her eyes and skid over her swollen cheekbone. "Check now."

Smudgy marks from his fingers stain her jaw. My stomach turns at what he's done to her. At the thought that this isn't the first time. She lived with him. She slept beside him. For months. Alone.

Fuck.

I gently shift her and scoot across the blood-covered floor to the vermin pickling in his own reckoning. Rage overpowers me the closer I get. I want to stomp on his face and press my boot to his throat. His hand is tucked under his shirt, and when I tug the shirt back, he's covering a hole in his belly streaming blood.

"West." His eyes flutter open. His voice is thin, withering, agonized. He grimaces, tipping his head back. Life leaks from his eyes as surely as it's leaking from his wound. "I guess you win."

I look back to Iris, who has pulled herself to a sitting position and leans against the wall. Even now, with him clinging to the last threads of his life, she's wary and guarded, watching him like, shot and bleeding out, he still might strike.

She lifts her hand, revealing a small ring in her palm.

"Lo told you your days were numbered," she says, her voice wobbling.

With eyes narrowed, she cups her hand to her mouth and blows over it.

"Fuck you, Iris," he says, voice rough and angry.

With one hand covering the bullet hole in her shoulder, Iris drags herself across the floor until she's beside me. A scarlet line of blood trails her.

"Iris." I pull out my phone and nod to her bleeding shoulder. "I need to call nine-one-one."

"No." She fires the word like a bullet, the last one in her barrel as she looms over Caleb. "Don't call yet."

"But your shoulder—"

"It's fine." Her soft mouth lopsides in a bitter smile. "I have a high tolerance for pain. Isn't that right, Caleb?"

Her gaze is locked on his—on the last vestiges of life draining from his eyes, from his body.

"As long as he's alive, I'm not safe and neither is my daughter. He tried to kill me." She draws in a long breath, her eyes narrowed. "So we wait."

She's my Iris, but I've never seen her like this. I thought I had seen all her sides, loved all her sides, but I've never seen this. Ruthless and beautiful and bloodied, she emanates all the strength and determination it must have taken her to survive.

And I've never loved her more.

We stand in silent vigil for the few minutes of life Caleb has left. His moans and his pain don't move me—they don't bring me satisfaction either. It's simply a necessary end. He deserves so much worse, but at least Iris gets to watch him die.

The absolute stillness of death settles over him. His gaze is vacant and fixed on Iris. I pass a hand over his eyes, closing them; denying him, even in death, one last glimpse of my girl.

I call nine-one-one and then turn my attention back to her. I take her face between my hands, aligning our eyes.

"He's gone." I press my forehead to hers, and the blood on her face smears against mine. I don't care. I wish I could share her pain as easily. I wish I could wipe it away like it had never happened.

"Yes. Yes." Her fingers dig into my hair and her head drops to my shoulder. She kisses my neck. "I love you."

I pull back, tilting her chin and erasing her tears with the back of my hand. Carefully, I kiss her, tasting her blood and her tears and her pain.

That night we first met, we couldn't have known what lay ahead. If she had only kissed me—if I had only pressed for more. If the night I won the championship, I'd managed to convince her that even though we'd just met, even though she had a boyfriend, even though it didn't make sense – we should take a chance. If I had looked closer and hadn't missed the signs. Life isn't a road that forks or a line of numbered sliding doors. There is no alternate universe filled with only right choices. There's just this one—just this life, and we go where our choices take us and grow wiser from our mistakes.

Standing on the porch waiting for the paramedics, I glance up at the blackened stretch of Louisiana sky. Life is a constellation of decisions, connected by coincidences and deliberations, painting pictures in the heavens. During the day, when things are brightest, we don't see the stars, but they are there. It's only in the contrast of night, when things are darkest, that the stars shine.

Iris is my constellation. She took the darkness as her cue to shine. It only made her brighter, stronger, and tonight, her hard-won glimmer lights up the sky.

OVER
TIME

"I have been bent and broken,
but—I hope—
into a better shape."

CHARLES DICKENS, *GREAT EXPECTATIONS*

EPILOGUE

IRIS

"**S**hitbag!"

I'm literally pulling my hair and grinding my teeth.

"Motherfucker, are you kidding me with this?"

I pace the floor and clench my fists at my side.

"Just . . ." I punch the air. "Ugggghhh."

My Lakers are playing. And as usual, I'm at war with the refs.

"Grrrrr." Another bad call.

I'm trying to keep my voice down. August is in his guest room reading to Sarai. We have these little "sleepovers" at his place from time to time, my concession since I haven't decided to move into his condo yet. I'm especially keen for these semi-regular events at times like this when he's coming off a long road trip and we haven't seen him.

The Lakers score.

Yes!

Even though I've been a Lakers fan since I was a kid, and even though

August knows that, I still feel a little disloyal. My Lakers *did* beat the Waves two days ago. I drove up to LA for the game and sat in the stands. I was torn, but I managed to sit on my hands whenever we—we, being the Lakers—scored. As competitive as August is, he gave me a "don't talk to me" look after they lost the game.

I wore his Waves jersey proudly, number thirty-three.

But my panties were purple and gold.

The doorbell rings when the game goes to a commercial, and I turn off the TV in case August finishes before I get back to the bedroom.

I stare dumbly at the pizza delivery guy standing at the door.

"Pizza for DuPree?" the pimple-faced teenager asks.

"Um, I didn't order pizza." *Would have been good, though.*

He peers up at the number over the door and back to the delicious-smelling box of pizza, and then squints at a little slip of paper.

"Pineapple and pepperoni pizza and root beer?" he asks. "That's not you?"

August.

"Oh, yeah. That *is* me." I laugh and turn back toward the living room. "Let me grab my purse."

"Already paid for." He hands it over, offers a small salute, and leaves.

I lean against the door, holding the pizza in the palm of one hand, clutching the root beer in the other. August knows me so well—he remembers that I like pizza and root beer when the Lakers play.

He knows me well, and we have no more secrets. No more shadows or shame. There are obvious disadvantages to Andrew leaking that file, but I can't deny the good it did. Yes, the darkest, hardest parts of my life were put on display for everyone to dissect and judge, but now I have nothing to hide.

And no one to hide my secrets from.

Caleb is dead. I've held onto my humanity enough not to take joy in it, but I can't say I mourned him. Never has 'survival of the fittest' been truer. There's no doubt in my mind that if Caleb had lived, I would have died. I almost did. His eyes were cruel until his last breath, and he tried to diminish me until the very end. And with him gone, it's like my entire existence exhaled.

There wasn't any question that it was self-defense. If the file released wasn't damning enough, the head wound, marks on my neck, and bullet in my shoulder testified against Caleb. I answered all the questions the police had, but I really wanted to leave it at that and go on with our lives.

But it's not that simple.

I'm in a relationship with one of the NBA's rising stars, one who leads a very public life. Two of the league's most popular players were ensnared in a "love triangle" that turned violent and tragic. One of them ends up dead, and the woman caught in the middle was holding the smoking gun. It was the juiciest basketball story in decades. In the locker room, after games, in interviews, reporters always found a way to bring up "the scandal." It was awkward.

August was evasive, impatient, ill-tempered. And I was . . . not sure. Not sure I was ready to talk about the things that almost destroyed me—to talk about my life like it was some telenovela. Like some sensationalized soap opera with a fairytale beginning, a villainous prince, and a grisly end. And the last thing I wanted to be was the poster child for domestic abuse, not with the way our culture finds ways to blame the victims.

But none of that was the ultimate deciding factor in why I finally spoke. I spoke because maybe there's some girl like me. Young. Vulnerable. Naïve. Flattered by his attention. Maybe she thinks his jealousy means he loves her more or that it's cute. Does she realize that slowly, surely, she's being cut off from her friends? Isolated from her family? Being molded into something she's not? Into what he wants her to be?

The heart speaks in whispers, but sometimes by the time we listen, it's too late. I learned that the hardest way. And maybe that girl can change her course before it's too late.

That's why I spoke.

I sat down with Avery Hughes one-on-one. She was thoughtful and compassionate, but she didn't let me get away with telling only part of the story. And I didn't want to tell it in sugar-coated half-measures. Once I decided to speak, I wanted to roar. Not just for all the women who might end up in a toxic relationship, but for those in one *right now*.

I get it. I know how real the fear is. That leaving doesn't always mean getting away for good. That it just might cost you your children. That leaving just might cost you your life. I know the system fails us too many times, protecting rights the abuser shouldn't have and offering us little shelter. I'm not recommending women kill their abusers. I just hate that our system leaves us with so many shitty options—difficult options that many survivors must negotiate even after leaving. Our choices are sometimes catch twenty-twos that catch us around the neck—that choke us and make difficult, dangerous situations more difficult and dangerous. Our laws don't make common sense and don't offer any real protection until the perpetrator's done something to prove he'll hurt you.

And sometimes by then it's too late.

The pizza burns my hand through the cardboard box.

"Shoot!"

I shift the box, propping it against my chest and grabbing it by the edge. I drop off the pizza and root beer in the kitchen and wander down the hall. The closer I get to the guest room, the softer I tread. I love watching August and Sarai together. My daughter is one of those kids you think is adorably precocious when you first meet her. After about the fiftieth question and a few of her "sage" ponderings, most search frantically for an escape. Never August. He answers her fiftieth question with the same patient thoroughness that he did her first.

By the time I reach the door, she's already asleep. My heart contracts at how beautiful she is, how peaceful. I've fought hard for that peace—to protect her from the violence that lived under the same roof we did the first year of her life. How many times did Caleb beat me, rape me with her just a wall away? And yet she hasn't been touched by it. If there is one thing I got right, I hope it was preserving her innocence while he stripped mine away.

August stands and sets the book on her bedside table. He doesn't otherwise move but stares down at her for long moments before bending to leave a kiss in her hair. My heart contracts again, harder, longer, watching him watching her. He loves her like his own. I know that. I also know he wants us here every night, all the time.

My beautiful prince in sweatpants.

His body has changed since I met him that night in a bar. He was leaner, lankier then. Playing in the NBA he has, by necessity, added more muscle, reduced his body fat to almost zero. The ridges of his abs, the chiseled line of his legs, and the cut of bicep where his shirt sleeve catches and strains prove it. All over, he's harder and more defined.

So am I. Harder. Defined by all the things I've experienced and what it took to survive. I've been through a lot since I was a college senior on the verge of graduating. I'm not that bright-eyed girl in a bar whose biggest concern was bad calls by the refs. I've had a daughter. I've lived through hell. I've killed a man.

I will never be the same.

Some things imprint us so deeply, we can never return to what we were before. But would I want to? Sure, I'm more guarded, but I like to think I have more compassion because I've known true suffering, and I hurt when I see it in others. I may be more cynical, but I like to think I'm wiser, too.

When I told my story, some said I was a hero. I'm not. I'm just a woman who ended up in a bad relationship with a bad man and had to fight my way out of it. I did what I had to do to protect my daughter and to protect myself.

That doesn't make me special, but it does make me a survivor. It's happening to women just like me and nothing like me all the time. To our neighbors, to our best friends, to our sisters. It's happening behind closed doors, or even out in the open, documented in redacted police reports or in a million views on viral videos that we judge and poke at and debate.

Even when I shared my story, everyone had opinions. I should have left sooner. I should have pressed charges. Why didn't I trust the system to "punish" him? Why didn't I tell everyone? Was it really self-defense, or was it revenge?

If you've never had to fight for your life in your own home, if you've never had someone you thought loved you hurt you the most, then you don't know. But I do. I know how it feels to wake up every day living in a nightmare and sleeping with a monster, and I told the world in my own words and on my own terms.

Maybe for women like me, after what we've lived through, what we almost died through, love is harder to come by. But it *can* come. August is living proof that it *can* come. Truly. Richly. After all I've been through, August is my reward.

When he sees me at the door, he startles a little, then grins and puts a finger to his lips, shushing me. He walks to the hall and closes the bedroom door.

"Don't shush me," I whisper-hiss with a smile.

"I don't want you to wake her up." He turns me by my shoulder and pops my bottom, making me squeak and jump a little. He urges me ahead of him down the hall. "I have plans for you."

He walks behind me toward his bedroom, and I'd know his footfalls anywhere.

They say *I'd follow you to the ends of the earth.* When he pauses, they say *I'll wait until you're ready.* And he has. August has asked me to marry him three times in the last year, and every time I've said no. It has nothing to do with not trusting him, and everything to do with not trusting myself. I know that sounds weird and I can't explain it, but these are the issues I work through in counseling.

"Plans?" I ask teasingly, turning to face him and walking backward. "What kind of plans, Mr. West?"

He gives me a gentle shove into his bedroom, closing and locking the door behind us. I'm immediately pressed into the door, crowded in the most delicious way by his big body. I'm crowded by his affection and pressed by his love. His hands, commanding and gentle, skim my sides and mold to my waist. He lifts my breasts with his thumbs. My breath hangs in my throat while I wait for a stroke across my nipples that never comes. He knows, damn him, grinning, his hands melting away. His fingers meet when he splays them across my back. He's so much bigger. Someone standing behind him wouldn't even see me on the other side of his broad shoulders. He's a wall and a fortress. He's twice my size, but I feel no fear. Only trust. Only sheltered.

"Road trips suck." His chin, a sexy scruff of bristles, scrapes the curve of my neck and shoulder when he kisses me there. "I missed you."

Cradling my head, he sinks his fingers into my hair and lowers his head to hover over my lips. For a few seconds, our breath mingles. We share the very air keeping us alive, and then our tongues touch, tease, and tangle. We torture each other with tiny licks and half-kisses until I need more, need to hold and clutch and grip him. I roam the hardness of his chest, caress his biceps, trace the strong sinew in his forearm, and search for his hands. I thread our fingers together, our palms fused by a connection as electric today as it was the night we met. He coaxes my off-the-shoulder sweatshirt completely off my shoulder, so my naked breast comes into view.

"Hmmmmm." The hungry monosyllable rumbles in his chest, rattles behind his lips. He frees his hands to scoop under my arms and lift me until my feet leave the floor. The wet, velvety warmth of his mouth surrounding my breast, the tantalizing bite of teeth and suction at my nipple, leaves me boneless. I'm limp and suspended in the air while he drinks from me like a man dying of thirst.

"August." My hips move reflexively, seeking friction, satisfaction. "Baby, come on."

"What?" he mumbles around my breast, the vibration of the word tightening my nipples and causing my core to clench.

I lift and curl my legs around his waist, thrusting slowly, deliberately. I burrow my nose through the thick curls to whisper in his ear, "Fuck me."

His mouth drifts to the other breast, swiping the areola lovingly with his tongue. With his hands sliding down to cup my ass, he walks us to the bed and lays me down gently. He stands there, watching me with the same protective reverence he watched my daughter, only there's also lust in his eyes. Passion. Hunger.

Not releasing his gaze, I tug the sweatshirt over my head and work my arms free of the sleeves. My nipples peak in the cooler air, and he fixes his eyes there, a hard swallow bobbing his Adam's apple.

I lift my hips an inch or so, just enough to hook my thumbs in my yoga pants and push them past my knees and over my toes. I toss them across the room and wait for his smile. He traces a finger over my purple and gold boy-short underwear.

"You little traitor," he says with husky humor.

My reply is a throaty chuckle.

We both stop laughing when he grabs the panties at my hips and jerks them off, throwing them to join my discarded yoga pants in some corner. His face sobers, and there are embers in his eyes. I want to stoke them—to blow on them. To enflame him the way he burns through me, like gasoline in my veins. A blaze in my heart.

Slowly, I bring my knees up and dig my heels into the mattress, opening my legs wide. He bites his lip and presses me open more.

"God, Iris. Yes, baby. Show me."

He palms my pussy. His huge hand covers it, possesses it. One long finger caresses me in the divide between the lips where I'm swollen and throbbing. The thickness of two fingers invades, presses, and hooks inside me. My back arches off the bed, straining against the pleasure. My hips thrust in time with his fingers fucking me. He's a conductor, and my body sings for him, my cry of release a note sustained, held.

I close my eyes and bunch my hands at my sides, holding onto this perfect sensation for as long as I can. When I open my eyes, August is staring at me, and the look on his face brings tears to my eyes. To have someone look at me like that and to have someone feel the way he does—it's the most humbling thing I've ever had. Every time he touches me, he restores my faith and reminds me what pure love feels like.

"I love watching you come," he says, one finger tracing the sensitive skin inside my thigh.

"Why?" I catch his hand and pull him toward me until he's up on the bed between my legs, and I move to my knees, facing him.

"You're so vulnerable." He tugs on a strand of my hair streaming around my arms and shoulders. "I love that you trust me with that, that you're so unguarded."

"That's because when I'm with you, I'm *not* unguarded." I kiss the back of his hand, blinking at tears. "You guard me. I know you'll always protect me."

"But I didn't. I missed what was happening, what he was doing." There's a sheen of tears over his stormy eyes, gray skies and rain. "You've been through so much, Iris. You can protect yourself."

"But when I'm with you, I know I don't have to." I lick my lips and taste my own tears, but now they taste like joy.

He traces a tiny scar on my hip that he probably never noticed before he knew about Caleb. The first time we made love after he found out, he asked about every little scar and nick he'd never thought twice about. But each scar told a story, and he wanted to know them all. He kissed all the places Caleb hurt me, and our lovemaking was my perfect revenge. Every soft, tender thing Caleb tried to deny me, I have with August.

"I wish . . ." August gulps, swallowing the emotion alive on his face. "I wish I could take it all away."

I cup his chin and catch his eyes in the dim light. "We don't get to take away the bad things, but it's okay." My smile is a work of triumph—a victory cry. "I survived them."

I reach between us and wrap my hand around him, relishing his grunt and gasp, his groan of pleasure as I stroke him long and hard, up and down. "Can we make love now?"

August spears his fingers into my hair, resting his forehead against mine, his breath laboring more with every pull. "I love you, Iris. So much.

I nod, lick his neck, and suck at his collarbone, one hand steadily pumping him between us, the other reaching up to skim over his nipple with my fingertips. All his air expels in one extended breath. With a growl, he grabs my ass and pulls my legs over his knees. I lock my ankles at the small of his back while he brushes my hand away between us. I sink onto him and moan. With our chests flush, his answering groan vibrates between my breasts. He pistons inside me relentlessly.

"August, harder," I beg, dizzy with pleasure.

With his lip between his teeth, his dark brows furrowed, he goes harder and deeper. He goes so deep he finds the remnants of my pain and soothes them. He goes so hard his love is an undeniable force that takes me by storm. There is room for nothing else. He takes up all the space, consumes my thoughts, and for a moment, remakes our memories so there's only ever been him for me and only ever been me for him.

It is sublime.

"We should have eaten this while it was hot," I say around a bite of not-quite-warm pizza, followed by a sip of tepid root beer.

"I wanted to eat you while you were hot," August says, his grin cocky.

My laugh bounces off the kitchen walls. "Such a cornball." I turn toward him on the high stools at the counter until our knees touch.

"And yet here you are." He laughs, leaning over to brush our noses together in an Eskimo kiss.

"And yet here I am." I roll my eyes and reach for the slice of untouched pizza on his plate. "You gonna eat that?"

He shakes his head and offers a wry smile. He only grabbed it to make me feel like I wasn't eating alone. He's deep in the season and eats like a Spartan solider.

"Thanks for this, by the way." I pop a pineapple in my mouth. "You remembered."

He runs a wide palm over my back, his touch warm through my silk robe. "Lakers means pizza and root beer. I told you I remember everything about you." He lifts my hair and then watches it fall, a small frown pinching at his brows. "So, um, when I was reading to Sarai, she had a question tonight."

"What's new?" I laugh and sip my root beer, eyeing him over my bottle.

"Yeah, I know, right?" A tiny smile quirks his full lips, but his eyes are serious before he drops his gaze to the counter. "I was kind of thrown by this one, though."

"What'd she ask?" I push my pizza away and give him my full attention.

"She asked if I was gonna be her new daddy." He watches me from under long lashes, gauging my reaction.

I cough a little, less from the bit of pizza lodged in my throat, more from the unexpected turn of conversation. Sarai had a few questions about Caleb in the weeks following his death. She barely knew him, but that word "daddy" carries significance. She only knows the man who told her he was her daddy is gone. One day, I'll have the hard job of the truth, but for now, she's satisfied. Or I thought she was. I sip some root beer to make way for a reply.

"Oh. Wow." I glance at him cautiously. "And what'd you say?"

He clears his throat and runs a hand through his hair. "I told her that I love her more than any daddy loves a little girl," he says slowly, not looking at me for a second before very purposely looking me right in the eyes. "And that I love you more than any daddy loves any other mommy."

The pizza may not be hot, but his words steam my heart.

"And I said that we're already a family." He takes both my hands between his. "And that one day, when the time is right, I'll be her daddy and I'll be mommy's husband."

I don't know what to say for a moment, so I leave it to the quiet to absorb his perfect response, and then I speak.

"That was . . . ahem . . . a good answer," I say, studying our joined hands. "I'm not surprised she asked, considering all that's happened. Well, and now that we're at your place so much, it inevitably raises more questions."

"Our place."

"What?" I look up with a frown.

"You said it's *my* place, but it's *our* place."

"Yeah." I wave a hand. "You know what I mean."

"But you don't know what *I* mean." He smiles, cupping his palms around my shoulders. "I'm adding your name to the title of the condo, and when we move into a house, your name will be on that, too."

Surprise immobilizes me, freezes me in place. Only I'm not cold. Warmth suffuses every cell of my body until I'm on fire under his hands.

"You don't have to do that just to prove a point, August," I finally manage to say.

"It's not to prove a point. If there's one thing I understand, it's team, and you and me"—he draws a line in the air between us—"we're a team, doing everything together. And when we do marry, I want to adopt Sarai." He holds up a staying hand. "I know it'll take some getting used to, but she's always felt like mine, and I love her. I want things as legal with her and me as they will be for the two of us."

This—what I'm feeling, what's washing over my reservations and fears— this must be what the Mississippi feels at that very moment every thousand years when its course resets: that deltaic switch. That monumental chrysalis. My heart resets in an instant. Or maybe it's happened in a series of patient, painstaking pivots over weeks, months. Maybe it started the moment August walked away from the greatest opportunity of his life . . . for me. When he took a chance on us. Maybe it started then, but his words show me right now.

"I know I've asked you to marry me many times, but—"

"Three," I say, almost absently. I'm so involved with examining this new space I just stepped into. "You've asked me to marry you three times."

"Yeah." He grimace–grins. "Thanks for the reminder. I don't want to pressure you. You know that. I understand your hesitation. After finding out what you went through with Caleb, of course I get it."

I watch him, my face serene, but my heart setting a breakneck pace.

"It's like this," he says. "My mom tells this story about my dad. How she'd watch him play, and he would hold the ball for the last shot. She'd scream 'take the shot,' but he'd watch the clock, holding the ball 'til the last possible second. Then at just the right moment, he'd take the shot. He had perfect timing."

August cups my face, his eyes intense and tender.

"That's what I want. I want to read the clock and know when the time is right for us. I don't want to keep asking you. It's . . ."

Hard? Disappointing? Embarrassing?

Who knows which word he'd use? He's never shown me any of those things when he asked before and I wasn't ready, but maybe he hid them. Maybe he felt them.

I slide off my stool and step into the *V* of his powerful thighs, setting my arms against his chest and linking my hands behind his neck.

"August, I love you," I say, twining my fingers in his hair.

"I know that." He closes his eyes, surrendering to my hands. "I love you, too. More than anything. More than everything."

He said he'd play me at the five, at the very center, and he's lived up to that promise every day that we've been together.

"I trust you with my life, with my future." Emotion scalds my throat, so I pause to steady my voice. "With my daughter."

He slowly opens his eyes to watch me. "I know that, too."

"And I want to wake up with you every morning."

"Youuuuuuu . . . do?" He settles his hands at my hips, splayed across my bottom, and narrows his eyes on my face, assessing.

"Yeah, but . . ." I search for the right thing to say—to let him know I'm ready. "I want the pancakes. Okay? I want the pancakes, August."

"Babe, I'll make you pancakes. Any time you want."

"You're not hearing me. What I'm saying is . . .the kids! You know, bursting into our room every morning? Your kids, August. I want to have your children. Our children."

He frowns and blinks at me like I might have been body-snatched and replaced by some amenable stranger.

"That makes me . . . happy." He looks more uncertain than happy, though cautiously ecstatic might be accurate, too. "But what do you mean? Are you saying . . ."

He watches my face with the same focus his father probably watched that game clock counting down. I've had reservations and fears based on the past, based on my mistakes, and on bad calls I made. But August is no mistake. He's not a bad call, and all that he wants, I'm ready to offer. All that he has, I'm ready to receive. One step forward will take me into the future, and I'm ready.

"What I'm saying is this, August." I tip up on my toes and smile against his ear. "Take the shot."

THE END

OTHER BOOKS BY
KENNEDY RYAN

THE BENNETT SERIES

When You Are Mine

Loving You Always

Be Mine Forever

Until I'm Yours

THE SOUL SERIES

My Soul to Keep

Down to My Soul

Refrain

THE GRIP SERIES

Flow (Prequel)

Grip

Still

AUTHOR'S NOTE

Thank you for taking this journey with Iris and August. It is at times a difficult one, but also hopeful. Most of all, it's uniquely theirs. I know the temptation is to tell ourselves this is fiction, and it doesn't happen this way in real life. Maybe I believed that, too, until I interviewed woman after woman whose stories sounded so much like this one. As a matter of fact, their stories, in many ways *are* this one. I didn't write this book until I'd interviewed survivors, and their experiences, their triumphs, their spirit have insinuated themselves into Iris's journey. If at times this felt real it's because so many of the things Iris experienced, I heard from women who survived the same challenges.

My deepest appreciation to the survivors, the social workers and the women's shelter staff who answered my questions and helped me understand.

If you need help, call the National Domestic Violence Hotline at 1-800-799-7233. Thank you again for your support. I hope you enjoyed *Long Shot*.

SIGN UP TO RECEIVE:
www.subscribepage.com/LongShot-bonus

YOU CAN STAY ABREAST OF MY NEW RELEASES AND SALES BY FOLLOWING ME ON BOOKBUB:
www.bookbub.com/authors/kennedy-ryan

AND ON AMAZON:
www.amzn.to/2pbMdtC

ACKNOWLEDGMENTS

I'm grateful to so many, but I MUST start with Paula and Natalie. The two of you became the face and spirit of survival for me. Hearing your stories inspired and empowered me to write this book. Your hearts are on every page, and you were with me every step of Iris's journey.

You are #ChangeYourCourse!!

My tribe is wide and deep. I'm sure I'm overlooking many, but the ones I can think of right now in my release daze are Dylan (#Bestie), Nana, Emma (#TeamHeavy), Kate, Stephanie (#PaperBag), Adriana (#GripzQueen), Ginger, Corinne, Leigh (cover BOSS!), Mandi, Chele (#MyHeart), Imani (My MEGAPHONE), Brittany, Margie (#DayOne), Melissa, Sara. To my beta boos - Jx PinkLady, Terilyn, Shelley & Christy. Thank you for reading this book before it was its best and helping me to get it there. Melissa, my PA, for putting up with my idiosyncrasies and list of ever-growing demands. Jenn and the Social Butterfly team. I know I'm extra, but you never make me feel weird for 3am PMs or last-minute ideas. Love you for that. Special thanks to Lucy Score and Kathryn Nolan for reading super early and giving me such incredible, insightful, constructive feedback. You really helped me navigate this touchy terrain so well, and I'll never forget it. Thanks to Lauren for your AH-MAZING editing superpowers, and to Tricia for the eagle eye-ness and all the squeals in the margins. :-)

Thank you to the readers in Kennedy Ryan Books! You guys are my favorite place online, and I stalk YOU!!! Thank you for all the unwavering support and love you give me.

To every person who has messaged me, emailed me, tagged me on an Instagram or Twitter post over the last year shouting about my books, thank you. Sometimes I feel like the things I write are an acquired taste. Every book feels like a new set of risks. You are my people. You "get" me and keep taking these rides with me off the beaten book path.

I love you for that.

Last, but certainly, not least.

To MY baller.

My husband, who shared with me his love for the game. Who answered all my basketball questions patiently and so enthusiastically, I had to shut you up. LOL! Who puts up with my screeching and hair-pulling when Golden State is losing. And my histrionics when my Tar Heels win.

You're my best friend, and I'd "play you at the five."

ABOUT THE AUTHOR

Kennedy Ryan is a Southern girl gone Southern California. A Top 100 Amazon Bestseller, Kennedy writes romance about remarkable women who thrive even in tough times, the love they find, and the men who cherish them. She is a wife and a mother to an extraordinary son. She has always leveraged her journalism background to write for charity and non-profit organizations, but enjoys writing to raise Autism awareness most. A contributor for Modern Mom Magazine, Kennedy's writings have appeared in Chicken Soup for the Soul, USA Today and many others. The founder and executive director of a foundation serving Georgia families living with Autism, Kennedy has appeared on Headline News, Montel Williams, NPR and other media outlets as a voice for families living with autism.

CPSIA information can be obtained
at www.ICGtesting.com
Printed in the USA
LVHW032312260319
611967LV00002B/318